House

OF THE

Raven

Ingrid Seymour is a *USA Today* bestselling author of over fifty novels. She writes new adult fiction in a variety of genres, including fantasy romance, urban fantasy, paranormal romance, sci-fi, and high fantasy – all with badass heroines and irresistible heroes. She used to work as a software engineer at a Fortune 500 company, but now writes full-time and loves every minute of it. She lives in Birmingham, Alabama with her husband, two kids, and a cat named Ossie.

Instagram: **@ingrid_seymour**
X: **@Ingrid_Seymour**
TikTok: **@ingridseymour**
Facebook: **/IngridSeymourAuthor**

BY INGRID SEYMOUR

House

OF THE

Raven

INGRID SEYMOUR

HEADLINE
ETERNAL

First published in 2024 by PenDreams

First published in Great Britain in this paperback edition in 2024
by HEADLINE ETERNAL
An imprint of HEADLINE PUBLISHING GROUP

1

Cataloguing in Publication Data is available from the British Library

ISBN 978 1 0354 2066 7

Typeset in 11/16pt EB Garamond by Jouve (UK), Milton Keynes

Printed and bound in Great Britain by Clays Ltd, Elcograf S.p.A.

Headline's policy is to use papers that are natural, renewable and recyclable
products and made from wood grown in well-managed forests and other
controlled sources. The logging and manufacturing processes are expected
to conform to the environmental regulations of the country of origin.

HEADLINE PUBLISHING GROUP
An Hachette UK Company
Carmelite House
50 Victoria Embankment
London EC4Y 0DZ

www.headlineeternal.com
www.headline.co.uk
www.hachette.co.uk

To Grey.
Kid, you blow my mind!

FRANKESIA

JABALTARIQ
SEA

CALENDAR ERAS

AV – After the veil
DV – During the veil
BF – Before the veil

I

VALERIA

"The Realta Observatory, a marvel to my old eyes, rose in days under the weaving of hands and the melodic hum of espiritu. I watched its creation—a sight that, before the veil, would have been deemed a miracle. I often wonder how Castella would be without magic."

Diego Fontana – Erudito de la Academia Alada – 1327 DV

*E*spiritu, the power to use magic, is almost dead in the realm. Many things in Castella are a constant reminder of how life used to be a mere two decades ago. The collapsed glass walls of the old observatory are one example.

Enormous shards of glass rise from the ground like icebergs. They refract the early afternoon sun, shooting rainbows onto the arid surrounding ground, while smaller shards sparkle in the dirt, fooling the eye with the suggestion of lost treasure. I feel like an insect in the presence of towering gemstones.

I've seen paintings of the structure as it stood back then, a magnificent building with a large cupola, a clever design held up by spells, the espiritu of long-gone fae immigrants, though they would simply call it magic. Humans never had enough espiritu for such grandeur, but at least we used to have some. After the veil disappeared, however, it all went away. Now only a few of the stranded fae possess the gift.

I stroll through the destruction, but the echoes of its past beauty don't escape me. Not for the first time, I wish I had seen the city before the veil disappeared and took all espiritu with it. Well, not all. Not yet.

"Val, home," Cuervo croaks from the top of the large shard where he's been perched.

Jago, my first cousin on my father's side, sits below Cuervo, making a show of looking exhausted. "You should listen to the chicken."

"Not chicken!" Cuervo croaks. The insult never fails to make him mad, just the reason Jago doesn't relent in its use.

They are both right. I shouldn't be here, but I'm tired of being locked up behind the palace's walls. This is the first time I've snuck out in weeks. Besides, Father and Amira, my oldest sister, think I'm attending my Tirgaelach lesson while my maestro thinks I'm down with a stomach ache.

I shake my head. Tirgaelach . . . what is the point? Even the fae still living in Castella don't speak the ancient language. Just like we don't speak Castellan. Over the two thousand years our cultures have been in contact, our languages evolved into what we speak now: Tiran.

Cuervo flaps his wings and flies down.

"Treasure," he croaks as he digs a hole in the ground with his sharp talon.

Cuervo's feathers are beautiful. They look like polished onyx, glimmer blue and black and purple, and oddly enough, even white when the light hits them just so. His beak is curved and sharp. Shiny too. He has perfectly round eyes that watch everything. He belongs to a rare breed of ravens that came from Tirnanog, the fae realm.

"What did you find?" Pushing away the rapier strapped to my waist, I kneel next to him as he uncovers a multifaceted piece of glass in the shape of a teardrop. This is not a broken-off piece of the observatory. It's not sharp. It is smooth, maybe a remnant of a chandelier or something similar.

I pick it up and hold it to the light between my thumb and forefinger. All the colors of the rainbow refract in the middle.

"Good job, Cuervo."

"You shouldn't indulge her, chicken." Jago comes up behind us.

Cuervo tries to peck Jago's foot, but my cousin moves out of the way, hands up. "Sorry. Sorry."

Sometimes their bickering drives me crazy, but these two are my constant companions. My days would be unbearable without them.

I stretch to my full height and place the piece inside my satchel. I'm making a necklace for Amira's birthday. I was missing the centerpiece, but I think I've found it.

Well, Cuervo found it. *Clever bird!*

I also found a pea-sized blue piece of glass that, once smoothed, can make a pretty ring for Nana. Blue is her favorite color.

Sighing, I decide it's time to get back before anyone notices my absence. I throw the hood over my head. I don't think many would recognize me, but better safe than sorry.

With Jago by my side and Cuervo flying overhead, I make my

way out of the dilapidated site and into the streets of Castellina, the capital city. The broken observatory lies to the east of the palace, and it's about a thirty-minute walk back. I keep my head low and my pace brisk.

"Mind if I take a detour from here?" Jago asks halfway to Nido, the palace.

I give him a narrow-eyed glare. "Where are you going?"

He shrugs.

Likely, he's after some man or woman or another. With his dirty blond hair, honey-colored eyes, and cheerful mood, he's popular among the single people of Castellina.

"Fine," I say, rolling my eyes.

He points a finger at the sky. "Cuervo will keep you safe." He leaves with a hop in his step, whistling a happy tune.

I'm sweating under my cloak, so I hurry my step. It's the peak of summer. Assaulted by an odd feeling, I halt as the hairs on the back of my neck bristle. Frowning, I look over my shoulder. The cobbled path is lined by a few businesses and official buildings. People mill about, immersed in their own affairs. No one is worried about me.

I keep going, but this time, my eyes dart in every direction. I wait for the uneasy feeling to pass, but it remains. Something is familiar about it. I've felt this way before, but when?

As I reach one of the nearby plazas, my eyes are drawn to the source of music and rhythmic clapping. Two men sit on low stools, one playing the guitar, the other one singing and keeping an intricate clapping pace—something known as *palmas*. A few members of the audience have joined him, their hands moving with

4

practice. What is most enthralling, however, is the singer's voice, so full of longing and pain. The duo is good, only missing a dancer tapping her heels and twirling in a red dress.

Despite the light atmosphere, my entire body is on edge. The area is busy with street vendors, people sitting outside crowded cafés, and denizens going in and out of the adjacent buildings, conducting business. Nothing looks out of the ordinary, so why do I feel this way?

A little girl runs toward the fountain in the center of the plaza. The performers finish their act, and cicada calls in the distance replace their song.

My ears begin to ring, and my mouth goes dry. I take several deep breaths. My heart pounds, and people walk past me, oblivious to my state of alarm.

Oh, gods! What's wrong with me? Am I sick?

A deafening explosion sends me flying backward. I land flat on my back with bone-crushing force. Dust chokes the air along with the panicked screams from people.

"Veilfallen!" someone shouts.

Coughing and disoriented, I sit up. My back protests in pain. Someone steps on my hand as they run past me.

"Ow." I yank it back and shake it, then pull my shirt over my nose, blinking at the floating debris.

"Saints and feathers!" I mutter as I peer through the dust and contemplate the madness: splintered wood fragments, brick chunks, overturned carts, the severed head of a statue, the severed arm of a person.

I look away, nausea tearing through my gut.

Cuervo's desperate croaks sound above my head, well past the thick cloud of dust that hangs above, choking the sky.

"Call for help, Cuervo," I shout, unsure of whether or not he can hear me over the screams and anguished cries.

A man stumbles by me, his eyes wide within a mask of caked dirt. His right arm is a stump dripping with blood.

I recoil, stand, and clamber toward a nearby wall, wiping muck off my face. Through the settling dust, I see the little girl by the fountain. She's curled up on the ground, a woman lying broken next to her. People run in every direction, and the girl doesn't dare move.

Without thinking, I rush to her, crouching low until I reach her. Wet streaks cut through the dust on her face.

"Are you hurt?" I ask.

She shakes her head and looks down at the woman, whose eyes stare blankly at the heavens. One side of her head is bashed in, probably due to a flying piece of stone.

"Is that your . . .? Do you . . .?" I don't know how to ask her if the dead woman is her mother, but the girl understands.

She shakes her head and sobs, "I don't know her."

I nod, relieved. The woman might still be someone's mother, but at least her kid didn't have to see her die so horribly. Not the way I saw my mother die.

"Let's get you out of here." I put my arms out, and the girl jumps up and hugs my neck tightly.

I'm about to run the way I came when I hear the organized marching steps of what must be Castellina's Guardia. Cuervo did as I instructed, I presume. As they round the corner, the neat lines of uniformed guards break apart and disperse through the plaza.

Thank the gods! Help is here.

However, my relief dies suddenly as arrows fly, making targets out of the helping guards.

Bastardos! When are the veilfallen going to stop killing innocent people?

I hold tightly to the girl and run away from the center of the plaza. When we reach the bordering buildings, she wiggles out of my arms and runs parallel to the wall.

"Come." She beckons with one small hand as she disappears through the door of a tavern.

I follow her in and come to a halt. A group of startled people blink at me, looking anything but friendly. The little girl runs into the arms of a bulky man.

"Nina." He crushes her to his chest. "I thought you were upstairs."

"I was feeding the fish in the fountain. She helped me." Nina points at me.

The man looks at my hood, gives me a distrustful nod. "Thank you?" It sounds like a question.

I throw the hood back to reveal my face, my ears. Everyone needs to see they aren't pointy.

"Princess Valeria?!" A woman says.

Wait, what? She recognizes me? Fantástico!

"Veilfallen are out there," I say to distract them, but also because we're still in danger. "Everyone, hide until the guards clear the plaza."

"Damn fae!" the burly man curses, taking Nina behind the bar counter where they duck out of sight.

Everyone else scurries behind furniture and closed doors. I walk to the window to take a peek outside. With a yelp, I jump back. Figures wearing heavy cloaks and cowls are headed this way.

"They're coming," I warn as I try to find somewhere to hide. There are many tables, but they will provide no protection.

The door bursts open. I whirl and draw my rapier.

Three veilfallen pile at the threshold. All I see are their eyes. Their cowls leave only a narrow gap between their brows and the bridge of their noses.

The one that stands in front glares at me, dark eyes feral. A scar cuts down his right eyebrow and across his eyelid, its trail getting lost under the cowl. He is massive, his shoulders as wide as the door, his hands long-fingered and strong. They curl into fists as his eyes flick down to my weapon and sparkle with amusement.

He takes a step forward as if I'm not there.

The conceited bastardo!

I take a step to the side and block his path, the tip of my rapier grazing his middle. "Where do you think you're going, veilfallen?"

"Let us pass, *girl,* if you value your life." His deep voice is calm, and it sends a shiver up my spine.

Girl? I'm not a girl. I'm twenty years old.

I stand firm. "You will not pass, and you will answer for your crimes." I don't know where the conviction in my voice is coming from, but I'm glad for it.

Out of the corner of my eye, I try to see if anyone in the tavern is coming to my aid, but it seems I've landed in the lower echelons of cowardice. Or is it the highest? No matter. I only need to thwart these criminals long enough for the Guardia to get here.

"We have to get out of here," one of the other veilfallen says, a female with violet eyes that shoot daggers at me. "I'll take care of her." She steps forward, but the leader puts a hand up.

"No need," he says as, with one callous finger, he pushes my rapier to the side.

Annoyed, I point the weapon back at his middle.

He pushes it again in the same manner and says, "You look familiar. Have I met you before?"

"No," I snap. "I don't associate with criminals."

"They're coming, River," the female warns.

I gasp, even as I try to hold back my surprise. River is the leader of the veilfallen. He is ruthless and has killed more innocent people than I dare count. I can't let him escape. Capturing him would be a huge blow to the veilfallen.

I'm prepared to do whatever it takes to stop him. If I have to—

He pushes my rapier out of the way once more. Though, this time that's not all he does. Moving faster than I can track, he steps forward, grabs my wrist, and squeezes it with viselike strength. The sword falls from my hand and clatters to the floor. Shifting to stand behind me, he twists my arm and wraps his other arm around my neck. I end up with my back flush against his hard torso as he walks backward, pulling me along.

My feet drag as I fight. "Let me go, bastardo."

I kick my legs desperately.

We move past the counter, and I see Nina and her father crouching there. She gives me a little wave.

Going limp, I become dead weight. Undeterred, River drags me down a long hall toward what I presume is a back exit.

"Slice her throat and be done with it," the female with the violet eyes says. "We do not need a hostage. We need to get out of here."

"Slicing Princess Plumanegra's throat would be unwise when we can use her as leverage," River responds.

What? He knows who I am, too? Dammit!

I suddenly hear my father's words echoing in my ears: *One of these days, someone will kidnap you for ransom.*

I always thought he was exaggerating, always thought I was too clever to get caught. Now, my ass is in the hands of the most feared criminal in all of Castella. Figuratively . . . the ass part, not the most feared part.

"Princess Plumanegra?" the female repeats, incredulous. "The future queen?"

"No. Not that one. The other one."

She leans down to look at me better. With a growl, I try to kick her but miss.

The other veilfallen, the one that hasn't said a word, throws a door open, and we spill into a narrow alley. He motions with one hand, urging them to hurry.

"That's not her," the female declares.

Whenever I sneak out of the palace, I hide my most recognizable characteristic, a streak of white hair that sprouts from the top of my forehead. A bit of a paste made from ground walnut hulls to match my natural golden brown color, and it's gone for a few days. Maybe I *am* clever enough, after all.

"That's right, you idiot. I'm not a princess," I bite the words out.

Within the blink of an eye, River whirls me around, pushes me against the wall, and grabs a section of my hair between his thumb and forefinger. He slides his grip along the strand, then shows his cohorts his stained fingertips.

Damn! I always thought I could blend in. I look just like any other Castellan woman: brown hair, brown eyes, olive skin. What gave me away? I bet it's that damn portrait they hung at the Biblioteca de la Reina. I told Father it was a bad idea, but he never listens to me.

"Help!" I scream.

He squeezes my throat, and my voice dies out.

"Will you look at that?" the female smiles with satisfaction. A lock of blond hair peaks from under her cowl.

I do my best to memorize her eyes, her height, and her build. I do the same with the others.

"Knock her out and throw her over your shoulder," she says.

River pulls his fist back, ready to do just that, but I'm not going down without a fight. If they take me, I may never see my father and sister again.

Using all my strength, I stomp on River's toes with the heel of my boot. Any normal human being would curse and holler, but not a damn fae. Still, his grip around my throat loosens just enough, and I'm able to reach down for the dagger sheathed at my thigh.

I don't hesitate. Instead, I let my instincts take over and cut at his wrist. When he pulls back, surprised, I drop to one knee and go for his leg. He jumps back as I try to stab him. Instead, my weapon slices as it travels downward, tearing through his trousers and opening a long gash.

He barely lets out a grunt. Anger flashing in his eyes, he tries to grab me again, but I slash my dagger from side to side, keeping him at bay as I back away.

Just as I think all three of them are about to jump me, the sound of footsteps comes from one end of the alley, and a group of guards appears. They come running down toward us without hesitation.

"This is the leader of the veilfallen," I scream, pointing at my would-be kidnapper.

There is a big reward for his capture—nothing wrong with giving the guards a bigger incentive to catch him.

River narrows his eyes at me. I stick my thumb between my index and middle finger and give him the fig sign.

"*Fuck you*," I mouth.

He reacts not at all. The male has ice in his veins. Instead, he turns around and sprints in the opposite direction, followed by his allies. He doesn't even limp. They're gone and out of sight before the guards even make it to where I kneel on the ground.

They stare at me.

"What do you think you're doing?" I demand. "Follow them."

A couple of them bristle at receiving orders from a random citizen. The idiots don't recognize me. *Really?*

I pull out the chain that hangs around my neck and show them the Plumanegra key, my family's symbol. It's a key shaped like a raven's feather. When they see it, they salute me.

"Never mind that. Capture them!"

As they rush down the alley, I'm not holding my breath for their capture. I know those cold-blooded criminals are gone. And there's one more thing I know. I'm in a heap of trouble.

2

RIVER

*"This night the fear of never seeing her again devours my bones.
I long for your embrace, Radina, my beloved mate."*

Kadewyn Zinceran – Fae Trader – 3 AV

My steps echo across the narrow passage. I would know these musty catacombs even blindfolded. The dank smell comforts me, the same as the torchlight reflecting on the ancient stone walls.

The others walk behind me, keeping their distance, carrying the loot. I hurry my step, eager to see what we got. We need funds to keep financing our efforts, to keep us fed, but I would be lying if I said that is my priority.

At the end of the passage, I walk into a concave chamber, remove my cloak and cowl, and cast them on top of an empty barrel in the corner. A table sits in the middle with many items already strewn on top of it. Obviously, others got here before us. Swiftly, my eyes rove over every single piece of what we've plundered.

The disappointment hits me, a familiar jab in the chest. I push it away as, one by one, everyone dumps their takings onto the table. I search once more, and once more, but I don't find what I've been looking for these last twenty years.

"Excellent plundering." Kadewyn, my second, pats everyone on the back as they pass by and walk deeper into the catacombs. He makes a mental calculation, then asks, "Where are Unmenar and Elassan?"

Besides him, only Calierin and I remain in the alcove. We exchange glances.

Kadewyn used to be a trader before the veil fell. He has a wife and daughter in Tirnanog. He hasn't lost hope that he'll see them one day.

"I didn't see them," Calierin says, her violet gaze turning dark, the way it does when she fights. She's an accomplished warrior, a member of the Tuathacath, one of the best fae warrior tribes in all of Tirnanog. She possesses magic capable of toppling buildings, which is useful more often than I'd like to admit. She was stranded in Castella while on a perimeter search of the veil. She was the only one of her regiment to be on the wrong side when the veil disappeared.

Everyone here has a similar story and lives before the veil's collapse, before we became pariahs in the human realm.

Kadewyn shakes his head, long silver hair swaying. "By the gods, they must be all right."

Calierin punches a fist into her hand. "We can't lose any more people. If only we'd gotten that stupid girl. We could have changed so much."

I grunt in agreement. The Plumanegras are my next target. I've been working on a plan to infiltrate their palace for some time now. I'll get to them sooner rather than later. Though Calierin and Kadewyn know nothing about what's coming. It is too risky to share.

My head snaps toward the entrance. I hear steps in the distance, but only one set. Some moments later, Elassan stumbles in, hands to his gut, blood seeping through his fingers. Kadewyn catches him and slowly eases him to the floor. We both kneel at his side.

"Get him some feyglen," Kadewyn says.

Calierin finds a bottle inside a hole in the wall and hands it over. I tip it to Elassan's lips, and he takes a labored sip.

Kadewyn lifts the male's shirt and examines the wound. He throws me a wary glance and shakes his head slightly.

"They . . . g-got Unmenar," Elassan says hoarsely.

"Dead?" Kadewyn seeks to clarify.

Elassan nods his head once, then goes utterly still. Dead, too.

Kadewyn closes the dead male's eyes. "May the winds carry your essence to the Glimmer."

I stand abruptly and turn toward the wall. How many more of my people must die in this godsforsaken, accursed realm? How can I feel guilt over those we kill when they do the same to us?

"Damn humans!" Calierin pounds a fist on the wall. She wears her anger on the surface.

Kadewyn leaves, then comes back with help. "See that Elassan is taken care of."

They gather his remains and take him further into the catacombs. They'll have no trouble finding a place for him, but he shouldn't have to sleep eternally in this rotten land. He should be laid to rest in Tirnanog and be forever protected by Faoloir, god of all creatures.

The excitement over today's plunder will be bashed by another friend's death. There is so little to enjoy.

When will we get out of here?

It's the same question I've asked myself for so long.

We sit quietly for an entire hour, passing around the bottle, wishing it actually contained feyglen instead of the cheapest human wine. Feyglen is made from grapes that only grow in Tirnanog. It is sweeter and stronger, what I need right now to put me out of my misery for at least a few hours.

"How do we divide it?" Kadewyn asks, breaking the silence. He points toward the trinkets on the table because that's what they are: jewels and gold from the human nobility who think strongboxes in guarded keeps can protect their gaudy accessories. But no lock is safe from Kadewyn's kind of magic.

"Rífíor?" he presses when I don't respond.

The humans call me River, mispronouncing the name I chose for myself when I stopped wandering this realm and came to the capital. The veilfallen correctly call me Rífíor, a common enough name in Tirnanog, but a fake one, after all. I will soon go by a third name. Will it suit me better?

"Same as always," I respond.

He nods.

After half of the pile is taken away and distributed amongst the poorest fae families in the city, every veilfallen will receive an equal part. They risk their lives every day. It's the least they deserve.

After paying everyone, Kadewyn returns with food and drink.

I guzzle the rancid-tasting wine in one go and ignore the chunk of bread and dry meat.

I stare at the ground and run a hand down my face, feeling the jagged edges of my scar. I'm still feeling annoyed that a human girl bested me. Fate put her in my path, and I allowed her to slip through my fingers. But that's all right. My new plan is already in motion, and perhaps this is the one that will ultimately lead me to the escape I yearn for, although I still fear my quest may not conclude anytime soon.

It's not that I'm jaded. It's simply that I'm beginning to think I deserve this curse.

3
VALERIA

*"I yearn for peace in the realm, but the other tribes remain
resistant. If only there were a means to unite us all."*

Lorenzo el Valiente (Casa Escalante) – Tribal Leader – 100 BV

Father hasn't said a word. He sits in his favorite chair in his study, arms crossed, jaw set. Amira stands behind him, looking just as stern. They are unified against me, as always. Against Jago, too, who shuffles from foot to foot next to me, making this a repeat of many past occasions.

Rey Simón Plumanegra the Third is a man of fifty with graying blond hair, olive skin, and clear blue eyes. He wears a closely cropped beard and is as fit as an ox. He likes hard labor and has never shied away from it. He practices with the Guardia Real in the lower courtyard every morning, rides his stallion in the palace woods in the evenings, and mucks up his own stall afterward.

Amira Plumanegra, my older sister, is twenty-five and the future queen. She acts as if she were my mother sometimes, but it's Father she resembles more and more as time goes by—not physically, mind you, temperamentally. He's shaping her to be the monarch Castella needs, which is taking all the fun out of her.

"I almost killed him," I say.

It's not an exaggeration. I was aiming for River's femoral artery when I tried to stab his leg. If I'd only been a little faster, we would be having a completely different conversation—not that this is much of one. It's more like a *let's give Valeria and Jago the meanest glares we can muster* type of situation.

Don't they realize I'm already immune to their evil eye?

"You have betrayed my trust. Both of you," Father finally speaks, his words lacking the anger I'm accustomed to.

This controlled lecture is far scarier than even that time he went blue in the face screaming at me.

I clear my throat. "Father, I—"

He cuts me off, putting a hand up. "I don't want to hear it. I've been working all day to ensure the injured are taken care of and those responsible for this attack pay for it. I have neither the time nor the desire to hear empty explanations about your appalling *lies*."

Amira winces. That is how harsh the last word sounds. It cuts me. Deep.

"I will deal with you later, Jago. Leave!" Father flicks a hand toward the door.

Jago rushes out without a backward glance. *The coward!*

Father goes on, "You promised me you wouldn't leave Nido without the Guardia Real again, and today you nearly got yourself taken by the veilfallen."

I consider denying it, but that would be another lie and not even a good one.

"From now on, you will be guarded from the moment you wake up till the moment you lay your head to rest," he decrees.

"What? Within Nido's walls? You can't confine me to the palace. You—"

He looks back at my sister. "Find a couple of guards who can watch her day and night. Inform them they are responsible for her safety."

I take a step forward. "I'm not a child. I don't need constant supervision."

"Your actions today make those words yet another lie."

"You can't keep me locked up. I've tried to respect your wishes, but life within these walls is not enough for me. I'm not allowed to go anywhere."

"That is untrue. You're welcome to accompany your sister and me."

"You know I have no interest in stately affairs."

"Instead your interests include dressing like a boy, playing in the dirt in dilapidated sites, and filling your head with things of no consequence."

"Father . . ." Amira rebukes him in a quiet tone.

Tears prickle in my eyes. He has never talked to me like this, has never called me out on any of my interests. It isn't fair, not when he's always encouraged me to be myself.

"It's time she hears it, Amira," he says. "She turned twenty this year. She is most definitely not a child, even if she insists on acting like one. She is to marry soon. Don Justo Medrano has made a fine proposal."

I do my best not to appear disgusted. "I have not agreed to that."

"Your acquiescence may become unnecessary."

"You wouldn't dare."

"I may not have a choice." Father runs a hand down his jaw, smoothing his graying beard, a distracted motion that means he's done with me. He stands up slowly and leaves without another word.

Amira sighs. "You really made him angry this time."

She looks tired and her golden brown hair, the same shade as mine, is not as neat as usual. She probably pulled at it in one of the endless council meetings she and Father attend almost every day.

"He has no right," I protest. "I'm practically a prisoner here. Hells, with a guard at my heels at all times, I *will* be one."

"You know the veilfallen have grown more dangerous this past year, and it's only getting worse. Today's attack is proof of that."

Damn veilfallen! A year ago, rumors that they were more organized began, and soon after that, news of a leader who had galvanized the once-dispersed groups of fae rebels was all anybody could talk about. Where did this male, River, come from? It's as if he sprouted out of the ground. The veil disappeared over twenty years ago. Why did he come to Castellina now? To ruin my life?

"I know how to take care of myself, Amira," I insist. "I don't need guards to follow me around the palace. What is everyone going to say?"

"You should have thought about that before you snuck out."

"You can't be in agreement with him. You have to convince him that a guard is unnecessary."

"You know well that when he makes up his mind, there are few who can convince him to change it." She stares pointedly at me.

Since I was little, I've always been the one able to cajole things out of him: a later bedtime, one more piece of cake, a birthday ball for my sister. With her expressive eyes, Amira is asking me, in no uncertain terms, that if I've failed to change his mind, what hope could she have if she tried?

"If I were you," she adds, "I would keep my head low for a *long* while. Maybe he will remove the guards if he notices good behavior."

I shake my head. "Do you hear yourself? Good behavior? I. Am. Not. A. Child. Whether or not he likes my behavior, I'm a grown woman. I'm not his puppet. He can't make me dance around to his tune."

"Valeria, please don't do anything stupid."

I huff. "I'm sure it doesn't matter what I do, you two will think it's stupid."

I march out of the study. I want to run to Nana to cry on her lap, but she doesn't need the anxiety my situation would cause her. Her health has been fragile lately. Besides, I need time to think about what to do next. My life can't continue this way. What Father wants for me—marriage to a lord with a fortune large enough to befit a princess—can't be the only path for me. There has to be something more.

There is no way I'll marry Don Justo Medrano or any of the other men Father has volunteered. I'd rather die.

22

My heart beats hard as I enter my room. I climbed to the fourth floor practically running. Shutting the door, I notice Cuervo perched on the balcony's marble railing. He flaps his wings when he notices me. The curtains sway in the summer breeze as I walk past the open balcony doors. I lean my elbows on the railing and peer beyond the palace walls toward the observatory.

The larger pieces of broken glass are still visible from this distance and sparkle like the lost jewels of a giant.

I sigh.

"I wish I had seen it," Cuervo croaks.

A sad smile stretches my lips. "I do say that a lot, don't I?"

He hops closer and bumps my shoulder with his head, his way of comforting me.

"I think you understand how I feel better than anyone," I tell him.

He bobs his head up and down in agreement.

"I was born twenty years too late, my friend."

What I wouldn't give to see Tirnanog, to visit my mother's village, to experience espiritu. Every time I think that this part of my heritage is lost to me, I feel a deep void in my chest, a space that will never be filled. I feel not only half-human and half-fae, but also half alive.

Not for the first time, I wonder why Amira doesn't feel the same way. I've asked her multiple times, and she says it's all in my imagination, that if I stop reading all those old history books, yearning for a world that may forever be outside our reach, I would feel much better. I often wonder if she wishes our mother wasn't fae, if she's tired of keeping that secret from everyone.

Either way, she's wrong. Some of those *old history books,* as she calls them, were relevant only two decades ago, for all the gods' sake. More than that, they describe the place where our mother was born. How can she just . . .?

Frustration mounting, I whirl and stomp back into the bed-chamber. I sit at the edge of my bed for a long moment. My nose itches due to the dust still embedded in my clothes. I rub it back and forth with the back of my index finger, trying to suppress a sneeze.

My mind whirls like carriage wheels, turning over and over and over. My whole future seems to flash before my eyes as my imagination flies with itself. Married to a stuffy, overweight, older man with a twisted mustache (I've never seen Don Justo, but this is how I imagine him.) Shipped to a faraway villa to *keep house* for him. Expected to part my legs every time he deigns to pause his duties for an obligatory visit to his burdensome wife. Required to pop heirs, preferably male and on the clock. Forced to ignore his many mistresses and illegitimate children.

At the brink of vomiting what little sits in my stomach, I leave my room, the seed of a decision embedding itself in the fertile soil of my tilled mind. With every step, my conviction grows. This idea has lived in the back of my head for a while now, but I've been afraid to look it straight in the eye. The further I walk, the fear that has kept me from taking action seems to peel off like dead skin and fall away in large strips until I feel lighter, and my steps gain a spring I've not felt in a long time.

I approach Father's private study. Here, the absence of guards is deliberate, as the room lies nestled deep within the heart of the palace. Instead, the guards are posted further out, protecting the perimeter doors that lead to this inner sanctum. This is the only way to have true privacy, he says. Secrets can't be kept if you have guards or servants roaming around, no matter how loyal.

The closed study doors are made of solid, dense fae blackwood, bearing an intricately carved depiction of a raven's nest resting on the branches of a tree. A vigilant mother raven stands watch over her chicks, silhouetted against the backdrop of broad leaves and a waning moon.

"So they are right then?" I hear Amira say on the other side of the closed doors. Her voice is raised, upset.

"Of course they aren't right," Father responds.

I press my ear to the door.

"Why did you decide to tell me this now?" Amira demands.

"You will be queen sooner or later. You need to know."

"And what about Valeria? Are you going to tell her?"

"Saints no!" Father exclaims. "With that bleeding heart of hers, who knows what she would do."

"But—"

He cuts her off. "You know I'm right."

"It isn't fair to her."

"Yes, but I'm protecting her."

Protecting me from what?

"When I'm gone," he continues, "it'll be your job to protect her."

"She is not a child, and you need to stop treating her as such. I think you cling to the idea that she is your little girl, and you're not allowing her to grow up, at least in your mind, but if you haven't noticed, she is a woman now."

He grunts in displeasure.

I want Amira to keep going, to tell him he can't keep treating me this way, but I also want to burst in and demand what secrets they're keeping from me. Except if I do, I know they won't tell me anything. Father will chide me for eavesdropping and send me on my way, without supper . . . if he still could. My best bet is to keep listening, and afterward . . . accost Amira for all the answers.

"Perhaps I will tell her one day," he says. "You know she sympathizes with the fae."

What? This has to do with the fae? Now I'm really confused.

"Not with the veilfallen, Father. Some live in peace among us. She feels for them as I do."

"Not as you do. You understand that *our* people are the priority. She does not."

Of course, we are the priority, but that is because we are the majority. We make the rules and control everything. But the fae have voices too, and they need to be heard. I wish he was as just to them as he is to humans, but there is no equality between us.

"Perhaps she's not so wrong, Father," Amira says.

I nearly gasp. Did she really just say that?

"Offering them a seat in the council may alleviate tensions," she adds.

"You know well we have attempted that already."

"But that was ten years ago. Maybe it's time for another try. Maybe a reasonable leader will emerge and—"

"There is no reasoning with outlaws, Amira. Have you learned nothing from what I've been trying to teach you?"

She says nothing in response.

Father has tried to make peace with the fae. It's true, but one should never give up on peace. There are plenty of fae who only want to live their quiet lives, even if that means doing so in our realm. Pointing fingers at us for the disappearance of the veil solves nothing, and a big majority of them understand that. Even if there is a group of bloodthirsty fae who don't. Father should keep trying, but maybe he's too stubborn for that.

Would Amira succeed where he has failed?

I shy away from the question as soon as it enters my mind. The only way I would find out the answer is if something happens to Father, and I would never wish for such a thing. I love him. He is a good father, and I think once we are past our differences, once he understands he has to let me carve my own path—even if it is not the path he has envisioned for me—we will get along just fine.

"I have to go," Amira says.

Shit! I tiptoe away from the door and hide behind a wide column, peeking out carefully.

"Please remember to keep this between you and me," Father calls out as the door opens and Amira glances back, a hand on the knob.

She huffs. "You made me promise, so you don't have to remind me."

She closes the door and heads down the hall at a clipped pace. Once her steps are but an echo, I come out of my hiding place and stand there, staring at the floor. Lost in my thoughts, I try to imagine what the secret could be.

"So they are right then," Amira said. Based on the rest of the conversation "they" refers to the fae.

The fae are right.

Right about what? That we are taking advantage of them? That we don't care about their well-being? That we hate them and want to expel them from Castella? That it is our fault the veil disappeared? The veilfallen accuse humans of all these things and more, so any guess is as good as another.

Still, none of these topics—no matter how delicate—feel like the kind Father should guard so jealously from me. It has to be something else, but what?

Snapping out of it, I walk past Father's door and go after Amira. At the end of the hall, I pause, wondering where she's gone. I check the time on a timepiece sitting on a narrow polished table. It reads half past thirteen hours. Also, today is a Wednesday so . . . I think for a moment.

Petitioners. She will be receiving petitioners at fifteen hours. I'm itching to talk to her, but I would just be wasting my time if I go searching for her now. Instead, I decide to go back to my room, take a quick bath, and change out of these dust-ridden clothes.

After that, I'll get my answers, then let Father know my decision.

I am leaving Nido. It's time I start living my life the way I see fit.

4

VALERIA

"A deafening boom rose at my back, and an instant later, a wave of white energy rippled through the forest and knocked me to the ground. I got up, dazed, and when I walked back the way I'd come, I couldn't find the shimmering veil. It was gone!"

Calierin Kelraek – Fae Warrior – 1 AV

After my bath, I feel human again. Half-fae and half-human, to be precise.

A simple tunic and worn leggings have replaced my dirty clothes. They are of an earthy hue that blends well with the walls. A worn leather belt cinches my waist and provides a place for my dagger, which I carry with me at all times. It was a present from Father. The hilt is shaped like a raven's body, and the cross-guard is its wide-spread wings.

I run a finger over the pile of books that sits on my desk. They are all *old history books*, like Amira likes to call them. They discuss Tirna-nog, espiritu, the veil, and how life used to be in Castella before our connection with the fae realm was severed for unknown reasons.

The veil's disappearance is the crux of my fascination with the fae. Why is it gone? Did the fae close it from the other side? They were the ones who opened it, after all, the ones with the knowledge.

Two thousand years ago, Aldryn Theric, a fae king from a long line, stumbled upon a split in the fabric of the ethereal plane. It is said he used his espiritu to widen the tear and cross to the other side. Right away, he knew he'd found something special and soon returned with his retinue to explore the new lands.

These fae pioneers remained in Castella for nearly two years, visiting the small tribes that dotted the land. It is well documented that King Theric befriended the members of one particular powerful family, my Plumanegra ancestors, who joined Theric and developed a human/fae alliance. In their minds, they foresaw two united races, working together to mutually benefit. They promoted trade and migration, a well-intentioned strategy that didn't anticipate the animosity that would eventually arise between the two species as the novelty of their acquaintance faded. Not surprising, really. Humans, even among themselves, find meaningless reasons to hate each other. For two races to quarrel seems only natural.

It was from King Theric's line that the Plumanegra's ability to shift into ravens came. In fact, my ancestors, at the time, went by the surname Escalante before they changed it to Plumanegra, which in the old Castellan means *black feather*.

I sigh. If only I could find a way to reopen the veil, then all of those fae who are trapped in our realm would be able to go back home and all this unrest would be over. The humans on the other side of the closed veil would also be able to return and stop their suffering. Unlike the fae, who can live for centuries, they're likely losing hope of ever reuniting with their loved ones. They are running out of time. Some probably already have.

Sadness sits heavily on my chest.

I open one of the books and trace the map that lies before me. Tirnanog used to border Castella to the west, but now they say that if one walks past the border, there is nothing but arid land. Beyond is the Eireno Ocean, and together Castella and that empty landscape form the Emerald Iberis Peninsula. To the south, the Jabaltariq Sea stretches eastward, its tranquil blue waters kissing the Eireno Ocean at the Strait of Jabaltariq. To the east, a vast mountain range separates us from Frankecia.

Some say Tirnanog is gone and all that is left of it is that dead land. However, most people believe it exists in a different plane. This is what *I* choose to believe. After all, two thousand years ago another country used to border Castella to the east. According to the history my sister trivializes, its name was Portus, and it's thought to have died out when their territory was cut off from the rest of the continent by the veil's sudden appearance.

I've read these books multiple times. The fae have always fascinated me. I have Mother to thank for that. Not many know she was from Tirnanog, specifically a small village called Nilhalari which she missed dearly and yearned to see again.

"Mother," I whisper, remembering her long brown hair and eyes, her gentle voice and tender touch.

I was eight when she died, but I still remember her beautiful face. She always used a glamour to disguise her fae features, except at night when we sat in our private quarters where only Father, Amira, Mother, and I were allowed after twilight. Then she dropped the glamour and became the most radiant being in existence.

I always wonder how it was for her to hide her true identity, to pretend she was human. Father says my grandfather would have never accepted the truth. He didn't like my mother from the start because she didn't come from an aristocratic family that could be traced back for at least a century.

A sound outside my room brings me back to the moment. I wait for a knock, but none comes. After a pause, I walk to the door and open it. I'm startled by the sight of a man standing right in front of me. He stands at attention across the hall.

I frown. "Who are you?"

"Princess Amira sent me," he says in a deep voice that makes the hairs on my arms stand on end. "I am to guard you."

He wears the Guardia Real uniform, tight-fitting black pants stuffed into black knee-high boots, and a black velvet doublet with leather straps to keep it tight to his wide chest and the House of the Raven coat of arms: a raven with its wings outstretched, painted over an ornate emblem. The standard issue rapier hangs from his narrow waist. He stares straight ahead at a spot above my head. He's tall, around six-foot-three, and has short jet-black hair and onyx eyes that seem to hold a million secrets he would kill to protect. His presence feels like a disturbance in the atmosphere, a palpable force of nature, as if he's harnessed the very lightning from the skies and will unleash it at the least provocation.

I've never seen him before, and despite myself, he commands my attention by just standing there.

"I . . . I don't need you," I say. "You can go."

Those dark eyes lower and meet mine. They go lower still and stare at my chest. I'm about to declare him a pervert when I remember my Plumanegra key is out in the open, hanging from a chain around my neck. I palm it and stuff it under my tunic.

"I said you can go," I repeat.

"I don't take orders from you," he responds with an effortless confident air, as though the realm itself bends to his will. Then he goes back to staring over my head.

"How dare you talk to me like that?!"

No response.

"You're fired."

Nothing. He just stands there as straight as if he swallowed an obelisk. His expression is blank.

"What's your name?"

Nothing.

Infuriating fool!

I march down the hall in search of my sister. She won't be in the petitioners' hall for another twenty minutes, but I'm determined to find her. The guard's steps follow behind me. I whirl around and glare. He stops, his expression as lifeless as the moles Cuervo sometimes leaves on my balcony.

"Who the hells are you?" I demand. "I've never even seen you around?"

"I'm new."

I wait for more, but he goes back to looking like a corpse. A damn good-looking corpse, but still, I might kill him, or Amira, or Father. Maybe all of them.

"Val!" Jago rushes in my direction as he sees me crossing one of the many Nido tapestry halls.

I wait for him to catch up. He looks chagrined. I feel chagrined.

"I'm sorry," he says.

"I'm sorry," I say at the same time.

We smile at each other like idiots.

"It's really my fault, Jago." I continue walking.

He keeps pace beside me. After a minute, he glances over his shoulder, noticing the guard following us.

"Who's your brawny beau?" he asks, his voice dripping with innuendo and his mouth stretching widely. The smile disappears when he takes in my displeased expression. "Um, on second thought, he looks like they dropped him on his face when he was a babe."

"Don't lie," I whisper.

"Well, who is he?"

"My personal guard."

"Since when do you have a . . ." He trails off. "No, he didn't!"

"Yes, he did."

"What a bastardo!"

I nod. Another day, I wouldn't let him call Father a bastardo. Today . . . I don't care.

"I'm sorry, Val. At least he's a sight for sore eyes."

"What about you? Has my father decreed your punishment yet?"

He shakes his head, looking worried. "Not yet, but I'm sure he won't assign a slab of delicious muscle as my guard. He'll probably order that I fuck an ugly goat every day for a fortnight."

"Would that really be a punishment for you? You're such a harlot."

He slaps a hand to his chest. "You wound me. Deeply."

We pass under one of the soaring archways that lead from the east wing to the center of the palace. Our steps echo on the marble floor and reverberate off the vaulted ceilings. Sunlight streams through the many rows of stained-glass windows, bathing us with colorful light.

As we approach one of the large doors that leads to the inner quarters of Nido, I stop. "Are you busy? I'd like to talk to you about something."

Jago narrows his eyes. "I'm already in enough trouble, Val. Maybe we should . . . I don't know . . . behave for a few weeks. Months?"

Jago has always been too afraid of my father, and with good reason. Father is inflexible with him. He shouldn't be. He should show nothing but compassion for his nephew. Jago's mother died at birth, while his father perished in a battle ten years ago. Uncle Julián was a general of the Castellan Army, and he was ambushed by a group of invaders and executed without quarters.

We are still fighting against this enemy: *Los Moros*, who come through the Strait of Jabaltariq wanting to retake our country. Two thousand years ago, before my family gained its shifter powers, Los Moros controlled our land. Later, King Anselmo Plumanegra drove them out, making strategic use of his new abilities. After that victory, the Plumanegra dynasty was born. However, since our espiritu disappeared two decades ago, their incursions have recurred with more frequency than we would like.

Despite the fact that Jago lost both his parents and was, therefore, my father's charge and only nephew, he receives no special treatment. On the contrary, he is expected to be perfect in all his duties as a royal member of the Plumanegras. When he was sixteen, he was forced to attend the Academia de Guardias, from which he recently graduated, and soon is expected to join the Castellan Army. Something Jago doesn't want to do. Not in the least.

"I promise this won't get you in trouble," I tell him. "I just need to talk to someone about it."

Just moments ago, I'd been determined to inform Father of my intentions. Now, doubts are creeping in. I could use someone to talk to before I take the final leap.

"What is it?" he asks.

I look in Guardia Corpse's direction. "Not here."

Jago considers for a moment. "All right, I have time."

We make our way back to my bedchamber. I let Jago in, then start closing the door on Guardia Corpse as he stations himself across the way. His onyx eyes hold a similar expression to the one the late king wears in the portrait that hangs above his head, which is to say: blank. Yet, I sense there is much going on behind that indifferent façade. I tear my gaze from him. Yes, he was definitely dropped on his face when he was a babe. I need to convince myself of that.

"Let's go out to the balcony," I say.

When we're standing out in the open, I close the doors behind us.

Jago frowns. "A bit excessive? He won't be able to hear us even if we talk inside."

Maybe, but I don't want to take any risks. I'm also glad Cuervo isn't here. That bird flaps his beak too much when he's overloaded with information. I shrug.

"So what is this all about? I'm very intrigued now," Jago says.

"I've made a decision," I start.

"What? Are you going to start playing the proper princess role and organize the All Saints' masquerade?"

"No."

"You'll start attending official meetings with your father?"

"Of course not."

"Um, you'll marry one of the lords he lined up for you?"

"Gods, no!"

"You'll—"

"Will you let me talk?"

He puts both hands up in defeat.

"I don't know how else to say it, so here goes . . ." I pause, make sure it still feels right. It does, for the most part. "I'm leaving."

His eyebrows go up, and he cocks his head as if waiting for more, but there isn't any more to say.

"You . . . are . . . leaving," he echoes, savoring each word, trying to tease out the meaning.

I nod.

"You already tried that, Val. He's not going to let you live at the summer palace until you become an old crone."

"That's not what I mean. I mean . . . I'm lea-ving."

Jago blinks rapidly, as if his brain is stuttering.

"Lea-ving," he repeats. "Leaving? Leaving?" He hooks his thumbs together and flaps his hands as if they're birds.

"Yes."

He bursts out laughing.

"Quit laughing. I'm serious."

It takes him a long minute to stop. "You . . ." he struggles to catch his breath, "you're serious?" He sobers abruptly.

I cross my arms and give him a *you think you're so funny* glare.

"Val, I'm sorry, but that's unrealistic."

Taking a step away from him, I let him have my meanest glare. "I thought you, of all people, would support me."

He considers my words for a moment, then flaps his mouth like a fish before taking a deep breath. "You know I'm always here for you, right?"

Reluctantly, I nod. He really is.

"Well, listen carefully because this is me being here for you . . . that's the worst idea you've ever had. You're a princess. You know nothing about living outside these walls."

"That's not true." I'm indignant. "I know more than Amira and many others who live here."

He shrugs. "That isn't saying much."

"I've been out there, Jago. I know the city. I can make my own way."

A drawn-out sigh leaves him. "That is terribly naïve. You've been to the destroyed espiritu sites, the shops on Colmenar Street, a few of the upscale taverns, some of the monuments, and that is it. You've never been to the outskirts of the city. That's where real Castellan life goes on for the majority of people."

"True. I can't deny that, but that's one of the first things I will correct."

"All right. Fine." He shakes his hands at the heavens and rolls his eyes. "Where are you going to live? What are you going to eat?"

"I'm not poor, Jago."

He scoffs. "You think your father is going to give you money so you can play house with the rubble?"

"I have a few valuable things that belong to me. I can sell them to get started, then I'll . . . make jewelry and sell it. I don't need much."

"Val, Val, Val!" He pulls on his dirty blond hair. "You know that *Tarta de Santiago* you like so much? Almonds cost an arm, a leg, *and* a testicle. This tunic you're wearing," he tugs at the fabric of my sleeve, "that is Malagasy silk, not homespun. That bed," he gestures to my large canopied bed, "It's made of fae blackwood from trees found only in Tirnagog, and has a swan down feather mattress. You haven't the faintest idea what you need."

"I don't care about material things and you know that."

At this moment, I hate him, hate him because his words have sliced through my resolve and have infected me with fear, increasing my doubts. What if he's right? What if I'm so spoiled and used to this comfortable life that I don't even know it?

I shake my head. No, I won't let him dissuade me. I can't keep going like this. I just can't.

"All right, how about this?" he says. "Have you thought about Nana? You'll destroy her!"

Gods, I could punch him in the teeth. This is a blow below the belt. Nana practically raised Amira, Jago, and me. She was there when Jago's father and my mother were alive, but after they died, her presence became ubiquitous. She made sure we ate, bathed, got to our lessons on time, had enough sleep and playtime. She also read to us, healed our scrapes, wiped our runny noses, loved us. She became our mother. I love her to death and don't want to cause her any heartache. Still, I think she will understand.

"My mind is made up, Jago," I say with resolve. "You might be right about everything, but if I keep living like this, under Father's thumb, I will wither like a leaf. And at the end of my life, when I look back, not following this instinct for freedom will be my biggest regret."

"Oh, Val." His face softens, and his honey-colored eyes fill with warmth. He pulls me into an embrace and squeezes me tightly. His chin settles on top of my head as a huge sigh fills his strong chest. "What are we going to do?"

I push away. "We?"

Jago nods. "Yes, we." A short pause. "Do you think you can teach me how to make some of those pretty necklaces that were a sensation with all the female servants?"

My eyes fill with tears. A year ago, I made necklaces for all the women who work in Nido. I used the prettiest shells I collected in the summer palace and spent weeks working on them.

"They were just humoring me." I fight back the tears.

"Oh, no, they were not. They wouldn't still wear them if they didn't think they're the greatest thing since the invention of the windmill."

A tear manages to sneak out and streak down my cheek. "You would really come with me?"

"To the end of the world."

"You idiot." I punch him in the arm.

"Ow, what was that for?" He rubs the spot in exaggerated circles.

"All those things you were saying I'm going to miss, you were talking about yourself, weren't you?"

He gives me a sad smile. After thinking for a moment, he says, "Only partly."

5

VALERIA

"Creatures with pointed ears are at my doorstep.
They must be devils, even if they look like angels."

Juan Anguiano – Castellan Farmer – 1 DV

Five minutes later, I slip through a side door of the petitioner's hall and search for my sister. She stands by the throne-like chair by the dais, getting ready to listen to grievances from Castellina's denizens. Emerito Velez, her royal counselor, stands by the door, waiting for her signal to start letting people in. Father and Amira take turns listening to petitioners once a month. I've asked them to let me help, but they told me the people would feel slighted if they sent *me*. I don't think they intended to make me feel irrelevant, but well . . . they did.

I march in her direction, grab her arm, and pull her aside.

"Did you, by any chance, instruct *him* to be an asshole?" I glance toward my assigned guard, who followed me in here but had the decency to stay by the door.

Amira frowns.

"Never mind." I cross my arms. "I don't want him."

"We've been over this." She glances toward the main door where Emerito waves impatiently.

"I don't want him nor *need* him," I insist.

"Take it up with Father. Look, I'm busy. Is there anything else you need?"

I sigh. "Who is he? I've never seen him. He won't even tell me his name."

"His name is Bastien Mora. You've never seen him because he just graduated from the Academia de Guardias. He comes with the highest recommendation from General Cuenca, who always sends his best recruits to the Guardia Real. Guardia Bastien is said to follow orders quietly, and be shrewd with the sword. Now, I really need to get started." She gestures toward the door where Emerito wears that annoyed expression that he displays like an emblem. He tugs his long beard for good measure.

I give her a pleading look.

She shakes her head.

My eyebrows draw together, and the question I really want to ask prickles at the tip of my tongue. I want to fling it forward like a slap.

What secrets are you and Father keeping from me?!

But this would be the worst time to ask. She has no time to answer. Feeling defeated, I pivot to walk away.

"Val," Amira calls.

I glance back.

"Spar later?"

I want to say *no* to be petty and hurt her feelings, but this is not her fault. I have no one else to blame but myself. I *have* been acting like a child, though not in the way Father means it. I have been allowing him to order me around as if I were not entitled to my own volition, as if he's the only one who knows what is best for me. But that job doesn't belong to him. Not anymore, and it is time I let him know that, even if it breaks his heart.

"Yes. I'd love to spar," I say.

There might be more than swords involved this time, but I don't tell her that.

With a loud croak, Cuervo lowers his head, gesturing toward the apple in my hand.

"You ate yours already, you glutton." I use my dagger to cut a slice and stuff the piece in my mouth. It's sweet and tart at the same time.

"Glutton," he repeats, eying me this time.

"But the nerve! Who feeds you, huh?"

He hops from one talon to the other and stretches out his wings. "Val. Val. Val."

"That's right. So hush your beak or I'll make quills from all your feathers."

At the threat, he flies from the parapet up to a perch staked to the ground.

We're in one of the east rooftop courtyards, waiting for Amira. There is a sparring area here, which we prefer, surrounded by small trees and flowerbeds full of rose and jasmine bushes. We are over one hundred feet off the ground, four stories of solid rock below us, and Castellina sprawls like a tapestry all around, its fringes ragged in the patchwork landscape. Nido is so massive that when I stand up here, I feel like a single blade of grass in a vast meadow, like a tiny bee inside a massive hive.

All around the courtyard, the parapets possess a repeating design that resembles Cuervo's perch. Father says that when he was young, he would shift, land on those perches, then propel himself into the open sky. Hours later, after soaring high above the city, he would return, feeling exhausted and exuberantly alive.

"I wish you could know how it feels, mis amores," he would tell Amira and me while we listened in awe, mourning the espiritu we should have inherited from him.

I yearn to fly. I do so in my dreams as if my body craves it, and it feels like the pain of a missing limb.

At this hour, the sun shines gently, and a summer breeze blows through the bushes, rustling their leaves. The air is like a warm caress, and it's times like this I thank the gods I'm not the first-born, and the job to govern falls to Amira.

She's late again, and I'm starting to wonder if she will come at all. Whenever we spar, we always do it at seventeen hours to avoid the heat of the day. I decided to postpone talking to Father until tonight. It's not something I look forward to.

Guardia Bastien Mora stands off to the side, peering curiously at Cuervo, his harsh expression showing the first sign of any emotion. For a second, I think he's going to ask me about the bird, but then he goes back to looking like one of the saint statues at the

Basilica de Castellina, stiff and polished. He would probably be one of those saints who are supposed to protect you like San Miguel or San Benedicto.

I'm curious to know if he perceives himself in that way, one of the devout adherents of the principal Castellan religion. Some of its members can be quite unbearable. Fortunately, following the arrival of Los Moros and the fae and their respective faiths, Castella now embraces religious freedom, allowing us to worship whichever deities we choose.

For my part, I prefer the fae gods Mother taught me about. I like the idea of multiple gods, all of them walking among us.

"I found Cuervo at the Realta Observatory a few years ago," I say, deciding to be friendly.

Like Amira, he's not to blame for any of this. It must be frustrating for him to be among the top new recruits and yet be tasked with guarding what he likely considers a pampered princess.

Even though he shows no sign of interest, I keep going.

"He was hurt, so I brought him home and repaired his wing. I thought he would fly away once he was healthy, but he stayed."

Guardia Bastien keeps up with his impersonation of a stiff wooden saint. I watch him out of the corner of my eye. His black hair is combed back perfectly and shines like Cuervo's feathers. I must admit, besides his stiff pose, there's nothing saintly about him. He is very handsome, and his full lips spell sin with a capital "S". Then there are his cheekbones and jaw. They're sharp, likely responsible for cutting more than one innocent hand attempting to trace their beauty. Blood was spilled, I'm sure. And those eyes, even though they seem empty as they stare straight ahead, their deep black is bottomless, able to draw a weak soul in with the purpose of never letting it go.

I glance down and smile at the ground as I cut another slice of apple.

"Guess who's not a saint, Cuervo?" I whisper. "Me."

I'm already imagining the poor guard naked. I'm even wondering if his chest is hairy or smooth. Not that I've ever lain with a man. I'm supposed to remain a chaste princess, but Nido has libraries. Plenty of them. And some of their books don't spare any detail.

"Saints and feathers," Cuervo croaks.

Sighing, I stand and offer Cuervo my last piece of apple. "*Tch,*" I click my tongue, and he takes it with one talon and bites a piece off.

I unsheathe my rapier and examine the blade.

"It's just you and me, buddy." I then point the tip of my rapier at Guardia Corpse. "You don't count because you're practically invisible."

Steps sound on the stairs that lead down from the small, adjoining armory. I turn and see Amira taking two down at a time, hurrying to meet me. I smile as her brown hair bounces on her shoulder, her cheeks flushed. She's wearing a dress, not her sparring gear like me.

"Late. Late. Late," Cuervo croaks.

"Shut up, you infernal raven." Amira comes to a stop in front of me and places a hand on her stomach as she catches her breath.

"Hey, it's not Cuervo's fault your tardiness has become a habit."

"It's not my fault either."

"Debatable."

"There were more petitioners than normal."

I roll my eyes. "You're wearing a dress."

"I'm well aware, but it's not a problem. I can beat you just the same."

"Unless you're hiding your rapier under your skirt, you can't." She didn't even think to grab a weapon as she crossed the armory.

She glances around and spots my guard. "You, give me your rapier."

Guardia Bastien frowns, but he hands over the sword after a beat.

His rapier is a standard issue, but it looks like he takes good care of it. Its sharp edge glints in the sun. Amira takes up her stance and immediately lunges, stepping quickly across the cobblestones. Viciously, she aims for my throat. I step back, parrying aside the rapid attack, then respond with one of my own.

Our blades sing, the sunlight gleaming off our narrow blades. Amira drives me toward the edge of the courtyard. She can beat me by steering me out of bounds of our predefined enclosure. I make use of my footwork to find my way back to the safe zone. General Cuenca taught us both, though he was only a *Teniente Coronel* when he still had time for us. The only reason Amira is slightly better than me is because she's older and had more time with our teacher.

Cuervo croaks. "Liquefy her."

Amira gasps. "You've been telling Cuervo you're going to liquefy me? I'm hurt."

Damn bird! Always repeating everything I say.

"It's a figure of speech," I say.

48

We feint, parry, lunge, and strike like a set of twins. We dance past each other, sweat in our eyes. The red sash around her waist slashes through the air as she twirls. The sharp blade glints in the sun once more as she tips it. Its spark blinds me, and as I blink, she sticks the tip of her rapier under my knuckle guard, jerks her hand to one side, and disarms me. My rapier flies off and embeds itself in the soft ground of a flowerbed, not before slicing a few red roses to shreds.

I curse. "Puta madre!"

"Language, Valeria." She retrieves my rapier and hands it back. "I told you the dress would be no obstacle."

I smirk without humor and sheathe my rapier. I want to confront her about the secret Father confided in her, but she looks tired and in need of some peace, so I let it go. For now. I shake my head, realizing that it's the second time someone hands me my ass today. I need a win.

Perhaps I'll get it with Father.

6

VALERIA

"When they come for their taxes, I hide the statue of my beloved Saint Agnes in the cellar. She guards our lambs, and their wool puts food in my children's bellies. What has Los Moros' god ever done for us?"

Francisca Oliva – Shepherdess – 35 BV

I wait until after dinner when I know Father is more at ease, unwinding from his long days of ruling Castella. He is a good king, a million times better than my grandfather.

Growing up, I was around enough adult conversations to pick up on different impressions. I hid under tables with Amira when everyone thought we were in bed or otherwise engaged, eavesdropping on countless gatherings—most inappropriate for children's eyes and ears.

During these occasions, we were glad to hear how beloved our father is, and how everyone thinks he fell far, far from the tree. If only the veilfallen could see that and stop blaming him for all their problems, then life for everyone would be much easier.

I knock on the door to the throne room. Three knocks, then two, then one. It's how he knows it's me, not Amira or one of his advisers coming to disturb him with some urgent duty. Oddly enough, he spends a lot of time in the vast room at the end of each day. I often wonder why. Maybe his private bedchamber feels empty without Mother. Maybe it holds too many memories. Though if that is the case, the throne room should be his least favorite place. That was where Mother was murdered.

"Come in," Father says.

"Stay here," I order Guardia Bastien.

He looks displeased.

"Unless you want to intrude on my private conversation with the king."

This works. He hangs back.

I walk into the throne room and find my father standing on the closest balcony, a glass of wine in his hand. He's peering down beyond the palace walls, at the thousands and thousands of lights that illuminate Castellina at night. Father says that before the veil fell, the streets were lit by fairy lights, not gas lamps. It took a couple of years to replace all of them, and during that time, crime spiked. People were afraid to go out at night. Now, it seems those dark times are creeping back. The denizens are afraid of the random attacks from the fae. These days, many are even wary of coming out during the day.

"Pour yourself some wine," Father says, inclining his glass toward a small table topped with more crystal glasses and a decanter.

"I need to talk to you."

"Haven't we talked enough today? I'm tired, Valeria. It's been a long day."

"I'm not marrying Don Justo Medrano under any circumstances."

He rubs his forehead and sighs. "At the moment, I'm not forcing you to do anything."

"I'm not marrying him or any others," I insist.

"That's nonsense." He comes in and sets his glass on the table. "I know you will do your duty."

"Not like this."

He frowns.

"I'm leaving, Father."

The frown deepens. "What is this about now?"

"I'm leaving Nido. I can't stay here to be smothered further. I've decided to live on my own, to carve my own path."

"Don't be ridiculous."

I hold his gaze to make sure he sees my determination.

"I won't allow it," he declares.

"What are you going to do? Put me in a dungeon cell?"

"You're being rash."

I shake my head, and when I speak, my voice is calm. "I've thought about it carefully, and my mind is made up."

"You can't just abandon your responsibilities."

"What responsibilities, Father? In your eyes, I'm incapable of handling the smallest of tasks."

"Exactly. So how do you expect to survive out there?" He jerks his arm toward the balcony and points at the city.

A wave of sadness hits me. "When did you decide I was worthless? Was it when I saved your life?"

"Don't put words in my mouth. I've never said you are worthless."

"You don't need to. Your actions speak for themselves."

"I only seek to protect you."

"From what? Life? Happiness? Because if that's the case, you're doing an outstanding job."

His face turns red with anger. He opens his mouth to speak, to shout more likely, but I cut him off.

"I'm not here to argue with you. I've done enough of that. I just thought you should know." I turn to leave.

"I won't allow you to make such a terrible mistake."

I face him again. "So you will put me behind bars then."

He clenches his jaw.

Pressing my wrists together, I thrust my hands forward. "Put the shackles on yourself then, because if you stop me, that is exactly what you'll be doing."

His face contorts with distaste. It's evident that the idea of personally restraining me is something he finds repulsive.

He thinks for a moment, then says, "If you leave, don't think I'll allow you to come back."

The words wound me deeply. It seems his pride is bigger than any love he claims to feel for me. "Don't worry. I don't intend to come back."

I leave him, fighting back the tears that pool in my eyes. Outside, Guardia Bastien scans my face for an instant, and the attention is enough to chase my tears away. Crying won't fix anything. As I lift my chin and keep walking, the walls that Father has erected around me begin to melt away, and the feeling is exhilarating. Tomorrow nothing will be able to stop me.

I hear someone headed in my direction. I'm not in the mood to see or talk to some random person, so I quickly slip through the nearest door and end up in a small waiting room. It's a familiar one. Since it is close to the throne room, Mother often arranged her workspace here in order to be near her husband, which means Amira and I spent a lot of time here when we were little.

Guardia Bastien follows me inside and stands by the door. He glances around, assessing the space, probably searching for exits through which I could escape.

"You don't need to follow me around anymore," I say. "You'll be glad to hear that this humiliating assignment is over for both of us."

He perks up at this, his bland expression going from dead to moribund. An improvement for sure.

"I knew that would cheer you up," I say, no attempt to hide my sarcasm.

Pacing along the back of a long sofa, I run a finger over its gold-trimmed back. I open my mouth to tell him I won't be here tomorrow, then shut it again. It's not in my best interest to let people know about my plan to leave. It wouldn't be conducive to anonymity.

With a sigh, I collapse in an armchair. The exultant feeling quickly wears out, giving way to sadness. Hurt taints my decision. I guess I expected Father to tell me he didn't want me to leave, that he would not force me to marry or expect me to be someone I'm not. Instead, he threatened me. It seems he would rather keep his pride than me.

Worse yet . . . I still have to talk to Amira and Nana. I can't put it off any longer. Well . . . maybe a few more minutes.

My eyes settle on Mother's sewing box for a moment. It's still here. No one has dared move it. I used to play with its contents after she died. Eventually, I stopped.

Next, my gaze roves over the painting across the way. The grand canvas is like a portal to the past. In vivid strokes and hues, it unveils a haunting scene, a raven soaring above a battlefield cast in shades of twilight and despair. The land is a tapestry of chaos, where once-bright banners fly bloody and tattered. Forgotten warriors lie strewn on the crimson-stained earth, silent witnesses to the Plumanegra might.

Yet, it is the raven that captures the essence of the painting. Its feathers, sleek and iridescent, appear untouched by the destruction. Its beady eyes, sharp and knowing, are the only real witnesses to the price Castella paid for its freedom from Los Moros. I've stared at this painting countless times, conflicted by its meaning, aching to soar and glide over the clouds. I blink, realizing I'm worrying at the key that hangs around my neck. Absent-mindedly, I stick it back under my tunic.

Almost of its own accord, my head jerks up. I listen. My ears begin to ring, and my heart jumps into a frenzy. I feel exactly the way I felt right before the veilfallen attacked this morning.

This time, there is something else . . . a thrum in the air, one I immediately recognize even though I haven't heard it in over twelve years.

"No!" I exclaim, jumping to my feet.

Without thinking, I run out of the waiting room and back the way I came.

I dart down the corridor, following the sound. My heart hammers. My feet pound the stone floor, keeping rhythm. Guardia Bastien joins me. I fear he will drag me back, but instead, he runs ahead, hand on the hilt of his rapier.

When he enters the throne room, he halts in his tracks. I watch his features with trepidation, attempting to predict the horror that lies ahead, but his expression is as inscrutable as ever, and that freezes the knot already stuck in my throat.

A second later, I cross the threshold, and it feels as though I've plunged into a recurring nightmare, and I'm tumbling head over heels. The scene unfolding before me distorts, melding with memories I've long wished to erase from existence.

Shaking my head to clear it, I skid to a stop. Father is standing, back to the dais, facing a glowing figure.

"Valeria, leave. Run!" Father holds a hand up in my direction.

No. He's crazy if he thinks I'm leaving him. I didn't abandon him when I was younger and he faced a similar threat. What makes him think I will abandon him now? I walk closer, wondering where his guards are.

"Go, Valeria!" Father insists.

I come to a stop next to him and stand shoulder to shoulder. "I'm not going anywhere."

"Then we're both dead," he declares.

"So long I've waited," the figure in front of us says.

At the sound of his voice, bursts of radiant light punctuated by thunderous waves of espiritu dance before my eyes, images from that horrible past.

I know that voice. It belongs to Orys Kelakian, the same fae sorcerer who murdered my mother all those years ago. How is this possible? He should be dead.

I killed him.

7

VALERIA

*"Saints and feathers! The little prince shifted
and flew out the window. Find him!"*

Esteban Colmos – King's Esquire – 10 DV

I was eight years old. My dress expanded around me as I twirled
and twirled.

"Look, Mother, I'm a bell."

She smiled that beautiful smile I was always trying to coax out of
her. It lit up my world.

"Indeed you are, my little pixie." Mother paused, a pair of pliers in
hand, mid-twist of a wire. She was making me a bracelet.

"You're going to fall and bonk your head," Amira said from her
desk. She was working on her letters and was annoyed that I wasn't
letting her concentrate.

I wobbled on my feet as my ears started ringing, and my heart sped up.

Abruptly, a thrum rippled through the air and dropped me to my
knees. My head and the entire room spun. Mother set down the pliers,
eyes snapping toward the door.

"What is it, Mother?" Amira abandoned her quill and ran to Mother's side.

I squeezed my eyes, willing the dizziness to go away. My heart hammered against my chest. It had never done that. I thought I was dying.

"Something . . . something is wrong." Shakily and with Amira's help, Mother rose to her feet and tottered toward the door, which she opened with a shaky hand.

The thrumming sound grew louder. I covered my ears with both hands. Mother turned her head to one side, wincing.

Brow furrowed in confusion, Amira stared from Mother to me and back again. She couldn't hear what Mother and I heard.

"Girls, stay here," Mother ordered, leaving the waiting room and closing the door behind her.

Even as my ears and heart pounded, I rushed to the door.

"She said to stay here." Amira tried to grab my arm, but I pulled away and followed Mother.

My sister came after me, but I was faster and slipped into the throne room, the source of the thrumming. Mother was on the floor, and Father was kneeling in front of her, trying to wake her up.

"Mother," Amira cried out when she crossed the threshold. She ran toward Father, nearly knocking me down.

Father glanced up, eyes red and wide. "Amira, get out of here! Take your sister."

Fear deepening on his features, his attention snapped toward an obscure figure standing in the middle of the room. A yellow light glowed all around the shape, creating a thumping contour, which moved in tandem with the thrumming in my ears.

Amira, obedient as always, grabbed me by the waist and started dragging me away. I kicked and screamed for Mother, and Amira only managed to move me a few steps before I slipped from her grip and threw myself near Mother's feet. I stared into her blank eyes, willing them to glance my way. They did not move.

"Mother," I sobbed, my small hand touching her ankle.

The light from the figure grew brighter, the thrumming intensifying by a similar degree.

Father pushed my shoulder. "Listen for once, Valeria. Go!"

I fell on my bottom as he took a step over Mother and blocked the ominous figure from view.

"You will pay for this," Father bellowed, his voice a mixture of rage and agony.

The thrumming reached a stupefying crescendo.

It can't be him. It can't.

Yet, the same glowing figure now stands in the exact same spot it did that day. Father also stands in the same place, shoulders squared, facing what looks like his wife's murderer. But it can't be. He's supposed to be dead.

The air thrums. My ears ring.

I try to peer through the terrible brightness, try to discern who stands within its folds. The shape is no more than a silhouette, but it matches the one in my memory. It feels like the same espiritu with the same attributes, the same signature.

Rage explodes in my chest. This bastardo killed my mother,

stole from Amira and me the joy of what used to be a perfect family. And now he's back, intent on taking what's left. I won't allow it.

I rush to Father's side. He startles at my presence and immediately throws his arm across my chest. "What are you doing? Get back!"

"I can stop him," I say, my rage boiling over.

"No, you can't," he says with certainty.

He knows I can. I did it before. I don't know how, but I did.

Guardia Bastien joins our side and unsheathes his rapier. His blade isn't fae-made, so it can't block espiritu. Still, Father looks relieved, and I can't lie. I feel the same way.

But all that relief washes away when Amira steps into view from behind the sorcerer.

Father shares my shock. It is evident in the way his entire being seems to wilt, as though all strength has drained out of him in one go.

"Amira, what are you doing?" Father asks, his words a croaky whisper.

"What needs to be done," she replies.

He shakes his head. "No. This isn't you. You are . . . good."

She scoffs. "And you know that how?"

The knot in my throat threatens to shock me. I struggle to breathe. Amira *is* good. She would never do something like this, which means—

"What have you done to her?!" Father bellows at the sorcerer.

Orys has now stolen my sister, too. But he should have never returned. I may not know or remember how I stopped him before, but I'm going to do it again.

As the thrumming of the sorcerer's espiritu snaked its way into every corner of my small body, something warm glowed in my chest. Like tendrils of smoke, that warmth moved to encompass the rest of my body until I felt an immense sense of calm and strength suffuse my entire being.

That monster killed my mother, and I will kill him.

This wasn't an appropriate thought for an eight-year-old. Nonetheless, it felt right.

I stood, abandoning Mother for only a moment.

I will be back. I promise.

Quietly, I stood behind Father as he faced his enemy. Amira wasn't a concern anymore. She was too paralyzed with fear and grief to try to follow Father's command anymore.

Father had no weapons. He only had his fury, desperation, and of course, his agility. It was legendary. He was said to have defeated many foes, even after he lost his ability to shift. Though it was against lesser opponents than this one.

He couldn't confront a sorcerer with only his hands. Standing there so brave and determined to fight, I later realized—once I was old enough to understand matters more deeply—that he wasn't seeking revenge.

He was seeking death.

Without Mother, the love of his life, he saw no path other than the one she'd been forced to take. In time, I also came to recognize that the love he harbored for my sister and me paled in comparison to his feelings for Mother. We weren't reason enough for him to want to stay. The knowledge hurt. It still does, but I have never been in love. If I had, maybe I would be able to understand him fully, and I wouldn't blame him for loving us less.

That infernal thrumming grew impossibly stronger. But the warmth that had enveloped me seemed to guard me against its effects. I no longer felt dizzy. Instead, I felt certain and empowered.

Heedlessly, Father lunged in the sorcerer's direction, a hoarse battle cry ripping from his throat.

What happened next I would never forget.

I lifted a little hand toward Father and said, "No."

The word was a command, and it was accompanied by a wave that rippled outward from my chest. As it traveled, it emitted its own thrumming, though it was quite different from the intruder's. Whereas his espiritu sounded like the elongated pounding of a hammer, what poured out of me was like the melody of a gentle violin.

Father came to a sudden stop, his foot hovering in the air. He was frozen, suspended. His blue eyes swiveled in their sockets, filling with panic.

Like Father, the sorcerer's espiritu also stopped. The room went blessedly silent as the horrible pounding came to a halt. The light around the male dimmed, and what had only been a silhouette up until now, solidified into a tall figure dressed in a long brown robe.

A pair of cold gray eyes stared at me from a handsome fae face.

The juxtaposition of evil and beauty was unsettling. As a child, I'd been accustomed to pretty things being good, or at least harmless. But I immediately realized how mistaken I had been.

Beauty can be sharp and lethal.

Cocking his head to one side, the sorcerer watched me with undisguised interest. "What do we have here?" His gaze scrutinized every part of me, placing special emphasis on my ears. "Half fae, I suppose?"

He directed the question at my immobile father. "What kind of secrets have you been keeping, Simón Plumanegra?" Now, his gaze slid toward my mother as she lay on the floor. In death, her glamour had dissolved, and her true nature was revealed.

Father's face went red. I imagined he was angry that this stranger had figured out the secret he'd so jealously guarded since he met my mother.

"What would your subjects think?" the sorcerer went on. "Their king cavorting with filthy batracios. What a scandal."

I later learned that "batracio" is a slur humans call the fae. It's a word from our old language that means frog or toad. People say fae might be as beautiful as princes or princesses on the outside, but on the inside, they are ugly and base.

The sorcerer went down on one knee and spoke in a tender, melodic voice. "Hello, princesita. My name is Orys. Would you come and let me take a closer look at you."

I glared at him, imagining him flat on the floor, staring blankly at the ceiling.

"I won't hurt you. I promise." He beckoned with one long-fingered hand.

His features were undeniably handsome, sculpted with an other-worldly grace. Sharp, angular cheekbones cast shadows upon his pale skin, and his eyes, the color of storm clouds, gleamed with unsettling intensity. Beneath this façade of beauty, however, lay a terrible dark-ness, a wicked edge that promised to strike like a serpent. He both captivated and repelled me in equal measures.

Yet, I was not afraid. Hatred boiling in my chest, I took a step forward.

A low growl escaped Father's throat. I ignored his disapproval and kept going.

Orys smiled kindly, but I could sense his malice, like an awaiting snare. I was only a pure child and the taint of his evil couldn't be disguised from my innocent eyes.

Behind me, Father continued grunting with effort, but I ignored him still. My full attention was on the sorcerer and the certainty that I could easily end him if only I got close to him.

Tentatively, he reached for me. I pulled back only to erase his caution. If he thought I was afraid of his touch, then he wouldn't be afraid of mine.

And so it was that, emboldened, he took my hand in his.

I sensed a gentle push in my being, as if he were trying to . . . read me . . . like a book.

His brow furrowed in confusion. "Who are you?"

The question was full of awe. A genuine smile stretched his lips. Gray eyes searched me and paused at my neck. Carefully, as if not to spook me, he snaked a finger under the chain I wore and tugged it until he pulled the necklace from under my dress.

His eyes grew wider still and a puff of breath escaped through his lips as he stared at the jewel. I perceived the moment his awe morphed into avarice. With a jolt of panic, I scurried away, pulling my hand away from his grasp even as he tried to tighten his hold.

For a moment, I feared that with our physical contact severed, I wouldn't be able to hurt him. Except I instantly realized it didn't matter. Even if he tried to hide in the confines of this realm or any other, I had the power to undo him.

I lifted a hand and splayed my fingers.

He pushed to his feet, espiritu thrumming again and light glowing all around him. With practiced ease, he launched an attack. I didn't have the sense to be afraid. I only had the certainty that he couldn't hurt me, or my father, or my sister. He had ended Mother's life, but that would be his last evil deed.

"Be gone and die," I said simply.

A surge of warmth emanated from my chest and coursed down the length of my arm. With swiftness surpassing even the sorcerer's, radiant espiritu burst from my fingertips. In an instant, as if he were nothing but a moth caught in a flame, a fiery whoosh enveloped him, consuming him in the blink of an eye.

All at once, the warmth left me, and I collapsed to the floor, the world around me fading to nothing. After that day, there was a white streak in my hair that forever reminds me of what I lost.

"This will be the last mistake you make, you asshole, because this time I'll make sure you never return." Even if I have to strangle him with my bare hands, I will make sure this bastardo never threatens my family again.

I vaguely wonder if Guardia Bastien will interfere—given that he's supposed to watch over me—but he does not. And it isn't cowardice. His expression looks as impassive as ever, no fear has entered it. Instead, he only seems . . . curious.

Shaking my head, I dismiss my quick assessment of him and focus on the real problem. The monster in front of me. I expect that warmth that enveloped me all those years ago to return as I square my shoulders and plant my feet next to Father.

"I'm counting on you to do your best. We have a score to settle," Orys's eerie voice speaks from the depth of the blinding glow. It reverberates through the room, along the thrumming of his espiritu. "It has taken me this long to recover and confront you again. Give me all you've got."

I clench my fists. "You will pay for what you did to my mother and for stealing my sister's free will."

"Amira Plumanegra is here of her own volition," the sorcerer assures me.

No. That's impossible. I shake my head, determined not to believe a word he says.

"I ordered you to get out of here, Valeria," Father says.

"I stopped him before. I will stop him now." I feel confident even as the empowering warmth in my chest remains conspicuously absent.

"No, you won't." Father sounds certain as if he knows something I don't, but in years past, he's maintained he has no idea how I defeated Orys.

"*How did I destroy that bad sorcerer, Father?*" I asked him more than once.

"*I don't know how it happened, amor. Maybe you inherited some espiritu from your mother, after all, but if you did, it's gone now.*"

"*What if it's just sleeping inside me?*" I wondered more than once, but Father never gave any credit to that idea.

And at this moment, that is what I'm counting on. The mere

possibility that I have some dormant espiritu inside me demands that I confront Orys. Not Father. He would certainly die while I may have a chance to survive. I have to believe it even if in the twelve years since Mother's death not a hint of espiritu has graced the tips of my fingers.

I take a deep breath, willing the essence of my very soul to strike Orys down. I don't want him to simply disappear like the last time. This time, I want his lifeless body on the floor, his vacant gaze fixed on the ceiling. I want to personally shovel dirt over his dead carcass.

I thrust a hand forward.

Orys lunges to one side and rolls over one shoulder, but it's all for nothing because my hand remains frustratingly normal. No light emanates from it. No espiritu delivers the killing blow I yearn to see.

The sorcerer stretches to his full height and the light that conceals him falls away. I gasp, horror seizing my breath. His once-handsome countenance is now grotesquely disfigured, appearing as if it is sculpted from melted wax. His mouth droops in a downward line, and his eyelids look like thin, crumpled parchment.

His gaze falls to my chest.

"I told you," Amira says.

Orys's destroyed mouth stretches into a grimace of satisfaction. "I had to see for myself."

Next, he lifts a hand and beckons toward my chest.

As if this is some sort of signal, Guardia Bastien steps forward and unsheathes his rapier with a *zing*. It seems he gave me the benefit of the doubt and patiently witnessed my ineffectual move, but seeing as all I did was wiggle my fingers at the sorcerer, Guardia Bastien has decided to act.

Raising his weapon, he quickly advances on Orys, then hacks down as if to split the male in two. Orys is quicker, however, and when he weaves his fingers and thrusts his hands forward, actual espiritu pours from them in a blinding torrent. The magic strikes Guardia Bastien squarely in the chest and sends him flying against the wall. He crumples like a marionette and doesn't get back up.

Father takes my hand, pulls me, and tucks me behind his back. Slowly, he starts backing away from the sorcerer and Amira.

"There is no escape, Father," my sister says. "Your time is over."

He takes another step back, still blocking me.

"Valeria, his time is over," she says to me. "It is our turn to shine."

What is she talking about? Father is still young and strong.

She goes on. "He keeps you under his thumb like a flea. Don't you want to be free to do whatever you want?"

"Amira, snap out of it." I try to circumvent Father, but he keeps me behind him, still making his way toward the exit.

She laughs. "I'm not his puppet like you are, and I don't have patience for your lack of conviction." She looks at Orys and says, "Take care of them."

He doesn't wait to be told twice and blasts a wave of energy in our direction.

I brace myself for the blast of Orys's magic, for death.

Instead, I'm hit from the side and go tumbling away from my father. I land on my back, the air *whooshing* from my lungs. Wincing at the pain, I realize Guardia Bastien is on top of me.

Scrambling, I push him away and sit up. "Father!"

He's on the floor, lying on his side and twisted like a discarded sparring dummy. I crawl desperately toward him. Grabbing his shoulder, I turn him on his back. His face is blank with death.

"No. No. No." I shake him. "Father, please." I press a hand to his cheek. His beard is soft against my palm. "Wake up. Please, wake up." Hot tears spill onto my cheeks, tracing twin paths that burn to the depths of my very heart. "I promise I won't leave you." I kiss his forehead. "I'll stay here and do whatever you want me to do. I'll marry whoever you wish."

He only wanted what he thought was best for me. I thought I would have the chance to show him there could be more than one path for me, but now our last interaction will forever be an argument we both wanted to win.

"I love you, Father. Please." I press my forehead to his chest and long for his strong embrace.

Amira comes closer. "Don't be pathetic, Val. His miserable life isn't worth giving up your own."

Strong arms wrap around my waist, but they are not Father's. They belong to Guardia Bastien, who picks me up and drags me toward the door. I fight feebly until I notice Orys walking in our direction. He's intent on me—his now-clouded gray eyes full of the same hatred I feel toward him.

Limp with grief, I let Guardia Bastien drag me away. We're almost to the door when it slams shut on a phantom wind.

"Where do you think you're going, you fraud of a girl?" Orys asks.

Guardia Bastien lets me go and produces a dagger. He stands protectively in front of me, but what hope does he have wielding a mere toothpick of a weapon against the blaze of espiritu? Only a fae-made blade would stand a chance, and there are few of those in Castella, like the one hanging on the wall in Father's bedchamber, La Matadora. What good is it doing up there?

"Stand down, Guardia Bastien," I say. "This sorcerer's quarrel is with me. You should leave and save your life."

He throws an incredulous look over his shoulder. He seems shocked, whether by the implication that he will flee like a coward or by my honorable offer to sacrifice myself, I don't know. When he doesn't run out the door and stands his ground, I decide it's the latter.

Definitely not a coward, but most certainly a fool.

"You should take her up on her offer, weak guard," Orys says.

Weak guard? Is he blind? Guardia Bastien is tall with wide shoulders and legs like marble columns. But maybe sorcerers measure strength by the amount of espiritu a person has, which amounts to zero between the guardia and me.

Orys flicks his hand carelessly, and Guardia Bastien's dagger flies off his hand and clatters to the floor. Fast as lightning, the guard pulls out another dagger from behind his back and flings it at the sorcerer. One flick of Orys's hand gets rid of that threat, too.

Next, my surprisingly loyal guard tries to go for Orys's throat. This time, he ends up frozen mid-lunge, his eyes wide as swiveling big marbles.

"Better," Orys says, smiling his twisted grimace.

A chill assaults me at the sight of the snake's amusement. Beyond him, Father's body lies still. I keep my gaze focused on my enemy, trying my best to keep my anguish at bay. Still, I notice Amira stepping over Father's prone shape as if he were only a bothersome obstacle.

Orys doesn't come closer. Instead, he waits for Amira, who casually makes her way to me. She stops a couple of feet away and scrutinizes me from head to toe. Her expression is annoyed, as if this horrible situation has been nothing more than one of the boring council meetings she complains about.

"He's gone," she declares. "For good."

My lower lip trembles.

"Aren't you happy?"

This can't be my sister. It just can't be.

Amira interlaces her fingers and nods. "I understand. You're in shock, but once it sinks in, you'll realize this is the best situation for both of us. I don't have to wait to be queen and rule, and you can be free to do whatever you want."

"Please, Amira, wake up," I say, my throat too tight for anything but a whisper.

"Do I look asleep to you?"

"Sleep isn't the only thing that can keep you dormant."

Amira dismisses my comment and steps closer. I immediately take a step back and put my hand up. "Stay away."

"There's only one thing I want from you," she points at my neck, "your Plumanegra key."

"What? What for?" It identifies me as a member of Castella's royal family. Everyone with the Plumanegra last name has one.

"It's just a . . . precautionary measure. You've always said you're glad I'm the eldest because you have no interest in ruling. It's the only reason you're still alive, and if that's the case, why should you care about a silly key?"

I don't remember a day when the key hasn't been around my neck. By tradition, it gets placed around every Plumanegra's neck on the day they're born. Every year until adulthood, it's resized without removing it. The last time a few links were added, Father was with me. He smiled proudly saying he couldn't believe I was all grown.

"I care because it's mine. Father gave it to me," I say, even though I know it's a mistake.

Amira's eyes flash with anger. She turns to Orys and points at Guardia Bastien. "Wake him up!"

Orys snaps his fingers, and Guardia Bastien staggers a few paces before he catches himself. He appears disoriented, his head and eyes moving from side to side.

"You're no longer required to watch over Princess Valeria," Amira says. "Understood?"

The poor guardia looks nothing but confused.

"You're relieved of the post, and if you value your station, you will obey me without question." She looks him up and down in a hungry way that is nothing like herself. Or is it? What if she did plan all of this? What if I'm wrong about her?

Guardia Bastien appears conflicted for a moment, but in the end, he thumbs his chest with one fist, clicks his heels, and bows slightly. "At your service, Queen Plumanegra."

I nearly choke.

Queen Plumanegra. It sounds wrong. So wrong.

Amira looks at me down her nose, satisfied. "Now, take the necklace she wears around her neck."

Guardia Bastien doesn't hesitate. Not for a second. Even though I try to fight back, he moves too fast and assuredly to be able to stop him. In no time, he has both my wrists in the grip of one hand while, with the other, he pulls the chain and breaks it with one abrupt tug. The metal bites into my skin and rubs it raw. I try to snatch it back, but he pushes me away and moves to stand next to my sister.

"Much better," Amira says, looking satisfied. "Now, you can go about your jewelry making, excursions into the city, cavorting with Jago and your parrot, or whatever it is you prefer to do. I promise no one will bother you as long as *you* don't bother anyone."

And by anyone she means herself? Or does she mean . . .? My gaze slides to Orys. If Amira is not being puppeteered by the sorcerer, what role does he play here? And if she is, what does he intend to do? Will he rule through her? Will he also kill her and install himself as king? Or is there another plan that I can't even begin to fathom?

My head spins. My heart aches.

Father is dead. I can't trust my sister, and the future of Castella may hang in the balance. The life I envisioned for myself crumbles as quickly as I built it. A new reality takes shape before my eyes, and it looks unlike anything I've ever imagined.

8

VALERIA

*"Don't fret, niña bonita. It's just the Basilica's bells.
They're tolling for the queen. She's with the saints now."*

Orquidea Rios – Castellina Resident – 10 DV

I pace in my room, my lungs pumping too fast, anxiety ripping me to shreds. I fear I'll go insane. There's a knock at my door. I freeze mid-step.

"Val, it's me."

I run to the door and fling it open. Jago stands there, his expression full of sorrow. I fling my arms around his neck and sink into him. He says nothing. He just holds me tight. Only two hours have passed since . . .

The news has clearly spread through the palace, but what news?

I grab his hand, pull him into the room, and shut the door. "What did she say?"

He furrows his brow. "She?"

"Amira. What story did she tell everyone?"

"Story?"

"Don't just repeat everything I'm saying, tell me what she said . . . what you heard."

"I heard from a guard that Uncle Simón is dead. I'm so sorry, Val."

"What else?"

He shakes his head.

"What else did you hear?"

"Nothing. I came straight here."

I whirl away from him and start pacing the room again.

"I'm confused. What's going on?" He comes close, tries to take my hands, but I don't let him.

Instead, I grab his shoulder and look him in the eye. "I need you to go out there and find out what happened to my father."

His mouth opens and closes.

"I want you to find out how he died."

"You . . . don't know?"

I shake my head. At this moment, lying is easier. I doubt I would be able to relate what really happened, and I don't need to add to his confusion.

He pulls me into a hug. "That can wait, Val. You're upset."

The hug nearly undoes me, but I push my emotions down and allow my mind to keep control of the situation. Calmly, I take a step back.

"Yes, I'm upset, but this is important. I need you to find Emerito. He will know."

Jago's light brown eyes scan my face. He's known me all my life, and he doesn't fail to see what I want him to see. "All right, I'll be back as soon as I can."

"Thank you."

He slips out the door. I engage the lock and go back to pacing. Thirty minutes later, as I'm on the verge of losing my mind, he returns. I throw open the door before he even knocks. His hair is standing on end, and his entire demeanor is worse than before.

"It's bad," he says.

Whatever he heard can't be worse than the truth, so I'm ready to hear it.

"Sit." I point toward an armchair in the corner near the balcony.

Jago collapses in it and runs stiff fingers through his hair, making the disarray worse. "Maybe you should sit, too," he suggests.

"No, I'm fine. Please, tell me everything."

He nods and begins. "I found Emerito on his way to the main council chamber. There's an emergency meeting happening right now. He didn't want to talk to me, but I insisted." He pauses, swallows audibly. "He told me that . . . Orys Kelakian killed the king."

I wait for more, but Jago is scrutinizing my face again, trying to read it as he does so well.

"You already knew," he says.

I nod.

"Then why did you send me out there?"

"What else did Emerito say?"

"He said they don't know how the sorcerer got in, and that Orys could possibly be associated with the veilfallen. Though, they don't think so. They have sent the Guardia Real in search of him. Amira has vowed to destroy him and all the rest."

Jago is still talking, but I'm not listening anymore. I press a hand to my throat, finding it difficult to swallow. They're spinning a lie as I feared, like clever spiders wishing to tangle all in their web. The question remains . . . Is Amira part of it? Or a victim like our father? And is Orys truly not associated with the veilfallen? Or is this a ruse to divert attention from the rebels?

"Val, are you listening?" He pushes to the edge of the armchair.

Snapping out of it, I kneel in front of him and take his hands in mine. "You have to listen to me," I whisper.

There's fear in his features as there should be. No doubt, his face reflects what he sees in mine.

"Why do I have the feeling I'm not going to like this?" he asks.

"It's all a lie," I say. "Well, most of it. Orys did kill my father. The sorcerer *is* back. I saw him."

"Puta madre!"

"But it was Amira who let him in."

His mouth falls open.

"She allowed it to happen, and I don't know if she did it of her own volition or if Orys compelled her."

"Oh, Val. That's . . . I just can't . . ." He squeezes my hands.

He believes me! My surprise lets me know that I was expecting Jago to tell me I'm crazy. I'm so grateful for his trust in me.

"She must have been compelled," he says. "There is no way Amira would do that. Is there?"

"I want to believe that."

"But?"

I walk away and run my hands through my hair in frustration. "Earlier today, I overheard her talking to Father." I've been turning this over in my head a lot. "They were talking about some sort of secret that he had just divulged to her, and that he made her promise not to share with me."

"What kind of secret?"

I shake my head. "I don't know, but it seems to have something to do with the fae."

"The fae?!" His blond eyebrows draw together.

Sparing no detail, I tell him everything I overheard.

"Very strange," he says when I'm done. "And it lacks sense in the way that jousting in the nude lacks sense."

If he knew my mother was fae, he wouldn't think so. I've been lying to my best friend for years. I've wanted to tell him so many times, but Mother and Father made Amira and I swear we would never tell. Even now, when I feel there's no one else in the world I can trust, I'm not sure I should tell him. I'm afraid he will hate me, and if he does . . . I'll be utterly alone.

We're quiet for a long moment, then I remember to tell him the rest. "She took my Plumanegra key." My hand goes up to my neck of its own accord. I find that I miss its weight.

"Wait. What?" He takes a moment to process this new bit of information, then works things out by speaking out loud. "She's afraid you'll try to challenge her, afraid you'll reveal the truth of what happened, but . . ." He trails off, then adds, "That makes no sense."

For the first time since I heard the thrum of Orys's magic, my mind takes over my emotions. "Yes, it makes no sense," I echo. "Everyone knows I am Simón Plumanegra's daughter. I don't need the key to prove that to the council."

"Exactly, and that's not the only thing the key does, Val."

My heart jumps to my throat as the realization hits me, then I'm running out of my bedchamber. I have to check the vault.

As we get close to the Plumanegra vault located at the heart of the palace close to Father's study, I hear voices ahead. Putting a hand up, signaling Jago, I slow down. I recognize my sister's timbre.

"It's Amira," I whisper. "Hide!"

He heads to the first door to our right, and I follow.

"It's locked."

My heart pumps so fast that I feel it will knock a hole in my chest. She can't find us here. I backtrack, running on tiptoes. I turn the next door's knob. It opens. We rush inside. The room is dark, and I sigh with relief as shadows envelop us. I don't close the door all the way and watch through a narrow crack as Amira walks down the hall, Emerito at her side.

"It should have been in the vault," she says.

"Maybe it's in her chamber."

"We'll have to look when she's not there."

The sound of their steps fades away. I press my back to the wall and slide down to the floor. My knees are too weak to hold me.

Jago sits across from me, peering at my face through the gloom. It looks like we are in one of the many waiting rooms that can be found in Nido. I'm not even sure I've been in here before.

"What is she looking for? Do you know?" he asks.

"There's only one thing I've ever kept in that vault." My mind races as I try to figure out this puzzle.

"What is it?"

Not even Jago knows—only Father and Amira. They've always known there's only one thing I consider precious enough for safekeeping.

"My mother's necklace," I say.

"What necklace?"

I lift my gaze from the floor and meet Jago's for only a second. I want to tell him everything.

"What necklace, Val?" He repeats his question.

"Um . . . you might have seen it a long time ago. It belonged to my mother. She gave it to me." I shake my head. "No. She didn't exactly give it to me. She . . . I don't remember." I scratch my head, finding a hole in my memories.

Gods, it hurts so much thinking about all of this.

"Why would Amira want it?" Jago asks.

"I don't know." And it's the truth. I don't have the faintest idea why she would go as far as to take my Plumanegra key to open my private nook in the vault. Does she want it because the necklace is of fae origin? Does it hold some kind of espiritu?

Jago rubs his jaw, thoughtful for a moment. "It *has* to be important. Why else would Amira be so secretive about it?"

I nod.

"Do you think it has something to do with the conversation you overheard? The secret your father told her?"

"I have no idea."

We are quiet for a moment longer, then he asks, "Where is your guard?"

"Amira relieved him from his duties. She said I'm free to do whatever I want."

"Strange. I don't want to seem paranoid, but he's new here. Maybe he has something to do with all of this?"

I consider this, but it doesn't ring true. "I don't think so. He defended me, Jago. If it wasn't for him I would be dead, too. He's only doing his job. Amira threatened to end his career. She's the queen now. He has to do what she says."

"Queen Amira," he says. "It sounds so strange."

I press both hands to my face and tell myself to be strong. Whatever is going on here, I have a feeling this is just the beginning.

"You know the next logical question, right?" Jago says carefully. "Um, where is the necklace?"

Lowering my hands to my lap, I meet Jago's inscrutable gaze. They are inscrutable, and his face is all sharp angles and hollows due to the lack of light. A bitter taste fills my mouth as, for the first time, an awful thought enters my mind. Is Jago also part of this nightmare? What if he—

No, it can't be. This is Jago, my heart says.

Your own sister betrayed you, my brain replies.

Jago jumps to his feet. "You know what?" He waves both hands. "I don't need to know. Don't tell me, all right?"

My shoulders slump in relief, but he doesn't notice. He is too busy staring at his feet as he thinks. "Unless it's in your room? Because Amira and that asshole are probably headed there."

"It's not there," I say, then decide that, in case they try to get to Jago, I need to lie. "In fact, I don't know where it is. I lost it a while back." I haven't worn it in a while. Amira hasn't seen it in a long time, so the lie will stand.

"You lost it?"

I rise to my feet. "Yes."

"Then you're screwed."

"Why?"

"You don't have what she wants, *they* want, whoever, so you'll be of no more value to them. Then your *next-in-line* status might sign your death sentence."

He's right, of course, but they killed Father and stole my Plumanegra key. I can't let them have the necklace, too.

Jago's next words are urgent. "We need to get out of here, Val. That thing is more than just a piece of jewelry, or they wouldn't be doing all of this to get it."

That is one of the thoughts that has been circling inside my head from the moment I was able to get my emotions under control.

Mother was always fiercely protective of that necklace. I had long assumed it was because it came from her homeland and held some sort of sentimental value. But what if there's more to it? Suddenly, I recall the words Father shared with me when I told him I wanted it days after her passing.

"Keep it, amor. It's just a trinket, after all."

Wouldn't he have known it was important? Mother told him everything, right? I have no idea. Honestly, I know nothing about their relationship besides second-hand accounts. Father never talked about her, and as a child, I didn't possess the maturity to grasp the nature of their connection.

"Jago, I can't leave," I say at the brink of tears.

My entire world has collapsed around me, and I have no idea what to do next. My life is in danger. I see the logic in Jago's words, but I can't leave Nido. Not now.

"I have to stay," I add with conviction.

"You can't."

"I must. I can't let them get away with murder, with usurping the throne, if that's what's happening."

"Don't be foolish. You have no power here. Amira holds all the cards."

"Perhaps, but if I run, I won't be able to live with myself. I have to expose the truth and show everyone Orys is behind all of this."

Because he has to be. I can't accept Amira isn't the person I believe her to be, and I'm determined to prove it to myself and anyone who dares doubt her.

9

VALERIA

"No, they don't come from Portus; they're a peaceful sort.
Los Moros come from the south, and they mean war."

Luis Castillo – Soldier (Casa de Cano) – 37 BV

Back in my bedchamber that night, I find signs that someone has been searching through my things. They are subtle, but I see them. The top drawer of my vanity is slightly open. The jewelry box on the mantle is misaligned. The covers on my bed aren't smooth.

"What now?" I ask out loud, my voice echoing in my loneliness.

"*Let's leave, Val. If we don't they'll torture you, and when you confess you lost the necklace, they'll kill you,*" Jago insisted when I told him to go to bed a few minutes ago.

But I can't run.

Amira said I could go about my life in Nido like I always have, and that's what I intend to do. Well, in theory, this is what I want her to believe, but in reality, I'll be working to get to the bottom of this. They're not the only ones who can deceive. I can, too.

Besides, the necklace isn't truly lost. I have leverage, and I will use it if it comes to it. I resist the urge to leave my room to retrieve it. The heirloom is safe where I last hid it, a place Amira would never suspect given its conspicuousness. I moved it from the vault to a place that felt more appropriate, more personal.

There's a knock at the door. I answer. A servant is here to deliver a note. I recognize the seal: Nana's. I retreat back into the room and set the note on the night table. She undoubtedly heard the news, and the note expresses her condolences. I know she would be here if she could maneuver the many stairs, but her pain must be too bad today to allow it. I can't read the note right now. I know I'll fall apart if I do.

I stare at the tapestry that hangs on the wall. It depicts a field with rows of colorful tulips, my mother's favorite flowers. We worked on it together as she taught me to embroider.

"How different life would be if you were still here, Mother," I whisper.

Shaking my head, I walk onto the balcony, wishing Cuervo was here so I could find some comfort in stroking his soft feathers, but he always sleeps somewhere else. I don't know where he goes. I just know he comes back every morning, bright and early.

Walking through the room, I put out the candles one by one. The servants light them at nightfall, along with a couple of gas lamps by the bed. I don't change from my tunic and leggings and curl up on top of the covers, leaving the lamps on. I'm afraid to invite the darkness in, afraid to discover that this loneliness has teeth and claws, like the childhood monsters of my imagination.

I shiver, though not from the cold. The room is warm with the summer air that comes in through the open balcony doors. No, I shiver from my effort not to cry, my effort to keep myself in one piece and not let my bones shatter into a million pieces.

"Forgive me, Father."

The next morning, bleary-eyed, I wake up early, take a bath, and dress in a new pair of leggings and a comfortable wool tunic I knitted myself. I slip on my favorite boots, a well-worn brown pair that Father's royal cobbler put together. The soles are made of supple leather, perfect for walking silently.

Cuervo's wings flap outside. I walk onto the balcony and find him perched on the railing. He peers at me with his small round eyes, looking for all the world as if he knows I'm hurting. I swear there is sympathy in his gaze.

He must have heard the news. He always seems to know what goes on in Nido.

"My father is dead," I say.

He inclines his head, driving his beak toward his chest, his way of saying *I'm sorry*.

"You knew?"

He bows again.

"What did you hear?"

"Rey Plumanegra . . . dead," he croaks.

"Anything else?"

He shakes his head, then hops closer and rubs his head against my arm, comforting me.

"Thank you, Cuervo."

We're silent for a long moment. I sigh. "I have to go. I need to find out what's happening. You can't trust anyone. Only Jago. Understood?"

He makes a few clicking sounds and tilts his head to one side. That white membrane in his dark eyes blinks, and I'm not sure he comprehends what I'm trying to say.

"Jago is a good friend," I say, trying to put it in simpler terms. "I don't like anyone else."

He thinks for a moment, then croaks, "Amira?"

"Amira isn't my friend. Not right now. All right?"

Tucking his head in, he gives me a confused look. The feathers on his head puff up. It may take him a moment to understand, but he'll get it. He's smart. I can trust he won't repeat something he shouldn't in front of my sister as long as I don't overwhelm him with too much information.

"If you hear anything interesting make sure to tell me, got it?"

It's not the first time I've asked him to eavesdrop. This is a concept he understands well. Through him, I've learned some interesting gossip like about the time Jago had a tryst with Fernando and Maria behind the stables. At first, I thought I'd misunderstood Cuervo, but Jago truly rolled in the hay with both of them. Simultaneously. Quite the accomplishment since Fernando always thought Jago wanted to steal Maria from him.

Cuervo turns away from the balcony, majestically spreads his wings, and launches himself into the sky. Watching him, I'm reminded of Father wistfully staring at the sky, a deep longing edged in his features. He always hoped the veil would reopen one day, and he would soar through the skies in his raven form once more. He used to talk about it when Amira and I were little. He wasn't afraid to appear vulnerable then. But in the past few years, he kept a tight lock on his emotions. I think it hurt him too much to think of all he'd lost.

Shutting my mind to my own vulnerable thoughts, I go back inside, pick up Nana's note, and break the seal.

My Dearest Valeria,

My heart aches today as I know yours does. The passing of your father will be felt across the realm, but nowhere as fiercely as it is felt here in Nido.

You have inherited his strength, wisdom, and resilience, and I have no doubt you will honor his memory by carrying his legacy forward. You and Amira are now the bearers of his torch, and I have every confidence that you will shine brightly, as he did.

During this time of sorrow, please remember that you are not alone. Come see me, my dear, if you need a shoulder to lean on.

Nana

This morning, I'm better equipped for Nana's encouraging words, and I manage not to shed a tear. Done reading, I fold the note gently, place it in a drawer, then leave the room.

I move slowly without making a sound. Whenever I hear voices, I slow down and listen carefully, hoping to catch something of interest, but I only run into servants, who go about their chores in hushed, respectful tones. Their moods seem to match mine. They liked Father. I know they did. He was a good king, who treated those around him with respect, no matter their station.

Except you. He never treated you with respect, my brain pipes in, but it's an unfair thought. Lately, we had our differences, but I know he would have come around. At least that's what I choose to believe.

A few times, before turning a corner, my heart speeds, fearing I will find Orys on the other side, but if he's still here, what are the chances I'll find him out in the open?

I'm up earlier than normal, hoping I will catch Amira during her morning meal, but when I make it to the first-floor breakfast sunroom in the east wing, she's not there. Yet, I see evidence of her earlier presence: an empty plate in front of her chair. The garden that extends beyond the enclosure is alive with workers and a gentle breeze. It all seems so mundane, but nothing is the same anymore.

I grab a few slices of orange and go in search of my sister. The next logical place is the main council chamber. The current state of things requires nothing less. I arrive a moment later and, judging by the amount of people loitering outside the door, it seems I came to the right place.

Emerito stands in front of the double doors, flanked by two guards in full uniform. He looks small next to the towering men and stands out like a parrot in an unkindness of ravens. He wears a puffy-sleeve doublet. It is blue velvet, embroidered with gold thread. Equally puffy short pants end at the knees and his stocking-clad feet are stuffed into too-pointed poulaines.

Every minister is here, too.

Ministro Genaro Covarrubias, minister of the exterior.

Ministro Eliseo Flores, minister of agriculture.

Ministra Eva Aquina, minister of war.

They all look haggard as if they haven't slept all night, which I imagine they haven't. I search the crowd for Guardia Bastien, but I don't see him.

After eating my last slice of orange, I wipe my hand on my leggings and march toward Emerito.

When people notice me, they lower their heads and murmur their condolences.

Ministra Aquina steps in front of me and meets my gaze. She was Mother's closest friend once, and she has always kept an eye on Amira and me, even if she is more adept at battle plans, infiltration, and whatever other things her ministry does.

"Valeria," she takes my hand and drags me aside. "How are you holding up?"

Immediately, a knot forms in my throat. I fight it and manage to swallow it down. "I'm fine."

She shakes her head. "This is a tragedy. Simón was so young. My deepest condolences. If there is anything I can do, you know I would move the heavens and the earth to help you. We are already doing everything we can to find that miserable sorcerer. Security has been reinforced at all of Nido's gates, and guardias are raking the streets of Castellina as we speak."

I'm tempted to suggest that she inquire about his whereabouts from Amira, but that might prove to be a mistake. I wouldn't be surprised if my sister is counting on a direct accusation from me. It would give her the chance to fling an accusation of her own. *Dynastic rivalry*, she would claim, then everyone would think me a traitor, hungering for the throne. I can't take that risk.

So I simply say, "Thank you, Ministra Aquina."

"You're here," Emerito says, noticing me for the first time. "Excuse us, Ministra Aquina, but Queen Amira is waiting for Princess Valeria."

I nearly choke at the word *queen*. Up until last week, she was saying she wasn't ready to be queen. Was she only lying in order to hide her true feelings? Was she yearning for the post all along?

Taken aback at the realization that Amira is expecting me, I walk forward. She must have sent someone for me, but they missed me since I left my bedchamber early.

Emerito rushes me into the council chamber, and I find Amira pacing the length of the long table that dominates the space. She is the only one there. The space is bathed in natural light, which comes from the high windows that flank the vaulted ceiling. At the far end, an imposing throne of polished mahogany stands upon a raised dais, the House of the Raven banner hanging above it.

"Your sister is here, Your Majesty." Emerito bows even lower than he used to just yesterday, steps back outside, and closes the door.

Amira appears as haggard as the ministers in the hall. She has dark circles under her eyes, and her normally glowing skin is lackluster.

"Good, I thought it would take a thunderclap to rouse you," she says.

"I slept well, so I got up early," I say from across the table. "A clear conscience helps with that."

She smirks. "I had a feeling you were going to be unpleasant."

"You killed Father, what do you expect me to do? Knit you a scarf?"

"I thought for an instant you might be smart about this whole situation, but then I came to my senses. You have never been a sensible person, so why would you start being one now?" She waves a hand in the air, then smooths her sage court dress. It is opulent, the neckline lined with jewels and fine lace. "None of that matters now, anyway. I have something important to talk to you about."

My breath catches. *Is she going to ask me about the necklace?* I do my best to appear nonchalant.

She goes on. "I'm afraid the life of leisure you envisioned for yourself simply cannot be. It turns out you still have a duty, the same one Father arranged for you."

"What are you talking about?"

"Your marriage to Don Justo Medrano can't be swept aside."

"I had already told Father and now I will tell you . . . I am *not* going to marry that man or any other." My words are firm and brimming with anger. Who does she think she is? She can't force me to marry anyone. She only wants to get rid of me, ship me to a faraway province, where I'll be less likely to uncover her treachery or challenge her right to the throne.

"What makes you think you have a choice?" she asks.

"There is always a choice."

"I am your queen, Valeria, and you are my subject. You have no choice but to do what I command you."

I lean over the table, placing my hands flat on its surface as I stare her in the eye. "Is this really you? If that sorcerer has some power over you, please give me a sign, sister."

Her eyes widen, then she seems to choke on words she's unable to spill out. She looks sick for a moment. I go around the table and seize her hands in mine.

"Amira, I'm here."

She shrinks from my touch, then bursts out laughing. "You really are naïve." She shakes her head, looking disappointed. "All that intelligence invested in foolish curiosity and daydreaming. What a waste of a good life."

My heart aches at the well-delivered jab. No one knows me better than Amira, except Jago, and she knows where to strike for major effect. As sisters, we've had plenty of fights, and her sharp tongue has left me crying many times, but this attack is vicious, striking to the very root of who I am.

"If this is really you," I say, "how did you hide your treachery so well?"

"Treachery? Don't be ridiculous! Maybe you didn't notice, but I was tired of being under Father's thumb. *Don't speak, Amira. You are here to listen and learn. No, Amira, I don't need your opinion right now. You don't understand the extent of the problem to begin to craft a solution. Talk to your sister, Amira. Make her see reason.* He was worse than Cuervo, constantly spouting the same things over and over. I just happen to have the courage to take matters into my own hands."

I shake my head, horrified by her words. They all ring true, which makes me doubt the idea that she's under anyone's influence but her own. I want so badly to believe she didn't plan all of this, but what if I'm wrong?

"Enough of this." She waves a hand in the air. "This is what's going to happen, whether you like it or not. You will travel to Aldalous with a small escort. Emerito will be part of the party. He will ensure you conduct yourself properly once you arrive.

Others will ensure you don't try to do anything stupid on the way there."

My first instinct is to yell and assure her that there is no way in all the hells she will force me into a marriage I don't want, but I manage to hold my anger back. I can tell there would be no point in arguing. She holds all the power here, and I hold none, so I try a different approach.

"You can't do this. I have to be here for Father's funeral." Another painful ritual where I won't be allowed to shed a tear.

The day Mother was laid to rest, I stood next to Father and Amira without crying. I acted exactly the way a Plumanegra princess should act. I honored her with my composure, ensuring the ceremony was regal and perfect. Nothing less than she deserved. I reserved my tears for the solitude of my bedchamber.

Still, I have to honor my father.

"There will be no funeral. He's already been buried."

"What?! You can't do that."

"I have."

"How will you explain that to everyone?"

"I don't have to explain myself. I am the queen. You are leaving tomorrow."

It takes a huge effort to compose myself, but I straighten, lift my chin, and ask, "Why do I have to do this? Why did you change your mind?" Does she not care about the necklace anymore?

"Don Justo Medrano is a very wealthy man, who commands a good number of troops, men loyal only to him. His villa is located near the Strait of Jabaltariq, where threat of invasion has increased in the past year."

95

Is this true? Or is she making it up? Father never mentioned it. Of course, he rarely talked to me about such matters.

"What Father didn't tell you," Amira continues, "is that he was selling you to the highest bidder. He wanted you to think that he was looking out for your best interest when in truth he was only looking out for Castella's future. But I won't lie to you. At least you can expect honesty from me. So here is the truth, Don Justo Medrano is from a less than—how shall I call it?—*desirable* background. He may be wealthy, but his riches do not come from honorable sources. His men are ruthless mercenaries, uncouth individuals who would do anything for gold. In that respect, they are not unlike their master. In short, by marrying a Plumanegra princess, Don Justo Medrano hopes to gain respect and social standing. If you don't agree, he has threatened to join forces with Los Moros."

"It sounds as if he would be better off marrying a Plumanegra queen," I offer with bitterness.

"Don't be silly. As queen, I will not lower myself or my throne. On the contrary, I shall make an effort to keep our royal blood pure." She pauses, then proceeds to finish the answer to my question. "If you don't marry him, he threatens to ally himself with our Moros enemies, which, as you can imagine, could be disastrous for our empire."

I don't know what to say. Amira watches me closely as the information sinks in.

"Now, do you see how you were nothing but a child in Father's eyes? He always tried to make everything seem like a silly game or adventure for you to undertake. He didn't think you were capable of handling the truth. But I'm not here to spare your feelings. I don't have time for that. I also don't have time for your childish rebellions, so go to your bedchamber, pack, and be ready to leave tomorrow at first light. Now, be gone."

Once more, her words cut me deeply. I bite my tongue and manage to keep back the tears that burn in the back of my eyes.

You were nothing but a child in Father's eyes.

Even as I try to deny her words, I see the truth behind them. He kept the Jabaltariq threat from me. He lied about why he wanted me to marry Don Justo, and he didn't share secrets with me that he shared with Amira.

After all her rancorous words, I don't know how I manage to speak firmly, but I'm glad I do.

"Before I do, share something with me," I say, considering that since she seems willing to reveal all the painful truths that were once withheld, she might be inclined to divulge more. "Yesterday, I overheard a conversation between you and Father about a particular secret . . ."

Amira's indifferent expression, which she donned while dismissing me, now tenses. "Eavesdropping is a nasty habit, Val."

"Don't act like you're perfect. We've done enough eavesdropping together."

"It is something I outgrew some time ago. Maybe Father was right to keep treating you like a child."

I wait for her to say more, hoping to trick her into revealing what Father confided in her, but she remains tight-lipped, giving nothing away.

"Is there a question in all of this?" Amira says, her expression relaxing as she slowly begins to suspect I know little of their furtive conversation.

"What was he hiding from me?" I demand.

She smiles widely, and I realize she's satisfied and relieved I don't know the secret Father entrusted her. *Puta madre!* I just wasted an opportunity to find out more. I need to be more shrewd. What if the secret has something to do with why she killed him? It can't be a coincidence. But what would drive someone to murder their own father?

"It's really nothing you should concern yourself with," Amira says. "Now, leave. I have a very busy day ahead of me. And don't do anything stupid. I don't need any trouble from you."

But what about the necklace?! I want to ask. Why would she send me away before demanding I give it to her? There's only one possible answer to that question—she found it! My fears kept me from retrieving it last night, and now she has it.

My legs falter as I take a step back.

No, no! She hasn't found it. She hasn't.

I take a deep breath and push my panic away. Calmly, I leave, perfectly aware that any further questions I ask of her will lead to more dead ends. I hold my head high as I walk past all of those waiting outside. My steps are firm and unhurried, but as soon as I turn the corner, I run.

Feeling as if my chest might cave in from fear and sorrow, I rush through the halls until I find myself alone in the waiting room by the throne room, the same one Guardia Bastien and I occupied last night.

I sit in the armchair next to Mother's sewing box. My hands

tremble as I lift the lid. Its small hinges creak with age. The top tray contains an array of delicate needles, their tips gleaming like silver. Beside them, spools of thread in a rainbow of colors rest in their slots, each one a potential tapestry waiting to be woven by eager fingers.

Further inside, a thimble, its surface bearing faint scratches from years of use, nestles beside a pair of elegant embroidery scissors with ornate handles.

I lift the tray and set it aside. My heart quickens as my fingers touch the concealed latch, almost imperceptible against the rich wood. With a gentle push, a hidden compartment is revealed.

There, nestled in a velvet-lined cradle, rests Mother's opal necklace. The jewel shimmers within its intricate golden framework. The metalwork is a delicate array of swirling vines. Carefully, I pick it up and set it on my palm.

"She didn't find it," I whisper in a rush of breath.

Then why hasn't Amira asked me about it? Why is she sending me away without doing everything she can to take it from me? There is only one logical explanation. She, or Orys, is afraid to make me aware of its importance, afraid that once I know I'll never relinquish it.

I turn the necklace over, my eyes roving over the small runic symbols etched on its underside. As I sit there, heart hammering, I wonder about its true origin, its connection to Mother's past, and the secrets it holds.

Quickly, I hide it in my bosom, replace the sewing box's tray, and close the lid. I sit quietly for a moment, willing my heart to settle.

Memories of happy times abruptly appear in my mind. Mother sat with me on this very chair, consoling me when I complained about the ache on the tips of my fingers because of my first violin lessons.

"After some time, you will build thicker skin on your fingertips, and playing the strings won't hurt anymore," she said, drying my tears with her tender touch.

"But I don't like the violin. I preferred the piano." The piano was much easier and didn't make my fingertips hurt.

Of course, I was lying. I much preferred the violin, at least when Maestro Clemente was playing it. He could draw the most beautiful melodies from the instrument, melodies that made Mother gaze out the window with a melancholic air. In those moments, I felt she was on the verge of telling me everything about her past, and I thought that if, one day, I could learn to play the way Maestro did, she would tell me everything. Sometimes, I still wonder if she would have shared her entire heart with me had she not died.

Slowly, I gather myself. I will walk through the halls carrying Mother's necklace with me and giving nothing away. At last, I stand, straighten my tunic, and leave the room.

Amira will not get this necklace, and she will not send me away. At all costs, I'm staying in Castellina.

On my way to my bedchamber, I resist the urge to glance over my shoulder. It's not easy, but I keep my steps unhurried. The few people I run into watch me closely. My heart pounds as I imagine

Orys looking through their eyes. I don't know if I'm being paranoid, but I feel . . . stalked.

I dab at my eyes with my sleeve, drying non-existent tears, pretending the pain that rages inside me has reduced me to a pathetic, blubbering woman—just what everyone expects to see.

At every corner, I imagine someone charging out to intercept my path and take the necklace from me. No one even talks to me. Maybe it's the fake tears. No one likes dealing with disconsolate people.

I make it to my bedchamber, and after making sure I'm alone, lock the door behind me. Through the open balcony doors, I search for Cuervo. He is not there.

Walking outside, I pull the necklace from its hiding place. Trying to convince myself that what I'm about to do is the best option, I click my tongue three times to call him. "*Tch, tch, tch.*"

Cuervo immediately swoops down from the battlements high above me, where he likes to perch. He lands on the railing.

"Hello, gentle don," I say.

"Hello, gentle señorita," he croaks.

I smile, then click my tongue once in approval. "*Tch.*"

"I need you to do me a favor." I stretch my hand out and show him the necklace.

"Treasure," he croaks.

"Yes. Very special treasure. I need you to hide it away from Nido. Do you understand?"

"Hide," he echoes.

"That's right. Hide it where no one but you can find it. Do you understand?" I ask again.

He inclines his head to one side, appearing unsure.

"Hide it. Only Cuervo can find it. Do you understand?" I insist.

After a moment of pondering, he croaks, "Safe."

"Yes! Safe!" I'm relieved. I know he gets it. "It's a secret. Don't tell anyone." I press a finger to my lips.

"*Shh.*"

"That's right, you clever bird. Now go."

He wraps his claws around the jewel and lunges into the sky, the chain glinting in the sun as he becomes nothing but a speck.

A stab of trepidation makes me place a hand on my chest. I don't know what I have just entrusted to a bird. The necklace could hold great significance, and now it's beyond my grasp. For all I know, my mother's heirloom is on its way to becoming nothing but a memory.

But the truth is, I don't actually believe that. I have faith in Cuervo, but if the necklace were to become lost, who is to say it's not for the best?

10

VALERIA

"No more bunnies, lad. 'Tis bear pelts the fae traders be seekin'.
They ain't got no bears in Tirnanog."

Juan Quiñones – Human Trader – 163 DV

Hand hovering near the dagger strapped to my thigh, I navigate Nido's labyrinthine corridors, my footsteps echoing through empty halls and shadowed alcoves. Each room I enter seems to conceal a threat, the disfigured sorcerer mumbling spells as he pulls the invisible strings that control my sister. My heart races as I search behind closed doors, lumbering furniture, and hidden passages.

Where is Orys?

The palace is a sprawling maze with no beginning or end. Each room I finish scanning seems to immediately transform into a new hiding place, leaving me to wonder when I'll ever complete a search in one room before I need to check it again. Doubt gnaws at me with every step. Is he really here? Or am I chasing a phantom? The vastness of the castle threatens to swallow my determination, and I fear that my task is futile.

As I approach Amira's bedchamber, my resolve strengthens. Maybe that's where Orys Kelakian is hiding. She's still busy in the council room and will be for days to come. I hope the new responsibilities sour in her mouth.

I expect a guard to be stationed by her door. When I realize the corridor is empty, I turn the knob and anticipate it will be locked. But the door offers no resistance, and I enter her room without trouble.

Inside, everything is tidy and in its rightful place. I notice nothing out of order, not even a quill on her desk. My own reflection in the full-length mirror tucked in the corner startles me. I resemble the very phantom I'm attempting to locate.

Breathing unevenly, I find myself wondering if Orys is ensconced in Amira's mirror, whispering evil deeds and curses into her ear while she brushes her hair at night.

Amira, what is happening? I need you right now. Father is gone, and I don't know what to do.

I shake my head. "You're wasting your time."

The truth is, I don't think I would find Orys even if I were able to see into every corner of Nido simultaneously. I have a feeling the sorcerer will reveal himself only when he's ready to be found.

Instead of wandering Nido like a lost soul, I need to find Jago and tell him of my plan.

"Leaving Nido today is not the same thing as yesterday, Val," Jago says.

We sit on a marble bench in the roof's sparring courtyard, the sun directly overhead. Our voices are little more than whispers as we huddle under the shade of a young acacia. Cuervo is nowhere in sight, and I'm grateful for that. The less he knows the better. It's best to keep things simple for him.

He did return after performing the task I asked of him and seemed to indicate everything went all right. Surprisingly, my mind is now at ease as far as the necklace is concerned—a good thing since I have many other things to worry about.

"Your father was going to let you go," he goes on, "but from the way you described Amira's ultimatum, I think she might chase you to the gates of hell to make sure you follow her orders."

"I don't care, Jago," I say. "I'm not going to Aldalous. I'm staying right here in the capital."

My plan to leave Nido is back on schedule. Amira—queen or not—isn't shipping me away.

Jago rubs the side of his face, frustrated. "And what do you think you will find out while living among the rabble? They can teach you all about washing your own clothes, but they know nothing of your father's secrets. You'll be so far removed from Nido that you'll be lucky if you catch a glimpse of Emerito's parade of ridiculous outfits."

"Nana can help."

"What? Nana? She's almost eighty years old, Val. Besides, it's dangerous."

Nana rescued me from trouble many times, but Jago is right. She's too old now. I'm grasping at straws.

"I'll figure it out," I say. "There are people within the palace who might help me." I think for a moment. "I can approach some of them while they're out and about."

"Oh, good. At least Nana will be safe. Who cares about everyone else!"

"You're a jerk, you know?"

We're quiet for a moment, then he frowns, looking worried. "I don't know, Val."

"If you're afraid, you don't have to come with me. I'll go by myself."

"Of course I'm afraid. I'm a pampered royal, a low one in the scheme of things, but still a royal. It would be hard enough to live in that wilderness," he gestures in the general direction of the heart of the city, "without having to worry about threats on our lives. It will be quite another to survive with the queen as our enemy. Have you stopped to think about that? We're too young to die."

I want to be mad at him, but I can't. I have no right to ask him to risk his life for me. Going against Amira might very well spell my end, but it doesn't have to spell Jago's.

"It's all right." I squeeze his hand.

"Oh, who am I kidding? Of course, I'm going with you."

My heart leaps with elation. I would be lying if I tried to deny my fear. Having Jago by my side will give me strength. I sense a test lies ahead, and I must do my best for Father, to avenge his death and ensure his legacy isn't tainted.

I throw my arms around Jago's neck. "Thank you, thank you, thank you."

"Don't thank me so much or I'll change my mind."

I put my hands up and concede. "All right, let's plan our escape."

"Ominous but exciting. I have to admit that last part."

Closing my eyes, I chew on my thumbnail. I need to go through everything in my mind before I start explaining. Once I'm sure of the necessary steps, I share my thoughts with him. "We'll meet at midnight in the old chapel in the west wing," I begin.

"Why there?" Jago scratches his head, confused.

"Because there's a secret passage there that will lead us out of the palace."

"A secret passage? Since when are there secret passages in Nido?"

"Since always."

"And how come I've only just learned of their existence?"

"Father told us to keep them a secret. I haven't thought about them in ages."

Jago huffs. "Just another reminder that I'm worse off than Cuervo in this family. If the palace were to catch on fire, at least he would be able to fly away while I'm consumed by the flames along with everyone else."

"I would never let you burn, cousin."

"I'm not so sure about that anymore." He pauses. "How long have you known about the passages?"

"Since I was nine or ten."

He throws his hands up in the air. "Saints and feathers, Val! Do you know the fun we could've had if you'd told me then? I feel cheated."

He's not wrong about that. It would've been fun sneaking out of the palace with him—not that we didn't find other means to do it. But when I was a child, I would have never considered going against Father's wishes no matter what. After Mother died, he was my hero. I looked up to him and sought his approval in everything I did. I felt starved for his attention when most of his time was devoted to Amira, his heir to the throne. If he had asked me to lunge into the sky from the top of Nido, I would've done it. So of course I didn't reveal the existence of the passages to anyone.

"Just be there at midnight," I say. "And don't let anyone see you."

"Of course I won't. Did you forget who you're talking to? I'm an expert at sneaking."

"And I, your apt pupil."

A smug smile stretches his lips. "I'm glad you recognize that. I'll go pack."

"I thought you had already packed." We were going to leave the palace today, after all.

Jago shrugs. "I'm not ashamed to admit I unpacked with a sigh of relief."

"I'm disappointed. How could you be relieved in any way after what happened yesterday?" I ask in a teasing voice. I know he likes his luxuries, but that doesn't mean he's not mourning Father's death, too.

"Valeria Plumanegra, do you really need to ask that question? You know me better than anyone. You know my philosophy."

"Of course, *minimum effort unless it leads to comfort*."

"Precisely."

With a shake of my head, I decide to leave it at that before he notices he's abandoning his philosophy for my sake.

Upon returning to my bedchamber, I come to a halt at the wide-open door and take a second look in disbelief.

Servants rush to and fro at Emerito's command.

"No, no, no." He picks a garment up from a large travel case, wrinkles his nose, and casts it to the floor. "No hideous leggings and tunics. I want the prettiest dresses and gowns only. At least seven of each."

I step into the room, blood roaring in my ears. "What are you doing?"

Nose still wrinkled, Emerito gives me a sidelong glance. "Getting your luggage ready for tomorrow's journey, of course."

Five servants enter and exit my closet, rummaging through my belongings, leaving nothing untouched. I see they've already been through my vanity as well. In the guise of packing for me, Emerito is searching for the necklace. I have no doubt about it.

I want to yell at them to get out, want to let them know I won't be going anywhere, but I manage to restrain myself. It would be unwise to do that. Instead, I'm tempted to walk away and save myself the headache, but that would also be inadvisable. The correct reaction here should be indignation, so that is what I deliver.

"This is unacceptable! How dare you invade my private quarters without consulting me?" I demand.

The servants freeze. They look to Emerito, their gazes pointing at the culprit.

The little man—he's a few inches shorter than me, even in heeled shoes—tidies his pointed beard and comes closer. "*The Queen* ordered me to take charge. And if you have a problem with that, talk to her."

We exchange charged glares, then he whirls, turns his back on me, and continues to supervise the servants' progress.

"Fine," I shout, "but I'm taking all the leggings and tunics I want." I march into the closet, grab an armful of my most comfortable clothes, and stuff them in one of the trucks, making sure to crumple all the dresses. "You, pretentious little leprechaun, will not tell me how to dress. If you have a problem with that, talk to my rapier. I'd like nothing more than to spar against you and reduce your puffy sleeves to mere threads."

One of the servants turns her face to hide a grin. I give her a wink that Emerito doesn't notice since he's too busy straightening his doublet and patting the sleeves down just to have them spring right back up.

Pleased with my work, I stomp out of the room and don't return until much later.

Everything I'm taking with me tonight fits in a small rucksack. I have one change of clothes, the few gold coins I had lying around the room, but most importantly, my jewelry. Selling it will be the only thing that will allow us to survive out there.

Earlier, I told Cuervo our plan. A glint in his eye told me he understood, and I'm confident he will meet us behind the palace. After that, he can follow us to our final destination, wherever that may be. I will rely on Jago to find an out-of-the-way inn. He knows Castellina better than I do.

It is almost midnight, so I sling the rucksack over my shoulder and take a deep breath. I'm ready to go. My only regret: not talking to Nana before leaving. I couldn't bring myself to do it. I would probably cry, and I don't want to worry her. With luck, this will be over soon.

Cautiously, I swing open my bedchamber door and cast a glance into the hallway. No one is there. I've been expecting Amira to send someone else to guard me and prevent me from doing exactly what I'm about to do. But perhaps she doesn't think I'm brave enough to disobey her.

She thinks wrong.

I ease out into the hall and silently close the door behind me. I'm wearing all-black clothes, and my long brown hair is arranged in a tight bun at the base of my neck. My leggings are form-fitting and comfortable and so are my supple boots. To complete my outfit, I wear a tunic and a long cloak. The cloak has a hood, which is pulled over my head.

My heart beats wildly and, though my breaths come fast, I feel as if I'm not taking in enough air. There will be guards stationed at different intervals from here to the old chapel, but I know this palace like the back of my hand, and I'll have no trouble avoiding them.

My boots only whisper as I traverse the long corridor.

"Going somewhere?" a deep, familiar voice asks from an alcove on my right.

Every muscle in my body turns to stone, and I can't move.

Guardia Bastien steps away from the shadows, his expression as deadpan as I remember. He looks neither angry nor satisfied that he has caught me sneaking out of my bedchamber.

As for me, I feel my own anger rising to my face in a heated wave that settles on my cheeks and betrays my emotions. My hand edges toward the dagger strapped to my thigh. Maybe I can carve some kind of emotion on his indifferent countenance.

But it would be untrue if I said I'm not intimidated by his sheer size. The man is well over six feet tall. Six-two? Six-three? Maybe there is a way to evade him without a physical confrontation.

"It's none of your business," I say, then keep walking.

After a few steps, I glance over my shoulder. "You're following me. It's uncouth *and* reeks of scoundrel."

Maybe he already knows he's a scoundrel because there is no reaction to the insult, not even the slightest twitch of an eyebrow.

I pick up my step. He does the same.

Whirling on him, I deliver the most withering glare I can muster. "If you don't remember, my sister, *the queen*, said I could go about my business as usual."

"That was yesterday. Today, *the queen* has a different opinion."

"And she told *you* that? A lowly, fresh-out-of-the-academy guard?"

"Indeed."

"Why?" I demand. "Why you?"

He shrugs with disinterest. "I have always found success in everything I do. It has ceased to surprise me, so I simply don't ask."

"I highly doubt that."

No answer again, only his usual indifference.

I keep walking, my thoughts churning. Amira doesn't trust me, so she's having me watched by a jerk who appeared out of nowhere, the same as the sorcerer.

If that's a coincidence, then I'm a pink unicorn.

As we walk past a large clock, its pendulum swinging away, I note the time. I can still shirk Guardia Bastien and join Jago before my cousin starts to worry that something is wrong, and I know just how to do it. One thing about being new . . . he doesn't know this place the way I do.

I make my way toward the greenhouse located on the third floor of the east wing, hurrying my step to make the most of the time I have left.

The sweet, citrusy fragrance of orange blossoms envelops me as I step into the glass enclosure. The expansive structure was commissioned by my great-great-great-grandfather as a tribute to his beloved wife. It spans two stories, and it's built on an intricate metal frame, a work of art in itself. The metal is masterfully wrought into twisting vines that shape portholes, benches, frames, and spiral staircases that lead to the upper level. Some of these details are meticulously carved in copper, which has acquired a pretty greenish patina over time. It's one of my favorite places in Nido, especially since Mother spent countless hours taking care of the plants. She offered special attention to the tulips, which have never looked the same since she passed away. Her brand of espiritu allowed her to communicate with plants, and her gentle touch seemed to revive even the most withered stems and leaves. I often wonder if I would have inherited her espiritu if the veil hadn't disappeared.

I spend a moment admiring the blossoms under the moonlight that filters through the glass. Leaning close as if they have ears to hear me, I tell the flowers how pretty they are. Out of the corner of my eye, I watch Guardia Bastien's approach. He's looking at me, probably thinking I'm crazy.

I suddenly glance in his direction and catch his curious stare. Immediately, his corpse-like expression returns.

Rolling my eyes, I weave between two rows of plants and make my way to one of the spiral staircases. It is narrow, so only one person can go at a time. Just to be obnoxious, I make my steps heavy. They clank loudly. Glancing down, I notice he has to stoop in order not to hit his head on the upper wrungs. Recognizing my chance, I start running.

"Hey!" he yells. "Hold it right there."

I reach the top, and like a child, blow him a raspberry. It's stupid, I know, but the jerk is so stiff I delight in being the complete opposite. I run with steps just as loud as I used on the staircase, but when I reach the end of a row of pink roses, I duck and step lightly. Silently, I reach the far corner, where there's a hole in the metal floor and a smooth tube running vertically from the ceiling, passing through the center, and extending all the way down to the lower level. Smiling with satisfaction, I take hold of the tube and slide down its length. I land on the first floor, my feet as gentle as a ballerina's.

"Where in all the hells are you?" Guardia Bastien hollers above.

With a spring in my step, I leave the greenhouse and rush to meet my cousin.

"I was about to go looking for you," Jago says when I arrive five minutes later. "What took you so long?"

The scent of aged wood and candle wax permeates the small chapel. Saint Francis' serene wooden countenance watches us from the altar. A circle of candles rests at his sandaled feet. There are four rows of pews facing him. Jago sits at the last one.

"I had to evade a certain jerk, the one who was dropped on his face as a baby," I explain.

His honey-colored eyes widen, then flick toward the door. "Are you serious?"

"Don't worry. I left him fumbling around in the Gloria Greenhouse. But we should hurry before he alerts everyone."

I walk up to the altar, pick up one of the candles, and hand it over to Jago.

"Hold this," I tell him, then climb the raised pulpit, and press a hidden button. A secret panel slides open behind Saint Francis, revealing a dark corridor. Right past the entrance, an oil lamp hangs from a hook. I retrieve it, remove its glass cover, and thrust it in Jago's direction.

Quickly, he uses the candle to light it, and we enter the passage. There is a lever on the wall, which I pull down. The panel moves back into place with a scraping sound, and the space grows dimmer.

"Very clandestine." Jago puts a hand on my shoulder as I lead the way. "I don't know whether to soil my pants or dance a jig."

I know exactly what he means. The fear of being discovered tingles over my skin, yet it's not the only sensation coursing through me. Even though what lies ahead is unknown and fraught with danger, I can't help the peculiar elation bubbling in my chest. For once, I'm following my own counsel—not only that, I have a purpose.

The passage winds, leading us to a set of narrow stairs. We

descend for several minutes, then spill onto a cavernous space with several arched doorways. I take the third one from the right and continue down another narrow passage. The silence is only interrupted by our steps and the sound of droplets feeding a puddle somewhere in the distance.

"Where are you taking me, Val? Don't tell me you've made a pact with the devil to use his realm as a shortcut."

"No, no pact with the devil, only with Bodhránghealach." He is one of the many fae deities Mother taught me about—the keeper of echoes, guardian of the underworld.

"Oh, I feel much better now, whoever Bocragelak is."

"Not Bocragelak . . . Bodhránghealach."

"Sure."

After five more minutes, Jago adds, "Are we lost? I feel like we're lost."

"No. I know exactly where we're going."

It's been a long time since Father showed us this particular passage, but I still remember the precise route despite the many detours in different directions. Father said their purpose is to confuse any pursuers. Yet, at every fork we encounter, I'm never hesitant and recall his instructions.

When we come near the exit, I stop and face Jago.

"What?" He blinks at me.

"The exit is straight through there." I point to the middle of three passages.

"So let's go." He starts, but I place a hand on his arm.

"Stay back, in case there's someone out there waiting for me. I'll let you know if it's safe to come out."

"Why wouldn't it be safe?" he asks.

"I don't know, but no one saw you, right?"

He nods.

"If I get caught, they don't need to know you're here, and I'll still have you as an ally."

He looks conflicted for a moment, then seems to decide it's a good idea. "All right."

I hand him the lamp and keep going. The way out of the passage is through several jagged rocks and draping vines. I push the greenery aside, even tear some of them down to clear the way, and finally, I stumble into open space. I blink at the darkness, letting my eyes adjust, and when they do, my heart sinks.

A group of guards led by Guardia Bastien surrounds me.

"Puta madre!" I exclaim, and this time I do go for my dagger, while belatedly Cuervo croaks a warning overhead.

II

VALERIA

"The once-magnificent Realta Observatory was constructed in mere days, crumbled to ruins within minutes on the day the veil collapsed. For miles, the sound of shattering glass was heard. For centuries, our astronomical eruditos will feel its loss."

Erudito de la Academia Alada, Diego Fontana XI – 10 AV

I lunge forward, dagger raised, and go for the closest guard. He is taken aback by my attack and is too slow to draw a weapon or build any kind of defense. Seeing as he will pose no opposition, I change the grip of my dagger and slam the hilt against his temple. He crumbles to the ground, unconscious, his knees unhinged.

The guard behind him steps forward. She has long hair arranged in a braid that begins at her hairline and goes down the middle of her head. She's more prepared and goes for a low attack, sweeping her leg toward mine in order to knock me off my feet.

I jump just in time to avoid being tripped and land in a crouch. I immediately spring forward, aiming for her middle. She falls backward and hits her head on the ground, hard enough to daze her. When I roll away, she stays there, blinking at the sky and shaking her head from side to side.

A third guard comes my way. This one looms large, standing at almost seven feet in height. I send a kick toward his stomach and nearly break my ankle. It's as if my foot struck a brick wall. I stagger back, taking several steps away from the mountain of a man. I think I've seen him around, guarding different posts around Nido.

"I don't want to hurt you, Princess Valeria," he says, coming at me with his arms outstretched. "Please, come peacefully."

"Hells devour you!" I give him the fig sign, whirl, and run.

I crash into a tree. I stumble back, shaking my head, and trying to dissipate the stars flashing in my vision. When I can see again, I realize that what stands in front of me is not a tree but Guardia Bastien. He stands as impassively as if a mosquito tried to ram through him.

He snatches my right elbow so hard I cry out.

"Enough of this foolishness," he says, relieving me of my dagger.

"Give it back. It's mine."

"I will, once we're inside."

He starts dragging me away. I fight to get free, but it's as if his fingers have turned to stone around my arm.

Cuervo sweeps in, talons extended toward my captor as he croaks in rage.

Guardia Bastien places a forearm over his head. "Shoot that thing." He points at a guard with a crossbow. The man hesitates.

"Don't you dare hurt him," I spit. "Let me go, bastardo."

Guardia Bastien continues dragging me along, even as I lean back with all my weight, trying to resist him.

Cuervo comes at him again. Guardia Bastien grabs the crossbow from the other man. I lash out and knock it to the ground.

Changing my tactics, I say, "All right, I'll go. Just don't hurt my bird."

I act resigned and start walking, then I perform a maneuver that has served me well in the past. I smash the heel of my boot into his toes. Or at least, I try. He moves out of the way too fast, and I miss him.

With an angry growl in the back of his throat, he shakes me. "Will you stop?"

My brain rattles inside my skull. The man is strong. *Damn him!*

"Unhand me," I shout. "You have no right to do this."

"I'm just following orders." He doesn't let me go, of course. Instead, he hurries his step and pushes me through the line of trees that surrounds the back of the palace.

"Is that what you're doing? Or is it something else?" I demand.

He glares at me sidelong, lips sealed. However, I sense he wants to say something.

"Why won't you answer me?"

"Whatever is between you and your sister is none of my business. Now, shut your mouth."

In an almost imperceptible movement, he slides my dagger under my satchel's strap and cuts. It falls to the ground where he kicks it, making the contents spill all over the place.

"Hey!" I protest, while his gaze hungrily peruses the strewn items. Disappointment washes over his face.

I shove him, rage getting the best of me. He's looking for the necklace. I know it.

He shakes me again. "Keep walking."

I struggle for part of the way, but my efforts are half hearted. He's too strong for me, and even if I manage to get away, there are half a dozen guards following behind us.

Twenty minutes later, he delivers me back into my bedchamber, leaving my dagger on a side table. It's only then that he lets go of my arm. I rub at the sore spot, sure that tomorrow I'll have finger-shaped bruises there.

I glare at him with the bulk of my hatred. There is no sympathy in his bottomless dark eyes.

"Stay here," he growls. "I would suggest you rest. You'll have a long day ahead of you tomorrow."

"What do you care?"

"You're right. I don't." He shoves me further into the room, then steps out and shuts the door.

"I hope you burn for an eternity in each separate hell, and I hope it's very, very slowly," I yell at the door, feeling as if my head is going to explode from anger. But it's useless. A lion could roar in that man's face, and he wouldn't bat a single eyelash. It's as if he's made of rock, and his feelings are shoved so far up his bottom that nothing can get through to them.

I stomp around the room, thoughts racing as I try to figure out another way to escape. If only I could fly like Cuervo, like Father used to do, I would spring wings and leap off the balcony.

Puta madre! How did he know where to find me?

It had to be Amira. She told him about the secret passages. How could she? Now Guardia Bastien and the others, all non-Plumanegras, know of their existence.

As I seethe in frustration, I find my feelings toward my sister morphing. She's doing this. She killed Father. She deserves to—

I shake my head. No, I can't lose trust in her. She isn't responsible for this mess. She's being manipulated by that miserable sorcerer, and I'm going to find a way to stop him. I won't give up, no matter what. He wants that necklace, and that's my leverage. He believes I have it and thought I would take it with me to Aldalous. He has no idea I overheard the conversation with Emerito.

Maybe Amira won't send me away. Maybe she only threatened to do so in order to unearth the necklace.

The thought fills me with hope. Perhaps in the morning, I will find that she's changed her mind, and a different scheme will be in place.

But why not simply ask me where it is?

That question has been ringing inside my head for a while now. The most logical answer is that she doesn't want me to know the necklace is important. But why not try some sort of subterfuge? Something like . . . *"Say, Val, do you remember Mother's necklace? I was thinking about it the other day, and I haven't seen it in so long that I can't remember what color it is. Do you still have it?"*

Anything along those lines would make more sense than all of this. There's only one explanation. This indirect approach means she really, really, really doesn't want me to know how important the necklace is.

After much pacing and worrying, I develop a headache. Reluctantly, I remove my boots and lie down. I beg for sleep if only to stop my mind from whirring, but it doesn't come. Dawn finds me sitting on a chair out on the balcony. Sunlight breaks through the clouds, cheery and warm—so at odds with the way I feel.

Cuervo finds me there. He lands on the railing and looks at me askance.

I lean forward, sitting at the edge of my chair. "Are you hurt?"

He opens his wings to demonstrate nothing happened to him.

"I'm glad. That was stupid. Don't ever do that again, all right?"

He makes a sound like a huff.

"I mean it, you hardhead."

Cuervo turns around and fans his tail feathers as if to scorn me for trying to tell him what to do.

"Watch it, Don Cuervo!" I shake my head. "That's all I need, a foolish bird taunting me."

With another huff, he leaps off the railing and flies away.

Sometimes I'm happy he has a mind of his own. Sometimes . . . not so much.

With a sigh, I get up and stretch my stiff body. I've just reentered my room when my door bursts open and Emerito waltzes in.

"Haven't you heard of knocking first?" I demand.

He ignores me, then waves a group of manservants in. "Take those three trunks and load them on the carriage." He points at the luggage stacked in the corner, then talks in my general direction. "We leave in an hour. Plenty of time for you to get ready."

"*Pathetic meddler*," I mutter under my breath.

His eyes flash to mine.

I give him a simpering smile. He has always doted on Amira, ever since she was little. He was waiting for the day she became queen. No doubt, he's the happiest man alive now. The closest adviser to the queen.

For the first time, I wonder if he has anything to do with Father's death and if he does . . .

"Emerito," I say, pronouncing his name with care and gravity.

My tone catches his attention, which is exactly what I want.

"Can I ask you a question?" I incline my head to one side, pointing to a corner away from the servants.

At first, he seems annoyed, but in the end, curiosity gets the better of him. Hands behind his back, he approaches me.

"This might sound like a strange question," I say, "but have you noticed anything strange about Amira?"

I pay close attention to his expression. Does he seem surprised? Confused? Suspicious? Angry? Any of these emotions might give away his involvement in all of this. But today, it seems Emerito has taken a page from Guardia Bastien's book. His features are impassive, giving nothing away.

"I'm sure I don't know what you mean, *princess*," he says. "Unless you are referring to the grief over the death of her father or her concern due to her new role as queen."

"Never mind," I say. "Perhaps what I've noticed is simply a sister's intuition. Perhaps it's nothing."

"I'm sure it is nothing." He pauses. "A word of advice, don't make trouble for her. Fulfill your duty. She has enough on her plate as it is without a spoiled brat making things harder for her."

"A word of advice to you," I say with an edge of threat in my voice, "don't let your britches get too big for yourself."

He looks me up and down with disdain. My threat means

nothing to him because he feels he has climbed higher than me in Nido's hierarchy ladder. And perhaps he has, and I've fallen far lower than I ever expected.

I turn to leave, invisible to the servants filing out with my luggage. I walk after them, but before I exit, Emerito has the last word.

"We leave in an hour, not a minute later."

I don't dignify his haughtiness with an answer, and instead leave the room in search of a strong cup of tea, something to fill my stomach. I don't bother to go to the sunroom where breakfast is always served. Instead, I find what I need in the kitchen, then go in search of Jago.

On my way to his chamber, I drink half of my tea and eat half of my fig pastry. His door is locked, so I bang on it with my foot. When he doesn't answer, I yell his name. He's a heavy sleeper.

At last, I hear grumbling inside. He lets out some colorful curses and yanks open the door. His belligerent expression falls when he realizes it's me.

"Val." He ushers me in and wraps me in a hug. "I'm sorry. I wanted to go out there and help you. You don't know how hard it was to do what you said."

"You did the right thing."

"Did I? It doesn't feel like the right thing at all. It feels like I abandoned you."

"If you had helped me, if they had seen you, I would not be able to take you with me to Aldalous. I'm sure Amira would force you to stay. We're leaving in an hour."

"Are you sure she'll let me go?"

"She has to. I'll think of something if she refuses."

He nods.

"I'll see you in my bedchamber in an hour then. I have to go see Nana. I've been avoiding it. Here." I shove the cup of tea and pastry toward him. "Breakfast."

He shrugs, takes it, and starts eating.

12

VALERIA

"If I regard it just so, it shimmers. See, by that tree branch.
What manner of thing is this? Stay here.
I shall climb the tree and inspect it more closely."

Aldryn Theric – King of Tirnanog – 0 BV

Nana gets up early. Her joints get stiff overnight, and she wakes up before the sun comes out to sit by the fire. She says the heat makes her human again. So I'm not worried about waking her up when I rap on her door. Her gentle voice welcomes me inside.

"Hello, Nana." As expected, she sits on her rocking chair by the fire, her gray hair falling to her shoulders, not yet pinned in her neat chignon.

She spreads her arms wide, and I can't help it. I crash to my knees in front of her and bury my face in her lap. I thought I didn't have any more tears, but Nana can always coax my emotions to the forefront with a simple gesture.

She smooths my hair, saying nothing. The chair rocks ever so slightly, a comforting motion. After several long moments, I pull away, dry my face, and rise to my feet.

"I'm sorry, child," she says, her gentle brown eyes full of sympathy. "Your father was so young. He had so many more years ahead of him."

I don't ask what she heard. I know she has been told the lies everyone else has, but I wonder what she would say if she knew Amira is involved.

"Not getting enough sleep, I see." She points toward the circles under my eyes.

I always stay up late into the night, reading or working on crafts. She hounds me about not getting enough rest. If only my concerns today were as simple as they were a week ago.

"But now, I understand the reason. Why don't you sit?" She points to the armchair opposite her.

I do as she says. The heat from the fireplace is stifling, the kind I allow in my bedchamber only in the dead of winter. She rocks gently, her fingers flexing on her lap. They are red, every joint nubby with arthritis. I know it hurts her, though she doesn't complain.

She sighs heavily. "I haven't seen Amira. How is she taking all of this?"

Many sharp answers fester on my tongue, but I hold them back. Instead, I say, "I'm not sure. She's very busy."

"Poor child. No time to grieve for her father." Nana shakes her head. "If you talk to her, tell her to come see me."

For the first time, I wonder about what Amira might be feeling if she's under the spell of that miserable sorcerer. Does she know what's going on around her? Is she actually grieving behind that mask of cold indifference?

Oh, sister! I'll free you. I promise.

"I'm not sure I'll have a chance," I say. "I'm leaving, and I've come to say goodbye."

She frowns. "Goodbye? Why?"

Gossip travels like the wind in Nido, but it rarely reaches Nana. Everyone knows she despises it.

"Amira is sending me to the Aldalous province. Alsur to be precise."

Her eyes widen slightly. "I thought that with your father's passing, you had escaped that fate."

"I thought so too, but Amira told me some facts that Father left out. Don Justo is threatening to join forces with Los Moros if he isn't given a chance to elevate his name through a royal marriage."

"Oh!" She rests a hand on her chest. "I am so sorry."

When I was little, I used to talk to Nana about marrying a handsome prince whom I loved with all my heart. I wonder if she's thinking about that innocent girl right now and if that's the reason her eyes now brim with such profound pity.

But I don't want her to worry, so I say, "It'll be all right, Nana. I'm happy to do my duty."

She reaches out and pats my hand. "I am so proud of you, my little Valeria. You have grown into a remarkable woman. You are willing to sacrifice for the welfare of the people of Castella. When Los Moros last occupied the kingdom, there was much suffering. They persecuted everyone who would not relinquish their religion for theirs."

My lower lip trembles, and I bite it to keep it from giving me away. I'm nothing like what she suggests. Even if what Amira says is true, I will not marry Don Justo. I don't possess a selfless heart. I'm not the kind of person who can sacrifice everything for the well-being of people I don't even know. That was never meant to be my path.

I stand up abruptly and press a kiss on Nana's wrinkled forehead. She smells of her lavender soap, a scent so familiar and comforting that I have to clench my teeth not to fall to my knees in another fit of tears.

Taking a couple of steps back, I put on my bravest expression. "I hope to be back soon, Nana. I would never let marriage keep me from seeing you."

She smiles gently, and her eyes tell me she won't blame me if I can't come back soon. She knows it might not be up to me once I'm married. Don Justo could easily turn out to be controlling, selfish, jealous, or any number of things that awful husbands sometimes are. The worst part is that the scant knowledge I possess about this man tells me he will be precisely that kind of husband.

An hour later, Jago and I walk out of the palace through a door by the stables. As soon as we exit, I notice one of the big carriages, led by two white horses, with my luggage already strapped to the top. Six guards stand behind the carriage, already mounted. One of them is Guardia Bastien. They're dressed in blue jackets, not the black of the Guardia Real.

Saints and feathers! Really?

I stare at him, wishing my eyes could shoot little daggers.

Cuervo shakes his feathers, perched on a nearby roof, which makes me notice him. Whenever we leave Castella, he always follows. I like knowing he's around.

Emerito is already inside the vehicle, waving a fan in front of his face. I refuse to ride with him. Absolutely not. I start toward the stables. I'm taking my mare. No question about it.

"Valeria," my sister calls behind me, and I'm surprised to see her, and out of the palace, wearing a dress far more regal than she normally does. As she comes closer, she looks Jago up and down. "Come to say goodbye?"

"No," I say. "He's coming with me and so is Furia."

Amira bristles. "That is not what we discussed."

"It's also not *not* what we discussed. I just made a few additions."

"I give the orders here," she says. "Get in the carriage."

I ignore her and keep walking.

"You will not ruin this. You have to be on your best behavior."

"Exactly. *My* best behavior. Not yours."

Amira follows me into the stables. Furia is eating hay in her stall, looking placid. I point to an attendant. "Saddle my mare as well as your best gelding."

The attendant, a young boy of no more than fifteen, takes a step to follow my orders, then freezes when my sister says, "Stop, boy. We don't need those horses."

As calmly as possible, I turn to face my sister. "I'm not asking for much, Amira. Only the company of my best friend and my mare. You're sending me away from home to do something against my wishes. Allowing me this small favor is the least you can do. You cannot expect me to ride with Emerito all the way to Aldalous. I will kill him."

Amira seems to weigh my request. I try to imagine what she's thinking. Is she worried that having Jago as my ally will cause trouble?

She turns her back on me and walks outside. Jago is reclining against the threshold, examining his nails. Amira glances to the left, pondering, and after a moment, she faces me again.

"All right," she says, "I'll allow it."

I do my best to hide my relief. My mare is fast, and Jago's gelding better be too.

An hour later, I'm seething. Guardia Bastien is holding my mare's reins, and Jago is riding behind the carriage, per the corpse's instructions. Arms crossed over my chest, I stare straight ahead at the road.

We have left Castellina proper and are on the Alcorcón trail, headed west. The trip will take five days and a hells of a lot of patience.

"This is ridiculous," I complain for the second time. I get no response from Guardia Bastien. He's looking straight ahead, his nose pointed slightly up as if he's scenting the road, but most likely he just has a sharp dagger stuck up his ass.

"Can't you at least let Jago ride by my side?" I ask. "Your horse is great to look at and offers far better conversation than you, but we have little in common."

Still no reaction.

"Gods! You're insufferable." Even as my mare marches forward, I sling my left leg over her and jump off, landing in a half crouch.

Guardia Bastien pulls on his reins, comes to a halt, and, in no time, is standing in front of me. How can he move so fast?

"What do you think you're doing?" he demands.

I flip my hair behind my shoulder and skirt around him without answering. If he doesn't deem talking to me necessary, I don't see why I shouldn't return the favor.

As the carriage crawls to a stop, I fling its door open and call Jago. "Come in here with me, cousin. Maybe you can help make this trip bearable."

He jumps off his gelding, ties it to the back of the carriage, and follows me in. Emerito looks annoyed, more so when Jago collapses next to him and thumps his shoulder.

"Hey, Emer," Jago greets him. "Got anything to eat? I'm starving."

"Don't touch me." Emerito dusts his shoulder with a sneer.

"Be civil, Emerito," I say. "You'll be stuck with us for the next five days. You wouldn't want us to . . . oh, I don't know . . . start singing bar ditties, would you?"

I'm not proud to admit that I've learned a couple of very lewd songs from Jago. He winks at me in approval.

"That one about the one-eyed barmaid is particularly good, don't you think?" my cousin asks.

"Your teachers failed you miserably," Emerito sneers. "God will punish you for your indecency."

Jago and I exchange a glance and nod. In perfect unison, we start singing. "In a tavern dark and smoky, where tales and spirits flow, there worked a one-eyed barmaid with two huge cheeks *below—*"

Emerito turns bright red. He looks sick and seems ready for an argument, but in the end, he presses his lips together and opts for looking out of the window, stroking his goat's beard. He knows he can't win against us.

I look around the compartment and find what I'm looking for, a food basket. They always pack one for long trips and customize it for the traveler, so I expect to find a slice or two of Tarta de Santiago. I'm smiling as I open the double lid, but my excitement evaporates when I notice what's inside: a jar of olives, pickled sardines, hard-boiled eggs, gazpacho . . . all things I don't like.

"Is there another basket?" I look around. Nothing.

I throw a nasty glare in Emerito's direction and set the basket on the floor. He really set out to make this trip as miserable as possible.

"What? No food?" Jago takes a look inside the basket. "Lentil stew? Whoever ordered this must be constipated. Yuk!"

Emerito sneers, his expression suggesting he truly is constipated.

The last time we took a trip like this one, Father was with us. We sang wholesome songs, told stories, and ate cheese, smoked ham, and bread. It was nothing like this.

Frustrated, I start climbing out the window and send Emerito into a nervous fit.

"What are you doing?" he demands, shrinking into his seat. "You're going to get yourself killed. You're nothing but a savage."

I'm tempted to kick him and pretend it's an accident, but I resist, and instead, make my way out, climbing dexterously and sitting on top of the carriage's roof among the luggage. The driver isn't too surprised. This particular man has seen me do this before. He only glances over his shoulder and offers me a friendly nod. Jago joins me a couple of minutes later.

"Much better," he says. "I would get ill if I sit next to that stuffy little man for too long."

Guardia Bastien pulls his horse next to the carriage and looks up at us.

"Get her down from there!" Emerito demands from Guardia Bastien. "It's so unseemly."

The guard's inscrutable dark eyes evaluate me and the roof around me. "Catch her if she falls?" he instructs Jago.

"Oh, she won't fall. She's like a monkey. She can out-climb anyone."

Guardia Bastien huffs then slows down his horse to take his position behind the carriage. He seems to like this arrangement, probably because he can keep an eye on me. I've been riding on top of the carriage since I was little. Father never objected, and if Guardia Bastien had, he would have gotten a piece of my mind.

I've been on this road before and know that our trip requires a few stops along the way. The first one is in a town called La Torre. It's a charming place with cobblestones worn smooth by years of history. Its whitewashed buildings are cozy and adorned with faded wooden shutters and terracotta tiles. Beyond its borders, golden fields of wheat surround it, as well as olive trees and vineyards that stretch for leagues.

There is only one small inn, and its owner must already be expecting us. I'm sure Emerito took care of sending a messenger ahead to prepare all of our hosts along the way. He wouldn't travel in anything but comfort.

At midday, I complain about being hungry, but Guardia Bastien refuses to stop in any of the villages along the path. So in the end, Jago and I have to content ourselves with Emerito's poor food choices.

We finally arrive in La Torre as the sun disappears on the horizon. The inn is a lovely little place, and as soon as I climb down from the carriage, my eyes are roving around, marking all the doors and windows, but most importantly, the stables where they will keep our horses. Cuervo flies overhead, surely in search of a tree on which to rest.

Jago and I discussed our plan in hushed tones when Guardia Bastien wasn't drilling holes in the back of our heads. Cuervo perched on the edge of the moving carriage, paying close attention. The plan is simple and involves a diversion that will give Jago time to retrieve the horses while everyone is distracted.

For now, a nice meal followed by a warm bath sounds delightful.

Stepping toward the inn, my eyes immediately catch sight of a prominent black bow above the doorframe. Pausing, I cast a glance along the row of doors lining the street, each adorned with the same somber bows. The sight sends a lance of sadness straight through my heart. Castella is in mourning for the loss of their king, and this is their way of showing it. Meanwhile, I, as the king's daughter, must press on without the luxury of grieving openly, concealing the pain that gnaws at me.

Shaking myself, I step inside. The first level consists of a tavern and an eatery. The owners are a married couple in their early fifties, whom I remember from a trip some years back. He is jolly, with a wide girth and graying hair. His wife is a still-beautiful woman, curvaceous and strong-boned from much hard work. Her hair is jet black, with only a few gray hairs in sight. They are friendly, much more so than my travel companions. It makes me want to stay here.

They treat us with deference, but not as much as usual, for which I'm grateful. Guardia Bastien advised me not to reveal my identity since it's being kept secret for *security purposes*. Whatever that means. No one has ever cared about Princess Valeria. Still, I appreciate the anonymity and the fact that no one seems to remember me. I'm older now, and Amira always gets all the attention. Luckily, I remembered to pack the ground walnut hulls to disguise the white streak in my hair.

The eatery is as cozy as I remember it. The same rough-hewn tables and chairs fill the space, though I don't remember the beautiful flamenco dancer mantillas hanging from the walls. They're absolute works of art. The most beautiful of the shawls, which the female dancers drape over their shoulders and arms, is made of black silk with an intricate embroidered design of vibrant roses as a focal point.

I sit down with Jago at a table for two. Emerito eats alone and so does Guardia Bastien, who sits in a far corner, never taking his eyes off me.

At first, I'm able to ignore him, but as I dip small pieces of bread in the gravy of my beef stew, I start growing nervous. There's something dark about Guardia Bastien. I can't exactly put my finger on it, but as I try to pretend he's not there, I find the hairs on the back of my arms standing on end.

"Are you all right?" Jago asks.

"I'm fine. It's just I wish he would stop staring at me."

"Who?" Jago starts to glance around the room, but I put a hand on top of his to stop him from glancing in the guard's direction.

"Bastien," I whisper, hiding my mouth behind my napkin, so he can't see I'm talking about him. "He keeps staring. It's not like I'm going to evaporate into thin air."

"Bastien, is it?"

I shrug. I'm tired of calling him Guardia Bastien.

"Ooh, maybe he likes you," Jago teases.

"Ew, no." I shake my head adamantly.

"*Ew*? There is no *ew*, no matter from which angle you look at it, my dear."

"Speak for yourself. The man is positively corpse-like. There is no emotion in him. I wouldn't be surprised if his heart is solid rock."

Jago rolls his eyes. "As well as other parts of his body," he jokes, then continues, "Clearly, you know nothing about men. The ones who hide their feelings are the worst. The deeper they bury their emotions, the more intense they are. Very dangerous. In fact, that's the kind of man you need to stay away from."

My eyes flick to Bastien for an instant. As they meet his gaze, a tingling sensation travels down my spine.

"Meh," I say. "I have absolutely nothing to worry about. Not my type."

"Like you have a type."

"Can you blame me? Every man who has ever shown any interest in me was only interested in my title. Honestly, if it wasn't because I'm very curious about," my gaze dances around the room and I lower my voice, "sex, then I would completely forsake the entire idea of marriage."

"Fair enough. There's always sex outside of marriage, you know?"

"You know, I know. Stop bringing that up. You also know it's not a possibility for me. At least not until I'm considered a spinster."

He looks up at the ticking clock on the wall and bobs his head from side to side. "Well, I guess you have a few more hours then."

I slap his arm, even though he's not far from the truth. It won't be long before everyone will consider me a spinster. Not for the first time, I find myself wishing I'd been born a man. None of this would be happening if I'd been that lucky.

To my chagrin, I can't finish my stew. My appetite shrinks and shrinks every time my eyes meet Bastien's. I set my fork down with a sigh.

"I'm going to my bedchamber," I tell Jago.

He reclines, crossing one ankle over the other, and nursing a tankard. "I'll stay up. See what . . . kind of excitement La Torre has to offer tonight," he says as he smiles at the pretty blond maid who served us.

I lean close and speak in his ear. "Don't have too much fun and forget our plan."

"Don't worry, I won't," he responds without even looking at me. I try not to let his attitude worry me. Whenever he spots someone he likes, male or female, he usually gets distracted. He has never failed me, though, so I resolve not to worry.

I swing by Emerito's table. "Please tell the person in charge that I require a hot bath in my bedchamber."

His eyes go wide, and his expression turns into a *how dare you?* sneer, but I don't give him a chance to say anything. Instead, I hurry up the stairs to the second floor, doing my best to ignore the burning sensation in the back of my head, which lets me know Bastien's eyes are following my every step.

The room assigned to me is called *Peineta Dorada* and has a golden flamenco hair comb painted on the door. Inside, the space is small, but I'm pleased by how clean and orderly it is. There is a metal tub in one corner, and the bed has a pretty canopy draping from its four posts. My luggage rests at the foot of the bed. I dig out a fresh pair of leggings and a tunic.

Soon, there is a knock at the door. "I'm here to prepare your bath, señorita."

Pleased by the efficiency, I call, "Come in."

I'm expecting someone or several someones carrying pails of hot water; instead, I'm taken aback by the appearance of a slip of a girl, no older than twelve. She wears a simple blue dress with a matching hair cap. She carries no water.

"Hello?" I say.

She curtsies, then walks toward the tub. I had assumed they didn't have internal plumbing—normally, small towns like this lack such luxuries—but it seems I was wrong. If I'd known, I would have drawn the bath on my own.

I busy myself with retrieving a few toiletries from my luggage, but when I don't hear the sound of running water, I glance back toward the girl. Her hands are hovering over the tub. Staring, I take a few steps in her direction and notice the water level rising inside the tub.

Espiritu! She's using magic to fill it.

My eyes flick upward, immediately trying to get a glimpse of her ears, but they're covered by the cap. I keep on staring and wait until she's done.

When she pulls away from the tub, she's surprised to find me watching. Her cheeks turn bright pink. Curtsying, she clasps her hands together in front of her and stares at the floor.

"I hope the temperature is to your liking, señorita," she says.

"You're fae," I say, stupidly pointing out the obvious.

She takes a sideways step toward the door, looking scared.

I'm half-fae, I want to say, so she doesn't have to feel afraid of me, but I bite the words down.

"Your talent is really amazing." I gesture toward the tub. "I wish I could do that."

A shy smile stretches her lips. It's surprising that she has espiritu. Her parents must be powerful and full-blooded. Since the veil fell, few of the fae trapped in Castella pass down the gift to their children.

I want to talk to her, want to ask her a million questions about her family. Where did they come from? Are they from the fae capital, Riochtach? Did they ever visit Nilhalari, my mother's village? And so many more questions that always assault me whenever I'm in the presence of one of the fae. But as always, I must hold back. No one can know my true heritage.

The child's meek demeanor likely stems from a lifetime of enduring discrimination, consistently treated as an outsider in our lands. No, Castella's citizens would not respond well to knowing their former queen was a full-blooded fae, and their current one is a half-fae.

I offer the girl my warmest smile to let her know I think nothing less of her because of her heritage, then let her go without revealing any of my questions.

While I luxuriate in my bath, I find immense pleasure in a whimsical notion. Silly as it may be, I imagine the water holds traces of espiritu and pretend it can reach into the depths of my being to rekindle the espiritu I once used to save my mother.

Being able to wield espiritu would be far better than having been born a man. Controlling espiritu would mean I would not be helpless and at the mercy of a meddling little man, a guard with a heart of stone, and a queen who may or may not be my sister.

If only . . .

13

VALERIA

"The fae healer will be here soon, my dear.
Just hold on a little longer. Please, please, do not fall asleep."

Conde Ricardo Luna y Figueroa – Conde de Mursiya – 725 DV

L ater that night, I put on a valiant performance. Around
twenty-two hours, I drape a robe over my nightgown and
walk out of my bedchamber. The youngest of the guards stands in
the hall, looking bored. He straightens when he sees me and acts as
if he hadn't been about to fall asleep on his feet. He blinks large
green eyes and twitches his thin mustache.

I give him a bleary-eyed look. "Can't sleep," I say, then head
down the corridor.

"You shouldn't leave your bedchamber, prin—" he cuts himself
short, then adds, "señorita."

I keep walking. "Why not?"

Guards are used to following orders without questions, so I
take advantage of that to stall him.

"Um . . . because of your safety," he stammers.

When I glance back, I find him checking out my butt. His eyes quickly snap to mine. He clears his throat.

"Am I not perfectly safe in your presence?" I ask with a suggestive smile.

Now, he's not only confused but also flustered. Of course he thinks I'm safe in his presence, but letting me go anywhere means breaking those unquestionable orders.

"I need some milk with a little honey, prepared just the way I like it. Not too sweet, not too plain," I say with a coy smile. "We have a long day ahead of us tomorrow, I need a good night of sleep if I'm to survive the rest of the journey."

I can see the moment he decides there is no harm in letting the poor princess get what she needs. His eyes soften, and a smile stretches his lips. He seems nice, and I like him for that. None of this is his fault. He's just doing what he's supposed to do.

We go downstairs, and as soon as I'm noticed, all conversations come to an abrupt stop. Every person—each a man—turns to look at me. Their expressions seem to indicate they've never seen a woman in a robe, no matter how decent.

I don't allow the crude stares to stop me. In Nido, I got used to them soon after I grew breasts. Every derelict, arthritic council member suddenly realized that I existed and subjected me to their filthy inspection every time they thought no one was paying attention.

Sashaying, I make my way to the counter in the back of the room, the young guard following behind. Before I make it there, Bastien gets up from his corner table and intercepts my path.

"You shouldn't be here," he says.

"That's the most perceptive thing you've ever said." I walk around him. "I should be in Nido, attending my father's funeral." My voice almost breaks at this, but I'm able to swallow the lump in my throat, hardening my façade.

"Get back to your room."

"Not until I get some milk." I reach the counter and give the owner a smile. "I can't sleep, and I thought some milk and honey might help."

"Of course, my dear," the man replies. "We'll get it right away." He instructs one of his helpers to get it done.

Behind me, Bastien chastises the young guard. "Weren't my instructions clear?"

"Yes, sir, but she insisted," he stammers, his expression fraught with panic.

A pang of guilt courses through me for putting him in this position, but I must ensure the image of me in my nightclothes is etched firmly in Bastien's mind.

See, I'm not trying to escape. I'm going to bed, I'm trying to say to him.

Also, if he believes this is my way of assessing the situation and planning an escape through the front door, he'll be less likely to figure out my real scheme.

"If you can't follow simple orders, perhaps your sole duty should be mucking the horses," Bastien spits.

"What was I supposed to do?" the young guard asks. "Deck her?"

"Not a bad idea," Bastien sneers.

I'd like to see him try.

"Get back to your room," he orders again.

I cross my arms over my chest. "I'm not going anywhere until I get my milk."

His eyes narrow, and his jaw ticks with irritation.

The inn owner regards us with curiosity, and Bastien seems to think better of making a scene. He wouldn't want to give anyone the impression that I'm being manhandled and forced to do things against my will.

While I wait, I glance around the room. Several of the guards traveling in our party sit there, nursing tankards. Their attention is still focused on me, though they are doing a very good job at pretending it isn't. I make a head count. Three of our guards are missing. That means they are outside, keeping watch. I imagine one guarding the front door, another one stationed in the back, and the last watching the horses. Three against two, not bad odds.

The helper returns with my milk, and the owner takes it and offers it to me. I cradle the heavy mug in my hands, enjoying the warmth and the scent of cinnamon and honey wafting from the delicious treat. I smile, then take a sip and let out an involuntary moan.

"Wonderful. Just how I like it. I thank you, kind señor."

"You're welcome, señorita."

Without a word to the others, I head upstairs. I'm tempted to say my soothing drink will help me sleep like a babe, but that would only make Bastien more suspicious. I'm also tempted to visit Jago's chamber to tell him how many guards are outside, but I'm sure he already made his own perusal. He knows the plan as well as I do.

Back in my room, I drink the milk. It's too rich and delicious to let it go to waste. I don't rest my head on the pillow though, lest the drink has its intended effect. Instead, I occupy myself with packing a bundle, using one of my tunics as a makeshift rucksack. It wouldn't do to escape completely empty-handed.

Before midnight, I peek through the curtains. After a few minutes, a guard paces into view. Without any pretense of subtlety, I throw the window open. He startles, but I do my best to ignore him and fan myself as if overheated. I can feel his eyes fixed on my delicate nightgown, its slender straps and plunging neckline. He will be lucky if his eyes don't fall out of their sockets.

Men! So easy to distract.

I pull away from view, leaving the window open. I'm not about to try to escape just yet. Besides, it's not time, so I sit at the edge of the bed and wait.

Thoughts of my parents assault me. I miss them so much. My sorrow quickly turns to rage as I think of Orys. He paid for Mother's death with his disfigurement. He will pay for Father's death with his life. I will make sure of it.

And Amira? Oh, Amira. If she is doing this of her own volition, it means I never knew her. And if she isn't, she will be devastated when she wakes up from the spell. That's if she isn't already suffering, trapped inside her own mind.

Gods! My heart hurts.

Shaking my arms, I stand up, change out of my nightgown, and throw it on the bed. I won't be needing such garments where I'm going. I attire myself in comfortable clothes and search through my luggage for the dagger and thigh strap I stored there, but they're gone. Damn them! They went through my luggage even after it was initially packed. Father gave me that dagger. They have no right. I stew for a long time, doing my best to control my emotions.

At last, it's time to go. The loud ruckus I hear in the distance is my sign. Cuervo is at the front door, doing his job of creating a distraction. His croaks are surely loud and obnoxious when he wants them to be.

I approach the window as silent as a cat. I don't see the guard and hope his attention is diverted by the commotion.

With my improvised rucksack tied to my back, I fling my legs over the windowsill and step carefully onto the ridge of the roof. The red-stained clay tiles aren't the best surface to walk on, but they seem stable enough. My steps are tentative at first, then more confident as the tiles hold. Hands out to my sides for balance, I hurry across the way on tiptoes. When I get to the other side, I stop, trying my best to ignore my heart's pounding rhythm.

I dare a glance down and around. I still don't see the guard, but I see Jago.

He's waiting for me in the shadows of the stables, his shape barely noticeable. He's mounted on his horse and has Furia with him. A smile stretches my lips. All I have to do is get down from here, run across the backyard, mount my mare, and we'll be on our way back to Castellina.

There is a tree close to the building. Shimmying down the sloped roof, I make it there. I locate a branch thick enough to support my weight, then jump and take hold of it. My hands hurt from the rough bark, but not too much. I have good calluses from sparring practice. Finding the right handholds and footholds, I make my way down to the ground and land in a crouch without a sound.

I stay there for a long moment, one hand on the moist ground as I watch for the guard. He's nowhere in sight. When I'm sure he's not coming, I cut across the yard, feet as light as Cuervo's feathers.

"Good job," Jago whispers.

"I think it's Cuervo you should praise."

I mount my mare, patting her neck, and calling her a good girl. "Let's go home." I pull the reins back.

Furia has only started to turn when I hear a voice from the inn's direction.

"Stop unless you want me to break his neck."

My blood turns to ice as I glance back and see Bastien silhouetted against the moonlight, holding a struggling Cuervo by the neck.

"Let him go!" I shout across the yard, the rest of my body turning as cold as the blood in my veins. If he hurts him, if he—

"I will let him go when you get off that horse and stand in front of me," Bastien says.

Hot rage fights against the cold fear for Cuervo's life. "You wouldn't dare."

"Try me." I can't see his face, but there's a frigid sound in his voice that leaves me no doubt he'll snap my friend's neck if I don't do as he says.

I hang my head and swallow the lump in my throat. "Thanks for trying, Jago."

"I'm sorry," my cousin says. "I really thought we would make it."

Slowly, I dismount and walk toward Bastien. When I stop,

I return his gaze with a steely glare, allowing all the resentment I harbor for him to pierce the air like a dagger, every ounce of my disdain unsheathed and ready to fight him.

"Let. Cuervo. Go." I punctuate each word.

Bastien unclenches his hand with an abrupt stretch of his fingers, and Cuervo weakly flaps to the ground. I fall to my knees and cradle him against my chest. His usually strong croaks sound hoarse and feeble.

"You are despicable." I slowly rise to my feet and hold the bastardo's gaze once more.

If he thinks he can intimidate me, he's mistaken. He will pay for hurting Cuervo, for forcing me into this journey, for keeping me from uncovering this plot, whatever it is. And if he's involved in any way in Father's death, I swear to all the gods I will slit his throat.

"Get back to your room," he says with his usual coldness and indifference.

"You are broken. You are worse than an animal. Who did that to you?" I demand, wanting to hurt him somehow, but getting through to this man is useless. His façade is so hardened that not even a blow from a hammer could break it.

He pushes air through his nose as if it's all the same to him.

I dig deeper. "I'd wager all that is dear to me that you're alone and unloved."

This time, there is a small crack in his expression, but it's gone so fast that I begin to question if I really saw it.

Without a word, he steps out of the way and extends a hand toward the side path that leads to the front door.

Holding Cuervo gently, I make my way back to my room where I tend to my friend, smoothing his ruffled feathers and caressing his little neck. As I lie down, he huddles in the crook of my arm, his beak resting over the back of my hand.

"Are you going to be all right?" I ask him.

He makes a small sound I know means yes.

"I'm glad. Please forgive me for getting you into this."

He lifts his head, turns it, and looks at me. "Friend," he says hoarsely.

And I know he means that he would do anything that I ask of him. A tear slides down my cheek. "I would do anything for you, too."

14

VALERIA

"I know Castella is where I was born, but I want to see Tirnanog, Mother. Do you think I ever will?"

Lenna Rogetorei – Fae Child – 10 AV

Dawn comes quickly, and after a short rest, Cuervo seems like his old self and jumps from the bed to the night table, looking up at the window. I open it and let him out, glad to see his wing beats are as strong as ever.

I get ready, go downstairs, and join Jago, who's already there. The guards watch us, and my food tastes like sawdust in my mouth. There is contempt in their gazes as they whisper in each other's ears. I know they think I'm nothing but a spoiled brat, unwilling to make any sacrifices for our realm and oblivious to the trouble I cause them.

But what do they know?

Soon, we're on our way. The sun is barely out, but Bastien seems determined to get us to Aldalous in the shortest amount of time possible. I'm sure they're all eager to deliver me to my supposed betrothed and get back to Castellina.

Well, I have five more days to try to escape.

The days are long, and the nights longer still as I try and fail to find a way to escape. Bastien watches me closer than ever, as if his life depends on it. After the third day of travel, I come to the conclusion I will have to wait until I get to Aldalous. I may not be able to fool Bastien, but Don Justo will be caught unawares. I may not know much about him, but one thing is for sure . . . he can't watch me every hour of the day.

While on the road, I hate riding inside the carriage with Emerito, but I hate looking at Bastien's dead-fish expression even more, so I endure it. Jago despises the stuffy cabin too, but he stays with me out of solidarity.

We play cards while Emerito watches in disapproval. He thinks cards are a sin, even if there are no bets involved.

"Games of luck are the devil's workshop," he says multiple times.

To me, card games are harmless and fun, certainly more so than Emerito, who only knows how to disparage those who are different than him. I can only imagine what he would think and do if he found out his precious Amira is half-fae.

For hours, I fan myself with a fan the inn owner's wife gave me in La Torre. It's made of light wood and lace, and I imagine it once belonged to a flamenco dancer, and she used it to enhance her fiery emotions as she twirled and stomped across a worn wooden floor. The fan isn't much help, however. Inside the carriage, the air is oppressive, charged with the stench of Emerito's heavy cologne. It isn't all bad, though. The little man provides endless entertainment.

Like on the second day, when he entered the carriage wearing a fake beauty mark on his left cheek. Since, he keeps rubbing it off with his handkerchief, and it takes him several minutes to put it back in place. During one of his efforts, the mark ended on the tip of his nose, and Jago and I exploded into laughter, while he demanded to know what was so funny.

For some much-needed relief, I sometimes stick my head out of the window. The breeze feels good as does the change of scenery. I search the skies for Cuervo but don't see him. He's trying to avoid Bastien, I'm sure.

On the fifth day, nearly lulled to sleep by boredom, I feel the carriage veer abruptly to the right. Blinking, I look out of the window and find that we're passing a small caravan. My curiosity piqued, I climb out, position myself on the roof, and watch the procession—Jago quickly following my lead.

Our guards give the travelers a wide berth as if they're infected with a disease. I can see from their wary but resigned expressions that they are used to this type of treatment, though no less hurt by its quotidian nature.

Much like the fae, the *Romani* are treated as if they don't belong in Castella.

Their troop consists of three wagons, one in the shape of a rectangle, built from wood, with only one door in the back. The other two have cloth tops that have seen better days. Three starved-looking horses pull the derelict vehicles.

Among the people that I can see are an older man, a middle-aged couple, two young men, a couple of children, and a beautiful woman around my age. There may be others inside, but I can't be sure.

They are dressed in a rainbow of colors. The women wear long, flowing skirts adorned with intricate patterns, and blouses embroidered with sun-bleached threads. The men, with their strong and weathered faces, wear vests and matching trousers crafted from sturdy fabric. All wear layers of scarves, shawls, and jewelry, as if each piece tells a tale of a distant place they once visited.

The beautiful young woman glares at me as we pass by. She has long ebony hair that cascades in curls down to her waist. Her eyebrows are thick and just as dark. Under them, heavily kohled eyes seem to hold a vast array of feelings: mischievousness, cunning, slight, anger, curiosity, and so much more.

I imagine she's surrounded by her family and has traveled all over the realm, free as a raven, able to see all the wonders Castella has to offer. I imagine nobody ever tells her what to do or who she should marry. All decisions are her own and for her sole advantage. Briefly, I wonder if she hates her life as I hate mine.

We leave them behind, and an hour later all I see is the dust their caravan stirs into the air.

"Do you think they would trade places with us?" I ask Jago.

"Who?"

"The Romani."

"Probably."

I wrinkle my nose. "But they're free."

"In one way, but not all."

I ponder his words and try to imagine in what ways they aren't free. They are bound to the road, to wander endlessly, I suppose. There is no rest or reprieve from their travels. I've seen them in Castellina, performing, trying to scrape a few coins in order to survive. They aren't free from everyone's stares and side-eyes, or the ignorance and hatred of those who think they're better than everyone else.

Jago is right.

"Since when did you become such a wise man?" I ask him.

He blinks and turns his eyes from the road. "Huh?"

I shake my head. Maybe he just knows what to say and when to say it.

The rest of the journey is tedious with nothing to offer any distraction besides fields of crops, expansive vineyards, and the occasional scarecrow.

The next day, we arrived in Aldalous province well after sundown. The town where Don Justo's villa is located, Alsur, is similar to La Torre with its cobblestone roads, whitewashed buildings, and terracotta roof tiles. However, the place has a different feel to it.

As we traverse the streets, I can feel the presence of the ocean to the east. Though the water remains hidden from view, its essence permeates the air. The salty tang in the breeze teases my senses, a reminder of the vast expanse of water that lies just beyond sight: the Eireno Ocean. Every building, every alleyway, is touched by the magic of the sea. Even the walls seem to breathe with the ebb and flow of the invisible waves.

I imagine a tranquil bay where ships gently sway at anchor. Or is it a tempestuous sea, its waves crashing against rugged cliffs? This will remain a mystery. I will not stay here to find out.

Don Justo's villa is located on the northern edge of the town, with many acres of wheat, extending from his backyard as far as the eye can see.

The villa is surrounded by an extensive white wall that keeps the interior from view. The wide wooden gates in the front are heavily guarded by four men who appear to have just been part of a tavern brawl. They are unkempt, their faces and arms scarred, their teeth missing. What isn't missing, however, is a wide array of swords and daggers strapped to their bodies.

A shiver goes down my spine, and I exchange a glance with Jago. They can't possibly mean to leave me here.

Even Emerito stares out the window with caution.

"Emerito," I lean forward and try to appeal to the wariness brewing in his eyes, "this place doesn't look safe. Are you sure you know what we're getting into?"

He swallows thickly but manages to compose himself and act as if he's perfectly in control. "The queen was clear in her instructions. You have a duty here, and she expects you to perform it."

"Are you really this cruel?"

He stares back from so high up his horse he might get a nosebleed. I hope he does and stains his ridiculous white and gold doublet.

Once the awful sentries have established who we are, they make us get out of the carriage. Without asking, they bring down our luggage and throw it on the ground to inspect it. Emerito's mouth falls open, but he says nothing. One of the men leers at me, wearing a twisted smile under a ridiculously long mustache. He smells of overripe cheese with a dash of spoiled fish.

I take a step closer to Jago. He places an arm around my back. The man grunts, then takes a step toward my cousin and shoves him.

"No one touches El Jefe's woman."

Jago staggers back and hits the side of the carriage.

"What is wrong with you?" I demand. "He's my cousin."

"More reason for him to keep away," the ogre growls.

I open my mouth to say something, but Bastien appears as if he has peeled away from the shadows.

"You will not mistreat anyone in my party," he says in an unequivocal tone.

The man turns slowly to face Bastien. There is a glint in his eye that suggests this is exactly what he wants: conflict. He must thrive on it, the way vultures thrive on carrion. He's a head taller than Bastien and twice as thick, but something tells me that's not an advantage.

"You don't give orders around here," the man spits.

"Perhaps, but I'm sure your boss would love to hear how you ogled his future wife the moment she got out of the carriage."

"That's a lie," he bellows as he steps forward to grab Bastien by the throat.

Instead, what happens is something completely different. In a flash, Bastien steps aside, hooks the man's foot with his own, and sends him sprawling to the ground like a fallen tree.

Our guards as well as Don Justo's laugh heartily.

"I've been saying you're getting clumsy in your old age, Bartolo," one of his fellow guards says between loud cackles.

Bartolo clambers to his feet, his eyes as incensed as those of an angry bull. Opposite him, Bastien stands calm, ice running through his veins. He has confronted worse challenges than this. I have no doubt in my mind.

Bastien and Bartolo face each other. The latter evaluates Bastien for a split second, judging the best way to attack. He takes several short steps to reduce the distance between them, then lunges forward, a massive fist directed at Bastien's jaw. Once more, my guard moves impossibly fast. He has ample time to trip Bartolo once more. This time, the big man doesn't fall but staggers, arms windmilling in an effort to keep his balance and what little is left of his dignity.

Huffing with rage and exertion, Bartolo clenches his fists. His upper lip pulls back, trembling. Straightening, he takes a deep breath. The effort to let this go is clearly monumental. However, judging by the vindictive look in his eyes, he will hold a grudge. If I were Bastien, I would watch my back every second of the day while in Alsur—not that I would be opposed to Guardia Corpse getting the beating of his life. As a kidnapper, he deserves everything Bartolo can give him. Not likely, I know, but I can hope.

After all the male posturing, we're allowed past the gate. Jago and I walk in rather than get back in the carriage like Emerito. Bastien follows close behind us, as well as one of Don Justo's guards assigned to the task by Bartolo.

"You're fast on your feet," the new guard tells Bastien.

As usual, Bastien offers no answer, unless a grunt qualifies.

"Bartolo's bark is worse than his bite," the man continues undeterred. "My name is Felipe, by the way. Welcome to Villa de la Paz." There is a slight note of sarcasm in his voice that makes me glance in his direction. *Paz* means peace in Castellan, and he doesn't think the name fits. He offers me a thin smile and bow. "Welcome, Princess Valeria."

I exchange a worried glance with Jago, then glare at Bastien. From his slight frown, I can tell he picked up on Felipe's tone. I already don't have the best opinion of Don Justo, and if not even his men can provide a good endorsement, maybe it's worse than I suspect. Or maybe I'm just reading too much into an innocent comment. Maybe this place is heaven on earth. Funny how that doesn't make me want to stay, not even a little.

"This way." Felipe guides us toward the front door of a sprawling one-story building. The walls are squat and perfectly white. The terracotta roof tiles are a vivid red and staggered in perfect rows. The doors and windows arch with grace and are adorned with wrought iron shaped into vines. Real vines around the metalwork enhance its beauty.

A woman dressed all in white waits by the door. Her hands are interlaced in front of her. Her hairstyle is severe, pulled tightly into a high bun, but her eyes are warm, even if slightly guarded.

She bows deeply. "Welcome to Villa de la Paz, Princess Valeria."

"Thank you."

"My name is Ynes Ayala. I am the *ama de llaves*." It's an old term for housekeeper that translates to *the mistress of keys*.

"She's my sister," Felipe puts in, which earns him a narrow-eyed glance from Ynes.

I've seen such glances before. She thinks her brother isn't behaving properly in front of me. The thing is . . . she doesn't know me. I don't care much for the stiff formalities offered in the name of my royal lineage. I love being a Plumanegra. I'm proud of my heritage and what my family and my ancestors have done for Castella, but I haven't earned the respect they bestow upon me. I have done nothing, and now my sister is pushing me onto a path where doing *nothing* is exactly what I'm supposed to achieve. That's not what I desire for myself, and I'll continue to resist the chains of a loveless marriage and a life without purpose.

"I regret to inform you that Don Justo is not here, Your Majesty," Ynes explains. "He had to ride further south to attend to some business. He left his deepest regrets and said you should make yourself at home."

A sigh of relief escapes me. Ynes's dark eyes don't seem to miss a thing, but I don't care. I don't plan to make things easy for Don Justo. If I ever see him, I will let him know right away that I don't want to be here. The more people know about it, the better.

I open my mouth to let her know as much when Emerito's rushed steps sound behind me. His handkerchief swings from side to side as he holds it aloft. He walks on tiptoes to keep his heels from sinking into the gravelly path.

Both Ynes and Felipe regard him as if he's a strange, exotic animal from a faraway land. He might as well be with all his finery. People out here aren't used to the likes of him. They wear homespun fabrics and work in the fields or boats, day in and day out. What do they know of velvet doublets and beauty marks?

"Your Excellency," Ynes bows deeply and throws a sidelong

glance at her brother, who quickly mimics her. She repeats the information she just gave us.

"How unfortunate." Emerito dabs his forehead with the handkerchief, embroidered with his initials. "When will he be back?"

"Tomorrow evening at the latest."

My heart sinks. I'd hoped *his business* would keep him away longer. But no matter, that simply means I have twenty-four hours to figure out an escape.

Ynes guides us inside the villa. It's a very nice place, clean, smelling of roses, and decorated with items belonging to the region: pottery, ship wheels, seashells, and carved furniture. She guides us through the middle courtyard, where beautiful rose bushes fill the ample flowerbeds. Artfully painted *azulejos* line the walls and arched entryways. The architecture is clearly influenced by Los Moros, as it's evident in the many ornate columns. The air is cool, perfect for sitting under the moonlight, reading a book while the sweet scent of roses tickles one's nose.

Except beauty is no substitute for freedom.

Ynes leads me to a large bedchamber with pristine white linens and a body-length gilded mirror. A copper tub sits in the middle of the room, already steaming with hot water and swimming with red petals. The pleasant scent of aromatic oils wafts in the air.

It's obvious that extra care has been placed into making the bedchamber perfect, but I would rather have a cot and a pail of water in a humble room, if it meant I could have a say in my own life.

I immediately let my eyes travel through the room, noting every window and door. There are plenty of exits, but there is the outer wall and Don Justo's guards as well as my own to contend with.

Things look grimmer with more potential eyes watching, but I don't let that bring me down. I will find a way.

"I can send a few of the maids to help you bathe, Your Majesty," Ynes says.

I shake my head. "No, thank you. I will be fine on my own."

She seems about to object, but in the end, she asks, "What about some dinner? I can have anything you would like prepared for you."

After the first day of travel, our food options were limited, so this sounds like a lovely offer. "If your cook knows how to prepare saffron rice, that would be wonderful. If not, anything savory would do."

"Our cook is excellent, and she can indeed prepare that. She can add shrimp if you wish."

"Oh, that would be divine."

"Is that your preferred dish?" Ynes inquires with a warm smile, her demeanor so kind that I can already sense how easy it would be to grow fond of her if I were to remain here.

"No. My favorite is cochinillo, but I wouldn't make your cook go out and find a suckling pig. Perhaps you can make sure my cousin, Jago, also gets some of the rice."

"Indeed, Your Majesty." Ynes starts walking backward toward the door.

"How is life here, Ynes?" I ask.

Her eyes open wide, and she appears a bit panicked at the question.

I elaborate, hoping to ease her into trusting me with what she knows. "How is the town? Is there a lot to do?"

She seems relieved, as I suspected, and has no trouble sharing. "If you like the outdoors, yes, there is much to do. The plains and hills are beautiful, especially in the spring and autumn. Fish are plentiful in the ocean, and there is ample game for those who enjoy hunting."

"Is that all?"

"There is a fair every April, and folk come from smaller towns to watch the dancers and bullfighters and to enjoy good food and drink. It's a very happy time for everyone."

I incline my head to one side, demanding more, but Ynes seems at a loss.

"We ran into a small troop of Romani on our way here. Are you expecting a visit from them? They always offer good entertainment."

"Romani do stop here every now and then," she says, sounding less enthusiastic about this subject.

"Are they not welcome?"

"El Jefe considers them lawless."

"And you? Do you think the same?"

She thinks for a moment, and I can tell she's pondering whether or not to be honest. In the end, I think she decides on the former. "Some are, but that isn't a trait exclusive to the Romani. There are many dons, lords, and kings who also partake."

"Well spoken, Ynes. I couldn't agree with you more. Thank you for the information."

She inclines her head. "I will be back with dinner in an hour to give you time for your bath."

"Perfect."

As soon as she's gone, I test every door and window. One door leads to a large empty closet, and the second one to a washroom. As I throw open the windows, I curse under my breath. Wrought iron bars cover them, leaving only a small gap toward the top, where the bars end in what look like spearheads. The windows face the inner courtyard, so why the bars? My eyes rove over the flowerbeds outside, then drift toward the windows beyond . . . windows without bars.

My stomach sinks. Maybe Father or Amira told Don Justo to expect a reluctant wife. I shake my head, not wanting to believe that they would willingly and knowingly put me in the charge of a man who would lock me up.

I rush to the door and test the handle. I sigh in relief when I find that it isn't locked. Would it be locked if Don Justo was here? Will I still be a prisoner when he comes back and I refuse to marry him?

Securing the door from the inside, I decide that I don't want to find out what that man will do. I will get out of this villa before he returns.

I take a quick bath and change into another tunic and a pair of leggings. My skin smells of roses and feels soft. I squeeze the dampness from my hair, enjoying how clean the strands feel.

Ynes comes back accompanied by a teenage girl carrying a tray with my dinner. The delicious scent of saffron and shrimp makes my stomach rumble.

"That smells amazing," I say.

"I hope it is to your liking, Your Majesty." Ynes guides the girl toward the door, ushers her out, and is about to leave too, but remains when I call her name. "What more can I do for you?"

"Can you tell me why my bedchamber is the only one with bars in the windows?" I ask, never taking my eyes off her face in order to examine her expression.

She seems to choke, and it takes her several hard swallows before she can answer. "I don't know, Your Majesty."

"Please, don't lie."

"It's not a lie." She closes the door and comes closer. "Don Justo had them installed a month ago. I don't know why."

A knot forms in my throat. A month ago?! Is it possible that Father knew then this would be my fate?

"Perhaps," I say tentatively, "Alsur is dangerous, and Don Justo only aims to protect me?"

Ynes winces slightly, which makes me think this conjecture is wrong.

I shake my head and swallow thickly, fighting back the anger that rises inside of me. It is directed at my father.

The housekeeper moves closer still, and when she speaks, she does so in a whisper. "Don Justo is extremely jealous and overprotective. That may be the true reason."

Her explanation makes sense, but her quiet delivery does not— not unless the jealousy and overprotectiveness she's referring to is the irrational kind, what should instead be called mistrust and possessiveness.

"I think I understand." I nod slowly, holding Ynes's gaze.

She smiles, satisfied that she got her message across.

When she leaves, I eat my rice, chewing carefully. I still can't forgive Father for arranging this marriage and concealing it from me, but at least he had decided to let me go. Amira on the other hand . . . she wants to ensure I find no escape from this distasteful duty.

Too bad!

I have a different duty in mind, and it involves avenging Father and bringing Amira back to her senses. One way or another.

15

VALERIA

"The child is blind. There is nothing to be done. I am sorry."

Eda Villanueva – Human Midwife – 25 BV

The next morning, I feel awful from lack of sleep. Before going to bed, I spent a couple of hours going around the house while the guard Bastien posted at my door followed me around. He appeared embarrassed the entire time, clearly uncomfortable with his orders to stop the princess from escaping.

We ran into guards and servants belonging to Don Justo. They watched us with curious eyes as I explored the many sitting rooms and museum-like spaces that held a variety of paintings and sculptures of clashing styles, the mesh of artifacts giving the impression of someone trying to pass as an art connoisseur and accomplishing the exact opposite.

I hope anyone who saw me assumed the guard at my heels was there to protect me and make me feel comfortable while I navigated my supposed new home. But if they suspect my plan is to run as far away from Don Justo as humanly possible, maybe they won't blame me. The problem is . . . based on my nighttime explorations, I decided that escaping the villa is virtually impossible. There is no gap in the wall, and there are too many guards everywhere. It was this realization that kept me from sleeping and had me tossing and turning all night, though it wasn't all for naught. I did come up with a feasible plan. I only hope it works.

I leave my bedchamber in search of Ynes and find her in the ample kitchen, directing the cook and maids, and instructing them in all the tasks to be performed for the princess and Don Justo's arrival later that evening. When she notices me standing by the entrance, she and everyone else curtsy and bow their heads.

"Good morning, Princess Valeria," she says. "I didn't expect you to wake up this early. I thought you might be tired from your travels."

"On the contrary," I say, putting on a vapid air, "I feel incredibly refreshed. It must be the ocean breeze having a positive impact on me."

"I'm glad to hear that, Your Majesty." Ynes turns to the others and claps her hands, causing them to blink and stop gawking. "Everyone, get to work." They shake themselves and do as instructed, some disappearing through side doors and others turning to the counters to knead bread and chop meats and vegetables.

I flip my hair to one side. "Ynes, I would like breakfast delivered to my room as well as help getting dressed."

"Certainly, we will be there shortly."

"Thank you." I whirl on my heel and leave, sashaying and looking all around as if I expect butterflies to start circling around my head. It's an act I've delivered a million times. Those who know me don't fall for it, but I can still get away with it every now and again.

My guard follows me, frowning. He can tell something is up, and I have no doubt he will run to Bastien to tell on me. There's nothing I can do about that, however, so I resolve to be more clever than him.

After breakfast, I instruct the maids Ynes assigned to me to find my lilac dress in my luggage. After they get it freshened and ready to wear, I let them do my hair and makeup. They are delighted to help me as I regale them with stories from Castellina and the royal palace. They want to know about my sister. Is there a dashing king somewhere vying for her love? Will she ever come to visit me in Alsur? Will I need their help when I go back to visit the capital?

Throughout the interrogation, I keep a friendly expression, even if their questions hurt. My father isn't ten days dead, and he's already forgotten. I'm glad when they leave me alone.

Carefully, I examine myself in the mirror and approve of their work. I definitely look like a *proper princess*. Father and Amira would be proud. I have always preferred trousers and leggings. Most of all, I prefer comfortable shoes, as opposed to the ones my feet are stuffed in at the moment. No way I'm going anywhere in them.

I'm on the way to the closet to exchange the heels for boots when there's a knock at the door. Jago pops his head in after a moment. I asked Ynes to deliver a message for me. She frowned when I told her I wanted to see him in my bedchamber.

"Perhaps," she suggested shyly, "you should meet him in one of the sitting rooms, Your Majesty."

I know she's only looking out for me. From the slight edge of fear in her expression, I can tell that inviting any man to my bedchamber, even my cousin, would be an issue Don Justo would take offense to.

To pacify her, I said, "Don't worry, I won't give Don Justo any reason for displeasure."

Ynes gave me a gentle smile, full of relief. It makes me wonder if she has suffered at the man's hands.

Jago blinks at my dress. "What is this all about? Have you decided to play by the rules and give the don what he's expecting?"

I glare at him.

He puts his hands up. "Sorry, it's just it's been a while since I've seen you in a dress like that one."

I go into the closet, kick my shoes off, and gather the clothes I left on one of the shelves. Sitting in an armchair, I slide the leggings under my dress, stuff my feet into a pair of woolen socks, then put on my comfortable boots.

Jago watches me all the while, stroking his chin. "You must have a plan."

"I do." I wiggle my toes in relief.

"So, is there a part for me this time?"

I winked at him. "Always."

He smiles and rubs his hands, a willing accomplice. "Tell me all about it."

So I do.

Meandering through the house sometime later, I take short steps to make sure no one sees my boots under the long dress.

A different guard trails behind me. I ignore him and make sure he has the most boring morning of his life. I fan myself and yawn, pausing at portraits of bald, fat men, who I'm sure aren't related to Don Justo and are here just for show. His fortune is new and stolen, so I doubt his ancestors commissioned such works.

One portrait out of the hundreds catches my eye. It depicts an extremely handsome man in his early thirties. He has clear blue eyes and blond hair framing a chiseled face. The painter has managed to capture an air of confidence and arrogance that is oddly alluring. A plaque at the bottom of the frame reads *Justo Ramiro Medrano*. What? This is Don Justo? No, I don't believe it. I'm convinced he looks like a wart-ridden, overfed goat. He must have paid handsomely for a double-dealing painter to lie on the canvas.

After a heavy lunch, I sit in the courtyard, smelling the roses and fanning myself some more. I haven't seen Bastien or Emerito all day, and I'm glad about that. Cuervo is here, perched on the roof and acting like a regular raven. I instructed him to keep his distance, especially from Guardia Corpse.

My guard stands next to one of the columns, pulling at the tight neckline of his uniform. He's dripping sweat and looking miserable. I'm not doing much better, not with two layers of clothes on, but it is little to endure if my plan works.

When the guard looks ready to fall asleep or faint from heat exhaustion, I stand and walk out the front door, sighing heavily.

"This place is so dreadfully boring." I look back at my guard. "Don't you agree?"

He nods, and I think that, like me, he would do anything to get out of here and return to the capital.

Distracted, I make it all the way to the front gate. The guards there stand at attention when I approach.

"Good day to you," I say, batting my eyelashes.

One of them positively blushes. He looks no older than me.

"What do you, gentle dons, do around here on dreadful days like this?" I ask.

The young guard opens his mouth to respond, but the other guard, his elder, cuts him off. "We perform our duties, Your Majesty."

I'm not sure if he's attempting to impress me with his diligence or trying to make sure the younger guard doesn't embarrass them by saying the wrong thing. I really hope it's the latter. I don't need a strict adherent to the rules at this moment. I need someone who can be flexible and enjoys life.

"That sounds as dreadfully boring as all of this." I spread my arms toward the house to illustrate the lack of . . . well . . . life. This place is dead, and I doubt Don Justo's return will make a difference. In fact, I have a feeling his presence will only make everything worse.

"I looked and the house doesn't even have a chapel," I complain.

"There is one right outside the villa," the young guard supplies eagerly.

"Truly?"

He nods, wearing a huge smile.

"Do you think you can take me there?" I incline my head to one side and innocently lick my lips.

"Of course, Princess Valeria," he responds.

"I don't think that's a good idea," my guard puts in.

"Of course you don't." I roll my eyes. "If you want to stay, go ahead." I step closer to the two guards. "These men work for my future husband, and I'm sure they know better than you what is a good idea and what is not."

He shuffles from foot to foot and glances toward the house, unsure of what to do.

After a moment, he seems to make up his mind and grabs me by the elbow. "You need to get back inside."

I cry out as if he's hurting me. "How dare you touch me? Let me go!"

"Hey, take your hands off her," the older guard commands, placing his hand on the hilt of his big knife.

My guard lets me go. "You don't understand. She—"

"She is the future lady of the house, Princess of Castella. Laying your filthy hands on her is a sin."

"That's right," I say. "I don't need you following me around the house or anywhere else. Leave!" I jerk my arm, *shooing* him away. "Don Justo has a battalion of excellent men at his disposal. They guard the villa and the city, and keep everyone safe from harm, including me." I approach the gate. "Now, I would like to take a pleasant walk to the chapel in the company of these two excellent gentle dons."

Both the young and older men look satisfied as they lift their chins and glare at my guard down their noses.

"Get replacements to guard the gate, muchacho," the older guard tells the other.

My guard looks right and left. If I'm being honest, he looks terrified. Guardia Bastien appears to be a shrewd commander, indeed. I feel sorry for my guard and for whatever price he's about to pay for letting me get out of the villa, but I can't let that stop me. Shaking his head at me, he takes several steps back, then finally turns and rushes toward the house in search of Bastien, no doubt.

Soon, two new guards take their positions by the gate, and I'm able to leave.

"Which way is the chapel?" I ask, even though I noticed a small building when we rode in last night, and I suspect that's where we're going.

"Just down the path, Princess Valeria," the young guard responds.

I hurry my step. I have to be out of here before Bastien comes searching for me.

The chapel is a quaint little building, tucked under a line of trees that extends behind it. It's built of ancient stone, its wooden door scratched and battered.

I throw the small door open and look inside. To my relief, there's no one there.

I glance over my shoulder at the guards. "I would like to pray in privacy."

"Of course, Your Majesty," they reply in unison.

After stepping inside, I quickly close the door and look around. Shafts of dusty sunlight pierce through the old windows. There are three sets of narrow pews on each side, presided over by the carved figure of a saint I don't recognize. Heat hangs heavily in the confined space, making the exposed beams groan overhead.

Moving fast, I retrieve a free-standing metal candelabra from a corner and use it to brace the door. I secure its top under the handle and brace the bottom securely against an uneven floor tile. With that done, I unlace the back of my dress and step out of it, leaving it in a puddle on the floor.

Shaking myself, I run toward one of the side windows, which, to my relief, is not locked and opens easily. Nerves sharp as daggers, I climb out, land on a patch of grass, and stay still for a few beats, listening. When it becomes clear that the guards are none the wiser, I run, staying right behind the church to avoid being seen. When I make it to the other side of a small hill, I start breathing more easily. However, I've learned enough about Bastien to still be wary. Despite myself, I keep imagining him jumping out in front of me like a ground-sprouting demon, moving in that effortless way he has. Cuervo flies ahead to offer a warning, but Bastien already bested him so I don't rely solely on him.

My eyes dart anxiously, scanning the surroundings, peering behind every gnarled tree for any hint of the man. It's irrational, I know, I should be worried about him assailing me from behind—not the front—but I can't help myself. Maybe he's secretly a sorcerer.

I freeze. *Oh, gods! What if he's Orys?*

The question pops inside my head out of nowhere, and it sends my heart into an even greater erratic frenzy. But the thought is ludicrous. Bastien can't be Orys. He was there when the sorcerer attacked, and even tried to help. *But what if it was all a big magical performance?* Orys is certainly powerful enough to project an image able to fool anyone, isn't he? Honestly, I have no idea.

Shaking my head, I quicken my step, jumping over falling logs and overgrown brambles. I can't get carried away with fanciful notions.

I hear a sound ahead, come to a sudden stop, and crouch. I hold my breath to better listen. Glancing over my shoulder, I make sure no one's pursuing me. Praying to all the gods, I take several deep breaths, obeying the demands of my pounding heart. Once my lungs are pumping steadily, I move forward, taking care to keep each step silent. Once I'm able to see past the trees, I realize that what lies ahead is a street with people milling about. I'm at the edge of town already.

But where is Jago? I search for him but don't spot him. He's supposed to be waiting for me somewhere around here. He left the villa an hour ago, riding Furia.

"The tracks go this way," someone calls behind me.

Oh, no! They can't be here already. What should I do?

I see no other alternative but to leave the woods. Casually, I recline against a tree at the very edge of the road, acting as if I've been there all along. Once I'm sure no one is paying attention to me, I meander down the cobbled path, which is lined by street vendors. It seems like it might be market day today, and it's to my advantage since many people are out and about, purchasing fruits, vegetables, cheese, tools, clothes, and all manner of goods.

I move away from the woods and to the other side of the street. Quickly, I turn the corner and press my back to the wall. Jago and Cuervo are nowhere in sight. Slowly, I peek around the building, back the way I came. My heart jumps as I see Bastien standing in the middle of the path, those dark eyes of his scanning every face like a hawk. I pull back and desperately try to find a place to hide.

The first thing I notice is a closed wagon with a painted sign hanging above its back door. It reads *El Gran Místico*.

I hurry up the step stool that sits right below the entrance and burst in, thinking of nothing but remaining free.

16

VALERIA

"I can see. I can see! I am not blind anymore. Bless the fae healer!"

Vicente Villanueva – Human Beggar – 5 DV

Blinking, I let my eyes adjust to the dim interior of the wagon. There are only two candles burning in each corner. The resinous scent of myrrh fills the air, as well as the sound of someone with long nails drumming their fingers. As my gaze sharpens, I discern a man seated behind a table adorned with a crimson silken drape. He wears a turquoise kerchief twisted and wrapped around his head to form a band. There is heavy kohl around his fierce green eyes and his dark beard is braided and adorned with colorful beads. El Gran Místico, I assume.

"Take a seat, dear," he says, gesturing toward the chair across from him.

There is a set of tarot cards sitting to his right and a veritable crystal ball to his left. He's a Romani diviner.

"Oh, I'm not here to—"

He cuts me off. "Of course you are." He glances pointedly

toward the door, as if he knows the reason I don't want to be out there.

Swallowing thickly, I take a seat.

He shuffles the cards with dexterity and lays the pile in front of me. "Take out three cards and place them in a row, facing down."

I frown. "I shouldn't. I don't have any money to pay you."

Swatting the air as though shooing away an annoying fly, he remarks, "No matter. It's not like the whole town is *beating down my door*."

The emphasis he places on the last few words causes a chill to run down my spine.

"Please," he nods towards the cards.

As I start to lift my hand from my lap, it trembles slightly, so I make a fist, take a few breaths to steady myself, then draw three cards and lie them in a row.

"The cards represent the past, present, and future. Now, flip the past, the one to your left," he instructs.

I do so to reveal a card with ten coins and three robed men under an archway.

El Gran Místico lifts an eyebrow as he looks at the card. "Wealth but perhaps also . . . strife. A strange combination, don't you think?"

Not from where I'm sitting. As a child, I suffered much after Mother's death. Her absence was a hole right in my chest, a hole nothing could fill for a very long time. And though now it does not gape, it's still very much present.

I turn over the next card, wanting to get this over with, but feeling oddly safe from Bastien.

The card presents a man trying to balance seven swords.

"Duplicity," El Gran Místico says. "It seems you aren't who you say you are."

What?! How can he . . .?

"I haven't said anything," I blurt out.

He shrugs one shoulder. "Not to me, at any rate."

I flip the last card over. It depicts a man wrestling a lion. I bite my tongue, afraid of what it may mean, given that the other two cards seemed eerily accurate.

"Fortitude," he whispers, rubbing his beard, the beads clicking together. "Lots of it. It can also mean power."

He regards me curiously, his thick eyebrows pinched. "Who are you?"

"Nobody."

"I don't believe you."

"It makes no difference." I look away at a set of shelves lined with bottles. They are held in place from bumpy rides by taut ropes extending from one side to the other.

Watching the man from the corner of my eye, I notice something . . . *different*. My head snaps back in his direction. I scan his face trying to spot what I perceived, but everything's the same. He kicks back in his chair and steeples his heavily-ringed fingers. I go back to glancing at the shelves. The same thing happens.

This time, I turn my head slowly, and just before I'm facing him fully, I realize what the difference is. His ears are pointed. He is fae!

"What seems to be the matter?" he asks.

"Your ears," I say in a low breath.

He stiffens for a moment, then relaxes again. "So . . . you have the blood."

How does he know? Because I saw his glamour? I've never done that before, never saw through Mother's glamour.

I shake my head and stand, the chair scraping the wooden floor. "I should go."

Turning in the cramped space, I reach for the door handle.

"I would hold for just a second before opening that door, if I were you," El Gran Místico says.

Over my shoulder, I give him a questioning frown.

"When you step outside," he goes on, "take a left, go to the front of the wagon, wait for five beats of your heart, then go into the tavern in the corner. Run there, don't walk. They have an exit in the back. Go out that way, and you'll be safe. For a time."

Is he serious? How can he foresee all of that? For all I know, he's a charlatan with marked tarot cards and a fake crystal ball. But then I look back at his ears, which keep flicking from round to pointed. He is fae. He has espiritu.

"You'd better go out. *Now*," he urges.

I make a split-second decision to trust him and open the door. Carefully, I step down and go around the wagon on the left side. When I get to the front, I wait and count.

One.

Two.

Three.

On the other side of the wagon, I catch a glimpse of movement in my peripheral vision. Slowly, I turn my head in that direction and see Bastien peering into the window of a dress shop. He pauses for an instant, then goes inside the shop.

Four.

Five.

I run toward the tavern in the corner and burst through the door. The patrons stare at me with deep frowns. I shake myself and begin walking with a casual air. No one is behind the counter, so I press past the doorway in the back and enter a small kitchen. The cook, a heavyset woman with her hair wrapped in a white cap, startles.

"Who are you? You're not allowed to be back here!" she says.

"Sorry." I keep pushing forward until I spot another door, which finally leads me outside. This time I'm in a narrow alley. The smell of garbage wafts in the air. A gray cat jumps off a wooden crate and meows at me. I wish I could pet him—I like cats—but I don't have time.

I look right and left of the alley. A caw alerts me to Cuervo's presence. He's perched on the roof of a building to my right. Without hesitation, I head that way. He takes flight, and I follow. Once on the market path, I weave through the stalls, following my friend, who leads me straight to Jago. He's standing at the edge of the woods, Furia's reins in his hand as he looks on, worried.

"Val, there you are!" he exclaims. "I thought that bastardo caught you."

"He's close. We have to go."

And just as I finish saying this, Bastien's voice booms behind us. "Stop right there."

Jago acts swiftly, guiding Furia into the woods, then helping me up with a firm grip.

I settle behind him and wrap my arms around his waist. "Let's get out of here."

Jago spurs the mare, and she takes off at a gallop. Her hooves pound the ground, and my heart meets their rhythm.

"Stop! I command you," Bastien's voice again.

I glance back and see that he's running toward us. Is he insane? He'll never catch up to us no matter how fast he appears to be. I'm starting to raise the fig when I notice a horse racing behind him. In an instant, the animal catches up, and Bastien jumps on it without even stopping.

What in Faoloir's name kind of horse is that?!

"Faster, faster," I urge. "He has a mount."

"What? How?"

I shake my head. I have no idea how Bastien does half the things he does.

Noticing a tall boulder ahead, I instruct Jago to go around it. He pulls on the reins, and Furia veers to the right. I lean in close to Jago's ear, my words pouring out as rapidly as they can. A crazy alternative to our initial plan has suddenly sprung to mind. I have no idea if it will work, but what's evidently clear is that if I remain on this horse, Bastien will catch me again.

"Don't stop for any reason," I say as adamantly as I can. "Keep going, no matter what. Go back to Castellina, I'll meet you there as soon as I can. You know where."

"What are you . . .?"

I don't hear the rest of his question because, as we go around the boulder, I leap off the horse. The impact with the ground is jarring, and it seems like every bone in my body is on the verge of breaking. Clenching my teeth, I ignore the pain and keep rolling with my momentum. I pass over a patch of grass that cushions my fall somewhat. As soon as I come to a halt, I scramble to my feet and hide behind the boulder.

Hooves pound on the opposite side as I crouch down, holding my breath and nursing my wrist. It hurts like all hells. The clamoring gallops swiftly fade into the distance, and I pray Bastien won't hurt Jago.

I straighten up to my full height and retrace my steps toward town. As I sprint through the flattened underbrush, I spot Cuervo perched on a tree branch, observing me silently. There's a subtle gleam in his eye, indicating that he took care to remain concealed, preventing Bastien from using him to track my whereabouts. I offer a nod of gratitude, and he responds with a nod of his own.

Jumping off the branch, he flies ahead. I know he will warn me if he sees any guards searching for me. Having just seen Bastien take chase in the opposite direction, I breathe a little easier and move with more confidence in my step.

Some minutes later, I find myself in front of El Gran Místico's wagon once more. This time I knock. I know exactly why I'm here, though I'm not sure it's a good idea. Something tells me I'll be safe hiding with the strange man. Bastien walked right by the wagon and didn't try to search it. Maybe that means he doesn't think I would hide among the Romani. Or maybe it means that El Gran Místico has protecting spells over his property. Whatever the case, I'm still free because of him.

But it's more than that, isn't it?

The door opens and a somewhat familiar face pokes out. It's the beautiful woman I saw on the road.

"El Gran Místico is taking a rest right now," she says. "Please come back later."

My heart sinks, and I'm about to beg or do whatever it takes for her to let me in when his voice calls from within. "Let her in, Esmeralda. She should rest."

The woman frowns but does as he instructs.

I swiftly enter, and a rush of relief washes over me, causing all the tension to dissipate from my body. My knees waver, and the pain in my wrist intensifies. I stagger backward, feeling light-headed. Esmeralda extends a hand and steadies me, guiding me toward the chair I occupied earlier, where I collapse with a sigh of relief.

She looks between me and El Gran Místico. "Who in all the hells is she?"

17

VALERIA

"I thought a seat in the council would be the answer, but the fae want what we cannot give them. This is Castella, not Tirnanog. My people come first."

Rey Simón Plumanegra (Casa Plumanegra) – King of Castella – 11 AV

"A repeat customer?" El Gran Místico responds in the tone of a question.

Esmeralda doesn't look convinced.

"A half-blood?" The charlatan tries again.

Anger rises in me. It's not his secret to share with others. I glare at him, but he seems oblivious.

"And why does she need to rest here?" she asks, narrowing her green eyes, which make a striking combination with her ebony hair. They are the same shade as El Gran Místico's. I wonder if he's her father.

My chest continues to heave at a faster pace than normal, making it evident that I'm exhausted, but can she guess why? Has she pieced together that I'm the one the guards are pursuing? What if she decides to turn me in, hoping to claim a reward?

Perhaps I made a horrible mistake. What reckless, impulsive notion led me here? I should have stayed with Jago.

My brain, like a rabbit constantly giving birth to ill-advised ideas, concocts yet another brilliant scheme: spill my secrets. Well, most of them, at least. Without a moment's consideration, my mouth is already in motion.

"I'm hiding from Don Justo Medrano's guards," I say. "I've been sent here to marry him against my will, but I want nothing to do with him. I've never met the man. I arrived only yesterday, and although he's currently absent from his villa, I've heard enough about him to want no part in it." The words come out fast and sharp, like daggers slicing a sparring dummy. It appears my tongue is equally swift and cutting.

They both fix me with quizzical expressions, their eyebrows arching in unison. Their eyes briefly meet, conveying an unspoken question: *Do you believe her?*

I wait for their judgment, not daring to blink. El Gran Místico is the first one to settle on a decision, and from his expression, it's a positive one. Esmeralda takes a little longer, but in the end, the belated sympathy in her eyes means more to me than his faster acceptance.

"If you've heard what we have about that mongrel, I don't blame you." She inclines her head toward my wrist. "Want me to take a look at that?"

I nod.

Esmeralda kneels in front of me and gingerly gathers my wrist in her hands. She moves it this way and that. I wince.

"I don't think it's broken," she says. "Badly sprained, but not broken."

"That's good," I say lamely.

"I'll get some strips and wrap it."

"I thank you deeply." I bow my head.

Esmeralda narrows her eyes as she examines my hair closely. I sit back, wondering if that damn white strip has become visible, and whether or not she'll immediately associate the streak with Princess Valeria Plumanegra, but it shouldn't be. I applied enough dark paste this morning to last a week.

"What's your name?" she asks.

I don't hesitate when I give her the fake name I've always used when exploring Castellina. "Catalina."

"It's nice to meet you, Catalina." The inflection she puts on the name lets me know she doesn't believe that's my real name.

I glance toward El Gran Místico, who looks amused, as if he not only suspects but knows more than Esmeralda does.

"Don't trust anyone, Valeria," Father's voice echoes inside my head. He would have me think that everyone, aware that I'm a princess, would seek to use me for their nefarious purposes.

"Surely there are good people in the realm," I would answer him, thinking that he was only trying to scare me into obedience.

But maybe he wasn't so wrong. The veilfallen tried to kidnap me. What if these people try to do the same? Holding the reins of my distrust in check, I decide to hold my judgment. I will be careful, of course, will watch all their movements closely, and will use what I learn to form my own opinions.

A couple of hours later, I sit inside the wagon alone. Esmeralda wrapped my hand tightly, and it feels much better this way. She thinks it will be fine in a few days, and so do I. They left me here, telling me not to worry, that I was safe in the wagon. Remembering Bastien's earlier lack of interest in searching for me here, I grow more confident in the assumption that the wagon is protected by some sort of spell. At some point, I drift off, lulled by the silence.

When the door opens, I startle and jump to my feet, but it's only Esmeralda. As the door closes behind her, I'm surprised to see that it's dark outside. A sudden apprehension stabs me right in the chest. I would like to know that Jago got away from Bastien. Except I don't believe he did, so really what I need to know is that he's unharmed.

"Have you . . . heard anything?" I ask, gesturing toward the door.

"There are a few guards still looking for you. There is a particularly grumpy one that seems relentless. He has come around three or four times already."

My breath catches. Somehow I know she's referring to Bastien, which means he must have caught up with Jago. Is my cousin back in Don Justo's villa? Is Don Justo? My stomach flips. I can only imagine the complexity of that situation. The overreaching man demanding where his supposed bride-to-be is, and Emerito attempting to find a diplomatic way to explain it all. They wouldn't hurt Jago, would they? If I could get a message to him.

"How come he hasn't tried to look for me here?" I ask.

"I think you already know why." Esmeralda's green eyes twinkle.

"Are you also . . . fae?" No matter from what angle I look at her, I haven't caught a glimpse of pointy ears, but I have to ask.

"Only a fourth. I don't have magic, in case you're itching to know. My great-grandpa on my ma's side was full-blooded, but he had no magic to pass down. He traded hides."

So many people in Castella have mixed blood, and so many hide it as if it were a stain to be removed. I wonder if it's the same in Tirnanog, if those with even the slightest hint of human blood are seen as less?

"What about El Gran Místico?" I ask.

Esmeralda laughs. "You don't have to call him that. He'll get a big head." She considers, then adds, "A bigger head, I mean. Call him Gaspar. That's his proper name. Anyway, he's also a fourth fae and has a good bit of magic for protective stuff and sneaky stuff too."

"Sneaky stuff?"

She points at the table with the tarot cards and crystal ball.

"I see. Is he your father?"

"Gods, no. What made you think that?"

"You have the same eyes."

She shrugs. "The color is common in our troop."

"I've never been able to see through someone's glamour before," I say.

"His glamouring magic isn't strong. Some people with the blood can see through it."

Esmeralda appears entirely comfortable sharing this information with me, even though we're strangers. It's as though there's an unspoken trust simply because we share a common ancestry. For the first time, I'm able to openly admit this one aspect of myself I've always concealed, and it's liberating.

"So yea, you're safe as a mole deep in its lair here," Esmeralda says. "Gaspar and I are wondering, what's your plan?"

"Plan?" I feel as lost as a mole *outside* its lair.

"Yea, what are you going to do from here? 'Cause you can't stay inside this wagon forever. Gaspar needs it for his work."

Oh, they want me to leave. Of course, what did I expect?

"I . . . I'll go." I start moving toward the door.

"No, niña." She touches my arm briefly, and I stop. "We're not kicking you out. We want to help you, but we have to know how."

As I breathe out in relief, a warm feeling spreads over my chest. These people know nothing about me, and they're willing to help me.

"That or they want to exchange you for a hefty bag of gold," Father's voice comes to my head in that eerie echo I would like to get rid of. That isn't the side of him I want to remember.

I think about it for a moment. How can they help me? There are a lot of things I can think of, like getting me in touch with Jago, so I can leave this town with him. That would be the perfect outcome, but I know it's not the most likely one. If I go back anywhere near that villa, I could get captured again. And getting these people involved in something like that could bring them terrible trouble. No, I can't do that. They're already taking a risk. I need to make it as easy as possible for them to lend me a hand. So with that in mind, I settle on what to say.

"Um, I assume your troop will be leaving Alsur at some point, right?"

She nods. "Yea, we don't stay for too long in any one place. Means trouble to linger for the likes of us. Matter of fact, we're leaving tomorrow. This is the end of our loop, then we'll be headed back to Castellina."

My heart leaps. "Castellina?" I repeat dumbly.

"Yea, you know the place?" The question seems sincere, which means she has no idea who I am, even if she suspects my name isn't Catalina.

"I've been once," I lie. "It would be a great place to hide from . . . all of this."

"That it would." She throws her hands out. "It's easy then. You ride with us back to Castellina."

"Do you think that's possible? No one will mind?"

"No, it's fine. There's always room for one more. You'll have to pull your weight though."

"I have no problem doing that. I'll do anything that needs to be done."

"Excellent." She hooks her thumb toward the door. "I have to get back. You stay hidden, and I'll get you some food. Also . . ." Her emerald eyes scan me up and down. "You need a disguise."

"Oh, great idea!"

She winks, and something tells me this is like a game to her. But it isn't a game at all. *Gods!* Maybe I should leave here on my own. Maybe I should steal a horse and ride as hard as I can back to Castellina. But that would mean leaving the protection of Gaspar's spell, the only thing that has kept Bastien from finding me.

I feel torn inside.

"Don't worry, niña. Everything will be all right," Esmeralda assures me.

That is how the next day, I find myself dressed in a colorful flowing skirt and a ruffled bodice, sitting in the back of a carriage, watching Alsur fade in the distance. Cuervo follows us discreetly. He has always been wary of strangers, and after what Bastien did to him, even more so, it appears.

Esmeralda says they will be stopping in two different places before reaching Castellina, two towns they skipped on their way south. She says they visited four others on the way here, leaving only two for the last leg of the journey since they're tired and ready to get back to Castellina for an extended stay.

"Business is better there," she says as she swings her feet and chews on a long piece of hay. "There are more people, and they have more coin to spend. Some of them outright waste it . . . their gold, I mean. I don't mind taking it when they're so loose with it. We have mouths to feed."

There are a total of fourteen people in her troop, four growing children among them, so I understand what she means. I feel embarrassed to see how little they own, how all their possessions fit in three measly wagons. They are forced to go from town to town performing and selling jewelry, fans, and other things they make.

"And if they don't make enough, they steal." Father's voice once more.

I shake my head, trying to remember if he ever taught me anything positive about our people. If this is how he felt about everyone, was he really a good king to them? I rub my temple.

"You all right?" Esmeralda asks.

"Oh, I'm fine, just a little headache."

"Don't blame you. That must've been an ordeal. I hate to say it, but your family . . . they're awful. Why would they try to marry you off to that bastardo?"

"Um, they think . . . it's the only way to protect their interests."

She huffs. "Well, that's selfish. What about *your* interests? What do you want?"

I get a bit defensive about her comment, and feel I have to speak up for my family. "They all have made sacrifices. I guess they figure it's my turn."

Esmeralda makes a sound in the back of her throat but says nothing else. She just chews on her piece of hay as the sun rises, and the path behind us stretches and stretches, leaving Alsur, and the province of Aldalous behind. I don't think I would feel too bad if I never returned.

18

VALERIA

*"What is the true religion, Padre? Should
I worship our saints? Or Los Moros' one god?"*

Marcio Hidalgo – Human Blacksmith – 50 BV

The troop travels much slower than we did with Bastien. It should wear on my nerves, not getting to Castellina faster than this, but oddly, it doesn't.

In fact, I'm enjoying myself.

We make stops whenever the mood strikes and spend longer than necessary eating, singing alegrias while attempting to mimic the moves of flamenco dancers, watching the kids play hide and seek with no boring lessons to interrupt their fun, lying on the grass under the stars, while the fire crackles and whispers the night's secrets, like we're doing now.

This is real freedom, I think with a sigh. No one wants anything from me. No one tries to tell me what to do or not to do.

"Have you always been with this troop?" I ask Esmeralda, who lies next to me.

"Yep. I was born into it. My ma joined it when she was carrying me. She never told me where she came from; another troop, is what I think. But I imagine she was running from my pa, who was probably a bastardo. Ooh, look at that!" She points at the sky, and I catch a glimpse of a shooting star before it disappears.

At the sight, a smile comes to me on its own and goes on unapologetically, almost as if I've had a glimpse of true happiness.

"I've been on the road since I was a babe," Esmeralda goes on. "Ma took me everywhere. She also taught me everything I know about healing, like binding broken bones and sprains." She gestures toward my wrist. "Gaspar taught me the rest."

She turns her head toward me and winks. The grass tickles her cheek. She's a true beauty. Those bright green eyes of hers could spellbind anybody.

The next day we arrive in Syvilia. The place is nearly as bustling as Castellina. The sun casts a warm, golden glow upon the cobblestone streets that wind through the heart of the city. The air is filled with the rich, earthy scent of market stalls offering exotic spices and herbs, while people from all walks of life go about their many endeavors.

Many of the buildings are adorned with intricate carvings that tell tales of battles fought and legends born. Towers and turrets rise majestically above, reaching towards the heavens. Cuervo flies from one to the next, keeping a wary eye on me.

Once they find a spot near the busy market, the troop works like a perfectly constructed timepiece, every part of the mechanism doing its job. Even the children have specific tasks they must perform to get everything in place.

Esmeralda assigns me simple responsibilities, similar to those of the children. I have to sweep the area where each stall will be set up. There's a space for El Gran Místico's wagon, and another for a long table where a woman named Prina will sell her pretty jewelry. I've been admiring some of her pieces, wondering how she puts them together. She certainly possesses a unique talent. I wouldn't mind learning a few of her secrets in the trade. I have always enjoyed creating things: drawings, paintings, jewelry, even embroidery. Maybe I'll get a chance to ask her later once she's not so busy.

Esmeralda's stall is a curious one. She sells a variety of ingredients in tiny bottles that she says are medicine.

"Snake oil salespeople, that's what they are," Father whispers in my ear.

To my chagrin, I have to admit I wouldn't take the remedies in those bottles without concern, though this doesn't seem like a problem to the Syvilia residents. They easily part with their coin as she bats her dark eyelashes and smiles with more charm than a cooing babe.

Gaspar also does good business. People go in and out of his wagon at a steady pace. Some walk out wearing smiles on their faces, while others seem discouraged by whatever news he gave them.

I stay out of the way, sitting on a low wall across the street, watching it all unfold with tremendous interest. Their lives are so different from mine. They are constantly moving, talking, gesticulating, charming anyone who comes near, all while remaining in a good mood, whether or not their customers purchase their offers.

At twelve hours, they cover their stalls and leave the children in charge of watching them.

Esmeralda walks up to me, shaking a small bag of coins in her hand. "Want to get something to eat?"

"I do." My stomach has been rumbling for a full hour now.

"Let's go explore. See what's new."

"Do things change much between your visits?" I ask, curious.

"Sometimes." She points toward a narrow cobbled path. "I know a place that sells the best stuffed cochinillo. We'll eat first, and then we'll explore. How does that sound?"

"Perfect! Cochinillo is my favorite."

We walk side-by-side. I admire the quaint, colorful homes as we move along the winding path. Many have black bows pinned to their doors, mourning my father. After a while, I'm quite turned around, lost actually. Ten minutes later, we arrive at a small tavern and find a table. No one pays us any attention.

"They didn't even have a proper funeral for Rey Plumanegra," a woman in a yellow dress says to her companion at the table opposite ours.

I stare at the table, my shoulders tensing.

"I know," her interlocutor responds. "It's an embarrassment. Unheard of."

"Perhaps Queen Amira isn't of sound mind. Imagine witnessing such a tragedy."

I try to ignore the conversation, but it's difficult, so I'm relieved when the two women begin talking about hat fashions instead.

Esmeralda orders two servings of cochinillo, which are accompanied by braised potatoes, a basket of bread, and a jar of wine. She pays in advance, and I get the impression the owner wouldn't service us otherwise.

"They'll take anything that isn't theirs if it isn't nailed to the floor," Father's voice says. *"That includes the food on your plate and the fruits of anyone's labor, including inn owners, farmers, street vendors, anyone who can fill their stomachs for free."*

"What's the matter now?" Esmeralda asks when she notices me frowning at the floor.

My eyes lift to meet hers. "Nothing, just . . ." I whirl a hand in the general direction of my head.

"You get lost in your mind a lot, huh?" she asks, though she doesn't give me any time to answer. "It's not good, you know? Constantly letting your mind turn round and round with your own troubles."

"Why is that?" I'm interested to hear why she thinks this.

"Thoughts go sour. Actions are better. If something is eating at you, do something about it."

I frown. "What if you can't do anything about it?"

"Then it's not a problem. Problems have solutions."

"Not always." I interlace my hands on top of the table and stare at them.

"Death is the only problem you can't solve."

Our food gets delivered, and I attack it with the intensity of someone bent on changing the subject.

"Who died?" Esmeralda asks, mid-chew.

My spoon freezes over the wooden bowl. The food is really good: the meat juicy, the vegetables tender, the bread freshly baked, but each bite I've taken suddenly turns to lead in my stomach.

"I don't want to talk about it." My words come out chopped like axe blows.

"Might help," she mumbles and wipes her mouth with the back of her hand.

I say nothing. If she thinks thoughts go sour, I think words go putrid. I don't need to tell her how tragically I lost my father, how much I miss him, how fearful I am for my sister, how lost we all are if Orys is controlling Castella's queen, or how I can't seem to remember anything positive about my father.

Since Mother's passing, the only person I've truly confided in has been Amira. Even Jago remains unaware of my mother's fae heritage. And although Cuervo is my friend, it's not like I can have real conversations with him.

Naturally, I lay the blame squarely on Father's shoulders. He warned me not to trust anyone with my secrets and planted the seed of fear and distrust in my heart. He impressed upon me that if the truth were ever revealed, it would not only bring harm to our family but to Castella itself.

I set my spoon down as an idea hits me. What if his negative talk about the fae, Romani, crooked and ambitious court members— in essence, anyone who wasn't Amira or himself—was solely to keep me from divulging the one momentous truth that would have condemned us all? What if he did it to protect us all? He loved a fae female deeply, after all.

But what could he gain by trying to shape my entire character around mistrust and fear?

"Fearlessness isn't a laudable character trait, Valeria." His voice is in my head again, providing the answer.

Father, did I always misunderstand you? Were you only trying to curb my impetus?

"Are you done?" Esmeralda asks.

I find that my appetite is gone, so I nod. She grabs the last piece of bread from the basket as her eyes track somebody behind me. A moment later, the bell above the tavern's door tinkles.

Jumping to her feet and going for the exit, she urges me to follow her. "C'mon, let's go."

She's out the door before I can even get out of my chair. When I join her outside, she grabs my arm and drags me along the sidewalk.

A heavyset man dressed in a tunic that reaches his ankles walks ahead of us. He carries a cane that taps with every step. When the man turns the corner ahead, Esmeralda makes me wait a moment before we turn too.

"What are you doing?" I ask.

"Following him."

"Why?"

"He's our first mark."

"Mark? What do you mean?" I ask, fearful of the answer.

"I need you to distract him," she whispers close to my ear.

"You aren't going to—"

"Shh." She presses a finger to her lips. "Don't ruin this. Don't forget you said you would do anything to pay back for our help."

"I did say that, but—"

"All you have to do is distract him. You want to get back to Castellina under our protection, don't you?"

Is she threatening to leave me here if I don't help her?

"Go." She makes sweeping motions with her hands.

"I don't know what to do."

"Well, think of something." She shoves me forward. I stagger and put out my arms for balance. My heart is pounding, and my mind produces one question after another.

Does Esmeralda want to kidnap this man? No, that's stupid. We couldn't carry him. Kill him? Not in broad daylight, and in front of passersby. Rob him? Yes, rob him. That has to be it. He looks like a well-to-do kind of man, the perfect target.

"What are you waiting for?" Esmeralda hisses behind me.

I can't be part of this. It's wrong. But if I don't do it, I have no doubt the troop will leave me behind, and then what? I have no money to pay for a horse or carriage ride back to Castellina, so in the end, I may end up a thief no matter what. The difference? I wouldn't have Gaspar's protection, and I might easily be captured by Bastien and brought back to Alsur. And that is definitely not an option, and Esmeralda knows that.

Swallowing my shame and honor, I hurry my step and catch up with the man.

"Gentle Don," I say, tapping his shoulder.

He jumps a little and turns around to fully face me. Beady eyes scan me up and down. His nose wrinkles and his upper lip twitches. I hadn't stopped to wonder about my appearance, but seeing his reaction makes me realize I'm a mess.

I haven't had a bath in two days, my clothes are filthy from sleeping on the ground, my hair is in tangles . . . I must look like . . . what? A Romani? A poor fae?

Undoubtedly, he's asking himself the same questions because he tries to catch a glimpse of my ears, but they are hidden under my messy hair.

The unwavering look of disgust on his face eases my guilt regarding my role in whatever scheme Esmeralda is concocting.

"I am new here," I say, "and I was wondering if you know a nice place to stay? A cheap inn, maybe?"

He looks scandalized, as if knowing about the existence of such a place would be a contaminant to his every thought.

"Go pester someone else," he sneers.

The way he looks at me and the venom in his words make a part of me recoil. No one has ever talked to me this way. I'm used to deference—too much of it—accompanied by smiles and bows. Despite myself, his treatment makes me bristle.

"I'm not pestering you. I'm just asking a question," my voice is haughty, dripping with entitlement, though that isn't all.

There's so much about this situation that rankles me. No one should treat anyone without respect only because they're different or because they have less than they do. Nana did her best to teach me as much.

I doubt this man even earned his own wealth and has a true reason to be so full of himself. He likely inherited everything from his father, like I did—not that I have more than the clothes on my back at the moment.

So who does he think he is?

For all he knows, he's talking to a princess of Castella, someone whose boots he'd bend down to kiss if he recognized it to be in his best interest.

I open my mouth to say something to that effect when Esmeralda comes toward us. Stumbling like a drunk, she crashes into the man's side. He lurches and prevents a fall by using his cane. His face disfigures into a mask of anger and repulsion.

Using all his strength, he shoves Esmeralda backward and sends her flying against the adjacent wall. She hits it with force and crumples to the sidewalk.

I'm stunned silent by the violence of the man's actions, and by the unadulterated disgust that drips off him. He looks as if he suspects Esmeralda has infected him with an incurable disease that will turn his skin to boils and his gold coins into lumps of coal.

"Filthy *gitana*!" he spits.

Blood trickles down Esmeralda's forehead.

I rush to her side. "Gods, you're bleeding! Are you all right?"

Sliding an arm around her waist, I help her stand. She leans her back against the wall for support, looking dazed.

I turn to the man, bent on dragging him and his mother through the mud with the most colorful language I can muster. But I find no words because he's sneering and patting his pocket, eyes wide.

"Thieves!" He comes at us, shouting at the top of his lungs.

Recovering remarkably fast, Esmeralda grabs my wrist and hauls me down the sidewalk, while the man runs after us calling us *thieves* over and over again.

By the time we round the corner, Syvilia's Guardia is after us.

19

VALERIA

*"It is unjust. The pretty fae boy uses magic to conjure his tears.
Alas, for me, shedding tears at will is no simple feat."*

Olallo Pardo – Human Actor – 335 DV

I run faster than I ever have. I'm on Esmeralda's heels matching her step for step. She's extremely fast and running quite unlike someone who just got bumped in the head. She weaves in and out of the many twisting alleys we traverse, like a hare leaping in fright. I worry that we might run into a dead end. I wish Cuervo was here to guide me, but I have no idea where he has gone. Luckily, Esmeralda seems to know what she's doing.

My heart has found its way into my throat. It has never knocked against my ribs this frantically, not even during my best sparring matches with Amira.

Scenarios run through my mind where I end up locked in a rotting cell under the watch of the Syvilia guards. Only the gods know what they would do to me, to us. I don't have my Plumanegra key to prove who I am. If I told them, they would call me crazy, white streak of hair or not. I would rather take my chances with Bastien than a group of random guards.

Ahead, the street is blocked by a tall wooden fence.

No! A dead end like I feared.

Esmeralda keeps going, undeterred.

"This way." She slides a board to one side and squeezes through the gap.

Relieved, I do the same. Once I'm on the other side, she puts the board back into place and keeps running. A moment later, we spill onto a busy street, lose ourselves in the crowd, then disappear amongst the trees of a nearby wooded area.

Esmeralda collapses on a fallen log and throws her head back, laughing.

I come to a halt, bent at the waist, and brace my hands against stiff knees. I struggle to catch my breath as she keeps cackling like a crazy person.

Staring in disbelief, I shake my head. "What was that about? You nearly got us arrested."

"Not even close," she manages between intakes of breath.

"Is that even real blood?" I grab her by the chin and turn her head to one side. There is a red streak that goes from her temple to her jaw.

She slaps my hand away. "Yea, it's real. That bastardo almost knocked me out. It was worth it, though." She pulls something from the folds of her skirt. "This is pretty heavy." A coin purse bounces on the palm of her hand as she assesses its weight.

"You *did* steal from him," I say incredulously. I don't know why I'm surprised, but I am, which only shows how naïve and unprepared I am for . . . for . . . *for everything*.

"Of course, you idiot. What did you think we were doing? Playing hide and seek?" She shakes her head, her expression full of annoyance and incredulity of her own.

"Stealing is wrong," I say, unable to help myself. Clearly, she doesn't care about the morality of it all. If she did, we wouldn't be having this conversation.

"If it's so wrong, how come the rich do it all the time? They take more than their fair share from other folk and call it enterprising. Yet when those who have nothing try to even the score, they're labeled as thieves and condemned to rot in jail forever."

"It's . . . It's not like that."

She spurts a laugh and rises to her feet. "I guess you wouldn't think so, rich girl that you are."

"I'm . . ." My instinct is to deny I'm rich because it feels like an accusation, but I trail off.

"What? You thought we wouldn't notice? With your fine leggings and tunic, hair as shiny as a show horse." There is so much contempt in her voice that she sounds exactly like that man. He talked to me with repulsion because he thought I was poor. Esmeralda is addressing me the same way because of the exact opposite.

Is this how everyone in Castella feels about people like me?

I grew up with the knowledge that Father was a good king, who did right by his people. I knew the fae hated him, but I imagined everyone else loved him. And now, for the first time, I contemplate the possibility that this isn't the case.

"I'm sorry," I say. "I'm no one and have no right to judge you or anybody else."

I turn away from her, conflicting emotions wreaking havoc

inside my chest and head. There is so much happening so fast that I find myself doubting everything I know. I thought my little excursions into Castellina had made me savvy and expanded my horizons, but now I realize Father thoroughly succeeded in sheltering me from the real world.

"I'm sorry, too," Esmeralda says. "I said those things in the heat of the moment. You seem nice enough, and you're down on your luck, worse off than we are, I wager. The troop is family, and we stick together, but you're all alone."

Her words hit me like fists pounding against my chest, and sudden tears start running down my face in a deluge.

"Hey, hey." She comes closer, and the next thing I know I'm in her arms, sobbing like I haven't sobbed in a long time—perhaps even since the day Mother died. The feeling of oppressive loneliness that pushes against me in this moment is not unlike what I felt when I lost her. Perhaps I'm just starting to truly mourn Father.

Esmeralda doesn't say anything. She only holds me tight and rocks slightly from side to side until my tears dry out, and I push away, embarrassed.

"I'm sorry. I don't normally cry like that." I hate crying in front of people. I hate showing any sort of vulnerability.

"I don't know what trials you've been through, niña, but they've left their mark for sure," Esmeralda says, holding me at arm's length.

I pull away and turn my back on her. Swatting at my face, I wipe away the tears. *The last few days have been too much*, I tell myself. *Of course you lost control. It's nothing to be embarrassed about.* And yet . . . I hate myself for letting my emotions get the best of me.

Luckily, Esmeralda seems to understand, and she changes the subject. "We can't go back to the troop. We'll stay here until night-fall, then meet them at the edge of town."

I clear my throat. "What you did won't get them in trouble?"

"Nah, they'll be fine. The guards might go looking for us, but they won't find us, will they?"

"But won't they figure out we came to town with the troop?"

She shakes her head. "They can't prove it. We're wanderers. We come and go in troops or alone. They would have to arrest every single one of us. They'd love to do that, don't get me wrong, but it wouldn't be practical."

"I suppose you're right."

"Of course I am."

Sighing, I ease myself onto a patch of grass and cross my legs. Nightfall is in six hours, so I may as well get comfortable.

20

VALERIA

"Princess Valeria made these earrings using bits of raven feathers. Aren't they special?"

Agata Cañero – Nido's Lady's Maid – 18 AV

Later that night, we are on the road again. Gaspar said the guards came looking for us and were extremely frustrated not to find us. He also said they ordered the troop to pack up and go, and that the guards didn't leave until their wagons were rolling away. Despite everything turning out all right, Gaspar seemed worried.

As Esmeralda and I ride in the back of one of the wagons, facing the retreating road once more, I notice that she appears ill at ease too.

"What's the matter?" I ask. "Shouldn't you be glad that you got away with . . . Um, I mean that there was no real trouble for you and the troop?"

She shrugs one shoulder. "Maybe, but they've never forced us to leave before."

My first instinct is to ask her why she's surprised it happened.

If robbing people is part of their repertoire everywhere they go, it's only logical that the authorities would wise up to the behavior. It is their job to keep their citizens safe, after all. Logically, this is what my mind dictates should happen. Yet, I say nothing, and instead attempt to look at things from Esmeralda's perspective.

I think of everyone setting up for a day of peddling their goods, items, or services they sell for a pittance because no one will pay them what is fair. I think of the long hours they spend traveling, sleeping under the open sky, and eating simple, too-small meals that leave their stomachs rumbling shortly after. So, isn't it our collective fault that they have to take what should be fairly given to them for their efforts?

Does the same happen to the fae? Are they treated just as unfairly?

Some of these Romani are also fae, Val!

Maybe not fully, but could that be part of the reason they're treated so badly? And if Romani who mostly carry human blood are treated this way, then the fae . . .

"That head of yours is at work again, huh?" Esmeralda nudges me with an elbow. "Anybody who sees your face would say you carry the weight of the realm on your shoulders."

I don't. That's supposed to be Amira's job, but what if she's lost? What if she has veered off course or Orys's influence has permanently erased her identity?

Shaking my head, I push that awful thought away. My sister isn't evil, and, one way or the other, she will find her way back.

"I'm glad I don't," I say. "My own load already feels unbearable."

"Imagine being Amira Plumanegra," Esmeralda says.

My heart jumps at the name, and I have to look off to the side to hide my reaction.

"The first queen in, like, two hundred years," she goes on, "taking over after a murdered king, that's gotta be tough. Not to mention those veilfallen folk, they're getting angrier at the Plumanegras every day. I wouldn't fancy being in her shoes. What 'bout you? Think you could handle all that mess?"

I shake my head, my eyes still averted. "No, but she can. I've heard she's strong, level-headed."

"And I've heard she's a spoiled brat, same as her younger sister. Apparently, Valeria Plumanegra likes to pretend she's a commoner when she gets bored."

"Does she?" I ask, nearly choking on the words.

"Yes, if you watch closely, you might spot her wandering the streets of Castellina. She paints that white streak on her head and wraps herself in a hooded cloak to hide her face. She probably thinks she's being all sly, but we aren't fools. We see her, but we leave her be. No sense in hassling a troubled child, is there?"

My cheeks heat up to an unbearable level. I want to yell at her, tell her that I'm not a troubled child, but I manage to keep quiet mostly because my shame is too immense to overcome.

"She probably thinks she's being all sly." Esmeralda's words echo in my ears, accompanied by a rebuke of my own.

You're not sly at all, Val. You're a complete idiot.

In the next town, everything is repeated, except the part where Esmeralda commits robbery. Instead, she remains by her stall, selling jewelry and playing with the kids when there are no customers. This time, at nightfall, we rest. Everyone is weary from lack of sleep, yet there is excitement in the air due to our impending arrival in Castellina tomorrow. The troop has been on the road for over a month, and everyone is eager for a visit to their more permanent stomping grounds.

I feel the same eagerness in the pit of my stomach, like a snake coiling and uncoiling, a snake that at any minute might sink its fangs into me, releasing a paralyzing poison that won't let me do what I need to do.

The next day, the troop rolls into Castellina from the south. Twilight paints the sky the way a painter must dream of. Different hues of blue and purple bleed into each other, and I try to pretend the heavens are welcoming me, letting me know everything will be all right.

As we pass near Nido, I try to retreat inside the wagon, but Esmeralda stops me. "Don't you want to see your new home? No one will recognize you here. You don't have to be afraid anymore."

I almost want to say, *"Maybe they won't notice me now that I'm not wearing a hooded cloak,"* but I clamp my lips shut and stick close to her as the wagons traverse from one street to the next, carrying us farther from the city's heart and into regions I've never explored, places I never even knew existed.

We've traveled west of Nido. That much I know because I can orient myself by the largest pieces of the broken observatory that jut into the sky and refract the dwindling sunlight.

After nearly an hour of driving through the city, we finally come to a stop. The cobbled street has given way to an earthen path lined by small, portable-looking shacks built in a tight row. Several people have come out to welcome the troop back. Most of them are old or disabled in some way or another. They get kisses on their wrinkled foreheads, and tight hugs from little arms clamping around their legs. Everyone is happy, smiling hugely and looking relieved. Do they worry their loved ones will not come back one day? Do they fear they might encounter hostility and violence on the road?

I stand to the side, nearly hidden behind one of the wagons as I twist my borrowed skirt nervously.

"Ma, this is Catalina." Esmeralda comes close, an older version of herself at her arm. The woman is probably in her late forties, but the gingerly way she moves makes her appear older. White hair frames the sides of her otherwise black hair, and her eyes are large and inquisitive like Esmeralda's, though they are brown, not green.

"Catalina was in a bit of trouble, so we offered her help," Esmeralda adds.

"Hello, Catalina. It's nice to meet you." She wears an unassuming brown dress, nothing like her daughter's colorful clothes.

"Nice to meet you too, gentle doña." I incline my head.

"Oh, so polite, but call me Leonor." She gives Esmeralda a raised eyebrow. "I've tried to teach this one manners, but . . ." She shakes her head in defeat.

Esmeralda rolls her eyes. "Let's get you back inside while we unpack."

For thirty minutes, there is a flurry of activity as everyone unpacks the wagons. They do it all in an efficient, eager way, as if they cannot wait to be under the roofs of their tiny homes.

I help Esmeralda bring her things inside. There's barely any room for everything in one corner, but in the end, each bundle finds a place.

Leonor lumbers toward a small hearth, tending a fire and preparing something that smells sweet. When we sit down at a rough-hewn table, she limps our way, carrying two steaming metal cups.

"Orange blossom tea," she says as I bring my nose close to the rim.

"Thank you."

"You're welcome, child."

There is a knock at the door, and Gaspar puts his head in.

"Everyone is all right in here?" he asks.

A shy smile stretches Leonor's mouth. "Hello, Gaspar. Would you like some tea?"

Gaspar slides in and closes the door behind him. "I'd love that." He has removed the band he wears around his forehead, and a full head of black hair falls around his face.

"I'll get it, Ma." Esmeralda prepares another cup.

Gaspar sits to my right. His knee knocks against mine. "Sorry," he says, but his green eyes are set on Leonor. "How are you feeling?"

"Fine," she responds. The one-word answer feels like an evasion. "How was the journey? Tell me all about it."

"Ma," Esmeralda's tone carries reproach. "How did *you* fare while we were gone? How's the pain?"

Leonor sighs tiredly. "Things are always the same here. Nothing has changed. I want to hear about what you saw, what you did. You know I miss being on the road."

Esmeralda and Gaspar exchange a glance, unpleased by her answer. I don't know how bad her pain is, but it's apparent that the fact it remains the same is bad news. Nevertheless, they relent and proceed to tell her everything.

They have tales for every town they visit and do an excellent job recounting them all. They're funny and witty and complete each other's sentences, making me wonder if they rehearsed what to say in order to draw out the laughter that now fills the small space.

I join in their merriment, once again feeling a pang of longing for the close bond they share, not to mention the deep affection. I can see it in the way Esmeralda's green eyes sparkle when her mother smiles, in Leonor's laughter at Gaspar's witty quips, and in the way he subtly clutches his hand into a loose fist each time her fingers graze his, as if he's attempting to preserve her touch in some way.

They also tell her how I ended up with the troop. She's most interested in this story, and it makes me wonder if she's worried someone will come after me and will cause them trouble.

I set my cup down, understanding that I'm very close to wearing out my welcome. "I'm very grateful to Gaspar and Esmeralda," I say. "I hope that one day I can repay you for your help." This is something I intend to do as soon as I can. "I should be on my way now." I jump to my feet.

Esmeralda follows. "What? No, you should stay. I'll make dinner. A feast. It's a tradition on our first day back, isn't it, Ma?"

"Indeed," she replies.

I shake my head. "I appreciate it. I really do, but I don't want to take advantage of your hospitality. It's more than enough that you have helped me get to Castellina."

"Where are you going to go at this hour?" Esmeralda asks. "It's late. It wouldn't be wise or safe. Stay the night at least."

I press my lips together, unsure.

"Ma? Gaspar?" Esmeralda enlists them in her efforts.

"I agree with her," Gaspar puts in. "It *is* late. You need a good meal between your ribs and good rest, so you can face the realm with new energy tomorrow."

"I second that," Leonor says.

A good meal sounds very tempting. We've eaten little more than stale bread on the road for the past several days. I will need the energy tomorrow, for sure.

"All right," I agree. "But you have to let me help." I'm not adept in the kitchen, but I remember a few things Mother taught me when I was little. She enjoyed cooking, and once a week, she took over the palace's kitchen to prepare something delicious and teach Amira and me what she knew. She never got a chance to show us everything she wanted.

They all cheer, and Esmeralda and I set to work on dinner.

The dinner is truly a feast compared to what they're used to.

Under the glow of a single candle, Gaspar slices a hearty loaf of bread that takes center stage. Warmth spills from within as the soft center is revealed. A bowl of stew consisting of lentils, onions, and garlic, simmered in broth, sits in front of me, its savory scent tickling my nose.

A small plate of goat cheese sits nearby, and judging by how sparingly they use it, I can tell it's a luxury they can barely afford. I refrain from taking any of it.

The tender lentils melt in my mouth, their earthy flavor filling me with pride. I helped cook them!

I sip water from an earthenware cup to wash everything down, and when I'm done, it all settles in my stomach like a load of stones. I yawn hugely and, for the first time, wonder where I'm supposed to sleep. There is one narrow cot against the back of the room, big enough for one person. I assume that's where Leonor sleeps, but I have no idea where Esmeralda lays her head down to rest.

"You look 'bout ready to pass out," Esmeralda says.

Gaspar stretches his arms over his head and makes a sound like a bear getting ready to hibernate. "I should go. My bones are so weary from so much travel that I wish I could stay right here." He looks at Leonor when he says this, and I'm sure he wants to add *with you* at the end of that sentence.

He drags his feet as he heads for the door. Leonor limps along. They exchange a few quiet words before he leaves, and then it's only the three of us.

Esmeralda and I make quick work of the dishes, while her mother gets ready for bed behind a curtained corner of the room. She emerges wearing a nightgown that was once white. Her gray-streaked hair is down, flowing in waves down to her waist. She's still a beautiful woman. I can only imagine how much lovelier she was when she was younger. Esmeralda definitely takes after her, and I presume Gaspar never stood a chance after he laid eyes on her.

Leonor settles on the bed. Esmeralda kisses her forehead and bids her good night. I stand in the middle of the room, eyes roving over the floor for a spot where to rest.

"C'mon." Esmeralda walks to the other side of a wooden beam and starts climbing a ladder I hadn't noticed. When she reaches the top, she pushes a trapdoor open and climbs through it. There's a loft cleverly concealed up there.

She pokes her head through the hole. "What are you waiting for?"

I make my way up the ladder and climb into Esmeralda's space. It isn't big, and I have to crawl on all fours to avoid hitting the ceiling, which is only a few inches above my head. Once I settle down, however, I find that Esmeralda's nest of blankets and pillows is quite comfortable.

"Welcome to my Nido," she says. "It isn't much, but it's mine."

"It's nice."

"Don't lie. I'm sure you're used to far better."

"Nothing was ever really mine," I say bitterly.

"Bah, forget all of that. Think of the future." She's sitting, taking all her bracelets off and placing them in a ceramic bowl. They clink one after the other until she's removed all of them. It's quite the task. She then removes her heavy necklace and earrings, and finally lies down, facing me. "Tomorrow is your day. Who knows what it'll bring."

I blink slowly as exhaustion weighs me down.

"Sleep good," Esmeralda whispers as I drift away.

I'm not sure what causes me to wake up, but my eyes snap open, and I find that I'm alone. I sit up abruptly, and instinctively flinch as the ceiling appears to loom closer. I had forgotten where I was.

I listen intently. The house is utterly silent.

Crawling, I approach the trapdoor, which is open. I stick my head through it and look down. It's dark, and I can't see very well, but I don't think Esmeralda is down there. I glance toward her mother's bed.

Is it empty?

Is that just a bundle of blankets?

My heart lurches and starts pounding. Something is wrong. I stuff my feet into my boots as quickly as I can, then scramble down the ladder. Breathing hard, I rush to the window and pull the curtain back. The first thing I see freezes my heart, and I can hardly draw breath.

Guardia Bastien Mora is here.

I retreat from the window, taking several steps back. Hands pressed to my chest, I'm surprised to feel the wild thumping that knocks against my breastbone.

How is he here? This has to be a nightmare.

Wake up, Val. Wake up!

The doorknob rattles. I head straight for the back window and throw it open. I start climbing out just as the door bursts into splinters, and two members of the Guardia Real rush in. I land outside in a crouch, but it's too late. A shadowy figure already hovers over me.

"Hello, princess." Bastien's deep timbre washes over me, sending a chill across my back.

Slowly, I stretch to my full height and meet his eyes.

"Your husband-to-be is very displeased," he adds. "He has even come to Castellina to fetch you himself."

My fists clench.

"You're relentless *and* resourceful. I'll give you that," he says. "But you should know better than to keep Romani for company."

Esmeralda sold me out. She knew my true identity all along. She brought me all the way to Castella just to do this. And I naïvely believed everything she said to me. I really thought she was my friend. My heart aches at the betrayal.

Stupid, stupid, stupid.

Father was right. People can't be trusted.

Everyone is out for themselves. No matter how nicely they treat you, how many smiles they bestow upon you, in the pursuit of their own interests, they will betray you, cheat you, lie to you. Like a hungry beast, treachery lingers in the shadows of trust, something my youthful innocence didn't allow me to see.

Father, did you have to endure such harsh lessons to grasp this truth?

I try to spit on Bastien's face, but I only reach the top of his leather armor. He doesn't even bother to look down or clean the saliva from the breastplate. Instead, he grabs my arm and drags me around the little house to the front, where a windowless carriage awaits.

I fight him, kicking and scrambling. "Esmeralda! You rat. You'll pay for this. I trusted you. I thought you were my friend." A growl of frustration leaves my chest. I know she's watching this, same as the other troop members, who are peeking out through their windows.

Literally lifting me off the ground, Bastien throws me into the carriage. I pound on the door as he slams it shut. I rattle the handle, but it's locked. I try the other side. The same. This can't be happening, not after all my efforts to get free. I'm back where I started.

"Mount," Bastien orders outside.

The carriage starts moving, clattering as it rolls over the uneven dirt road. I pound and pound on the door to no avail. Tears of rage slide down my cheeks.

Bastien and Esmeralda will pay for this. I don't know how, but one day, I'll make them regret treating me this way. Esmeralda thinks she's better than the rich people she robs, but she isn't. She's worse. She's a backstabber and betrayed me for a handful of coins, no more. She sold me like a pound of meat at the market. Well, she better watch herself from now on because, somehow, I'll get that pound of flesh back.

When my arms are numb from pounding on the carriage walls, I sit and rake my fingers into my hair. My scalp is sweaty and dirty. I can smell myself, and I feel disgusting.

I'll find a way. I'll find a way.

Amira can force me all the way up to the altar, but I'll never willingly marry anyone. The only answer the priest will get out of me is a fist to his groin, the same as Don Justo. And after that, they'll all pay: Bastien, Esmeralda, Orys, even Amira, if it comes to that.

21

VALERIA

"They can keep their wooden saints, but they will follow our laws."

Abu al-Mohads – Caliph of Carduba – 77 BV

Soon we leave the dirt road and we're back on the cobbled streets. The carriage still rattles, but the ride is slightly smoother. I imagine Bastien thrusting me in front of my sister and perhaps Don Justo, if he is truly here in Castellina. It will be humiliating, but it doesn't matter what they do or say, I'll make their lives a living hell if they force me to do anything I don't want to do.

At least I will see Nana. I wouldn't mind one of her tender embraces, and the soothing sound of her sweet voice. And Jago . . . I'll see Jago as well, right?

I wonder where Cuervo is. If he'd been near, he might have been able to warn me of Bastien's presence, but I can't blame him for enjoying that which I don't have: his freedom. As long as he's all right, that's all that matters, though.

A deafening sound explodes all around me as something crashes against the carriage and sends it lurching to the side. I slide down the bench as the vehicle teeters precariously, then tilts and begins its descent down what feels like a steep slope. Arms and legs twisting into knots, I go tumbling, careening from the floor to the side, then to the ceiling and back again. My ears are assailed by the splintering of wood and the agonized screams of men and horses.

There is a loud splash, and the carriage starts filling with water.

Oh, gods!

I stand on the ceiling of the carriage, my boots half-soaked. We have rolled into the Manzanar River. It's the only explanation. The river travels west to east across Castellina and must be crossed to get to Nido.

Fear bubbles inside my chest. The carriage will sink, and I'll drown. Maybe this was the plan all along, to get rid of me.

I start pounding on the door again, crying out for help. I watch the water closely, expecting it to rise, but it doesn't.

My relief lasts for only an instant, then the door is thrown open and a figure wearing a heavy cowl that reveals a set of dark eyes—one of them scarred—stands outside.

River. The veilfallen leader!

He grabs me by the shoulders and yanks me out of the overturned cabin. Without a preamble, he throws me over his shoulder and runs.

I kick and pound my fists against his back. "Let me go. Let me go!"

How is he here? What is going on? A horse kicks weakly, stirring the water. He's lying on his side. The poor animal will drown. Someone should help him, but the men lie sprawled on the river bank, moaning.

I keep fighting. I buck and jerk from side to side as hard as I can.

River grunts as he rearranges his hold on me. "Stop or I'll knock you out," he rumbles as he turns the corner into a narrow street.

He runs up the road with that speed the fae have. I peer down the length of the distance we've traversed, hoping to see one of the royal guards coming to my aid, but there's no one. I'd prefer to face a human guard any day than contend with a fae, let alone River of the veilfallen.

I continue struggling, even as my limbs grow weak and my hope drowns. I can only imagine what the veilfallen want with me, and none of the things that come to mind are any good.

River weaves through the labyrinthine streets and alleys, causing my head to spin and leaving me disoriented. I have no idea in what part of Castellina we are anymore.

Eventually, he enters a three-story building and shuts the door behind him. It dawns on me that my cries for help have fallen on deaf ears. No one ventured to assist me, all choosing to remain safely behind closed doors, unwilling to endanger themselves. Does this mean Castellina has descended into lawlessness? Does it imply that the night belongs entirely to the criminals?

Father feared that our capital city would become such a place. Were all his efforts in vain?

River swings me down, and the room turns. My stomach convulses, and I vomit. He jumps backward to avoid getting my sick on his boots. Collapsing to my knees, I empty the rest of my dinner onto the floor. The rancid scent of stomach acid stings my nose. I push away and wipe my mouth with the back of my hand.

The room we're in is dilapidated, furnished with broken chairs and layers of dust. River stands silhouetted against the moonlight that cuts through a small, broken window. His shoulders are wide and so is his stance.

"Valeria Plumanegra, you are a hard person to track," he says, his voice calm and those dark eyes watching me closely through the small slit in his cowl.

Slowly, I rise to my feet, eyes roving around the room, searching for an exit.

"You won't get away this time, princess," he says.

"How is your leg?" I glance down at the place where I stabbed him.

Fae heal quickly on their own. Most of the time, they don't even get scars, not unless the attack is magical in one way or another, which makes me wonder about the scar across his eye. Did he get it here or in Tirnanog? He looks to be in his late twenties, but for all I know, he's hundreds of years old. Some fae can live to be a thousand. I can't even fathom what that must be like.

He ignores my question. The fact that he carried me here at full pelt is answer enough. He pulls out a dagger and aims it at me. I take a step back and hit the wall. I'll give him a matching scratch in his other eye if he comes closer. Before I can even move, he's on me, hard body flush against mine, the tip of the dagger at my jugular.

His free hand travels the length of my body, over my breasts, my rear, between my legs. A flush of embarrassment heats my neck, my cheeks, even my ears.

He steps away, and I lash out, growling. "Animal!"

Why didn't he ask if I was carrying any weapons? He didn't

have to paw me up and down. Not that I would have told him if I did.

"What do you want with me?" I don't want to be on my way to Nido with Bastien, but I would rather not be in the clutches of yet another bastardo.

"I don't mean you harm," he says, lifting his hands to show me they're empty. "I just want to talk." I find his calm demeanor infuriating. The man has ice in his veins.

"Talk?" I scoff. "Well, you forgot the tea and pastries." I glance around the room. "You could have dusted, at least."

There's no hint of amusement in his eyes. In fact, there's no hint of anything. He just goes on staring at me, never breaking eye contact as if he were trying to pry my mind open by will alone.

"My condolences on the passing of your father," he says.

Anger rises in my chest at his sheer audacity. As if he wouldn't have killed Simón Plumanegra with his own hands if he'd had the chance, as if it's not a distinct possibility that Orys is working with him, or *for* him.

My gaze falls to the dagger strapped to his thigh. What if I went for it and—

"You won't be fast enough," he says, guessing my thoughts.

I take a few steps to one side to get away from my vomit. Its acrid smell is making me nauseous again.

"Keep my father's name out of your mouth," I say, my eyes still roving the room, cataloging every aspect of it as my brain tries to figure out an escape. There is a set of stairs to my right that might offer a way out since the front door is out of the question. If only I had inherited my mother's fae speed.

"Fair enough." He inclines his head. "Let's talk about you, then."

"You're wasting your time. Whatever you want, whatever you think you can accomplish by kidnapping me, it's not going to work."

"We'll have to see."

I cross my arms. "Talk then. What do you want? I don't have any money if that's what you're after. I don't have any power. I've never cared about befriending council members or gaining political favors of any kind, so I can't help you there either. And if you hope to use me as leverage with my sister," I laugh, "good luck. She hates me, and she'd rather be rid of me."

Saying those words hurts. The last time I saw my sister, I felt the hatred I speak of. What I've yet to find out is if it's real.

"Good thing I'm not interested in any of those things," he says.

I frown, confused. What else could he want?

Out of the corner of my eye, I glance toward the stairs, judging how quickly I can climb them and whether or not River can catch me.

"Your mother," he says.

Every muscle in my body freezes. My mother. My fae mother. Why would this veilfallen bring her up? Did he use to know her when she lived in Tirnanog?

"What about my mother? She's dead," I say.

There's a slight change in the tension around his eyes.

"Did you know her?" The question is out of my mouth before I can stop it.

I think I already know the answer, and if I'm right, then I think

I also know what he wants. River aims to use that knowledge as leverage. No one, no one can know my mother was fae. It would be chaos. Fae haters in our council would immediately work to remove the Plumanegras from the throne, a century-old dynasty that has always served Castella well. Many would seek to install themselves as leaders, and there are few, if any, who would do it out of selfless reasons.

"I did know her," River says, confirming my fears. "Loreleia Elhice."

That is her fae surname, which Father erased from our lips the moment Mother revealed it.

"You will never utter that name," he said, casting Mother a reproachful glare.

"I knew her," he repeats. "In Nilhalari, sometime before she came to Castella and met your father."

My breathing is agitated, and the escape I've been planning up the stairs is all but forgotten. For the most part, Mother's life remains shrouded in mystery to Amira and me. While she was alive, she would tell us little stories about her previous life, but always when Father wasn't around. When he was present, she dutifully followed his orders not to speak of the past. When she died, any knowledge we might have gained died with her. Despite our constant nagging, Father rarely spoke of her again, and when he did, it was only to insist on the lies we were to tell the rest of the world.

Now, standing in front of someone who could tell me the things I've always craved to know, I find myself disarmed, my attention completely captured by this male from whom I should flee. There is a side of me I crave to understand better, a feeling of absence that nothing seems to fill.

"What do you know about her?" I ask, my voice a near plea that lets River know he has me in the palm of his hand.

His eyes crinkle a little, and that's how I know he's smiling. "I know she had in her possession a very important amulet."

22

VALERIA

"'Tis the hardest wood I've ever handled.
My saw barely scratched it before it dulled. Fae blackwood, is it?"

Juanes Hernández – Human Carpenter – 101 DV

A knot forms in my throat, and I nearly choke. Mother's necklace. River is after Mother's necklace. Any doubts that he's working with Orys fly out of my mind.

You're so stupid, Valeria! One mention of your mother and you forget who you're dealing with. He wasn't looking for a weapon when he pawed you. He was looking for the amulet.

I don't let myself think twice. I turn and sprint up the stairs, taking two at a time. River is after me in an instant, his hand reaching out and nearly catching the back of my skirt. But he's heavier than me, and one of the steps splinters under his weight, slowing him down.

Reaching the top, I find a decrepit chair sitting in one corner. I pick it up and hurl it at River, who is nearly upon me again. The chair hits him square in the face, and he stumbles back.

I run toward the only source of light in the dark space. It leads me to a broken window. I don't hesitate. I push through it, scratching my arm in the process, but find a foothold outside, which allows me to shimmy along a narrow ledge.

River sticks his head out and claws at the air, trying to grab me. He throws the window open. Pieces of glass fall out and shatter.

I keep going, my back pressed against the wall as I take small shuffling steps. The next house over is only two stories tall. If I reach it, I can jump onto its roof.

River squeezes his considerable bulk through the window and steps onto the ledge. I move faster and nearly lose my balance. Glancing back once more, I see that he isn't faring so well. He's too big for the narrow overhang, and that's slowing him down.

I finally make it to the end. Leaping sideways, I land on the other house. A couple of roof tiles come loose and clatter over their neighbors, making a racket. Whoever lives here likely just had the fright of their lives.

I climb, stepping gingerly over the tiles. I make it over the apex of the roof and swiftly approach the edge on the other side. This time there aren't any trees to help me descend, but there are a few bushes below that will cushion my fall.

Carefully, I sit on the edge of the roof, letting my feet dangle. Twisting to take hold of the edge, I slide off. For a couple of seconds, I dangle in front of a second-floor window, but my fingers lose their grip, and I plummet, landing unceremoniously in the middle of what turns out to be a rosebush.

With a whimper, I attempt to disentangle myself from the

thorny monster. My skirt rips in some places, and threads get yanked and stretched in others until I finally manage to break free.

I hear River above. A clay tile flies near my head and breaks to pieces on the ground. Limbs tingling with my energy-charged blood, I press my back to the wall and hurry alongside it until I reach the last house on the block and turn the corner.

I'm faced with an open road. Nowhere to hide that I can immediately see. I run, head turning right and left, trying to spot somewhere to conceal my presence. If I just keep running on this open street, River will easily catch me.

My hope has nearly been spent when I hear the trickle of water. I move in that direction and, behind a mound of grass, spot a drain. It is narrow, big enough for me, but not for River. The prospect of climbing inside isn't palatable, but I'm out of alternatives. Ensconced in there, I can at least keep out of his reach, and who knows . . . maybe it leads to freedom.

I get closer. The stink of sewer hits my nose like a physical blow. *Gods! I can't go in there.*

But I have to. Holding my breath, I get on my hands and knees and crawl inside the dark, dank sewers. My gag reflex makes me convulse. My head hits the top of the pipe as I jerk. The suffocating stench of filth and decay assaults my senses, finally making me retch and choke on the putrid air. My fingers tremble as I navigate the slippery, muck-covered path. The echoing sounds of distant droplets and the scuttling of unseen creatures in the shadows intensify the dread that gnaws at my mind. As I creep deeper, I can't help but wonder if escaping River is worth descending into this wretched underworld.

I keep pushing through the darkness, my hands and knees sinking into the thick, lumpy slush. Pushing my mind far away from this place, I imagine I'm crawling through a pleasant brook edged by sweet-smelling flowers.

When I'm far enough into the pipe, I pause and listen. I can't look back. The space is too tight to do anything but move forward. There's a trickle ahead, but I think I hear something behind me. I remain in place.

"Where the fuck did you go?" River's voice is amplified inside the pipe. "Are you in there?"

Gods, please!

He grunts and curses and stomps.

"No. No way that fucking princess went in there."

I hear retreating steps. He's leaving. I remain frozen for several long minutes. He seems to be truly gone, but I can't be sure. Making up my mind, I decide to keep moving forward. Eventually, I come to a fork with a shaft of moonlight cutting through its middle. I glance up and see a hole high above my head. I could climb out that way, but I'm afraid it's too soon to leave the safety of the pipes.

Three other pipes shoot from this fork. I choose the widest and crawl, crawl, crawl. After ten minutes, I begin to worry. I'm about to turn back around when I spot light up ahead. I hurry forward, and at last, I come out on the other end. Making no noise, I get out of the pipe. I'm on high alert, expecting River to be here waiting for me. I'm not about to let my guard down. I have two very shrewd men after me. Everything is quiet, however.

The drain has brought me to a section of the Manzanar River.

When I confirm there's no one around, I walk along the bank, upriver and away from the drainage where the current is clean. Heaving from my own stench, I entirely submerge my body in the cool water, dunking my head and scrubbing everywhere. While still submerged, I take off my clothes, one garment at a time, and scrub and scrub until my hands hurt.

It's a near-impossible feat getting back into my wet clothes, but I manage. Feeling weighed down, I trudge out of the water and discover a secluded spot along the shore—a small open space encircled by dense bushes. I settle down, reassured that I'm well-concealed from view, shielded from anyone passing along the pathways that run on both sides of the river.

After a few minutes sitting there, I start to shiver. It's warm during the day, but summer evenings can be cool. My teeth rattle, and my arms tremble even as I tightly hug my legs. I lie on my side, curled up into a ball, and wish for warmth that never comes. What does come, however, is sleep. At last, I drift away but take my shivers with me into a host of feverish nightmares.

I wake up with a jolt and scramble backward on hands and knees. There's a figure sitting next to me. I get tangled in a heavy coat that's been draped over me.

Blinking, I clear my sleep-blurred vision. "Jago?"

"The one and only," he says, wrinkling his nose. "What an unsightly princess you are."

"Jago!" I lurch forward and throw myself on top of him.

My arms wrap around his neck, and he teeters precariously but braces himself with one arm as he hugs me with the other.

"It's good to see you too, Val." He thumps my back. "Even if you abandoned me to that good-looking bastardo." He holds me at arm's length. "Though judging by your state, it seems I got the better end of the deal."

"How are you here?" I ask.

"A little bird told me where to find you."

"Cuervo!" I glance around, looking for him. He's nowhere to be found.

"He flew off a little while ago. I've been here for almost two hours. I hated to wake you up, you looked so cozy in your . . . nature bed. Quite the statement for you. I doubt it'll become a fashion with nobility, though. Unlike those raven earrings you used to make. Vanity only goes so far."

"Stop all your nonsense and tell me what happened?"

"*I* want to know what happened to *you*. How did you end up here, smelling like a latrine?"

I shake my head. "You go first."

"All right, don't get feisty. After you jumped off the horse, Bastien, naturally, caught up with me. The devil jumped from his horse to mine and knocked me senseless to the ground. I hit my head and cracked it open. Bled all over the place, too. But maybe it was worth it. I had a good roll with him and got to feel all his delicate and not-so-delicate bits."

I wrinkle my nose in disgust. "I'm not interested in hearing about that."

"You should be. The man is . . . hard."

"Focus, please."

"All right, all right. He threatened to strangle me if I didn't tell him where you were. I have the bruises to prove it." Jago pulls his collar down and shows me the dark finger marks that circle his neck.

"I'm sorry."

He shrugs. "Don't be so sorry. I gave in and told him you'd jumped off by that boulder, and he got back on his horse and went looking for you. I thought for sure he was going to find you. I've been holding my breath for days."

"So then what? Everyone came back to Castellina?"

He nods. "Everyone, including your betrothed."

"Don't call him that. He's nothing to me. Besides, I knew he was here."

He raises his eyebrows.

"Bastien told me. He found me last night. That's why I ended up here."

"He found you? How?"

"I was betrayed. That troop of Romani that was in Alsur, I rode here with them."

"You trusted a bunch of Romani? Are you insane?"

I hate that I want to rise up to their defense even after what Esmeralda did, yet a part of me does. I still want to believe that people are good: Romani, fae, humans, all of us. Father couldn't be right. However, it's not so easy to believe after what happened.

"It was stupid of me, I know," I say. "I didn't think they would recognize me, but they did, and . . . well, they also know I'm . . . half-fae."

"You're what?!"

I nod.

"So . . ." he speaks carefully, "your mother . . . she was . . ."

I nod again. "I'm sorry I never told you. Father made Amira and I promise."

Jago rubs the back of his head as he stares at the ground in shock. "I'm going to need a lot of time to process this, you little *half-batracia*." He gives me a sidelong glance and a smirk.

"Hey!" I punch him. "I hate that word."

He holds both hands up in apology for the awful joke, but I'm relieved there's no real judgement in his voice. Why did I ever fear he would think less of me?

"If the council finds out . . ." He trails off.

"I know, and now that Romani troop knows."

"I wouldn't worry about it, all right? Who's going to believe them if they claim such a thing against a Plumanegra princess?"

Maybe he's right. "I just don't understand how they recognized me."

"Oh, Val. The entire city knows who you are." His eyes are sad. "You're like their pet princess. They watch over you, make sure no one bothers you."

"You knew that?!" Tears waver in my eyes.

He nods gently. "I'm sorry. I didn't want to disillusion you."

"Father *was* right," I say absently. He could see me for the naïve fool that I am.

"About what?"

I shake my head. "It doesn't matter."

"What now?"

I keep shaking my head. I have no idea. All along, I thought that I could hide in Castellina, but as everyone's *pet princess*, what hope is there of blending in unnoticed?

Pressing a hand over my eyes, I fight back the tears.

"Hey, hey." Jago pulls my hand away, then wraps me in a hug.

"Maybe I'm deluding myself. Maybe I'm meant to go to Alsur with Don Justo and bury my head in the sand. I can't go against Amira and the entirety of the Guardia Real."

"We don't have to figure it out right now. You need to rest, clean up, eat, then you'll feel much better. We can find an out-of-the-way inn. There, we can regroup, then you'll know what to do."

"Will I?"

"Of course."

I sigh. "I also need to figure out how to evade River?"

"River? As in the leader of the veilfallen?"

I nod.

"What does he have to do with any of this?"

"Hells if I know."

"I'm so confused."

After I explain everything, Jago is flabbergasted. "This plot is thick as Bastien's arms, Val."

"I wouldn't know about that."

We sit in silence for a couple of minutes, then I say, "Your plan sounds good. I need to think."

"Good." He climbs to his feet and offers me a hand. "Maybe we'll think of something on the way to this little inn I know."

I'm wrapped in a sheet, my hair loose, wet, and smelling of lavender. My stomach is full, and the sweet, yet spicy taste of anise still lingers in my mouth. Jago is out, getting me new clothes, and Cuervo stands on the windowsill, shifting his weight from one talon to the other.

"Thank you, Cuervo. That was the best tomato soup and the best bath I've had in my entire life, and I owe it all to you."

"Val, friend," he croaks.

"You're my friend, too." I reach out and pet his neck with the back of my index finger.

"Oh, Cuervo, what do I do? How do I free my sister?"

I still refuse to believe she's doing all of this of her own volition. She loves me and loved Father and only Orys is to blame. And all because of my mother's necklace.

"Necklace," Cuervo croaks as if reading my mind.

Doing a double take, I look at him in surprise.

"Yes, Cuervo. The necklace is the key. The necklace that River called an *amulet*."

"Amulet," he repeats.

"Yes, amulet. Are you keeping it safe?" I ask.

He bobs his head up and down.

I pace the room, the length of the sheet trailing behind me. "What is so special about that necklace? Maybe it's worth a fortune." I shake my head. "No, that's not it." I've seen some of the courtiers wear far more valuable pieces. "Maybe it has some sort of power like I initially thought? But if it does, why did Father let it be my toy after Mother died? I have to find out more. But how?"

Frustrated, I collapse on the bed, lay my head down, and get some much-needed rest.

When Jago returns with my clothes, I'm awake. My hair is dry, cascading in waves over my shoulders. He has two paper-wrapped bundles, which he sets on the dresser that sits in the corner.

"I got some of your favorite leggings and tunics from Woven Whimsy Wear. Also, a dress in case you decide you need a real disguise." He winks. "I think everything will fit. I have your measurements, cousin."

"What time is it?" I ask. There's no clock in the room, and I've completely lost track. When I woke up, a possible plan was sitting in front of me, some crazy idea I must've hatched in my dreams. Now, I'm restless to act.

"Thirteen hours."

"Good. We still have time."

"Time for what?"

"We're going to the library."

He scratches his head, making his blond hair stand on end. "Not my favorite place. Why the library?"

"To see if there's anything I can find out about Mother's necklace."

"Why would the library have information on your mother's necklace?" He clearly thinks this specific outing will be a waste of time.

At first glance, it does seem that way, but the more I think about it, the more convinced I become. "If the fae want that necklace so desperately, it means it's important."

"I'm not denying that, but the library? You're overreaching."

"Maybe, but what if it's *that* important?"

"Important enough to warrant a book or a scroll being written about it?"

I nod. "It sounds ludicrous, I know, but it's the only idea I have."

He sighs. "All right, but do I have to come?"

I give him a narrow-eyed glare.

"Fine, fine, I'll help you fetch books, but you do the reading. Deal?"

"Deal." We shake on it. I have a feeling he's going to be busy, running up and down the stacks to get me what I need, anyway.

"I don't mean to rush you or anything," he says carefully, "but what do we do after that? Is your plan more . . . fleshed out?"

"It is." I smile, cocking my head to one side.

"You minx. What have you concocted?"

"I'll tell you all about it after I change."

I *shoo* him out of the room and dress quickly. Once I'm ready, I open the door and drag Jago back inside.

"Hey, this is one of my nicest jackets." He smooths the lapels I carelessly crumpled. He blinks and looks me up and down. "The dress, huh?"

"You said I needed a real disguise. Do you think this will fool Castellina's nosey dwellers?"

He smiles. "I got something else for you." He reaches for the unopened package. "One more small touch and no one will know who you are." He pulls out a small tin of brown paste and proceeds to cover the white streak in my hair.

23

VALERIA

"You can play with my necklace but only for a moment.
Understood, my little pixie?"

Loreleia Elhice – Queen of Castella – 9 AV

"Saints and feathers! I feel ridiculous," I say as I walk down
the sidewalk arm-in-arm with Jago.

"From the way everyone is staring, it's working." He waves as we
pass a woman about my age. She looks at me with a mixture of
alarm and jealousy. I don't see how both emotions go together, but
apparently, she both approves and disapproves of my outfit.

The red silk and damask dress Jago got for me came with a
bodice, which he made sure to lace in such a way that my bosom
feels as if it might burst forth at any moment.

My heels are precariously high, and I'm afraid I'll trip and break
my neck. There is no way I'm letting go of Jago's arm.

"I thought the point of a disguise is to avoid being noticed," I say.

"You already tried that, and all of Castellina knew who you
were. This is perfect."

"But everyone's looking at me."

"Exactly. When you skulk around in a cloak, they all pretend they don't see you because they know you don't want to be seen. Now, you're accomplishing the opposite. One more thing," he leans closer and whispers in my ear, "they know their little princess hates dresses."

Nonsense. The only reason they don't recognize me is because they're spending all of their time staring at my breasts, not my face.

When we reach the library, we walk up the front steps, which are flanked by two raven statues made from obsidian. They gleam in the sunlight, reminding me of Cuervo. He stayed back since, according to Jago, the bird is a dead giveaway of my presence, another beloved pet of Castellina's residents.

Fantástico!

We cut across La Plaza de Tierra Madre where a once-grand fountain dominates the center. Water trickles weakly from spouts around the goddess Achnamhair—fae mistress of the land, sea, and everything in between. Her marble semblance presides over a chariot, guided by two ferocious lions. I've read that globes of water used to levitate overhead, their colors changing with the seasons and the mood of the spell that kept them afloat. Just one more of the wondrous sights that were present in Castellina during the veil years.

Though built after the veil, the Biblioteca de la Reina is a magnificent place, rumored to be the envy of the entire continent. It's one of the few projects Father initiated that inspired me to participate. Mother's love for books, which she passed on to Amira and me, made constructing the library in her honor a cause I had to be part of.

Once inside, I'm struck by the place's beauty as usual. The entrance is adorned with intricately carved tulips, Mother's favorite flowers. The moment I cross the threshold, a hushed reverence envelops me. I wish she could have seen this. The soaring, vaulted ceilings, adorned with constellations in their frescoes. Sunlight filters through towering stained-glass windows, strategically avoiding the bookshelves in order to protect the books.

Rows of bookshelves, carved from dark mahogany, stand proudly, holding volumes that whisper secrets of centuries past. Gilded tomes, leather-bound classics, and scrolls from far-off lands fill the shelves, a treasure trove of human knowledge.

In the heart of the first level, a grand statue of Queen Loreleia Plumanegra stands tall. She's depicted in regal attire, her posture reflecting both strength and kindness. My throat aches at the sight.

How I miss you, Mother.

I swallow hard as we approach a tall counter, where a thin man of about twenty-five stands scribbling in a large ledger. We stop in front of him, and he regards us over round spectacles. He has a long nose and a mop of curly red hair that tickles his thin eyebrows. A black band with the wings of a raven embroidered in gold thread wraps around his bicep, carefully stitched to the sleeve of his jacket. This marks him as an erudito graduate of the Academia Alada. Only the best students in Castella are admitted to the prestigious learning center. There are few available spots every year, and they're given to the brightest of the brightest, no matter their economic background. There's one requirement, however—the student must be human.

This is a topic I argued about with Father many times. There are bright fae born in Castella who deserve a spot. They are also our citizens. He countered that it wasn't our responsibility to educate them—not when they had always considered our education methods subpar to their own, not when there aren't enough spots for our own people. How could he love Mother so much and at the same time scorn her people?

"Good afternoon," I say.

The erudito reappraises me, which involves glancing down at my cleavage, then over-correcting to look anywhere else but there.

"May I help you?" he croaks.

"Can you direct us to the section where I may find books on Tirnanog and the fae in general?"

"Certainly. Take the stairs to your right to the second floor. From there, go to the end of the stacks. The last ten rows will contain what you're looking for."

"Thank you."

"He wanted to eat you alive," Jago whispers as we climb the steps.

"I never realized how distracted men can be over something as simple as a pair of breasts."

"Oh, there's nothing simple about it. Many joys can be derived from—"

I put a hand up in front of his face. "I don't want to hear it."

"Honestly, you should educate yourself to know what you're missing."

"I'm pretty sure I only like men, Jago. I told you this before. So why don't you tell me about the joys of *their* many attributes instead."

"I could, I could, but then they would blame me for corrupting you."

"Who would blame you?" Father is gone. He was the one Jago was always afraid of.

He gets my meaning but says nothing else. Perhaps he still feels a duty to protect me. Father always told him he was the big brother I never had, and therefore, it was his job to take care of me.

When I turned eighteen, I had a brief lesson from Nana on my duties as a wife. At the time, I was mortified by the conversation and wanted it over with. I didn't even ask any questions despite my curiosity. I still remember what she said, however, and the images her words painted in my mind have been replayed many times over. I looked at them from every angle, and my questions only multiplied. Good thing there are libraries to do just that: answer young women's curious queries.

"How is Nana?" I say, reminded of her. "Have you seen her since you've been back?"

"I have. We ate breakfast together yesterday morning. She's very worried about you."

"Did you tell her I'm all right?"

"Of course. I know how to lie like the best."

When we reach the top of the stairs, we hurry down the corridor, passing several people with their noses buried in thick tomes. At the end, we enter a section in which each bookshelf is labeled *Fae Studies*. Underneath that title, there are smaller ones such as: Fae History, Fae Religions, Fae Philosophy, Fae Languages, and more.

Jago puts hands on hips and regards the shelves as if they're his enemies. "Are you sure we need to do this?"

"There's more to life than leisure, sex, and parties, Jago."

"Maybe, but books?"

"Quit complaining and let's take a closer look at all the sections, so we can decide where to start."

We walk up and down the aisles.

"Here is a section marked *Fae Magic*. I say we start here." Jago calls from two aisles down.

"*Shhh*," the rebuke floats from across the way.

"Sorry," Jago says.

"*Shhh*," once more.

I walk around to where he stands. He's about to say something else, but I press a hand to his mouth and shake my head. *Quiet* isn't something Jago does well.

Nodding at the books, I grab a stack. Jago does the same, and we find a place to sit in a corner outfitted with a round table and cushioned chairs.

Sitting, I make myself comfortable and start on a book titled *Enchanted Realms: Fae Magic Unveiled*. The leather-bound tome is as thick as Jago's head. I turn the pages and run a finger down the table of contents: Spells and Rituals, Faerie Beasts and Creatures, Riddles and Challenges, Fae Artifacts and Relics.

I immediately jump to this section.

"No pictures?" Jago whispers as he looks over my shoulder.

"Why don't you grab one of those books and help me?"

"Nah, I think I'll take a nap. Your bird woke me up early today, pecking at my window like his feathers were on fire." Jago takes a seat, slumps back with his arms crossed, and closes his eyes. "Let me know when you need more books."

I shake my head, knowing I wouldn't trust him to read everything thoroughly anyway.

Eagerly, I begin to read, perusing through the different books, carefully examining the relevant sections. It takes me one hour to go over three of the books in the first pile.

Jago is snoring lightly, looking content while I'm starting to get a headache from squinting at the tiny script.

As I pull a new book closer, I realize I need to hurry or it'll take me days, if not weeks, to get through a small fraction of these books. I finish the next three books in half an hour. Still not fast enough, but if I move much faster, I'll likely miss what I'm looking for—if it's to be found here at all.

I thump Jago on the forehead. His eyes roll as he struggles to wake up.

"I need more books," I tell him. "You can put these ones back."

He drags himself out of the chair, picks up the books I've finished, and returns a moment later with another pile. He looks at his pocket watch and frowns.

"I take it you haven't found anything of interest," he says.

"Not yet. It's so frustrating. Why is the necklace so important to everyone?"

"I told you that trying to find knowledge here would be a waste of time."

"Where else can I look?"

He shrugs. "As long as you're willing to spend a lifetime here, going through all of these books shouldn't be a problem." He yawns hugely.

"Either make yourself useful or go back to sleep." I pick up the next book and dive in.

Jago takes another nap.

We repeat this process for another two hours. With every new pile of books, my frustration grows. After his third nap, Jago complains about being hungry.

"I've never seen anyone so consumed by his own physiological needs," I snap at him.

"We've been here too many hours already. It's unnatural."

"Leave then. I don't care!"

He looks guilty at that. "I'll stay, and I'll help." He reaches for one of the books and begins turning the pages, his honey-colored eyes moving quickly from left to right, then back again.

Another hour passes. I find the mention of something that catches my attention and makes my heart leap.

Someone coughs lightly. "Excuse me, señor, señorita, it is now closing time."

I glance up from my thick tome, bleary-eyed. The red-headed man who was servicing the counter earlier is here, looking apologetic. For the first time, I realize the library is quieter than quiet. It seems we're the only ones left.

Jago lets out a sigh of relief, stands, and stretches his arms to the ceiling, a little roar sounding in the back of his throat. "I guess we'll have to come back tomorrow."

I shake my head. "No. Time isn't a luxury we possess."

He shrugs, glancing from me to the librarian as if saying *what do you want me to do?*

I stand and reluctantly shuffle from behind the table. It was ambitious to think I would find what I needed here, and even more so to imagine I would find it today. Still, I hoped. Maybe if I had a few more hours . . . a thought occurs to me.

The librarian is staring fixedly at the floor. I stop in front of him, and he startles. His gaze lands right on my cleavage.

I clear my throat.

The ceiling becomes very interesting to him.

"Dear Erudito," I say, "I very much need to continue my research."

"I'm sorry, señorita, the rules are strict."

"But surely you can make an exception in my case."

Jago comes closer and hisses in my ear. "What are you doing?"

The librarian finally looks me in the eye. His gaze roves over my face, and I see the moment he realizes who I am. How could he not when that huge portrait of me hangs in the vestibule so prominently for everyone to see?

"Princess Valeria." He bows deeply, his right forearm draped across his middle. "My apologies, Your Majesty. I didn't recognize you."

"It's all right . . . um . . ."

"Erudito Manuel Pineda, Your Majesty."

"It's all right, Manuel. You were busy doing your job as you should be. Now, about overlooking that small rule for me, will that be a problem?"

"Of course not, Your Majesty. I will remain here for as long as you need me to allow you to continue with your very important work."

"Oh, you're a dear."

"And if you need any help, I'm at your service."

"As a matter of fact, I have just read something very interesting about a beautiful opal called The Eldrystone. You wouldn't happen to know anything about that."

"I'm sorry, Your Majesty. My studies revolve around human sociology, not fae lore."

I hang my head. "That's a shame."

"But perhaps . . ."

"Yes?"

"There is an additional collection of fae texts that are too valuable to keep out here for general use."

My heart leaps.

He digs in his pocket, pulls out a key, and holds it up. "I happen to have the key to that private section right here."

I exchange a glance with Jago. If I'm to find the information I need, it will be there. I know it.

"You have saved the day, Manuel," I say.

He blushes bright red, making a smattering of freckles I hadn't noticed before stand out.

"Guide the way, please," I say cheerfully.

He takes us to the fifth floor, past several doors marked with *Eruditos Only* signs. At last, we arrive at a wooden door carved with intricate vines.

Manuel slips the key in the lock and ushers us in. "This is it," he says proudly. "I will be outside if you need me."

It's immediately apparent why this space requires restricted access. Only three medium bookshelves stand in a file, but the large, gilded tomes that grace them rival even the most valuable tomes in Nido's libraries.

The air feels different, thick with the scent of aged parchment and charged with an otherworldly energy that sends shivers down my spine. I feel as if time itself slowed the moment I stepped over the threshold. These shelves must hold treasures beyond imagination, old knowledge from the fae realm, my mother's realm. The books are unlike any I've ever seen—ancient, ornate, and adorned with intricate engravings of mythical creatures and symbols. Each book seems to hum with hidden power, as if the very words within them yearn to escape their pages. I approach one of the shelves, carefully running my fingers along the spines. The titles are in a script that's both beautiful and unreadable: Tirgaelach.

"It's your mother," Jago says.

I follow his gaze to a spot above the door behind us and find a portrait of my mother that I've never seen before. She looks resplendent, her eyes wide and full of light, the way they looked when she dropped her glamour to display her full fae features. Only her pointed ears are missing.

At the bottom of the gilded frame sits a golden plaque.

In memory of Loreleia Plumanegra. Beloved wife and mother.

"She was beautiful," Jago says, stepping next to me. "I barely remember her face. I mostly remember her kindness."

I rest my head on his shoulder. "I miss her so much."

"Sometimes I think it's good I don't remember my parents. It would hurt to miss them that way."

I face the bookshelves again, wondering why that unique portrait hangs here, why in this room with all these books.

Stepping lightly as if afraid to wake up the ancient texts from some deep slumber, I approach the shelf, run my fingers along the edge of the wood once more, and allow myself to feel the eerie power that seems to radiate from each tome.

When I get to the end, I continue on to the next bookshelf, then back to the first one. In this last one, a gilded tome seems to shine brighter than the others. I carefully remove it, lay it on the lonely table in the center, and lean over it.

"This one speaks to me," I say as Jago comes behind me.

"If it said it likes your boobs, it's a dude and you shouldn't trust it."

"A little respect, please."

He groans. "I'm nervous, all right? And when I'm nervous, joking makes me feel better."

I turn to look at him. "You feel it too, don't you?"

"Um, feel what?"

"There's . . . power in this room."

"Is that what it is? I thought it was the smell of old dust making me dizzy."

"Sit and be quiet." For once, he doesn't argue. He sits at the table and bounces his knee.

I ignore the nervous tic even if it makes the table rattle a bit. Instead, I focus on the book, too nervous to sit. I turn the pages slowly. They are soft and shine like mother-of-pearl.

My gaze roves over the words. They're written in the blackest ink, in a scroll I can hardly comprehend.

Tirgaelach became a dead tongue centuries ago—the same as Castellan. Fae and humans alike speak Tiran now.

For the first time, I regret all the lessons I ever skipped. If I'd been present, I might be able to comprehend more than an odd word here and there.

The tome contains illustrations. They're skillful beyond belief, lifelike depictions that play tricks on the eye, artfully melding shadows and light to convince the reader that the objects portrayed are tantalizingly within reach, as if one could touch them.

"I've never seen illustrations like that," Jago says.

"Me neither."

I keep going, admiring the images, representations of royal crowns, daggers, swords, suits of armor, and more.

Jago leans closer. "Is it some sort of military book?"

"Maybe. Too many crowns and tiaras, though. Could be about their monarchy."

A few pages down, my theory is confirmed.

"Look, it says Theric." I point out one word that seems to jump off the page, and I immediately recognize from my history lessons.

"That's the surname of their royal family, right?"

"I'm surprised you remember that." Jago and I sat in lessons together when we were little.

"I *did* pay attention. Sometimes."

The fae king at the time the veil disappeared was Korben Theric. In our lessons, we learned that he was a fair king, the great-grandson of Aldryn Theric, the male who found the rip in the veil and opened it wider.

Vaguely, I wonder what King Korben thinks of the veil's

disappearance. Is he glad contact with humans has been cut off? Does he worry about the fae folk trapped in this realm and unable to go home?

Father said that when humans and fae used to cross the veil freely, things were better. Per his account, things weren't perfect. There was still tension between our races, but the benefits far outweighed any squabbling. Trade was good. Espiritu flowed freely from their realm into ours, giving our family the power to maintain a peaceful kingdom for centuries. Now, we're in constant conflict with the fae and are being attacked in the south by our old enemies, who wish to regain control over Castella and its vast resources.

"So this book is about the fae royal family and their accoutrement?" Jago says.

"It appears so."

As I continue to flip through the pages, my heart suddenly seizes in my chest when I reach the midpoint. There, before my eyes, is an incredibly detailed rendering of Mother's necklace, nestled within the pages of a tome of untold age.

"That's it!" Jago exclaims. "I haven't seen the thing in a long time, but I remember it."

I nod, breathing shakily. My eyes rove over the page. The Tirgaelach scroll unravels before me, but I can only read a few of the simplest words.

Jago points at the book. "You have to take this to Maestro Elizondo. He can decipher it for you. If you can trust him, that is. What do you think it says? Maybe your mother was a Theric."

"No. She wasn't. She was born in a small village."

"What if she was lying? What if her father wanted to marry her off, and she ran away? It would be perfect symmetry."

I shake my head. I always sensed that Mother kept secrets. Everyone is entitled to those. Lies, however, it would hurt me deeply if she knowingly deceived me. Could this possibly be the secret Father confided in Amira before he died?

"I need a copy of this," I say.

"We can just . . ." Jago goes for the book as if he's about to tear out the pages.

"No!" I slap his hands away. "Are you mad? Every book in here is invaluable."

"I was just trying to save us some time." He rolls his eyes.

After a quick search of the room, I spot a stack of loose parchment, an ink well, and a quill. I gather the materials and begin copying the text with painstaking slowness.

"This is going to take forever. You should let me—"

"I would feed you a pound of strawberries before I let you hurt this book." Jago is allergic to the fruit. He breaks out in horrible hives and struggles to breathe if he eats them.

"Are you saying you value that old parchment more than you value your favorite cousin's life?"

"You're my only cousin, Jago."

"Exactly."

"The strawberries wouldn't kill you, but they would teach you a lesson."

"I will never forget how little you value my life." He stomps away, presses his back to the wall, and slides down to the floor to wait while I fill up the sheet with the tilting scroll.

It's only the second hour of a new day when we leave the library. We are bleary-eyed, and so is the librarian, but he seems pleased to have helped us.

"I'm forever in your debt," I tell him as he ushers us out the front door.

"I only did my duty, Your Majesty." He inclines his head, cheeks glowing brightly.

"Don't hesitate to come to Nido if you ever need anything."

His cheeks turn redder still. He remains behind us as we descend the marble steps. A shiver runs across my back, the feeling that someone is watching us making my skin prickle.

I glance all around, but the streets are deserted at this hour. There's only a slight breeze that caresses the leaves in the trees and makes them sing.

"What is it?" Jago asks.

"Nothing. Let's go. We should get some rest. We have a long day ahead of us."

We hurry down the sidewalk, headed back to the inn. I hold my breath at every corner, afraid a band of veilfallen will assault us. I have nothing of value with me, but the pages I've carefully folded and slipped down the front of my dress. I doubt River would see any value in dry ink and parchment. He only cares about stealing and causing chaos.

But luck is on our side today in more than one way, and we make it safely back to the inn.

24

RIVER

"I must say, I do appreciate Los Moros' beautiful architecture."

Maria de Alsedo – Duquesa de Castellina – 98 BV

When Valeria Plumanegra walks out of the inn, I nearly don't recognize her. She's wearing a provocative dress. Her face is enhanced with makeup, and her locks are arranged in a way that makes their ratty state of last night only an unpleasant memory.

She's hanging from her cousin, and they walk with purpose, headed where? I don't know, but I can only hope they're on their way to retrieve the amulet. My chest pumps with heavy anticipation.

I follow at a safe distance. Passersby are distracted by her new appearance. She crosses their path, and they don't recognize her. Dressing this way was a clever idea. She is attractive, I suppose, and the dress is revealing enough to draw the eye away from her face.

I'm also dressed to distract, humble human clothes and a cap that hides my ears. I walk hunched over, my head down. Some of the most distrustful denizens take closer looks, then hurry their

261

pace or move out of the way to avoid me. The majority of people, however, don't see through my disguise and ignore me.

After I follow them for several blocks, Valeria and her cousin head up the Biblioteca de la Reina's steps and go in. I stay on the other side of the street, hidden under the shadow of an awning.

For a moment, I struggle with the decision of whether or not to follow them inside. This can't be their final destination. The Eldrystone wouldn't be safe in such a place, or would it? I do remember someone mentioning the place was built in Loreleia's honor. Maybe this *is* the most logical place for its safekeeping. Maybe they built a vault for it.

If that is the case, I ought to remain here, bide my time to let Valeria secure the amulet, and then . . . I forcefully suppress the hope that starts to surge within my chest. I know better than to let my desires grow.

On the other hand, what if this is merely a diversionary path? They might only be passing through the building, hastening toward a rear exit in an effort to evade pursuers.

Not that they know with certainty that they're being followed. Valeria thinks her trip through the sewers delivered her to safety. Little does she know I meticulously orchestrated her feigned abduction and allowed her to escape.

I anticipated she would escape through the pipe. It was her only option. I also foresaw she would choose the wider passage that led to the river, so once I made sure she wouldn't reemerge, I hurried to the exit point and watched her come out. Pathetically, she immersed herself in the river to wash, then nestled by the overgrown bushes like a lost animal. She believed herself secure, blissfully unaware that I lurked nearby, monitoring her every move.

What I didn't count on was that godsforsaken raven fetching Jago, that clown. The cousin is harmless, however. It's the bird I'm wary of. If he spots me, he will ruin everything. So far I've been able to evade him, but I'm worried my luck might run short. If I get my hands on the creature, I swear I will snap its neck. I can't have my plan ruined by a bird. Too much depends on that amulet.

In the end, concern for their escape drives me into the library. If The Eldrystone is here . . . My hands itch with possibilities. I may hold the amulet today. Finally, after so long.

I take the front steps two at a time and push past the heavy wooden doors, wondering if the amulet has been here all along, so close within my reach.

"May I help you?" a puny man with red hair and spectacles asks as I walk in. He looks me up and down. I don't fit the appearance of the library's regular visitors.

My eyes rove over the large space. On the second floor, on the landing that oversees this area, I spot them.

I read a sign that points toward the stairs. It reads *Foreign Studies*. The second floor appears to contain tomes relating to other cultures.

"I need some reading material on Andalous battles against Los Moros," I say.

The man scrutinizes me. He pays close attention to my cap and the scar over my eye. I should have had Calierin apply a powerful glamour, but I didn't think it necessary. The scar marks me as an undesirable individual. It speaks for me before I have the chance to open my mouth. Most of the time, I don't care. It makes people properly afraid. Other times, it's an inconvenience.

"Your kind isn't welcome here," the man says, his voice trembling. I can tell it took every shred of courage he possesses to tell me that.

"And what kind might that be?" I ask.

His mouth opens and closes, but no words come out.

"The kind that writes papers on the socioeconomic impact of war?" I ask.

He reevaluates me. The wing-embroidered black band around his left arm lets me know he's an erudito from the Academia Alada, and the glint in his eyes tells me this might be a topic of interest to him. Maybe now I fit his idea of someone worthy of this sad place.

What he doesn't know is that in Castella, I may be a thug, but in Tirnanog, I used to be something else entirely.

The man shakes his head, dispelling the momentary curiosity that the scholarly topic brought out in him.

"I'm afraid I'm going to have to ask you to leave." He extends a hand toward the door.

I want to jab him straight in the mouth and knock his teeth out for daring to treat me as if I were garbage.

I lean closer, my gaze drilling into his. He inclines back, practically shaking in his shoes. He knows well I can paint the wall red with his blood, and that's just a fraction of what I'd like to do to people of his ilk.

"You're a maggot," I growl, "and will die a maggot, and if I cared enough about mere insects like you I would dance on your grave.

But you're hardly worth my time." I ease back as he withers under my stare.

"Don't . . . ma-make me call the Guardia," he manages in a stutter.

I huff and walk out. No number of guards could stop me if I wanted to raze this place to the ground, but that wouldn't serve my purposes. Instead, I wait outside for a few minutes, reclining against the outside wall, close to the door where I'll still have a view of the inside whenever the door opens.

A few people walk out. If they notice me, they quickly glance away. I wait some more.

Some moments later, a man pushes the door open with his foot, balancing a tall pile of books. He can barely see over the top. I hold the door open for him. He issues a *thank you* that he quickly regrets when he catches full sight of me.

I resist the temptation to trip him and watch him tumble down the steps, his precious load scattering all over the ground. It irks me how petty I've become. I ignore him, and it gratifies me to know that I can still rise above, if only because I have better things to do.

The puny erudito's back is to the door. I'm up the stairs before he can blink an eye. Humans are pathetically slow. They only best us because their numbers are greater, but they're like ants attacking a weak, fallen foe.

Most of the patrons don't notice me as I walk the length of the second floor. They're busy in their studies or research, noses buried in their work.

I spot Valeria and Jago at the end of the stacks. They are exploring books in a section marked *Fae Studies*.

I enter one of the aisles several rows removed from where they stand, and carefully approach until I can hear their conversation.

"I take it you haven't found anything of interest," her cousin says.

"Not yet. It's so frustrating. Why is the necklace so important to everyone?"

"I told you that trying to find knowledge here might be a waste of time."

"Where else can I look?"

"As long as you're willing to spend a lifetime here, going through all of these books shouldn't be a problem."

I stand frozen, processing what I just heard. Valeria Plumanegra doesn't know what the amulet is, and she's here to try to figure it out? I shake my head as the notion takes root. She's not trying to keep the amulet because of its power? She thinks it's just a necklace? And they're here only to do research? Impossible.

She wouldn't risk her life for something she thinks is nothing but a pretty trinket.

Slowly, I backtrack and find my way out of the library. I wait for the princess to come out. It takes hours and spends all of my patience until I'm pacing back and forth like a caged animal. When they finally emerge well after midnight, I follow them back to the same inn.

I clench my empty hands, the memory of how The Eldrystone used to rest in my palm, haunting my senses. Once more, my hopes are shattered, and my endless wait and banishment persist. Despair beckons, but I resist. I've never stood nearer to my goal. The amulet will find its way back to me. It's only a matter of time.

25

VALERIA

"This blade, my lord, is a gift, skillfully forged by the most adept fae blacksmith. It is invulnerable to the weave of magic."

Llewelur Virsier – Fae Emissary – 1699 DV

The royal guards at Nido's gates can't believe their eyes as I walk up to them, alone. Jago will come in later. It won't be a stretch for Amira to figure out that he's still helping me, but his absence might delay the realization.

I'm wearing the same dress from yesterday, with the corset tied even tighter, and my breasts straining against the fabric.

I also have makeup on and keep resisting the temptation to rub it off, wondering if this is the sort of thing one ever gets used to wearing all the time.

The white streak in my hair is fully visible now.

"Princess Valeria." The guard in charge bows and orders the others to let me through.

Once inside Nido, I make my way to Father's study, Amira's now. That is the most likely place to find her at this time of the day.

My pointed heels make too much noise on the hardwood floor, and my dress rustles like a leaf-strewn lawn in autumn. These damn clothes announce my presence in every possible way.

At the double doors, I knock firmly and try to draw courage from the mother raven carved on the blackwood. My heart trembles, and my mind screams for me to run away. This could be the worst idea I've ever had. This could land me exactly where I don't want to be.

There's still time, Val. Hide! I glance right and left, feeling trapped.

The door opens. Emerito stands on the other side. At first, he doesn't recognize me and looks annoyed at the interruption. But slowly, his expression changes, giving way to surprise.

"Va-valeria?" he stammers.

"*Princess* Valeria to you," I say, my tone as patronizing as what he uses on everyone below his station.

He stands frozen.

"I'm here to see Queen Amira."

He has the look of someone whose thoughts are drowning in molasses. Maybe he'd been expecting to never see me again.

"Emerito, what is it?" My sister's voice comes from inside the study.

I push past the still-dumbfounded Emerito and march toward the desk that occupies the center of the room. Amira sets her quill down and looks up. I'm expecting to see a reaction similar to Emerito's, but she just stares at me with cold indifference.

"Look who has decided to stop playing hide and seek," she says. "Why are you here? You wasted enough of our time already."

"Hello, Valeria, I'm so happy to see you. I'm glad you're all right,"

268

I say in a high-pitched voice. "Nice to see you too, Amira, my dear sister."

She reclines in her chair and crosses her arms, unamused. "Well, are you going to tell me why you've decided to come back?"

She's not my sister. This can't possibly be Amira. Her expression holds none of the love and sympathy I'm used to seeing there.

I take a deep breath. If somebody, namely Orys, is forcing her to play a part, it's time for me to play mine. She and Father are right. I need to stop acting like a child, though that doesn't mean I'll turn into the adult they hope for.

"I have come to my senses," I say. "I was wrong to think I could survive on my own." The words taste rank in my mouth, even though I don't mean them. "I'm here to do as you ordered."

Behind me, Emerito coughs as if he has choked on his own saliva.

"Is that so?" Amira asks.

I nod.

"I don't believe you. I think you're here to play more games."

I bow with a bit of chagrin. I'm trying not to overdo my performance. It's a precarious balance.

"I don't blame you," I say, "but I promise you I'm serious. I do, however, have certain conditions."

"You're in no position to set conditions, Valeria."

"I will not ask for more than my due. You dispatched me to Alsur like an old piece of luggage to be married off in obscurity, as if I've done something wrong."

"But you have, sister. You dared disobey my orders, and people are discovering very quickly that this is not something I will tolerate. It seems even you've learned that as well."

I want to jump over the desk, shake her, and ask her what's wrong with her, but that led me nowhere before, so I smooth my dress instead and refrain from jumping.

"I have," I admit between clenched teeth. In this case, it's fine to let my irritation show for the sake of balancing my performance. "The last few days taught me some valuable lessons."

Emerito chuckles. I look at him sideways and register the satisfied smirk on his face. He's enjoying this far too much.

"I nearly died two nights ago," I say. "You sent Bastien for me, and the carriage was attacked, as I'm sure you've learned. I had to wade through the sewers to escape."

Amira's face twists in disgust, just the effect I was going for.

"Foul," Emerito sneers.

They have no idea that I would go through much worse to make those responsible for Father's death pay. They don't know that despite the hunger, cold, and lack of regular baths, I've never felt more alive than during the time I spent outside these walls.

"Bastien said the veilfallen took you." Amira rests her elbows on the table and steeples her fingers. "So it's true, you escaped?"

"I did. It wasn't easy or sanitary, but I thought for sure they would kill me if I didn't . . . forgo my sensibilities. It was then that I realized there isn't a safe place for a Plumanegra to hide in this city. I would never be able to have a peaceful life, wouldn't have the freedom I crave."

The best lies are sprinkled with the truth, Father used to say, so I give Amira something she would expect to come out of my mouth. She knows freedom is what I want most.

"As it stands," I add, "I would be freer in Alsur."

"Hmm, you bested the veilfallen. Again. Not many get to do that. Their attacks have been relentless in the last few days. They keep besting us, and you just . . . escape." She says the word *escape* as if getting away from River was a game I played.

She's considering this as if it were the most important piece of information I've offered so far. I frown. This is what she's choosing to focus on. Why?

"I'm not an easy target," I say, "and you know that."

Father made sure we both trained in self-defense and weaponry. He said he never wanted us to be damsels in distress, that we should be self-sufficient in every aspect of our lives. Amira shouldn't be surprised by my ability to defend myself.

"Yes, but . . ." She lets the word hang.

"But what?"

Waving a hand in the air, she dismisses the whole thing. "Never mind. What matters is that you are here and have *come to your senses.*" The way she says the last bit makes me think she doesn't believe me or suspects I'll still cause trouble. "What are these conditions you're talking about?"

All right, this seems to finally be moving in the right direction.

"I want Don Justo to court me properly. I want an engagement party, a ball here in Nido. I don't want people to gossip and say I was spirited away because I got pregnant or some such nonsense. And I want a long engagement."

"Fine."

All the fight goes out of me. I didn't expect her to agree so readily, especially to the long engagement part.

"I have a request of my own," she adds.

And . . . all the fight rushes back in.

"What request?" I ask.

"I want you to give me Mother's necklace." Her brown eyes watch my reaction closely.

I'm genuinely confused, and I'm glad that's the expression showing on my face. I wasn't expecting this at all. Not after all the subterfuge.

"Mother's necklace?" I shake my head.

"Yes."

"Do you mean the one with the opal?"

"Precisely."

"Why?"

"It turns out it might be of some importance," she says.

"Really? Says who?"

"The veilfallen are looking for it."

My jaw hangs open. Yet something else I wasn't expecting. "Why would the veilfallen want Mother's necklace?" I ask, feigning ignorance.

"I don't know."

I sense she's not telling the truth. She knows why. If only I'd been able to get Maestro Elizondo to translate those pages already. Jago has them. He's keeping them for me. I was afraid to walk in here wearing the evidence.

"That sounds insane. The veilfallen want a useless necklace Mother let us play with. That makes no sense." I glance toward Emerito, wondering how much he knows.

"It stands to reason that it may not be as useless as we might have imagined," Amira says.

"How do you know they want it?"

"Our spies came across that bit of intelligence. We need to keep it safe and find out why the fae want to get their hands on it."

"Well, it's safe, all right," I say, "because I lost that thing a long time ago."

Amira stands up abruptly, her chair scraping the floor and nearly toppling over. "What do you mean you lost it?"

"I mean I lost it."

"You did not!" She nearly shouts, which confirms my suspicions that she's lying. She knows exactly why the veilfallen want it, and whatever the reason, it's also why *she* wants it.

"I'm sorry, Amira. I was a child, and I used to play with it all the time as you might remember. Then one day, I must've left it somewhere. Maybe someone took it. Maybe it fell through a crack somewhere. I wasn't worried about it. I just found something else to play with."

"You're lying."

I blink. "Why would I lie about something like that? If I had it, I'd gladly give it to you. Hey, wait a minute!" I pretend to think hard about something. "Before I left for Alsur, someone searched my room. Did you have someone go through my stuff?" I let all the indignation I feel color my words.

"Of course I did not."

Such a liar.

"Well, someone did," I say. "Do you think it was . . . a veilfallen spy? Oh, gods. Maybe Orys is working for them, after all. Is that why he killed Father? For that useless trinket?"

"Let's not get carried away," Amira says.

"But what if—"

My sister cuts me short. "It's not your job to worry about these things. It is mine. All I want you to do is to think about where that necklace could be and to pacify Don Justo. He has accosted me every day since he arrived, demanding the presence of his promised bride. He has gone as far as to make threats that would endanger our position in the south. We have enough with the veil-fallen. We need Don Justo to keep Los Moros in check. So you see, you do have some very important tasks to perform."

The way I see it, my tasks align not at all with hers. Task number one is to protect Mother's necklace and find out why it's so important. Task number two, find Father's murderer. Task number three, free Amira from whatever spell that sorcerer has on her. And task number four . . . Give Don Justo the boot. Eventually.

I incline my head. "As you wish, my queen."

"Don't mock me."

"Oh, lighten up, Amira. There's no need to become a different person just because you're queen now. We're still sisters, you know. You can count on me, talk to me if you need someone to listen."

I wait for a little warmth to enter her expression. Amira has always been serious, and Father praised this quality because he said it would help her be a stern, yet just, ruler. However, no matter the circumstances, she maintained a tender side. She may have kept it hidden, but not all the time. Not with me.

"You can leave now." She picks up her quill and goes back to writing, acting as if I've already left.

Emerito has remained quiet, absorbing every bit of information. He smirks stiffly as I make my way toward the door.

My heels click down the corridor as I make a loud exit, but when I reach the end of the hall, I take off my shoes, pick up my dress, and run back the way I came. Pressing my ear to the study door, I listen.

"Yes, she's lying," Amira says. "She still has the amulet."

Shit!

"Are you sure?" Emerito asks.

"I am."

Emerito says, "I guess you know her better than anyone."

"We still need to keep a close eye on her, need to keep searching. We have to find that amulet."

Silence, followed by steps.

I whirl and run back down the hall and turn the corner just as I hear the door open.

Breathing a sigh of relief, I make my way to my bedchamber. My mind is a battlefield of conflicting thoughts, each fighting to get to the frontline. I desperately need to think.

26

RIVER

"A son, yet Carolina has passed away."

Julián Plumanegra – Castella General – 20 AV

I followed her back to Nido. She walked right up to the gates and gave herself up. It was hard to watch her go, hard to allow her to slip through my fingers, but what other choice did I have?

Valeria Plumanegra didn't take The Eldrystone with her to Alsur. If she had, it would have been on her when I searched her. The amulet is in Nido. It has to be. It's the only thing that makes sense.

So yes, I had to let her go back, though that doesn't mean I'm done with her. If she found out about the amulet's power during her little research session at the library, she won't be able to resist retrieving it this time.

Everything makes so much sense now. I thought she was an artful deceiver, biding her time, but she was just ignorant of what she held in her possession. Now, curiosity and greed will be her downfall.

"So what have you decided?" Calierin asks, sitting across from me. We're in our usual hideout in the catacombs, drinking stale wine. Candles burn inside nooks in the walls, filling the space with flickering light.

"It is time to act," I say.

"Finally," she throws her hands up in the air.

"Are you sure?" Kadewyn asks, wiping the back of his hand across wine-tainted lips. He has always been the most cautious of us.

"I am sure," I say.

"Damn Orys Kelakian! He robbed us of the pleasure of slitting the king's throat. I guess the simpering queen will have to do." Calierin laughs drunkenly.

She isn't the only one who feels that way. Simón Plumanegra bears the blame for my exile. For two decades, I dreamed of exacting my vengeance. It took me long enough to find him, but how could I have guessed that the man who interceded on Loreleia's behalf as she escaped Tirnanog with The Eldrystone was the King of Castella? The man responsible for the fall of the veil.

It wasn't until I stopped feeling sorry for myself, put an end to my aimless wandering through the countryside, and arrived in Castellina that I finally discovered his true identity. Here in the capital, one can hardly escape Simón's portraits affixed to walls in all public places. His subjects loved him. There's no doubt the Plumanegras have served this realm well. But it was the Castellinians' obsession with their king that allowed me to happen upon one of these portraits at a cheap tavern.

I instantly recognized him: the foe that changed the course of my life.

Ever since that day, I made it my mission to end him. I joined the disorganized veilfallen, became their leader, and strengthened their cause. That was one year ago; too late, I now know.

That fucking sorcerer stole my chance. Evidently, he had nurtured a deep-seated grudge against Simón Plumanegra. Aiming to take the king's place, he attempted to kill him twelve years ago but failed miserably. Everyone believed Orys dead, but as it turns out, he had been nursing his wounds, lying in wait for a second chance. He got it, without a doubt, and now, he's up to something else, lurking in the shadows and manipulating events from afar. We've made several attempts to locate him, but the powerful sorcerer remains elusive.

It enrages me that I didn't get the chance to confront Simón once more, but even though one of my goals has slipped through my grasp, the primary one still stands: The Eldrystone and its return to its rightful owner.

"I wouldn't mind doing away with that bratty princess, too!" Calierin adds, not privy to my main objective.

My veilfallen brethren think this is all about fighting our oppressors. They have no idea this is much more than that. But I can't trust anyone with the knowledge. The less people know about the amulet, the better. Too many already covet its power. I've learned through painful experience that, no matter how virtuous someone appears, the hunger for power can darken their heart and lead them to the worst type of betrayal.

I've been with Kadewyn and Calierin for a year, and they have given me no reason to think ill of them, but I know no one ever shows their true self.

Everyone lies.

Every.One.

"The bratty princess is not our priority," I lie as if to prove the point to myself.

I need everyone to focus on Amira Plumanegra while I worry about her sister.

Throwing my head back, I down the rest of the wine.

Soon I will hold the amulet in my hands again.

Soon.

27

VALERIA

"I find myself conflicted. Los Moros have contributed to our knowledge in abundance. Yet, many have suffered greatly under their rule."

Manrrique Guillen – Erudito de la Academia Alada – 45 BV

My heart still pounding after eavesdropping on Amira, I make it to my bedchamber. The door is thrown open, and when I step inside, my heart sinks heavily into the pit of my stomach.

My room, *my room*, the place where Mother soothed me to sleep after childhood illnesses and night terrors, is destroyed.

Numbly, I place one foot in front of the other and walk further in. My furniture is gone. My belongings have vanished, leaving behind broken walls and floors littered with debris underfoot. In one corner, I discover the tulip tapestry that Mother and I once embroidered together, now abandoned. I lift it gently and hug it close to my chest, tears welling in my eyes.

Amira didn't even have the decency to mention they'd destroyed my bedchamber searching for Mother's necklace.

I want to run back downstairs and yell at her. I want to shove her and slap her and . . .

Gods! What is wrong with her?!

My arms tremble and tighten around the tapestry as if to strangle it.

"Sad," a voice croaks behind me.

I turn and see Cuervo perched on the balcony's railing. I approach him, the weight of the sadness he just named heavy in my soul.

"I don't have much from Mother, Cuervo."

I hang the tapestry over the railing and beat on it. Dust floats up in a cloud and gets carried away by the wind.

"I made this with her. Well, I made this flower and this one."

With a trembling finger, I point to two small crooked tulips.

"They're ugly, but she told me they were beautiful, better than the first ones she made when she was little."

Cuervo's eyes are full of sympathy as he looks up at me. Seeing such understanding in his expression snaps me out of my emotional spiral. I can't let despair take me. I have a mission, and I won't accomplish it by feeling sorry for myself.

Taking a deep breath, I get my thoughts in order, realigning my plans with all I've learned today. Once I'm calm, I take the tapestry and leave in search of Jago. I find him sleeping in his bedchamber, shirtless and drooling on his pillow, a bottle of wine on the night table.

"Wake up!" I slap his cheek.

His eyes roll as he struggles to keep his lids open.

"Really? Did you have to get drunk first thing?"

He sits up. "I'm not drunk. I only had two glasses of wine." Yawning hugely, he stretches his arms over his head.

"Oh, good." I make myself comfortable in a cushioned armchair and watch as he jumps off the bed and finds his shirt.

"How did your meeting with Amira go?"

I tell him every detail of our conversation.

"Be careful what you wish for." Jago shakes his finger at me. "You wanted adventure since you were little, and now you're in the middle of a conspiracy."

"Look," I say in a no-nonsense tone, "I need you to find Don Justo and tell him that I will have breakfast with him tomorrow in the sunroom. East wing."

Jago frowns, clearly displeased by the assignment.

"I don't want to see him yet," I say. "I want to delay any interaction with him as much as possible."

"Um, why not have one of the servants deliver your message? It doesn't have to be me. The man is a dolt, and I'd rather someone twist my nipples—they're very sensitive, mind you—than see his face again. I already had to ride five days with him from Alsur, thanks to you."

I clear my throat. I thought about this long and hard. "I understand, but I was thinking you could act as my representative in all official matters."

He sits at the edge of the small desk he keeps in one corner and gives me a slow blink. "Official matters? Since when do you care about those?"

"Since I came to terms with the fact that it's the only way I'm going to figure out who killed Father?"

He huffs and crosses his arms. "I don't want to have anything to do with *official matters*, and you know that. I thought we were of the same mind."

"Maybe it's time we grow up, Jago."

"And end up like our parents?" He walks to the night table, grabs the wine bottle, and takes a long swig. "I'd rather not."

"What then? What is your plan?"

"I have no plan." The smile he gives me is one of his most fetching ones. He's proud of this.

"And you expect to go on like that your entire life?"

He shrugs. "I see nothing wrong with that."

Slowly, I stand, the heat of anger filling my chest. "So you're saying that your aspirations amount to being a drunk and a cad who sleeps with anything that moves."

His eyes widen. "A drunk and a cad who sleeps with anything that moves?" he echoes. "Is that what you think of me?"

I want to take the words back as soon as they're out. I can see the hurt in his expression and hate that I sound exactly like Father. But maybe he was right.

He sputters a laugh. "That *is* what you think of me. At least you didn't call me a leech. Your Father used that word once."

I shake my head. "That is horrible. I would never—"

He cuts me off. "My father and my mother gave this kingdom enough, and what did they get in return? A stately mausoleum in an abandoned cemetery? You think that might have been enough to buy their only son a quiet existence."

I can do nothing else but stare. I have no words for him because I never knew he felt this way, never knew that Father—

"Simón Plumanegra never saw any value in me because I didn't aspire to be the captain of his Guardia Real, because I don't value violence, because I don't think life is a prescriptive formula everyone needs to follow." His voice is several octaves higher now, and his cheeks are red with the fervor of his words and feelings.

"I'm sorry, Jago." Still holding the tapestry, I incline my head and walk toward the door. I stop and stare at the floor for a moment before I reach for it. "I will find someone else to help me. I didn't mean to offend you."

I don't look back as I exit. I'm too embarrassed to do so. Father thought there was only one way for a Plumanegra to live their life, and that was in the service of Castella. He was selfless in that way, but he was unable to understand that not everyone was like him. Duty isn't the sole measure of one's existence, and while some might feel lucky to be a Plumanegra, it doesn't mean that is all they would ever want to be.

As I meander down the least frequented halls in Nido, I realize the irony of my situation. It seems I'm growing up to be exactly who Father wanted me to be.

Regardless of that, I understand Jago. I can't lie and say I'm not disappointed. I want him by my side in this. He, Nana, and Cuervo are the only beings I trust at the moment. But I won't force him or guilt him into doing something that goes against his nature. At least I learned that much after being asked to do the same so many times.

Five minutes later, I find that I've wandered all the way to my favorite sparring courtyard. It seems my mind can't quiet down despite the fact that I already have a plan. I roll up the tapestry and leave it in the armory.

Outside, I lean against the battlement, allowing the crisp breeze to caress my face. My gaze drifts across the woods and city encircling my home. Clouds drift lazily across the sky, a stark contrast to my racing thoughts. Castellina sprawls beneath me, with distant blue-gray mountains tracing the contours of the valley.

The realm of the Plumanegras stretches far and wide, a legacy that has endured for nearly four centuries. The fae magic, that ancestral gift, has been instrumental in maintaining our enduring dynasty, a rarity among neighboring kingdoms. While elsewhere, disputes, internal strife, uprisings, and conquests create new kingdoms in the blink of an eye, Castella is different in this regard. But what if we have reached the end of our road?

It must have been what Father was worried about.

Since we lost our espiritu, things have changed. There are the veilfallen, deep within the kingdom's womb, and Los Moros to the south, hoping to reclaim what was once theirs.

Now, our king is gone, and his daughter, his replacement, may not be the person he hoped. And even if she is, perhaps she's not strong enough to take his place—not if she has fallen under the influence of Orys's malevolent powers. Could it be that the task falls to me now?

Anxiety clenches my throat at the very thought.

A sudden noise from behind startles me, yanking me out of my reverie and grounding me in the present. I whirl, clearing my throat and the choking sensation that nearly stole my breath away.

Of course, the choking sensation returns as I see who stands behind me: Guardia Bastien Mora.

I wait for him to say something as I stare at his stern face, but not a word comes out of him.

"Do you want something?" I demand.

"Your sister sent me to watch over you."

Now, it's a laugh that chokes me. "You can't be serious. I'm sorry. You might have been a top cadet at the academy, but as a personal *guard*, you're a failure."

The satisfaction that floods me when his mouth twists and a muscle ticks in his jaw is very . . . well . . . satisfying.

I walk closer and stop a few feet away from him. I thrust my chest forward and put on a self-important air. These things don't come easy to me, and I feel extremely awkward. However, I'm hoping practice will make me perfect.

Bastien's dark eyebrows draw together as he scans me, his eyes subtly sweeping over my attire, and even though it happens quickly, I don't miss the glance directed towards my décolletage.

I smile inwardly.

"Pray, do enlighten me, why would my dear sister burden me with such a disappointment?" I circle around him as he remains steadfast, his gaze seemingly fixed on some distant point as though I've vanished into thin air. Still, I sense there is much he'd like to say.

"Are you in league with her?" I dart around his left flank to peer into his face and gauge his reaction, but it remains as inscrutable as ever.

I continue pacing around him, arms behind my back. There's a small ledge to his right, a three-inch brick barrier that encircles the flowerbeds. I step on it and walk along its length. Balancing, I go from one end to the next, and on the way back, I stop and face him.

His profile captivates me, and I'm struck by his sheer perfection. His jawline is impeccably chiseled and angular. The bridge of his nose rises gracefully before descending to a subtly upturned tip. His brow and chin exude strength, and his lips are neither too thin nor overly full, striking the perfect balance. Wavy black hair is swept back from a slight widow's peak, resembling the texture of soft silk.

My foot slips from the ledge. I yelp and throw my arms out, but I know I'm going to end up ensconced in the rosebush behind me. I'm just on my way down, but I'm already mortified.

Bastien's strong arm wraps around my waist and pulls me upright. As he sets my feet on the ground, I find myself standing against his hard body, his arms embracing me tightly.

He's looking down at me. I'm looking up at him. Something passes between us. I don't know what it is but it feels slightly like . . . recognition.

But that makes no sense.

Abruptly, he lets me go and takes a step back. "Dainty shoes don't seem to suit your usual agility, princess. It seems I don't have to worry about any escape attempts while you're dressed in this manner."

I glare at him, nostrils flaring. Clenching my fists, I take a moment to ease my temper, and when it passes, I know what I need to do.

"You're absolutely right," I respond, forcing a smile with that air of haughtiness that makes me feel like a harpy, even though this man deserves every bit of my disdain. "But that isn't the only reason you and my sister shouldn't worry. You see, I'm back for good. As I told Queen Amira, I've come to my senses. I'm here to do my duty, and since you're here, and I have no one else to do my bidding, I want you to find Don Justo and inform him that I'm ready to meet him tomorrow for breakfast in the east wing sunroom. Good day, Don Bastien."

I turn on the heel of my traitorous shoe and march out of the courtyard, resisting the temptation to glance over my shoulder to see Bastien's reaction. I can well imagine it, though.

I'd wager it's corpse-like.

When I get to my destroyed bedchamber, I find Jago waiting for me. He's on the balcony, feeding Cuervo grapes and making clicking sounds with his tongue.

"Hey," I say, unsure whether or not he's still mad at me. I hope the fact that he's here means he isn't.

"What the hell happened here?"

I set the rolled-up tapestry on the floor and shrug.

He shakes his head. "Such bastardos. I can't believe they did this." He gives Cuervo the last grape and turns, wiping his hands on his pants. "I'm sorry."

"*I'm* sorry," I say at the same time.

"No, I was being an ass. Of course I'll help you."

I shake my head. "It's all right, Jago. I understand. I shouldn't have assumed anything. I was out of line. I've been dragging you into all my troubles despite knowing how you feel about what duty has stolen from you already."

"True, I don't care about any duties as a Plumanegra, but you're my friend, and my most beloved cousin, so . . ."

"You don't have to do anything you don't want to."

"Oh, get off your high horse, and let me help."

"A high horse has nothing to do with it. I found someone else to help."

"Who's the poor sucker?"

"Bastien."

"Bastien?"

I nod. "If he's going to be hanging around me, he can make himself useful."

"Do you mean he's still your guard?"

"Yes."

"That makes no sense. You left him in the dust in Alsur. Well, actually, you were the one left in the dust while he chased me," he says thoughtfully. "But you know what I mean."

"Jago, I want to apolo—"

Jago turns to face the open sky. "You're right about me. I have no purpose. My life—"

"You don't have to—"

"Let me talk."

I shut my mouth, stand next to him, and watch the sun play on the observatory's broken walls in the distance.

"Uncle Simón was hard on me," he begins, "but he was hard on Amira and you, too. I know he loved us and wanted the best for us. He did what he had to. He challenged us, never settled for less than our very best. And even if our best wasn't good enough, he never gave up on us." He pauses. "I thought we would have more time, Val. I thought he would be there for a long time." He swallows thickly and blinks repeatedly up at the sky. "I miss him," he says, blowing air through his nose.

"I miss him, too."

He faces me, then wraps me in a hug. "I'm so confused. I thought I hated him."

"He loved you, Jago. He may not have said it in so many words, but I saw the way he looked at you sometimes. He used to say that even though you look like your mother, you were just like his brother, stubborn and brave."

"No brave," Cuervo croaks. "Chicken."

Jago and I pull apart, give Cuervo a sidelong glance, then burst out laughing.

We stand in silence for a few minutes, watching fluffy clouds float by.

At last, I sigh. "I should go see Maestro Elizondo."

"Need me to come with you?"

"No, though if you're still willing to help there's something you can do for me."

"What is that?"

"It might be unpleasant, but it doesn't involve Don Justo."

"Then I'm all ears."

28

VALERIA

"I'm well aware my kin disapprove, but my love for this human female knows no bounds, and I'm not afraid to proclaim it to all. I will wed her and remain in Castella."

Padraig Theric – Fae Royal Knight – 2 DV

Before Bastien gets back on my tail, I go in search of Maestro Elizondo. I got the parchment I copied at the library back from Jago. It's hidden under my corset, safe from prying eyes.

I know my teacher likes to spend his afternoons reading in the south library, a quiet space, far removed from the bustle of the big library in the center of Nido.

When I get there, I find him hunched over a large tome, using a magnifying glass to peruse its contents.

I quickly pull the copied parchment out and smooth it over. The sound of crinkling paper makes him look up. One of his eyes looks comically large through the magnifying glass. I repress a laugh and instead offer him a gentle smile.

"Princess Valeria!" He sets his implement on top of the book and blinks with exaggeration. "What a pleasant surprise for me and these humble books." He gestures at the bookshelves. "And wearing a dress. I forget the last time I saw such a thing."

"Hello, Maestro Elizondo. It's so very nice to see you, too."

He's a man in his late seventies. The top of his head is bald with white wisps of hair on the sides that extend down to a long beard. He wears robes like a monk, even though he isn't one. He once told me that when he was young, it was his mother's desire for him to follow the saints' path. He had been a faithful, obedient son until he found out that texts other than religious ones would be outside his reach. It was then he decided facing his mother's wrath was nothing compared to a life that denied him his passion for learning.

At that point, he left the seminary, but not the robes. He said they're far too comfortable to give up.

"What brings you here, your majesty?" His curious gaze is already fixed on the rolled-up parchment in my hand.

"I was visiting the Biblioteca de la Reina the other day and discovered a small section filled with fae books I'd never seen."

"Oh yes, the private collection."

"You've been there?"

"Of course, I've read every single tome there. It's impossible to find that many works in the old fae language anywhere else in Castella. I would be remiss not to visit that place. Often."

He knows I have an interest in the fae, and he never mentioned this collection.

Maybe it's because they're all written in Tirgaelach, and you never show interest in his foreign and ancient languages lessons, you idiot.

Going around the table, I unroll the parchment and place it in front of him.

"I was hoping you would translate this for me," I say, taking a step back and releasing a shaky breath.

My body tingles with nerves. The irrational desire to run out the door assaults me. I fear this is the point of no return and everything hinges on his next words. What I glean from him might propel me into a vast unknown for which I may not be ready. But what other alternative do I have?

Maestro Elizondo's dark eyes move from side to side. After only a couple of lines, he stops and shakes his head.

"What is it?" My heart jumps into my throat, and I can hardly swallow past the lump.

"This looks like a five-year-old wrote it." His tone is disappointed, the same one he uses when I turn in my Tirgaelach writing assignments.

"I know I'm terrible at it. I just want to know what it says."

"If you took your lessons more seriously, you would."

"I know."

"And you would not have to depend on an old man, who might soon go blind from cataracts."

"You don't have cataracts."

"My father did, and I fear he might have passed the curse on to me." He looks truly terrified at the prospect. "What will I do when I can't read anymore? There are so many books, so much to learn, and I can only make small dents no matter how many hours I devote each day."

The man is positively theatric. His eyes are the dark brown of rich soil, not a speck of white in them, but he likes to wax dramatic, and it's best to let him or he gets grumpy.

I wait patiently as he bemoans his nonexistent cataracts. I'm distracted scanning the papers and books on the table when he says something that pulls my attention back.

"If only the veil hadn't collapsed or The Eldrystone were on Castella and not Tirnanog." He sighs heavily.

"The Eldrystone?!"

Is that name mentioned in the parchment? I saw a brief mention of an opal named The Eldrystone in one of the books I initially checked, something vague about it being a powerful amulet.

Maestro Elizondo goes on. "Yes, The Eldrystone. With that amulet, no malady could stop me from fulfilling my life's dream."

"What is it?"

"I wish to read every single book in the realm."

"No," I protest. "Not that. I mean what is The Eldrystone?"

"Did you learn nothing in your history lessons?"

I open and close my mouth, unsure of how to respond. I did acquire some knowledge, but it's evident I wasn't paying close attention when my teachers covered The Eldrystone.

He pauses, stroking his white beard thoughtfully. "Actually, this isn't your fault."

"It's . . . not?" This is news to me. He always blames me for all my educational shortcomings.

"I now recall your father requesting us to leave all mention of The Eldrystone out." He taps his chin. "An odd request. Perhaps he felt the veil would forever remain beyond our reach, and you would have no need to commune with the fae royal family as his father, and his father's father once did. Shortsighted, if you ask me."

"Will you please tell me what The Eldrystone is?"

He looks up at me with a frown as if he's trying to decide whether or not to uphold my father's wishes now that he's gone. Maestro Elizondo remains quiet for so long that I start to fear he will refuse, but in the end, he looks down at the parchment.

"Very well. I will translate, but it won't be perfect. It's hard to improvise these things."

"That's all right. Improvise away."

"I'll start here." He places a finger mid-parchment and clears his throat. "The Goddess Niamhara made her subjects in her image. Given that she had full control of all natural forces in the realm, logically, many of her subjects inherited similar abilities. Some could draw energy from nature as she did. Thunder, wind, animals, plants, water, fire, and more. Many used their powers for good, but as she had granted her subjects free will, some sought to do evil. Fearing for their future, she devised a way to keep a balance, a conduit that allowed its bearer to channel all of her power when used for the prosperity and well-being of all."

"So . . . are . . . is . . . the conduit," I can barely frame my question, "is the conduit The Eldrystone?"

Maestro Elizondo nods. "That is correct. Legend has it that thousands of years ago, Niamhara gave The Eldrystone to the most loyal of her subjects, a young farmer by the name of Othano Theric. He went on to bring his people together and create an unchallenged era of progress and greatness."

The fae king who opened the veil bore the surname Theric, I know that much. And from the sounds of it, the Theric dynasty has endured for millennia, making the Plumanegra lineage seem trifling.

"It's . . . it's impossible," I mumble, addled by the news.

"What's impossible?"

I force myself to focus on Maestro Elizondo. "That . . . I mean . . . that the Theric family still rules Tirnanog. Because they do, don't they? I remember Mother mentioning King Korben Theric."

"Yes," he nodded, a sagely expression on his face. "It seems quite impossible given our human standards. I'm certain it has only been accomplished by the power of the amulet itself. As you well know, this magic also extends to your family, the Plumanegras. King Aldryn, Korben's great-grandfather, discovered the veil and opened it wide for fae and humans to use as they saw fit. It was his brother, Padraig, who married one of your ancestors, passing along his shifting magic to his offspring. That is how the House of the Raven was born. How, through espiritu, the Plumanegras have also endured through many centuries. It is all very interesting, don't you think?" He wears a satisfied smile as he always does whenever he expounds on topics he enjoys.

"And so . . . what happened to The Eldrystone?"

At the moment, I'm not interested in my lineage, and he's missing the point. The Eldrystone. I'm shocked the thing has a name. No one gives names to inanimate objects unless they're trouble. Take Father's sword: La Matadora. In the old Castellan, it means

The Killer, and it certainly has lived up to its moniker. This doesn't bode well.

Maestro Elizondo says, "The amulet was passed down from Theric monarch to Theric monarch, of course."

"So it's real. It's not just a legend?"

"There's no way for us to be sure," he said. "But let's explore that thought." He stands and starts pacing the room, his eyes lost in some imaginary creation of his brain. He really likes *exploring* ideas.

Normally, this would be my cue to stare at the imaginary creations of my own brain, but this time I'm riveted.

"The fae have the ability to wield magic," he started. "That is something completely different from us humans. Innately, we have no such powers, and our saints have granted us little more than our own free will." He scoffs at this. Even though he once meant to be a monk, he seems to hold a general contempt for Castella's religion.

He goes on. "This magic has to come from somewhere. Somebody had to give it to them, and the fae say it was Niamhara. Much like humans are modeled after their saints, fae kind is supposed to be created in her image. Therefore, they inherited her ability to draw power from the earth and all its elements.

"Once we take this axiom, then what is explained in your parchment is only a logical succession of events. Naturally, some fae would have used their magic for good, while others used it for evil. A benevolent creator, like any parent, would seek to help their children get along and thrive. It seems The Eldrystone did just that." He stops pacing and looks up at me in surprise, as if he'd forgotten I'm here.

Frowning, he scrutinizes my face. "But why the sudden interest in The Eldrystone, Princess Valeria?"

I consider my answer carefully. Of course, I cannot say I suspect Mother's necklace is The Eldrystone. That would lead me to reveal she was fae and not human, and that isn't something that would benefit anyone.

Also, the fact that Father forbade our teachers to mention the amulet . . . There had to be a good reason.

Although, the harder I think about it, none of it makes sense. If Mother's necklace is Niamhara's conduit, why did she have it and not King Korben? Why did she keep it with her and not locked up somewhere? Why did Father never ask for it when it could have solved so many problems? And why, oh why, did he let me keep it as a toy? This is the question that haunts me the most. So no. I can't be honest with Maestro Elizondo.

Moreover, I can't tell him that my sister seems to be possessed and in search of the powerful amulet. There's only one thing that seems safe to mention, so I take a deep breath and let it out.

"It appears that the veilfallen are searching for The Eldrystone here in Castellina."

"What a ludicrous idea!" he exclaims. "What would make you think that?"

"Um, rumors." I wave a hand vaguely in the air.

"Who would start such rumors? They make no sense."

"How should I know? We can explore the idea on how rumors get started, I suppose."

He waves a finger at me. "Don't get smart with me, young lady."

I roll my eyes but turn sideways so he can't see it. He still scares me when he uses that tone. I'm supposed to outrank him, but the man will always be an authoritative figure in my life, just like Nana. They practically raised me.

"The veilfallen want what any disadvantaged group of people has ever wanted," he says. "Whoever is making up these fanciful ideas is only trying to distract us from the real issue. Wouldn't you say?" He taps his temple, and I can almost hear him asking *haven't I taught you to think?* which is the typical question that accompanies the gesture.

I force a laugh. "You're right. It's absolutely ridiculous."

He inclines his head, raising an eyebrow, another gesture of his with a meaning I know well. *Of course I'm right.*

I take the parchment from the table and roll it up tightly. "Thank you for helping me satisfy my curiosity. I must go now."

He watches me as I walk to the door, and since he must always have the last word, he says, "I will be waiting for you tomorrow for your Tirgaelach lesson. We can work on improving your calligraphy so it doesn't look like a toddler's."

I sigh heavily and shake my head. Continuing my studies is the last thing I want to do right now, but a niggling notion has taken root in my mind. I have wasted a lot of my time being a brat and thinking I know better. But if I truly did, I would know how to read this parchment. All those times I didn't listen to Maestro Elizondo, I wasn't only wasting his time, I was wasting mine, too.

After talking to him, I find one of the housekeepers and instruct her to find my furniture and restore my bedchamber to its original state. She seems flabbergasted, unaware of what happened, but I have no desire to explain, so I tell her I trust she will get it done.

After that, I head to my bedchamber, and I encounter Bastien waiting by the door. He looks down at the parchment still rolled in my hand. I resist the urge to hide it behind my back.

"Looking for me?" I ask in a singsong voice.

He ignores my question. "I delivered your message to Don Justo. Any other tasks you would like me to perform?" He takes a slight bow that is more mockery than anything else. The parchment crinkles as I tighten my fist.

He smirks.

"As a matter of fact, yes," I smirk back. "Why don't you jump off the east tower?"

I keep walking, without waiting for a retort. The door shuts behind me with a satisfying *thud*. "What an insufferable man."

"Insufferable," Cuervo croaks from his favorite perch on the balcony.

"Say *that* again."

"Insufferable," he repeats.

That makes me smile and helps me push Bastien out of my mind. Instead, I busy myself with burning the parchment and watching it crumble to ashes in the fireplace.

After there's little more than black soot left, I go to Cuervo.

Caressing his neck, I ask, "Are you all right?"

He bobs his head up and down.

"I'm sorry I haven't been able to spend much time with you. My life is out of control." A warm breeze blows a lock of my hair loose. Cuervo's beak snaps at it playfully, trying to catch it.

We share a silent moment, looking out at the beautiful sight that is Castellina. The Manzanar River sparkles in the distance like a diamond necklace left behind by a giantess.

"Cuervo," I whisper, "one day soon, you have to take me to the necklace. I need to know where it is."

"Treasure," he says, then he blinks his beady eyes and stares into the distance. "Treasure," he repeats more insistently.

Slowly, my gaze follows his toward the observatory to the east. Cuervo does a little jump and flaps his wings once.

"There, huh?"

The place where he and I have spent countless hours searching for *treasure*. It makes sense why he picked that place.

"And it's safe?" I ask, worried because others also go there to retrieve beautiful crystals that dazzle the eye.

"Safe," he repeats.

"Good. We'll go soon."

"Soon."

29

VALERIA

"You will leave out all mention of
The Eldrystone in Amira and Valeria's lessons, understood?"

Rey Simón Plumanegra (Casa Plumanegra) – King of Castella – 11 AV

Before nighttime, my bedchamber gets efficiently restored while I eat dinner with Nana. She has many questions, but I manage to pacify her with what can only be called lies. I don't want to worry her though. She is too fragile and deserves her peace.

After that, I instruct the reliable housekeeper to have my chambermaids tend to me in the morning—a request that also leaves her flabbergasted since I haven't needed their services in years—I retire to my room and spend an hour setting every little thing just right.

Finally, I lay my head to rest and when sleep finds me, so does a vague dream with the trapping of a nightmare.

The next morning, I'm tired and in a bad mood, but I treat the chambermaids kindly as they help me get into one of my elaborate dresses. I couldn't do it on my own. I selected one that shows considerable cleavage. I have a feeling it might offer me help with Don Justo.

When they're done with me, I look like one of the many debutantes who attended Amira's birthday party ball last year. Excessive ruffles, too much makeup, and too many lacquered curls.

"Perfect," I tell the girls, making sure to make eye contact with each one of them. They seem eager to do a good job even though I barely know them.

After they leave, I pace alongside my bed. The notion that the most powerful instrument ever created in all the realms is hidden somewhere in the rubble of the old observatory has me on edge. More than once, I have to stop myself from calling Cuervo and asking him to retrieve The Eldrystone. I could use it to unmask Orys and defeat the veilfallen and Los Moros, but I'm terrified. Bringing the amulet back to Nido could be disastrous. I have no idea how to use the jewel's power, and I fear that my actions will only cause it to fall into the wrong hands.

When it's time to leave, I walk out of my room and find Bastien there. He was standing in the same spot when I came back from dinner with Nana last night. Did he even move? I examine his face to see if he appears tired, but he looks as fresh as a dewy rose.

"Good morning, princess." He bows slightly.

"Good morning to you, too," I say with matching mockery.

Holding my head high, I march down the hall, dreading my meeting with Don Justo.

"Just the way I like to begin each day," I mumble under my breath.

Bastien appears at my side. "I'm sorry."

Frowning, I turn to look at him. He sounds and looks sincere. Have all the hells frozen over?

"I shouldn't add to your already . . . complicated life," he says.

"Did someone hit you over the head?"

He blows air through his perfect nose in amusement. "Many times. Hazards of the job."

"It smells as if you're calling a truce."

"You could call it that."

I narrow my eyes and say nothing. A truce? No, I can't trust Bastien. This change of heart seems too sudden and convenient—not to mention out of character. It has to be some sort of trick.

He must be following orders from Amira, my most sensible self says inside my head.

But if he failed so many times to do his job, why would she still trust him? Again, I find myself wondering if he is Orys or in league with him. And again, I dismiss the idea because Bastien was there when the sorcerer attacked, and he tried to help Father and me. I rub my left temple as a headache blooms there.

One thing at a time, Val.

Right now, I have to take care of Don Justo.

When I arrive, I take a deep breath and put on my most pleasant face before stepping into the sunroom. My heart pounds with nerves, and I steel myself to face the mysterious man I've only been told about.

When Don Justo hears my approach, he shifts his gaze from the beautiful garden view and turns to me.

My expectations shatter, and I blink in surprise at the sight of the man who stands in front of me. I hadn't trusted the portrait of him I saw in Alsur. I thought it was an exaggeration from the artist, a paid-for commission meant to render him in the best possible light.

But now, looking at him across the food-laden table, I realize that the portrait did absolutely no justice to the man. Don Justo is every bit as handsome as he was depicted and more to boot.

Before me stands a striking figure, his presence commanding every bit of my attention. He possesses a tall and imposing frame, every muscle beneath his clothing chiseled and defined. His sun-kissed blond hair falls in effortless waves, framing an angular face and looking as thick as a lion's mane. Piercing blue eyes, like shards of cerulean ice, hold a spark of unwavering confidence and a hint of arrogance.

I stand there, feeling intimidated by his raw presence. He may be handsome, but something about him conveys latent savagery. I don't like the way he's scanning me from head to toe, making me feel as if he's going to pounce at any moment.

Involuntarily, I glance askance at Bastien. He stands at attention by the door, and I'm glad of it—a ridiculous notion since he's also my enemy, isn't he? Besides, I don't need him. I know how to defend myself.

"Good morning," I say, pushing away my bafflement and apprehension.

He walks around the table and comes to stand a few paces in front of me. He bows deeply, reaches for my hand, and presses a gentle kiss between two knuckles.

"It is a pleasure to finally meet you," he says, his words polished but somehow forced.

"The pleasure is all mine."

He pulls out a chair for me and helps me sit, then takes the place across from me. He gives a moment's consideration to Bastien.

"Is he your guard or your servant?" Don Justo asks.

"Both."

Bastien's mouth twists slightly, which gives me enormous satisfaction.

"I must say, dear Princess Valeria, that I was rather disappointed not to find you at Villa de la Paz."

Those blue eyes hold mine, and I sense the shrewd quality of his character that I heard about from members of the court.

I reach for a bowl of fruit. Making sure my movements are calm and unhurried, I serve myself a few slices of orange and apple, then set the bowl down.

My response is as unhurried as my movement. "My apologies, Don Justo. You should know that I am a willful woman and hate being ordered about. I wanted to remain in Castellina for my father's funeral, and that comfort was denied to me."

As he mulls over my answer, I watch him closely. If he wants a submissive wife, I want him to know he's looking in the wrong place. Perhaps a little clarity will send him away.

"Willful, huh?" He leans back, savoring the word with a smile. "I do love a challenge."

Well, it couldn't have been that easy, could it? Of course it had been wishful thinking on my part. He wouldn't allow something as trivial as my stubbornness to get in the way of his ambition.

I clear my throat. "I will not be a challenge, of course. Not if I'm given what I want, what I'm used to." I spear a piece of apple with my fork and take a dainty bite.

"You will not lack for anything, I assure you." He seems affronted by the suggestion that he might not be capable of providing for me.

Maybe this is an angle of attack. "I am a princess."

"I'm well aware of that."

"I told my sister I will not be married off like some sort of nuisance she wants to get rid of. I want it done the right way."

One of his fine eyebrows goes up. "Meaning?"

"Meaning that I want a proper engagement party and a proper wedding at the Basilica de Castellina, presided by Archbishop Septimo Aquila, of course."

Now both of his eyebrows are up, looking as if they might join his hairline to make his majestic mane even thicker.

"I . . . I wholeheartedly agree." His mouth stretches into a huge smile that shows his back molars.

As I suspected, he's immensely gratified by this. He wants so badly to get higher in the rungs of Castella's social ladder that I couldn't have provided him with a better set of news. He has no idea the Castellan *crema de la crema* will eat him alive.

He interlaces his fingers, which are blunt and coarse. It is in this roughness that the mercenary is, at last, revealed. "You should have everything befitting a princess, and I would hate to be the one to rob you of that." He reaches across the table and places a rough hand on top of mine.

I resist the urge to pull away, but it turns out to be a mistake, as he interprets it as some sort of encouragement. He rises from his seat and circles the table, seizing my hand and pulling me to my feet.

Without any sort of prudence, his stare lingers on my cleavage before belatedly meeting my eyes.

"You're delightful and more appetizing than I imagined," he says, acting as if he's giving me a compliment. Except I'm not a scrumptious dessert for him to devour. I'm a woman of intelligence and strong, independent will.

In a flash, his arm goes around my waist, pressing my body tightly against his. A wave of revulsion rolls up from the pit of my stomach. He angles his face, and my revulsion mixes with a heavy dose of panic. He intends to kiss me.

Bracing both hands against his chest, I try to push him away, but his grip is firm.

My first kiss cannot be with this man, with someone who would force me. I want to scream, but if I do, everything will fall apart. This went well. I bought myself the time I need to unravel this mystery and, perhaps, even save myself from a lifetime as this brute's wife.

I can't scream. I have to bear it.

"Princess Valeria," Bastien's deep voice breaks through my disgust and panic. "I'm sorry to interrupt, you asked me to remind you about your Tirgaelach lesson with Maestro Elizondo."

With a reluctant growl, Don Justo releases me and glares at Bastien. I take two quick steps back and do my best to appear shy rather than ready to pull out a dagger and stab him right through the neck.

"My apologies," I say. "I do have a full schedule today, which includes meeting with the best seamstress in all of Castellina to talk about the proper wedding dress for a princess."

Don Justo seems to like this, so I add, "I would suggest you talk to the best tailor as well. I want our wedding to be the talk of the town."

At this, he looks a bit frazzled. I wouldn't be surprised to learn he feels out of his league when it comes to fashion. He's dressed adequately, but he's far from the likes of Barón Miguel Rubio de la Concha and Duque Luis Tinto Gallegos, two of the most eligible and fashionable bachelors in Castellina's upper circles.

"I will certainly do so." And with that, he bows and leaves, though not without giving Bastien one more nasty glare.

30

VALERIA

"These Castellan's must make room to plant rice. We will teach them how."

Tariq Zuhr – Moro Settler – 98 BV

"Why did you do that?" I ask Bastien as we stand alone in the sunroom.

He shrugs and goes back to staring straight ahead.

I snatch a pastry from the table and walk out. I only ever seem to eat on the run anymore. Bastien follows me at a distance, almost as if he isn't doing his job. Anyone looking on would never guess he's supposed to be keeping an eye on me.

When we're almost to my bedchamber, and no one's around, he finally comes closer.

I turn to face him. The way he acted in the sunroom is still bothering me. "I know you don't like me, so why did you lie to . . . save me from that jerk?"

He thinks for a moment, then says, "Because I hate bullies."

For some odd reason, his answer disappoints me. I thought he would at least try to deny that he dislikes me, but I guess I'm just a job to him. Expecting even a hint of friendship from someone stuck with me might be asking too much.

Back in my bedchamber, I go back to pacing along my bed like a lunatic. I can't get the amulet out of my head. If it gets lost, worse yet if it falls into the wrong hands, I could never forgive myself. Maybe I should ask Cuervo to bring it back. I could—

No! I shake my head so forcefully that a few strands of hair come loose. *The amulet is safer outside of Nido.*

Besides, what am *I* supposed to do with it? I'm not the right person to hold such power, not that I could wield it. I'm just a half-fae whose espiritu was a one-time fluke, who—

My legs give out, and I fall to my knees as a memory hits me like a lightning bolt.

I was wearing Mother's necklace the day she died, the day I saved Father from Orys's first attack. I had totally forgotten. She was letting me play with it after I pestered and begged her.

That warmth in my chest . . . it didn't come from me. It came from The Eldrystone. All along, I've been so sure I possess espiritu that it never occurred to me the power came from a different source.

Gods! I cover my face with my hands and weep. I could have saved Father. If I'd known, if I'd understood what happened that day when I was but a child, I could have finished Orys before he had time to take Father away from me.

Why? Why did you hide the truth from me, Father? Why?! And why did my memories fail me?

My chest heaves with huge sobs that I attempt to drown in my hands. I don't want Bastien to hear me, to learn how weak I am. Clenching my teeth, I push my despair into the darkest corner of my being and stand. My legs tremble, and I barely make it to the bed, where I sit at its edge and take deep, calming breaths.

This isn't the time to fall apart, Valeria.

After a few minutes of this, my mind clears, and my rational self returns, giving way to another realization: The Eldrystone isn't a legend.

The Eldrystone is real.

Up to this moment, I hadn't truly believed that my mother's necklace was the same one Maestro Elizondo had read about in the parchment. And if it was, then it meant that the story about Niamhara creating the amulet was nothing but lore, concocted to instill the belief that the Theric family was divinely favored among the fae.

Yet, the question remains: how was Mother—a self-described humble fae—in possession of the most powerful object in existence?

A knock at the door brings me back to reality. I scrub at my face to erase any evidence of tears and call, "Who is it?"

"Maestro Elizondo and Nana." Nana's old voice comes from behind the closed door.

Still shaky with emotion, I stand, frowning. What are *they* doing here? Nana hasn't been in my bedchamber in a long time. The stairs are too hard for her joints to maneuver. And Maestro Elizondo? I don't think he's ever been up here.

Still confused, I open the door and let them in.

Nana's arm is looped through Maestro Elizondo's. They hobble in together, and it's like the blind leading the blind, though I suppose he's in slightly better shape than Nana. Even if he's a year older, he doesn't suffer from her malady.

"What a surprise! Please, come in. Sit." Curiosity overtakes me. Whatever brought them here has to be related to my conversation with Maestro Elizondo. I see no other explanation.

He helps Nana sit in one of the armchairs, then takes the opposite one. I remain standing, the restlessness that fills me increasing its tempo.

"What brings you here?" I ask.

They exchange a loaded glance.

"It's about what we talked about yesterday," Maestro Elizondo whispers behind his hand.

There's no real need for secrecy here, but I also feel the need to talk in low tones. "And Nana knows something about it?" Why else would she be here?

He nods. "We were having breakfast together this morning as we sometimes do," he glances fondly towards her, "and we got to talking about . . . well, you know. The thing is, Serena seems to think that you may be right about that," he clears his throat, "*important item* actually being here in Castella."

I take a knee in front of Nana. "What makes you think that, Nana?"

"You probably think your mother's origin is the best-kept secret in Castella, and perhaps it is, given how few know it. Yet, more people than you suspect are aware of it. Marco and I have known the truth for many years."

"You have?"

She nods. "Since we were always close to you children, King Simón thought it wise to confide in us."

It makes sense, but for some reason, it saddens me. All my life,

I've never been able to talk freely about my mother with Nana or Maestro Elizondo. It hurts to realize that two of the closest people I have in all of Nido could have been my confidants all along.

I glanced over at Maestro. "So yesterday, you knew that there was a possibility The Eldrystone was actually here."

"No, child," he shakes his head. "There are many fae in our realm, and I would have never guessed that any of them could be in the possession of such a powerful object. Not even your mother."

So it must've been something Nana told him that changed his mind. I turn my gaze to her.

"I spent many nights with you, Amira and your mother when you were growing up." She smooths her already smooth skirts, her eyes distant as if lost in a memory. "She had a necklace, very beautiful. She always tried to keep it hidden, but I saw it on several occasions, hard not to when you were babies and she was nursing you. I noticed how protective she was of it, especially in the beginning. A few times, I observed her looking at it, and there was this . . . heaviness in her manner. She was a gentle female, always happy and ready to offer a smile, and it was strange to observe such somberness in her expression. I always suspected there was a story associated with that necklace, something to do with her fae home. I had quite forgotten about it until Marco mentioned it."

"You see," Maestro Elizondo says, "I have actually read the book from which you copied that passage you brought me. I have seen the illustration that goes along with it, so when I described it to Serena, she immediately thought of Queen Loreleia's necklace."

After the realization I had moments ago, I hardly need more

proof that Mother's necklace is actually The Eldrystone, but hearing them talk so solemnly doesn't fail to cement the knowledge further.

"Child," Maestro Elizondo pushes to the edge of his chair, "do you have it with you?"

I tense, and the most ludicrous idea occurs to me: what if Amira sent them?

Doing my best not to give anything away, I stretch to my full height, shake my head, and lower my eyes to the floor. Nana knows how to read me better than anyone, and I'm afraid she might see the lie in my features.

"No, I don't have it," I say. "I used to play with it, and I lost it."

"Lost it?" Maestro echoes in shock.

"This is madness!" I exclaim, feeling I need to put on a performance to convince them. I would love to trust them, to have someone else to confide in, but I can't take that risk. "There's no way I held *The Eldrystone* in my hands, that my father allowed me to play with it after Mother died. That makes no sense."

I peek at them from the corner of my eye, trying to read their reaction. They appear flabbergasted.

Maestro shakes his head and strokes his beard. "You are right. That seems highly unlikely. Perhaps he didn't know what it was."

I hadn't considered the possibility. I should have, but Mother and Father were so close that the possibility doesn't seem natural. They loved each other very much, and I can't conceive a world in which she kept something so momentous from him. No, he must have known.

"Maybe he didn't know," I echo, trying to diffuse this situation.

"Or maybe . . . maybe it wasn't The Eldrystone. Maybe it was a replica of some kind."

Maestro Elizondo nods. "Y-yes. Yes. Yes, that is extremely likely." He seems ready to dismiss everything with this explanation. After all, this is easier to believe than the alternative.

Nana, on the other hand, doesn't seem so easily swayed. I can tell she wants to believe Mother was in possession of The Eldrystone, but does she believe I lost it?

Oh, gods! How I want to trust Nana, but what if she has fallen prey to Orys the way I suspect Amira has?

"Whatever the case," Maestro Elizondo says, "we need to tell your sister about the veilfallen."

Shit!

The curse word bursts inside my head, but my cheeks heat as if I actually spoke it out loud in front of Nana. She would pull my ears so hard they would come off.

What now? If they talk to Amira, she'll figure out I know Mother's necklace is The Eldrystone—not just a trinket. And if she figures that out, she will definitely not believe that I lost it. Instead, she'll think I want it for myself. Worse yet, sharing their knowledge with Amira might get them in trouble.

"Perhaps," I start tentatively, "it would be best not to talk to her."

Maestro Elizondo looks at me as if I'm stupid. He has given me this look plenty of times, so I'm not offended.

"We have to," he argues. "If the veilfallen think the Pluma-negras are in possession of The Eldrystone, I can't even begin to imagine what they might do." He stands, his back straighter than normal, which means he's determined to tell Amira.

"Um, Amira already knows about the rumors," I say.

"You didn't mention that."

"I . . . I made a mistake." My mind races trying to come up with something. "I wasn't supposed to tell anyone about the amulet. She trusted me with the information from her spies. So if you talk to her, I'll get into trouble. Please don't tell her."

He frowns, looking uncertain.

I try again. "She's already mad at me for leaving Alsur. I'm sure you've heard." I try to look chagrined at the gossip I know has already reached his ears.

They both raise their eyebrows and exchange a glance, which confirms my suspicions. They know I've been *gallivanting* all over Castella, which I have no doubt is the word everyone is using to describe my escape from a marriage to that bastardo.

I go on. "She'll kill me if she finds out I'm not safely keeping state secrets."

Maestro Elizondo shakes his head. "I hope you haven't told anyone else."

"I haven't!"

With a sigh, he waves a hand in the air. "I'm glad she knows."

I smile. "Me, too."

Nana makes as if to stand, and he rushes to her side and extends a hand. She takes it, and as she stretches her rheumatic joints, she offers him a smile that makes him beam. I've always wondered if, when they were young, there was something between them. I don't dare ask, though. I like my ears right where they are.

As they make their way out of my bedchamber, I find that my restless energy from earlier has doubled.

I spend the rest of the day drowning in fabric and helpful assistants armed with little cushions stuffed with pins. They turn me this way and that, tacking lengths of silk to my body and asking me if one shade of white is nicer than the other. I have no idea. All I know is that hours later when I return to my bedchamber, I'm exhausted and determined to never wear a wedding dress in my entire life.

Still restless and itching to tell Cuervo to retrieve the amulet, I return to pacing the length of my bed. My head starts pounding, then I realize there's only one thing that will calm me down.

Rolling my shoulders, I go into my closet, discard my dress in a pile, and change into my most comfortable tunic, leggings, and boots. Quickly, I braid my hair and tie it with a smooth piece of leather. I leave my room and have to roll my eyes when Bastien follows me at a distance like a grumpy shadow.

In the armory next to the sparring courtyard, I retrieve my rapier and go outside.

From the top of the tower, I realize Castellina is alight in breathtaking twilight. The sun, a radiant orb of molten gold, has begun its descent behind the distant hills, casting a warm, amber glow over the landscape.

The city below seems to settle with a gentle hum, as the first stars twinkle into existence in the gradually darkening sky. The buildings, their windows reflecting the fading sunlight, shimmer like jewels in a sea of stone.

To the west, the horizon blurs into a delicate palette of pastel hues—pinks, lavenders, and soft blues. The sky is a canvas painted by the dreams of an artist. Wisps of clouds catch fire, igniting in shades of coral and tangerine and making me pause long enough to cut my anxiety in half.

Now only a good bout will get rid of the rest.

"Pull out your sword," I tell Bastien.

At first, he doesn't react. Instead, he watches me for a moment, then finally obliges, pulling his rapier from its ornate scabbard. The blade emerges with a sharp *swish*. The sound resonates with purpose, a declaration of readiness. With these rapiers in hand, we are armed not only with steel but with tradition and the unspoken language of combat. For a moment, I stop to wonder if challenging him is a mistake. But really, I don't care. I need this.

"En guardia," I say.

He whips his rapier up and down, cutting the air, then strikes a ready pose, his weight evenly distributed, knees slightly bent.

Letting go of all the feelings I've been harboring for days, I lunge forward and cry out, "To the touch."

"To the floor," he says instead, making this even more interesting than I expected.

31

VALERIA

"Alas, I cannot choose. Our saints, the one god of Los Moros, or the many of the fae. Yet, I've made peace with all the choices and so will everyone else. We will not quarrel over religion."

Rey Alfonso Plumanegra (Casa Plumanegra) – King of Castella – 591 DV

Under this rooftop haven and the burning clouds, our swords clash. The sun sets over the sprawling city below, its warm, golden hue dimming slowly. A breeze sweeps through, carrying the scent of jasmine and rose.

Bastien, rugged in his guard uniform, exudes confidence, his dark eyes locked on to mine. I meet his gaze. I want to make him pay for his relentless pursuit of me, for his inflexible adherence to orders, for the way his lips are always sealed even though his eyes seem to tell me he's holding back.

I leap back, my off arm extended backward for balance. Members of the Guardia Real have perfect form, and he's not the exception.

Fluidly, I twirl my rapier, daring Bastien to make the next move.

He strikes. I parry, my footwork lithely putting some distance between us. I feint. He retreats a step and makes an approving sound at my display of skill.

He, a highly ranked cadet, is caught off guard by my agility. What he doesn't know is that I also learned from the best, and I learned to be precise, but also unpredictable.

Our rapiers clash again, sparks flying. I push the attack, drawing closer. Bastien's muscled body moves with grace, parrying my strikes. The tension grows thick between us.

Like two dancers following an unheard tune, we move across the courtyard, our feet barely making a sound over the cobbles. Our swords are another story, though. They sing as they meet, their shrill voices gradually growing quiet when we pull apart and reassess.

Sweat breaks along my hairline and trickles down my back. My limbs tingle with energy. I feel alive, and everything else is forgotten. Only this moment matters. Only beating Bastien and making him pay in this small way matters.

A breathless flurry of quick exchanges follows. I anticipate every strike and dance out of the way. His attacks come more swiftly. He aims at my upper chest and springs forward. I react instinctively, redirecting his blade to the side with a well-practiced circular motion.

With his attack deflected, I seize the opportunity. My riposte is immediate, a lightning-fast counterattack. I lunge forward, extending my arm and blade just below his protective guard. My body is fully engaged in the motion, and my blade finds its mark, making contact with the target area with a satisfying *clink*. The impact is controlled but forceful, a testament to the hours of training and muscle memory.

"I won," I say.

He shakes his head. "I said to the floor, not to the touch."

I huff. "Convenient. But have it your way."

He probably anticipated I would be faster than him. His muscular bulk makes him slow. That is why he called *to the floor* instead. But no matter. The bigger they are, the harder they fall.

I'm ready for our next exchange in this intricate dance of blades. He's a more challenging opponent than Amira. I'll give him that.

Just to make a point, and so there is no doubt in his mind as to who is better, I go for another touch, this time higher. With a swift move, I graze his cheek with the tip of my rapier, leaving a mark. He touches two fingers to his face and is momentarily stunned by the sight of blood.

Narrowing his eyes, he lunges at me. I parry and lightly jump back out of his way, my feet moving as if the steps belong to a well-memorized waltz. He follows, and I have him right where I want him. I seize my chance and lunge, rapier aimed at his throat. He's forced to take a step back.

I know each of this courtyard's cobblestones by heart. Maybe it's an unfair advantage, but he asked for it. Right behind him, there is a stone slightly uneven with the rest. The back of his heel connects with it, and he loses his balance. He is agile and immediately tries to compensate in order to keep his footing, except I won't let him.

I press my advantage, my rapier pointed straight at his heart this time. His dark eyes signal the very instant he knows he has lost, but there is something else in that inscrutable gaze, a combination of pride and relentless determination. He isn't the type to accept defeat.

He's fast as he reaches over and seizes my wrist with his offhand. My heart races as Bastien's warm fingers tighten around me, pulling me close. My body crashes against his, and we fall. His back hits the ground. Our rapiers clatter, discarded. I'm on top of him, practically straddling his well-muscled body, which I can feel along every inch of my own.

Our gazes meet. The air seems to crackle.

The heat of embarrassment starts climbing up my neck, but I won't let this awkwardness spoil my win. With a quick, fluid movement, I draw the dagger I took from the armory and raise it. Right as I'm on the verge of pressing the blade to his neck, he deftly entangles his legs with mine, seizes my wrist, and rolls.

Now, he's on top, and I'm pinned underneath, his hips ensconced between my legs, his nose nearly touching mine. His eyes fall to my lips. Our chests rise and fall in unison as our breaths mingle, creating an intoxicating blend. The air itself is electrified.

Bastien's expression is unlike anything I've ever seen in him. There is a mixture of emotions washing over him, some appear to be the same ones churning within me at this very moment, but there are others I cannot decipher.

The sun has dipped lower on the horizon, bathing us in a deeper shade of gold. His eyes burn brightly as our lips remain tantalizingly close.

I feel him grow between my legs, pressing against my middle. A delicious sensation such as I've never felt floods my body, and I suddenly realize I want him to kiss me.

I want my first kiss to come from his chiseled lips.

Oh, gods!

My eyes flutter closed of their own accord. I'm feeling as if I'm about to float straight to the sky from ecstasy, when he jumps to his feet, leaving me bereft on the ground. My lids spring open. I jerk to a sitting position and wrap tense arms tightly around my chest, as if I'm covering my nakedness. I'm fully dressed, yet I feel exposed.

Before he turns away, I notice the erection tenting his pants. It's . . . it's . . . I don't know what it is, but I'm intimidated by the size.

"I'm sorry, princess," he says, but he doesn't sound sorry. He sounds angry.

At me? At himself? I have no idea because all I see is his back and the tension across his wide shoulders.

"That was . . . inappropriate," he says, his voice low and gravelly. "It will never happen again. Once more, my apologies."

He still doesn't face me. He only turns his head slightly to show his profile.

My embarrassment grows. I have no idea what to call or even think of what just transpired. My brain struggles to process it and put a name to it.

When we first started sparring, there was only my anger, but as the tension dissipated, something else came to the surface. I was exhilarated by the intensity of our match and our proximity. Then our bodies collided, we became one, and a different emotion came over me: desire. Yes, that's what it was. I've never felt it before, but I recognized it. And I know he felt it, too. He can't deny it. The physical proof is evident.

Inappropriate, he said, but isn't that for me to decide?

Slowly, I climb to my feet and take a step in Bastien's direction. His head snaps forward, away from me, and an invisible wall seems to appear between us. His rejection is like a punch to the gut. My anger reappears, and it's worse than ever.

"You lost," I snap, wishing to humiliate him the way he has humiliated me with his rejection. "And you're a sore loser."

He says nothing.

I pick up my sword, and as I wrap my hand around the hilt, I try to draw strength from it, willing its steel to enfold my heart. I don't like what I'm feeling. Not at all.

As I walk past him, I keep my head high. Before opening the door, I pause with a hand on the knob and glance back. Bastien is facing me now, though he still isn't meeting my gaze.

"Please deliver a message for me," I say coldly. "Tell Don Justo I'll meet him for breakfast tomorrow again."

"Yes, princess," he responds, eyes reflecting what little light is left on the darkening horizon.

I don't lose my composure until I hang the rapier in the armory. After that, I start down the hall, my strides picking up speed until I'm running.

I'm so confused. I've attended many balls where good-looking, eligible bachelors vied for my attention, and I've never felt even a fraction of what I felt on that roof.

When I reach my bedchamber, I slam the door shut. I feel as if something has been building inside me since the day I met Bastien, and I haven't been aware of it. Or maybe I've subconsciously camouflaged my emotions as animosity. I've been too busy trying to hate him, but the truth is that I'm attracted to him.

"Oh, gods! Why now? As if I already don't have enough trouble."

"Troublemaker," Cuervo croaks from the balcony.

I can barely see his silhouette against the darkening sky. Shoulders slumped, I walk out there.

Troublemaker. Father sometimes said that was my middle name. He said it enough times that Cuervo learned the word.

"Maybe Father was right, Cuervo. Maybe I am a troublemaker. I think I've just made the situation entirely more complicated than it needs to be."

Cuervo bobs his head up and down, as if agreeing with me.

"Saints and feathers! With a friend like you who needs enemies?"

I leave him behind and take a hot, hot bath, submerging my head and shutting my eyes to the world.

Scrubbing with vigor, I try to wash away the lingering feeling of Bastien's body on top of mine, but I only manage to send an electrifying jolt down to my core, one that even makes my nipples pebble into points.

Gods! What is this feeling?

Nana tried to explain, but either her words were lacking the right descriptive quality or my imagination had no way of conjuring the precise notion. Either way, if this is the way attraction between a man and a woman is supposed to feel, I'm doomed.

I get out of the bathroom, wrapped in a towel. Involuntarily, my feet take me to the door, where I press a palm flat on the wood and listen.

Somehow I know Bastien is standing out there. The ludicrous idea of walking out wearing only this towel, hair dripping wet, assaults me.

"A woman must remain chaste for her husband," Nana's voice echoes inside my head.

During those lessons, Amira and I always scoffed and argued that if the same requirement isn't set on men, women shouldn't have to adhere to it. Nana is a liberal woman, and we know she agreed with us, even if she never said so. She always kept her lessons proper as she was supposed to do, but we know better.

Amira isn't chaste by any stretch of the imagination. She's had several trysts with men she's felt attracted to.

"If you find someone who makes you feel star bursts right here," Amira pointed at her chest after telling me about one of her escapades, *"you go for it, little sister. You don't listen to that nonsense about chastity."*

I agreed with her at that moment. The problem . . . I'd never felt anything remotely like a star burst. Not until today, and I'm afraid. This feels too immense to control, too deep not to fall and get lost forever.

Turning, I press my back to the door and slide to the floor.

"I have no time for star bursts," I mumble. "Now I need an eclipse."

32

VALERIA

*"I despise my hideous visage, but not as much as
I despise that half-blood child."*

Orys Kelakian – Fae Sorcerer – 14 AV

The next two mornings, I wake up tired. Lately, I've been
spending half the night thinking of Bastien outside my
door, and the other half lost in dreams that seem to be getting
increasingly disruptive and more vivid.

I've also been eating breakfast with Don Justo, as our engagement ball is organized. Every meeting with him is just as unpleasant
as the first one. However, since I'm a quick learner, I haven't allowed
him to come too close and assail me with unwanted advances. The
only allowance I've made is to let him caress my hand and squeeze
my fingers between his clammy ones. The reason: to gauge Bastien's reaction. The result: his corpse-like expression doesn't twitch
even a bit, yet he's unable to control the telltale flush that climbs to
his cheeks, a clear sign that Guardia Bastien Mora is very much
alive.

Seeing him stew gives me pleasure, but it leaves me terribly unsatisfied. Moreover, I suspect my behavior isn't helping, as my strange, feverish dreams now feature him.

Each night follows the same pattern, from start to finish. It all begins with Bastien and me sparring, clashing our swords and moving around each other just as we did that evening. As the dream progresses, I find myself lost within Nido, frantically racing in search of Amira. I navigate through the labyrinthine rooms, acutely aware that if I don't find her, she will die.

When I finally locate her, she's in a broken pile, her gaze vacant as it fixates on the ceiling. She bears no wounds, no signs of physical harm whatsoever. Yet, no matter how much I shake her and beg her not to leave me all alone, she remains in an unbroken slumber, never stirring.

I wake up panting, and my nerves only settle when I see Amira in passing, if I see her at all. She seems bent on avoiding me. Otherwise, I remain in a constant state of anxiety, worried that I will lose my big sister, my confidant, my playmate, my shelter when things get tough, my advocate, my only connection to the family we once shared. My friend.

During the day, I sneak around the palace, searching for Orys in people's faces, trying to find any hints that will alert me to his presence. I mingle among the servants, guards, courtiers, and council members, hoping to uncover the truth, but it's all in vain.

"Everything all right?" I startle at the sound of Bastien's deep voice.

I'm in one of the small, seldom-visited libraries, feigning interest in a book while my mind endlessly cycles through the same questions, grappling with the same lack of answers that has plagued me from the beginning.

I glance up and notice that I'm tapping my foot at the same time that I bite on my thumbnail, all my energy finding an escape through restless fidgeting.

"Sure, everything's all right," I want to say, but what comes out is, "What do you care?" Angry at myself, I press my lips together into a severe line.

So far, I've managed to treat him with the same cold indifference that he uses on everyone else. I don't want him to know that his aloof attitude even after what happened between us hurts me.

He glances toward the door as if concerned someone will come in. Reluctantly, he comes closer, pulls the chair across from me closer, and sits.

I set the book on my lap and close it, intrigued by this uncharacteristic behavior.

"I do care," he says, his expression looking conflicted as if he's lying or he's finding it hard to admit.

My gut tells me it's the former, but another part of me—my heart, I assume—wants to believe it's the latter. Father always told me to listen to my instincts, so I do. Besides, why should I believe him when he's only made my life harder since the first moment I met him?

"I'll believe that when rapiers learn to wield themselves," I say.

"I'm not supposed to be here," he says.

I frown and shake my head, confused. "What do you—?"

He puts a hand up. "Let me explain."

It goes against all my instincts to make this concession, but my heart wins this time, and I nod.

"The queen did . . . relieve me of my post." He looks mortified at this.

"What do you mean?"

"She's angry at me because I failed to keep you in Alsur. She ordered me to fix it and sent me to get you after the Romani woman gave you away. But I failed there, too. So she demoted me. I'm supposed to be mucking the stables."

My mouth is hanging open. "Uh . . . h-how are you here then?"

"The chain of command is long and Nido is a big place," he says by way of explanation.

He means that there is an excessive number of intermediaries between my sister and the individuals who issue direct orders to ordinary soldiers. Those at the pinnacle of the hierarchy are aware that Bastien has been relegated to the stables, but somewhere in the chain of command, communication has broken down, and no one in the lower rungs either knows or cares about my detail. In addition, Nido's vast size compounds the problem. Anyone who might recognize that something is amiss is unlikely to cross paths with us, which also explains why Bastien consistently lags far behind me. It gives him ample time to hide or pretend he's doing something else should a superior possessing full knowledge of the situation happen to come along.

I sit stunned into silence for a long moment, then finally ask, "Why are you doing this? If they find out, you'll be in a heap of trouble." Is he really risking his military career for me? No. Why would he do that?

He shrugs. "I highly doubt it. Your sister seems too preoccupied with other matters. I don't know what, but after what she did to the king, I just . . ." He shakes his head, unable to find the words. "I'm supposed to follow orders," he continues, "and I did that to keep you safe, even in Alsur. I thought you would be out of harm's way since your father wanted you there, then I met Don Justo and realized I was wrong. Now, I'm disobeying Amira's orders for the same reason. That sorcerer is out there still or maybe here in Nido. But of course, no one is going to find him if your sister is in league with him. She . . . I don't know. I'm sorry. It's not my place."

Wow, I never knew he could speak so many words at once!

"Please," I say, "keep going. My sister what?"

His dark gaze roves around the room. "It's nothing specific. It's just she's up to something. Emerito as well. He searched your luggage before it was loaded onto the carriage the day we departed to Alsur."

Yes, Amira is definitely up to something, whether of her own accord or not. And of course, Emerito, her loyal pet, is doing all he can to help her. I know that. What I don't know is how much he knows. Has Amira revealed we're dealing with The Eldrystone? Would she risk sharing that knowledge with him? I suspect she hasn't—not when he could decide to keep the amulet to himself if he finds it.

My eyes rove Bastien's handsome face. "So you're saying you're risking everything you worked so hard to accomplish to protect me?"

He doesn't answer right away. Instead, his expression grows tense. It takes him a long moment, but at last, he nods.

"Then why don't I believe you?" My gut is still squirming, festering with distrust. What if Amira put him up to this?

She's been waiting for me to do something stupid. She's watching me closely, and no one has been closer than Bastien. Do they think I'm that naïve? Maybe they do. Maybe there's a way I can use this to my advantage.

"So . . . what do you think I should do?" I ask with an edge of innocence to my words.

"I don't know." He appears bewildered that I would ask such a thing from him. "I don't really know your sister. I have no idea what any of this is all about. I thought *you* might."

Either he's a good performer, or he really knows nothing.

What and how much can I say without risking my position? Does he know of The Eldrystone? Would Amira have told him? No! All I can do is play the victim. I don't know if that can help, but at least it won't risk my safety.

"Oh, Bastien," I blink rapidly, trying to conjure tears, "I wish I did know something, but I'm so confused. I feel like all Amira wants to do is get rid of me. Before Father died, she at least understood me. Now, she barely talks to me and wants to force me to marry that awful man. I thought she loved me, but . . ." I trail off and place a hand over my eyes.

"Have you—sorry for what I'm about to say—but have you considered that she might not be under the sorcerer's spell? That she acted this way to become queen?"

I let out a huge exhalation as if someone punched me in the stomach. I wasn't expecting to hear this from him. "She . . . she would never," I protest, finding that my defense of her is unequivocal. "She's not that kind of person. She loved our father." Now real tears are pooling in my eyes.

"I'm sorry, princess. It's just the entire situation is . . . very strange. There is secrecy surrounding your sister at the moment. In case you don't know, everyone is talking about it."

"They are?"

"Yes. There's even talk that she may not be fit to be queen."

This is why all the council members were acting so strangely around me. Backstabbers!

"Oh, gods." I shake my head, and without a preamble, my thoughts force themselves past my lips. "If the council proposes a vote against her, and it passes unanimously, they could declare her unfit to rule."

I look up from my lap, and my gaze locks with Bastien's. He nods, appearing less tense now than when he first took a seat, as if this is what he had wanted me to know all along, and now that he has gotten it off his chest, he can finally breathe easily.

Seeing him like this, I find myself undone. "You still haven't answered my question. Why are you doing all of this? Why risk yourself for someone you barely know?"

There's conflict in his eyes, and I can't even begin to understand why, but when he leans forward and puts his hand on top of mine, nothing else seems to matter but that touch.

"Because I . . ." Again, there is hesitation, but he seems to find the strength he needs to go on. "Because I like you."

The words have a definite ring of truth, yet his eyes tell me he's lying. I pull my hand away.

"I don't believe you, Guardia Bastien Mora."

He swallows thickly and lowers his head, but when he looks at me again, I see something I didn't expect: resolve.

"I don't blame you," he says. "If I were you, I wouldn't believe me either. This nest is full of vipers hiding around every corner. It's smart of you to be careful, to distrust. It's a trait I think your sister would have found useful before getting tangled with Orys."

What? I feel like there's something I should be able to grasp from this strange response, a light that would illuminate all the secrets he seems to keep, but all I can do is wonder why he sounds like an entirely different person.

After a brief bow, he resumes his position near the door. As he stands there, his expression stoic, his gaze fixed upon a sconce on the wall, I sense myself plummeting even faster and farther than before. Ever since the day Father died, I've been sinking deeper and deeper into the depths of an unforgiving sea, and despite my miraculous survival so far, the pressure has become overwhelming, and my chest hurts.

I'm definitely drowning.

33

VALERIA

"I told him it was called an eclipse, but the ignorant
peasant insisted it was an omen from the saints."

Ibn Ziyad – Moro Astronomer – 103 BV

The engagement ball is in two days. I don't know how I will manage to go through with it. My nightmares have gotten worse, and I feel as if I'm waiting for something: my inevitable drowning, perhaps.

Momentum is building. The tension rides the air like an electric current, a storm brewing inside of Nido that will soon unleash itself.

I know I have to do something, but what? So far my efforts have yielded nothing. I didn't even find out about the council's concerns.

Standing alone on the balcony of my bedchamber, I glance toward the observatory. It is nighttime and moonlight refracts from the larger pieces of glass, behemoths bigger than the tallest buildings in the city.

Maybe The Eldrystone is the answer to everything. I might be able to use it to find Orys and free my sister from his hold. But I must admit I fear it. I fear being unable to wield it. I fear delivering it into the wrong hands. I fear being ensnared by its power.

Maybe it would be best if The Eldrystone is forever lost because how could greed for its power not bring about more tragedy than it already has?

A warm breeze blows my hair, and I close my eyes and inhale. It is past midnight, and my exhaustion runs bone deep. I should be in bed, but I'm afraid of the dreams that will inevitably come. Begrudgingly, I get in bed and slip under the covers. When sleep finally takes me, the nightmare inevitably comes.

Bastien and I spar under the twilight sky. Beautiful colors glimmer in our blades as steel meets steel. We dance. We push into each other, lean closer and closer, our gazes locked. My arms and my heart tremble. We push, jump back, and begin a new dance.

I want our dance to last forever, but a voice beckons me. I follow it. The voice grows desperate as I walk through Nido's halls, many of them unrecognizable. I thought I'd explored every corner of the massive palace, but I'm lost, and nowhere closer to the voice, to Amira. She's calling for help!

I reach a closed door. The walls around it throb, as if built around a beating heart. Rivulets of blood begin seeping from the wood and stone. Desperately, I pull on the doorknob, calling out my sister's name. The door doesn't budge. My hands slip, sticky blood soaking them. I try again. The door breaks open. A wave of blood slams into me, flushes me down the corridor. I sputter, coughing crimson. Something hits me. I claw at my eyes to clear them.

A set of wide-open eyes stare at me from a pool of blood. They belong to Amira.

BASTIEN

I slip into Valeria's bedchamber as I've done every night since she's been back. Moving quietly through the shadows, I search the area for signs of the amulet. My eyes rove over every surface: night tables, vanity, mantel, armchairs. It's unlikely she would leave it lying around, but I can't be too thorough. I peruse her closer for a moment, then approach her bed.

There's no sign of the amulet on her pillows or bedding. The hope is that she will retrieve it, tempted by the desire to test its power, and what better time to do it than at night? But so far, there's been no sign of it, not even when I search the room more closely when she's not here.

I'm about to retreat when she begins breathing hard. Her arms thrash, pushing away the covers. It appears as if she's having a dream of some kind. She wears a silk gown that sticks to her, outlining her body.

Squeezing my eyes shut, I take a deep breath. *Don't look. Don't look.*

It's what I tell myself every night as I'm tempted to watch her sleep and contemplate her beautiful features without reserve.

But like every night, I fail, and this time, it's not only her face I admire.

Guilt tears through my chest as I follow the flawless shape of her breasts through the thin silk. My mouth goes dry, and my fingers twitch. I want to reach out and touch her.

I want so much more than that.

Her mouth parts and a small moan escapes her. I lick my lips and wonder what it would feel like to kiss her, to slip my tongue in and taste her.

Shaking my head, I take a step back.

No. You can't. Don't be fooled. Don't lose sight of why you're here. She is no different than the rest.

VALERIA

I sit up with a start, my silk gown sticking to my body. At first, I'm disoriented, but some survival instinct sends a jolt of energy straight to my chest, telling me there's danger. My still-blurry eyes scan the room.

A shadow looms nearby.

I go for the knife under my pillow, but the figure, a man, jumps on top of me and restrains my arms with his knees as he straddles me. He presses a hand to my mouth, stifling my scream.

"Shh, it's me, Bastien," he says. "Don't scream or you'll get half the Guardia Real in here."

Buckling, I curse from behind his hand, but the insults I've directed at his mother come out muffled. I'm angry. Beyond angry. I'm going to kick his ass. Again.

"I thought I heard something," he says, "and I came to check, but I think . . . you were having a bad dream."

I'm breathing hard, but I make a conscious effort to calm down. When I do, he slowly lifts his hand and shifts his weight from my arms, setting me free. He watches me carefully, as if he expects me to start screaming at any moment, but all I can do is grind my teeth.

"Are you all right?" he asks.

"I will be once you get off me," I sneer.

"Are you sure you want me to do that?" His voice grows husky.

I'm taken aback. Ever since our sparring match, he has shown me little more than indifference, and now he's here—not only inside my bedchamber but in my bed and on top of me. Part of me wants to shove him away with matching indifference, but a bigger part wants the exact opposite. Despite myself, I find my anger morphing into exhilaration.

My heart pounds harder. I want to grab his jacket and pull him towards me, let him be my first kiss. But I won't make it so easy for him. He has to shed some of his pride and propriety, if he wants this, and from the hungry look in his eyes, I think he does.

"Are you really here because you heard something?" I ask.

"Of course."

I'm not sure if I believe him. "And does ensuring my safety involve you straddling me in my bed?"

He's serious at first, then a lopsided smile stretches his mouth. "Certainly."

"No, Don Bastien. It does not, and I highly doubt they taught you that at the Academia de Guardias. So why are you doing this?" Now, my own voice is husky and suggestive.

"Well, you were reaching for the knife you keep under your pillow. I might be dead if I hadn't acted quickly."

"I'll grant you that, but I'm not trying to kill you now, and you've had plenty of time to get off my bed. So what is this all about?"

"All right, princess, I'll tell you what you want to hear." His voice is a rumbling whisper that feels like a caress over my skin. "But you should know that my job isn't easy. It hasn't been since the first day I laid eyes on you. In fact, I think I'm in an unfair position."

My chest is visibly moving up and down. The intense way he's looking into my eyes, the heat of his body close to mine, the caressing timbre of his words . . . I'm a feather drifting in a breeze of his making.

"I can't stop thinking about you, princess. I stand out there, wondering what you're doing behind the closed door, wishing I could be in here instead. For days, you've been the only thing on my mind." He pauses. "There it is. Is that what you wanted to hear? Does that make you happy? The lowly guard is obsessed with you?"

He starts to move off, his expression now angry. Is the idea that I'm a princess and he's my guard really what bothers him? Something tells me there's more to it, but what?

I snatch a fistful of his jacket and force him to stay.

"Kiss me, Bastien," I say, hoping that the invitation will break down the imaginary barriers he sees between us.

He hesitates.

"I want you to be the first man to kiss me," I add, my voice carrying a slight edge of desperation.

His eyebrows go up, revealing his surprise.

"It's true. No one has ever kissed me, and I want it to be you. It doesn't matter what happens afterward. Tonight, I want it to be you."

Slowly, he moves back to hover directly on top of me. He wets his lips, the tip of his tongue traveling along the length of his upper lip. The small action sends a lighting jolt to my core, the same sensation I felt the other day, and I have a name for it now: lust. It's delicious, and I want more of it.

Bastien tilts his head to one side and very slowly lowers his mouth to mine. There is conflict in his eyes, and I fear that at any moment, he'll pull away. I want him desperately to stay, and this is not wholly up to him. To prove that, I lick my lips the same way he did.

With a rumbling growl in the back of his throat, he drapes his body over mine, his mouth capturing my own.

I meet his kiss with as much fervor as he offers me. His mouth explores mine as if to memorize it, tracing my top and bottom lips. I do my best to memorize him as well. That chiseled mouth is on mine, and I'm filled with awe because I wanted this and thought it would never happen.

Just when I think it could not feel any better, his tongue slips in and brushes against mine. I let out a breathless gasp. Encouraged, he deepens his kiss, his tongue flicking over the corners of my mouth, the length of my bottom lip, then it slips back inside, expertly stroking with a suggestion of more, but what else could that possibly be?

The tips of my breasts are tight. Something is building inside me, and I want the *more* his tongue seems to promise.

His hands move up and down my sides. I grab one of them and

slowly slide it toward my chest. He seems to fight me for a split second, then his large hand cups my breast, covering it in its entirety. He squeezes, and I arch against him. His thumb traces circles around my nipple, and when it's as hard as it can possibly get, he flicks it, making me moan.

All the while, he's kissing me, but he has abandoned my mouth and he's tracing my jaw, moving upward until he nibbles on my earlobe.

I never knew one could feel so much. Star bursts are nothing compared to this. And it doesn't stop there. He shows me more as he kisses his way down my throat, my collarbone, the edge of my gown, and the swell of my breasts.

"Bastien," I moan his name.

He freezes, his mouth hovering over my breastbone, his breath just as out of control as mine. After several deep breaths, he slowly pushes away and slides off the bed.

I sit up with a jolt, feeling as if he has taken all the warmth with him.

"What is it?" I reach out a hand. "Please, come back."

Turning to face the balcony, he shakes his head. "It's not proper."

"The hells with proper! It's right. It feels right."

Another shake of his head. "It's *not* right."

"Why? Because I'm a princess? Because I'm supposed to get engaged the day after tomorrow?"

"That and many other reasons."

"None of that matters. I know you want me, and I want you. What could be more right than that?"

I push the covers away and get out of bed. My feet pad over the soft carpet.

I take his hand and stand next to him. He's looking out the open balcony door. Dark gray clouds meander across the night sky. I interlace my fingers with Bastien's. The strength of his hand is comforting around mine. Despite the desire burning inside me, despite how close we were, I feel the same barrier between us.

I don't trust him, and I wonder if things would be different under other circumstances, if Father was still here, if my life hadn't changed its course. There's no way of knowing. There's no way to dispel this pervasive doubt that casts a shadow over every action I take.

"Danger lurks, Val," he says in an eerily low whisper. "I can feel it in the air."

Cold fingers slide down my back, and I have to clench my teeth not to shiver.

He turns, and we face each other. Gently, he presses his mouth to my forehead. "Ready yourself." Letting go of my hand, he bows, then leaves the room.

The door barely makes a sound as he eases it closed, yet a sense of finality washes over me. Unmoving, I stand in the darkness, the delicious feeling of Bastien's presence and the weight of his body on mine fading one beat at a time, retreating until it feels completely out of reach.

34

VALERIA

"Why can't I shift, Father? Carola and Benito can, so why can't I?"

Fatima Plumanegra (Casa Plumanegra) – Princess of Castella – 784 DV

Jago walks next to me as Bastien lingers many paces behind. I glance over my shoulder and briefly meet his eyes.

"What's going on with you two?" my cousin asks.

"What? Nothing."

"I've never heard you deny anything faster than that. Not even the day of the stained-glass window incident." He thinks for a moment, then asks, "Did you sleep with him?"

I roll my eyes. "Of course I didn't sleep with him."

He moves his head from side to side. "*That*, I believe. You took your time to answer, which means . . ." he snaps his fingers. "I know, you two kissed."

How does he always do this? I can never keep any secrets from him.

"Yep, that's it." He nods, satisfied. "How was it? As good as I suspect?"

"Just be quiet, Jago, and take me to her."

"Fine."

"Was it hard to find her?" I ask, wishing to change the conversation.

"Very. She's a slippery one. You didn't tell me she is pretty."

I huff. Of course he would say that. "She would sell your soul to Bodhránghealach for a copper, and she would use her beauty to lure you there."

He shrugs. "She didn't seem all that bad."

"Are you saying that because she batted her lashes your way?"

"Maybe."

Jago leads me to go to a section of the palace I haven't visited in a long time. When I was little, I made it my goal to explore every corner of Nido, whether or not I was allowed. The four dungeons located at each cardinal point of the lower level fell into the *out-of-limits* category, but I managed to get as far as the iron door of the west wing cells, which is where we are now.

Two guards stand at either side. They bow their heads and let us pass. Only a few years back, they would have dragged me back upstairs.

A dank smell welcomes us. A jangling sound of jewelry that I recognize comes from one of the cells to the right. I turn that way and find Esmeralda pacing. When she sees me, she stops mid-step.

"Hello, Romani girl," I say.

She lowers her eyes sheepishly, looking as innocent as a dove.

"You thought you could get away with betraying me?" I demand.

She mumbles something.

"Speak up. I know you aren't shy." Anger makes my words as sharp as daggers.

"I'm sorry, Princess Valeria," Esmeralda says.

"You knew who I was from the beginning." The recrimination comes out before I can stop it, and so does the hurt in my voice.

She nods.

"Is anything sacred to the likes of you?"

Her emerald eyes snap up to mine. "The likes of me?"

"Now, that's the fire I'm used to."

"We wouldn't exist if it weren't for people like you," she shoots back. "And what is so bad about me anyway? That I have no money to feed my sick mother while you live in a fortress palace and lack for nothing?"

"I would have helped you."

"Like you helped us before?"

I have no comeback for that. While Mother was alive, she ran the charities and did work for the poor. She always made sure Amira and I helped. I loved it, loved spending time with her doing things for people in need. But after she died, I lost my taste for the task because it reminded me of her absence.

"You even hate your own kind," she spits. "The fae suffer as much as we do."

"I don't hate the fae or the Romani." I think of warning her to keep her mouth shut about my fae blood, but Jago is right. No one will believe her even if she scatters the truth to the four winds.

"Since your father died everything is worse. We're hungry, and the veilfallen and their chaos isn't helping things," Esmeralda says.

347

Is it? I have no idea. I've been too busy trying to figure out who killed him, trying to unravel what's going on with my sister. But what does Esmeralda know or care about that? I'm wasting my time. She would never understand the poor, rich princess.

I turn away from her and start to leave. "I'm wasting my time." She can stay in this dungeon until I remember she exists.

"I regretted it right away," she says.

My foot freezes mid-step.

"I haven't even been able to spend the money that guard gave me." She lets out a mirthless laugh, then collapses on the stained cot by her side and peers at me sideways. "Be careful princess, El Gran Místico asked me to deliver a message."

Something in her voice is like a command to the hairs on my arms to stand on end. With a shiver, I meet her eyes. "What message?"

"Danger lurks. Ready yourself." She glances away and stares at the wall, seemingly resigned to whatever fate I've decided for her.

The shiver bleeds into my bones, and I feel ready to break.

"Danger lurks, Val," Bastien's voice echoes in my mind alongside Esmeralda's. *"I can feel it in the air. Ready yourself."*

An unsettling feeling of foreboding washes over me like cold water. Hastily, I leave the dungeon, Jago following closely. Bastien waits beyond the outer hall and stands at attention when we approach. The direction of his gaze changes several times, but it never comes my way.

Once we are out of earshot from the dungeon guards I turn to Jago. "Let her go."

"What? It wasn't easy to catch her," he protests.

"Just let her go." I leave him there, Esmeralda's words still echoing in my mind.

Danger lurks. Ready yourself.

Ready myself. How?! What can *I* do?

The answer begins to creep into my thoughts, and I avert my gaze from it. It feels like everything and everyone is pushing me toward The Eldrystone. But if I trust my instincts, if I heed my intuition as Father taught me, I will keep my distance from that amulet. Doing otherwise feels like tempting fate.

35

VALERIA

"Amira, Valeria, and Jago are the children I never had."

Serena de la Aguila – Royal Governess – 12 AV

Danger lurks. Ready yourself.

I sit in my bathtub, arms wrapped tightly around my legs, chin resting on my knees. The water has gone cold, but I barely notice.

When a shiver runs up my spine, I climb out and dry myself. Draped in a towel, I make my way to the closet, where an immense dress dominates most of the space. A wooden mannequin holds it in place, preserving its pristine condition and preventing it from creasing.

The seamstress declared it her masterpiece, second only to my wedding dress, which she has already started. I whirl away from it, mad that the whole affair is for Don Justo's benefit.

I will have to stand by him, talk to him, dance with him, pretend that he means something when all I feel is contempt.

The towel falls to the floor as I pick a silk nightgown and pull it over my head. The fabric caresses my skin, causing goosebumps to break out. I rub my arms, feeling strangely sensitive even to my own touch. I let out a shaky breath and walk to my bed. My hand freezes as I pull back the sheets. I stand there, unmoving, for several minutes, trying to understand the feverish sensation that seems to roll over my body like sun-warmed water rolls over the beach.

The memory of Bastien's lips on my collarbone and his large hand on my breast appears before my eyes.

"If you find someone who makes you feel star bursts, you go for it, little sister."

What if I don't have another chance? What if the danger I've been warned about ends it all and I never feel this way again? In a split second, my heart makes a decision, determined to follow Amira's advice. I walk toward the door, bare feet padding over the rug. The texture tickles my soles, making me aware of how sensitive every inch of my skin is.

Pushing away the fear of his rejection, I open the door. Bastien is standing a foot away, his fist raised as if he was about to knock.

He lowers his hand as those dark eyes rove over my body.

"W-would you like to come in?" I say.

His chest moves like big bellows. His angular features seem sharper, wild somehow, and I feel like prey to his predator.

"I should not," he answers hoarsely.

"Do you often refrain from doing what you want? Because I have a habit of doing precisely the opposite."

I reach for his hand. Our touch is electric. He blinks slowly. He felt it, too. I know. Pulling gently, I guide him inside and close the door.

A few candles burn over the mantle and combined with the moonlight seeping through the balcony, I can see him well enough. His eyes are dark pits that hide everything from me. I know nothing about this man, and yet I want him. The emotions coursing through me right now, the intensity with which his eyes consume me, I understand that this is no ordinary connection. This attraction isn't something that can be contrived or taken lightly.

"Take me. Make me yours." I press a hand to his cheek and guide his lips to mine.

His mouth is a breath away from mine when he stops and says, "We should not, Valeria. *I* should not. You'll hate me later."

"It's only you and me tonight. There's no yesterday, no tomorrow. Only this moment matters."

These words pierce through his defenses like a rapier through flesh, unleashing his ill-restrained desire. His mouth crashes into mine. I meet his kiss with matching fervor. His arms wrap around me, and we stumble until my back is to the wall and his body is flush against mine. His tongue slips into my mouth, warm and insistent.

My body shudders as he growls like a wild creature. His hands caress my shoulders, cup my face, slide down my sides. They're everywhere, and yet it's not enough. I need more. The spark we set alight the other night has lingered between us, steadily heating up, and now it has finally erupted, igniting a pyre that may consume us.

His strong hands slide down my backside, and abruptly my feet come off the floor, and he's pinning me against the wall, his middle pressed to mine, his hips moving rhythmically. I throw my head back as he rubs against me, the feeling is exquisite, and I can't fathom how it could get much better, but something tells me it will.

His tongue traces a path up my exposed neck, then he bites me hard enough to make me hiss. As if taking this as a sign, his kisses slow, growing tender. Carefully, he leans back, carries me toward the bed. There, he sets my feet on the floor, as if needing my permission to go further.

Wrapping my arms around his neck, I kiss him on the mouth. His eyelids flutter closed, and I can't believe a touch from my lips can penetrate his strong barriers so easily. My hands slide down—over his chest and abdomen—enjoying every well-defined ridge and valley. I don't know what about this man makes me brave, but my hands slide further down, moving over his length.

Gods, he's big.

He groans and takes this as his permission to do as he pleases. Lifting me off the floor with ease, he sets me in the middle of the bed and resumes kissing me, his lips more determined to explore every section of my body.

In turn, I kiss him. His mouth, his jaw, his neck. He tastes of freedom and abandon, two things I never thought I would find in a man.

I feel his body and hardness through my thin nightgown, but it isn't enough.

"This isn't fair." I push him away and sit.

He blinks, his eyes dark pits of lust. I give him no time to formulate a thought and work on the buttons of his jacket. When that is done, he throws it on the floor and quickly slips his white shirt over his head, revealing the most beautiful male body I have ever seen.

The royal guards train on Nido's grounds and shirts have always been optional. I've seen plenty of bare chests, but none as perfect as Bastien's. The moonlight seeping past the balcony plays over his golden skin, and I'm jealous of the way it touches him all at once. I want to do the same, so I settle for the closest alternative and let my eyes drink him in.

The width of his shoulders, his expansive chest muscles, the dips and crevices of his abs, the way his torso tapers down to his narrow waist and begins to form a V, the dark hairs traveling down from his navel and disappearing under his trousers.

I touch the tips of my fingers to the silver scar across his chest. It's subtle, shining under the silver light only when I tilt my head to look at it askance. It's three jagged lines, running parallel to each other, like claw marks.

Bastien grabs my hand and presses it to his lips. He bestows a kiss, then puts my index finger inside his mouth and sucks it. My core responds and suddenly I'm aware of something slick between my legs. He pushes me back down, nostrils flaring. He glances down and smiles wickedly.

Oh, gods!

He's kneeling between my legs, his trousers still in the way, but the way his hands are slowly sliding from my knees toward my hips makes me forget all of that. He pushes my nightgown to my waist and growls between his teeth when he realizes I'm wearing nothing else.

"Damn, princess, is there anything about you that won't make me lose my mind?" he asks, as he places a hand over my belly, his thumb settling at the apex of my mound to trace a circle. "I will come back to you," he adds, leaning down to press a light kiss on my navel before he trails a path upward, all along pushing my nightgown up and up until I take it off in one swift motion and discard it without a second thought.

I'm too busy watching him kiss his way to the tip of my right breast, where he stops to suck and tease with the tip of his tongue. My nipples harden to aching nubs. He cups my other breast, then pinches it between thumb and forefinger. Chills travel to my toes. My scalp tingles.

It feels as if I've gone to heaven, then he returns his attention further south, and I learn there's a heaven within heaven.

Tenderly, he parts me with his finger, then slides his tongue from my center back to the apex where the entire universe seems to concentrate. The tip of his tongue concentrates there, tracing circles, causing me to moan with need.

Of their own accord, my hips lift off the bed. Head thrown back in ecstasy, I squeeze the sheets between trembling fists. Something builds inside of me, momentum that seems terrifying and exhilarating at the same time. Bastien laps and sucks, sucks and laps. He's breathing hard, his face buried between my legs as he devours me with uninhibited delight.

A wave of tremendous release washes over me and suddenly I'm screaming, tremors assaulting my body. I'm falling, falling, falling, and then Bastien is there, holding me tight to his chest, kissing my temple, whispering my name against my ear.

I bury my face in his neck and continue shuddering, pleasure rolling from my core in exquisite cycles and leaving me helpless in this man's arms.

When the delicious assault passes, I start kissing his neck. He responds with a moan of his own. My hands reach for his trousers and despite the shaking of my fingers, I undo the buttons.

He gets out of bed, stands, and removes his pants. They drop to the floor revealing the extent of his beauty. I'm embarrassed by the way his erect length consumes my attention. Here is something I've never seen, and I'm immediately fascinated. I want to know all there is to know about this part of him.

Eagerly, I push to the edge of the bed and sit in front of him. I'm careful as I wrap a hand around him, my thumb stroking the underside. His eyes close. He throbs in my hand, and I smile at the response. He is soft and hard all at the same time.

A small drop of liquid shines at the very tip. I lap it away with my tongue, and he nearly melts into me. It seems like an impossible task, but I take him into my mouth and revel in the feel of him inside my mouth. My hand pumps all the way down to the base, then back up.

With a sudden growl, he pulls away from me and returns us to the center of the bed, where he positions himself on top of me once more. His tip presses against my center, and I barely have time to bemoan the change in positions because I'm shocked by the anticipation of what he will do next.

"This," he says. "*This* is what I want."

"A bit selfish, don't you think?" I manage in a breathless gasp.

"This is not about altruism, princess. I want to fuck you. This night, you are mine."

Mine. Mine. Mine.

I like the sound of that word on his chiseled lips. "Be selfish then."

His expression—no, his very features—seem to change. His eyes devour me, lust brimming from their dark depths. His nose and jaw are sharper, his eyes more luminous. He's so beautiful that words aren't enough to describe.

And when he thrusts his hips once, his shaft pressing against my core and causing the most delicious ache, words cease to matter. There is only the pressure between my legs, the way he tears me one bit at a time, until I'm full to the brim with him, until he's touching the most tender parts of me, his body flush against mine, his wall undone as he surrenders to this feeling of belonging to each other.

Mine. Mine. Mine.

He is also mine.

Bastien thrusts in and out.

I arch in pleasure as he fills me so deeply and so thoroughly that tears slide from the corners of my eyes. Once more, he drives me to that tense momentum, that space that feels full of possibilities even though there is only one outcome.

I sway at the very edge as he ebbs and flows. For a long moment, I teeter precariously, my fingernails digging into his back. Together, our bodies rock and we scream in utter delight. It feels like a release of self, that taste of the ever-elusive freedom I crave.

He shivers and collapses into my arms, our chest, our hearts, our souls, touching. He is utterly at my mercy.

Mine. Mine. Mine.

36

VALERIA

"The wound of words is worse than the wound of swords."

Moro Proverb

My stomach twists itself into tight knots as I walk down the grand staircase that leads to my engagement ball.

Fabric drapes around me like spun moonlight, a delicate combination of silvery threads that shimmer gently. The bodice of my exquisite dress is adorned with intricate lace, painstakingly woven to resemble delicate snowflakes. The skirt billows in cascading layers edged with tiny pearls that catch the light and resemble glistening dewdrops on a morning bloom. The sleeves are sheer, veiled with lace that reaches my wrists, giving the impression of gossamer wings. A silver diadem, adorned with precious gemstones, nestles atop my head, its ethereal glow matching the gown's radiance.

Jago walks next to me, my hand perched on his arm. He wears his academy uniform and looks dashing. I appreciate his company, but I wish Bastien was here instead. A different guard has been in his post all day. I hate the twitch in my heart that his absence causes—the same twitch that has been there since I woke up this morning and found him gone. My bed felt empty and cold, the same as my heart.

I can't help but wonder why he isn't here. Is it because he doesn't want to see me next to Don Justo? Does he care enough for that? I know I would hate to see him with someone else.

"You don't look too bad, cousin," Jago says.

"You don't look too bad yourself."

"Where is grumpy face?"

I shrug, trying to appear indifferent, but I can't fool Jago, and his raised eyebrow is practically a condemnation.

I lean closer to whisper in his ear. "I slept with him."

He pulls back to better look at me, as if he'll be able to discern the sign of my new womanhood. His surprise only lasts for a few seconds, however, and he immediately does what he does best: tease.

"Saints and feathers! What is Don Justo going to say?" He fans himself by batting a hand around his face. "He'll return you on your wedding night once he finds out you are soiled!"

"You know well I don't intend to make it that far with that vapid man."

"I didn't think we would make it *this* far, and yet here we are."

The melody of a tranquil waltz permeates the hall as we approach the ballroom.

I scoff. "Things haven't gone as I hoped. I'm just buying us some more time, so we can figure out how to solve this."

"I don't know, Val. I'm starting to think this is a hopeless endeavor. Amira . . . she . . . well, maybe you're wrong about her, and this is how it's going to be from now on."

I can tell from his own uncharacteristic hesitancy that he's been holding this opinion for some time.

"I am *not* wrong," I argue. "That's not my sister. It can't be. Now, shut your mouth. We're here."

He steps back and bows. "Don't trip."

When I was seven, during one of the first parties my parents allowed me to attend, my foot got tangled in my dress, and I went tumbling down the steps like a helpless kitten. Jago has never let me forget it—not that I would, even if he didn't tease me. Everyone laughed at me, and I was mortified. That was the day I swore dresses were evil, and I vowed never to wear them again. How thoroughly I lost that battle, too. Father didn't let me get away with it during any official events. *Princesses wear dresses, not trousers.* I have to admit, they have their uses, and I'm going to put this silver monstrosity to good use tonight.

I turn the corner and head toward the twenty-foot-tall, gilded doors. They lead to the grand staircase and are flanked by two pages, who bow then pull them open to let me in.

The din of voices, music, and the glow of too many crystal chandeliers assault me, overwhelming my already addled senses. To make matters worse, two pages on the other side of the doors blow on matching horns and obnoxiously announce my arrival.

The chatter stops and every set of eyes in the place turns my way. I stop at the top step, two black marble columns carved like the feathers of a gigantic raven standing at my sides.

Now would be the perfect time to be loyal, I warn my feet.

Affecting the self-important air that court demands, I start my descent, dress swaying back and forth with every step, heeled shoes tapping on the marble.

I incline my head as I meet people's gazes. Conde Salvador Almolar, a nobleman who once asked Father for my hand in marriage and who sports a mustache resembling a dog's tail, raises a wine glass in my direction as if to say *it's a shame you didn't choose me*. Conceited bastardo!

I scan the ballroom in search of my sister, but it appears she has not yet arrived. This will be her first social event as queen, so I assume she's determined to outshine me. Good thing I don't care about being the center of attention. I want this to be over already.

Don Justo strides across the center of the floor, stops before me, and kisses my hand.

"You look enchanting tonight," he says, his mouth still on my knuckles as he peers up at me from under perfect eyebrows.

"Thank you." I curtsy.

Smiling hugely, he tucks my arm under his elbow and proceeds to parade us around the room like two preening peacocks. His posture is so stiff, he appears as if he swallowed a rapier. Yet, all the young women's eyes are set on him. Only a few seem interested in me—or more precisely my dress.

Despite Don Justo's constipated look, I can tell he's enjoying himself tremendously. It's disgusting, really, though it has an advantage: he's so lost in the attention and adulation he barely notices me.

After I spend half an hour introducing him to a mental list of people he seems to be checking off, he's engaged in conversation with General Cuenca, talking about troop numbers and Castella's effort against the veilfallen and the ruffian River.

I stand forgotten off to the side, and when I see the perfect opportunity to excuse myself Don Justo barely acknowledges me.

Breathing in relief, I snatch a glass of wine and step out into the small balcony reserved for Plumanegras only. Whoever's idea it was to create these sorts of safe spaces throughout Nido . . . I love them!

I sip my wine, then set the glass on a small mosaic table.

"You're the most beautiful woman I've ever seen."

Each word slides down my spine like a caress. I turn and face Bastien. He's reclined against the wall in the dark. He takes a step forward and a beam of moonlight illuminates his face. My entire soul aches at the sight of him. He's so devastatingly handsome.

The memory of his jaw sliding against mine flashes before my eyes, and that wanting ache that seems to have wormed its way to every corner of my body redoubles. I want to reach out and touch him, but he feels as distant as the Strait of Jabaltariq right now.

"I am *not* going to marry him." The words are out of my mouth before I can stop them.

"No, you are not," he agrees.

My heart turns stupid and falls into a ridiculous daydream. He's here to tell me he won't allow me to marry Don Justo, to ask me if—

"But you won't marry me either," he adds, killing my daydream before it is fully realized.

"Who says I want to marry you?" I snap, hurt driving the question out of my mouth.

He smiles deprecatingly. "The look in your eyes, I suppose."

"Why are you acting like this?" Something about him seems altered, or perhaps he's back to being himself, and it was last night that was different.

"I'm leaving," he says with finality. "I'm transferring to Qadis."

"What? Why? Is this my sister's doing? Because I can—"

He shakes his head. "It's not your sister. I asked for a transfer."

The pain that tears through my chest feels like a thousand daggers raking down with vicious force. Last night, he was so tender, so careful, that he made me believe he cared.

All men are the same, Val. Jago has told me this many times, and his words come back to haunt me now. *They get what they want, then they're gone.*

I'm such a fool to think that what I perceived in him were echoes of my own feelings, when all this bastardo wanted was his own selfish pleasure.

He never lied to you, Val, a derisive voice says inside my head.

Our exchange last night becomes clearer in my mind

"A bit selfish, don't you think?" I said.

"This is not about altruism, princess. I want to fuck you. This night, you are mine."

I focused on the word *mine* when I should have focused on the word *this*.

He was honest. For him, I was always a one-night encounter.

"I see." My voice is steady, and I'm proud of my inner strength.

Yes, it hurts to find that I can be easily deceived, that despite my pluck, I'm still the child Father warned me about. But this isn't the first time my heart has been shattered to pieces. I lost my mother and my father.

Bastien Mora is nothing compared to that.

I go on. "I must extend my best wishes to you, though you need not worry. Nido will continue its existence just as it always has. Over the course of centuries, countless souls have passed through here. Your brief stay hardly registers as noteworthy."

I'd like to say that there is a small flinch in his stern expression, but I'm afraid it's only my imagination.

Inhaling deeply, I gather strength from the air. "Now, if you'll excuse me, I must return to my party." I walk away so fast that, this time, my feet almost fail me.

"Goodbye, little princess."

BASTIEN

I hide back into the shadows once more as Valeria walks back into the party.

Frivolous chatter and laughter flow out the open door to taint the night. I inhale sharply, still unable to forgive myself. I ruined everything and now I must leave. I can't stay here—not after what happened, not after I lost control of myself.

Being close to Valeria Plumanegra was my best chance to get The Eldrystone, and I've spoiled it with my ridiculous behavior. I acted like a weakling, forgetting all I ever learned from my past experiences with females.

Squeezing my eyes tightly shut, I try to push away the memories of last night, but they rise like mirages, tempting me further. Her skin under my touch, her lips trembling against mine, the maddening heat inside her as I took her fully . . . it all conspires against my focus.

But she is inconsequential, a cog in this faulty reality that only my ownership of The Eldrystone can repair.

My only hope is that my withdrawal from Nido won't matter after tonight. Everything could be precipitated through Amira Plumanegra. Valeria will find herself with no other alternative but to bring out the amulet at last. The allure of its power, the promise that it can remedy all her troubles, will be impossible for her to resist.

And it will be this hunger to be almighty that will spell Amira and Valeria Plumanegra's undoing.

The memories of the young princess will fade with time. She will leave no mark on me, just as she claimed I would leave no mark on her. Though perhaps I'm wrong about this.

I won't soon forget my lack of control, something I'll need to remedy, so nothing similar ever happens again.

VALERIA

My chest aches with my effort not to cry. I want to walk out there and rage in Bastien's face, demand why he's doing this, but instead, I keep walking, holding myself with the aplomb of a Plumanegra. I've been through worse when I was less than half my age.

I'm grateful when I find Jago sitting quietly in a corner, nursing a glass of wine.

He perks up when he sees me. "There you are. Is everything all right?" As always, he finds it too easy to read my expression.

"It's just Don Justo," I lie. "I wish I could push him off the balcony." This manages to get him off me.

"All those ladies would be terribly mad at you if you dared touch a hair on his coiffed head. They might throw *you* off the balcony instead." He gestures with his glass, pointing at a gaggle of young women surrounding my supposed betrothed.

I'm about to tell Jago what the ladies can do in no proper terms when the horns ring again, this time with The Monarch's Fanfare.

The music stops. The dancers freeze mid pirouette. Everyone faces the stairs. At the very top, Queen Amira stands transformed. I haven't seen her in several days, but it might as well have been a hundred years because she is virtually unrecognizable.

Jago and I stand slowly.

"What the hell . . ." he murmurs.

I shake my head, unable to comprehend. My breath catches, and my heart clenches with shock at the sight.

My sister's face is entirely covered with black makeup, her eyes white pools in the endless darkness. Her dress is unlike anything I've ever seen. Woven from iridescent raven feathers, it cascades around her like a waterfall, an ominous sea of obsidian plumes that seem to undulate, ready to take flight. The crowd stares in awe and uncertain fear, just like I do. Amira's magnificence is undeniable, but it's also terrifying. This is not our way.

Emerito steps forward and lifts a hand. The fanfare stops. "Esteemed Castellans, bow to the Raven Queen."

No one does anything. They just stare.

"Bow!" Emerito orders as Amira explodes into a cloud of black.

A collective gasp comes from the guests.

The cloud disperses into hundreds of ravens all croaking, flapping their wings, and weaving through the chandeliers, obscuring their light.

An unkindness of ravens.

37

VALERIA

"Methinks the Plumanegras lay eggs.

How else might they sprout wings and become feathered friends?"

Jester of Castella Royal Court – 1757 DV

Everyone is bowing now, but it's from fear as the ravens swoop down, talons extended.

In the place where my sister stood just a moment ago, there's empty space.

How?! How is she doing this?

The question booms in my head as I crouch, avoiding a scratch to the face. We don't possess the espiritu for that anymore.

Jago throws an arm over me and forces me down. "Did you know?!"

I shake my head. "Amira has no espiritu."

I'm the only one who ever showed any signs of magical powers, which now I know came from the amulet.

At the thought, my heart seizes. *The Eldrystone!* Did Amira find it? *Oh, gods!* That has to be it. But how? Only Cuervo knows exactly where it is, and he would never relinquish it. I'm about to run out of the ballroom to go in search of Cuervo when my ears start ringing, and my heart picks up a desperate rhythm. *Gods!* Something bad is about to happen.

An explosion rocks the floor.

The very air quivers as espiritu tears through the room with an ear-splitting roar. The chandeliers shatter into a thousand glittering shards, their radiant crystals raining down like deadly hail. The walls groan as they splinter, and the tapestries tear to tatters. The dance floor trembles and cracks, sending guests tumbling. Chaos reigns, a whirlwind of panic and clogging dust. Acrid smoke saturates the air, and the bitter taste of espiritu fills my mouth.

My ears ring. I lift my head and try to see through the cloud of dust. Immediately, I'm transported to that day at the plaza after the veilfallen's attacked.

"They're h-ere." My throat is filled with grit. I cough, looking around. "Jago." He's several feet away from me, lying on his back. I crawl in his direction. "Jago!"

He doesn't answer.

When I reach him, I see blood streaming down his temple. I grab the collar of his jacket and shake him. He moans, eyelids fluttering, though he doesn't fully open them.

"You're all right," I say in relief.

I help him sit up. He's dazed but is able to steady himself after a few shakes of his head. "What just happened?"

Ravens still croak above, flying in useless circles. But why do that? Why not help? I push the questions away as I assist Jago to a standing position. He steadies himself with the aid of a chair. Turning away from him, I look around at the chaos. Is this Orys's doing? Or the veilfallen's?

Danger lurks. Ready yourself. Bastien's and Esmeralda's twin warnings ring inside my head like tolling bells. This is what they meant. Gaspar, El Gran Místico, possesses espiritu that grants him foretelling abilities. I've seen what he can do. But what about Bastien? How did he . . .?

My eyes search for him, and my heart and mind war with each other. The former wants him to be all right, unscathed, while the latter brims with suspicion. I don't see him anywhere. All I see are broken bodies—some frozen in grotesque shapes, others staggering in confusion, trying to find an escape or searching for loved ones.

A hooded shape steps over a body, parting the floating dust particles.

Veilfallen!

The figure throws his hands up in the air and electric espiritu pours forth in a crackling spider web. The still-unbroken chandeliers tremble and refract rainbows of light. The ravens cry out in unison as the electricity hits them, their calls resonating throughout the ballroom. For an instant, they seem suspended in midair, then they plummet and smack the floor one after the other and lie there twitching.

"No!" I cry out. "Amira." I take several steps toward the closest raven, a small broken shape that is slowly turning to smoke.

I stare in disgust. That wasn't part of Amira. That was a cheap magic trick. Whirling, I search the top of the marble steps.

Where is she?

I start running in that direction, but Jago grabs my arm and stops me.

"No! Look." He points with his chin.

More veilfallen are pouring into the ballroom, all hooded and armed. Where are the royal guards? Why aren't they here fighting? Have they already been defeated?

"We have to get out of here, Val." Jago starts pulling me toward a side door.

I shake my head. "I have to find Amira. I have to help her."

"And how are you going to do that?" He looks at me as if I've gone crazy.

The place is crawling with the veilfallen. I'm wearing a stupid dress, and I don't have a weapon. I don't have anything. Except . . .

I grab Jago's forearms and pull him close. "Go to my bedchamber, call Cuervo, and tell him to get the necklace for me."

"What? The Eldrystone? I thought you lost it. You lied?"

"I don't have time to explain. Please."

Jago's face twists into a grimace. "That may not be the best idea."

"What other choice do we have?"

"We can run."

"No, we can't. Just do it!" I beg. "I can't leave Amira."

"What is a necklace going—?"

I cut him off. "Go and do what I said. NOW!"

Without waiting for an answer or protest, I take off running toward the staircase. That was the last place where I saw Amira, my sister, who I now know, without a doubt, is under the influence of that bastardo sorcerer.

She couldn't possibly be in possession of The Eldrystone. That raven swarm was a deceitful ploy unworthy of Niamhara and the ancestral espiritu the Plumanegras once held. There's only one plausible explanation for the deceptive ruse meant to fool the entire court: Orys orchestrated it.

My dress *swishes* around me, cutting my steps short. I walk around a body, then backtrack as I realize it's a guard.

"I'm sorry," I murmur, removing his rapier. It gives that satisfying metallic whisper that always boosts my confidence.

I rush awkwardly up the steps, jumping over debris, hoping my dress doesn't catch. When I reach the top, I notice Emerito crouching behind one of the marble columns that frame the landing. I rush to his side.

"Where is Amira?" I demand.

He looks at me in a strange way and slowly rises to his full height, never breaking eye contact.

"You're too late to save her." His eyes flash, and in one blink, they change color, going from brown to cold, clouded gray.

I take a step back. Slowly, his features morph, giving way to Orys's grotesque, twisted countenance. His drooping mouth attempts something like a smile.

Without hesitation, I raise my rapier and lunge, aiming for his middle. With an effortless wave of his hand, he sends me flying backward. As my bottom hits the floor, the sword clatters down the steps, and I keep moving, sliding along with terrible momentum. My back collides against something soft that lets out an *umph*.

Head swimming from the impact of Orys's espiritu, I sit up and look back at what I hit. Amira lies in a heap, the whites of her eyes showing, her face peppered in sweat and the black makeup running down.

I whirl and kneel in front of her. "Amira!"

She gives no sign that she knows I'm here.

"Amira! Please!" I lightly slap her face several times. "It's me, Val."

Her eyes roll around, all white, no sign of her irises.

"No, please, no," she mumbles feverishly.

"Stop! They're mine," a female voice yells behind me.

I glance over my shoulder to see Orys marching toward Amira and me, but there's someone behind him, someone wearing a heavy hood: a veilfallen.

Bright espiritu explodes from her hands. Orys whirls just in time to counterattack.

The veilfallen are fighting Orys! I thought they were working together, but it seems I was wrong.

The muddled red of Orys's espiritu clashes against the veilfallen's white attack. Blinding light pierces my eyes. Jerking my face around, I focus on my sister. I have to get her to safety. Hooking my hands through her underarms, I start pulling her toward the gilded doors. Her feet drag behind her. Black feathers from her dress litter the path as we go.

Orys crouches, seems to dig deep, then pushes forward. The veilfallen's feet come off the ground. She growls with effort, teeth bare.

My back hits the double doors. They don't open.

"Shit." I let go of my sister to twist the knob. I open one of the doors a crack, then pick Amira back up. When I glance up, a red sphere is rushing toward my chest. Orys doesn't intend to let us go.

Puta madre!

38

VALERIA

"I deserve better than a second princess, yet one can never predict what fate might befall the first."

Don Justo Ramiro Medrano – Master Mason – 20 AV

Orys's espiritu hits my chest and sends me flying backward again. Amira slips from my grasp. The back of my shoulders and head hit the door, and I crash to the floor. Splitting pain bolts down my spine. I sit up, dazed, and crawl back to my sister.

The sorcerer has the veilfallen female suspended in mid-air with one hand, a torrent of espiritu flowing through it, while with his other hand, he points menacingly at me. He doesn't even spare a glance for his adversary. His piercing glare is fixed firmly on me.

"You are not going anywhere until you give me the amulet," he says, his voice sounding as if he's inside a tunnel.

Ignoring him, I try to pick up Amira again. No matter what, I have to take her to safety. Orys growls in frustration, flexes his opposite arm downward, and the veilfallen hits the floor with a sickening crunch. Orys then turns his entire attention on us.

I scramble, trying to pull my sister through the doors. My shoe slips on the marble floor. I stumble. The bulk of my dress makes it hard to move.

A host of royal guards arrives at last and engages the veil-fallen. Swords crash, filling the room with the sounds of battle. I catch a glimpse of Don Justo heedlessly confronting one of the intruders. I may not like that man, but I must admit there's bravery in him.

"Heed my words, girl," Orys sneers.

Someone get this bastardo! But there seem to be too many veil-fallen and not enough guards.

"The amulet!" Orys demands, advancing in our direction, flexing his fingers as if preparing them for his next attack.

"I don't have it. I told you I lost it." I manage to drag Amira back a couple of feet.

"That is a poor lie. I am not stupid. You want its power for yourself. You're greedy like your mother. I learned enough about her from your sister to know what she was. Such a tool did not belong with her or a half-blood like you. Now, give it to me unless you want me to snap her neck."

As he finishes the sentence, he abruptly jerks his right hand upward, and Amira slips from my grasp once more. His espiritu compels her to stand, and with grotesque, uncoordinated steps, she starts walking toward him.

I clutch a handful of her dress and try to hold her back, but she eludes me. Her head hangs to one side, and her arms lie limp at her sides. She's standing up only because he bids her to do so. Once more, she's his puppet. Rage engulfs me.

I glance around, searching for something, anything, that I can use as a weapon. There's nothing.

"Let her go!" I snap.

"I will, once you give me the amulet. If you don't, I will kill her. I am tired of this game. I thought you would be unable to resist its allure and would bring the amulet out in the open, but you are smarter than I gave you credit for. It was not all wasted time, though. It has given me the opportunity to spread my tendrils through the council. Castella will be mine, and humans will pay for the way they have treated us."

"Is that why you're doing this? To gain control of Castella?"

"It was at first. If it hadn't been for you all those years ago, my people would be the ones treating *your* people like refuse. We would be in control, and you would do our bidding. It took me over a decade to recover from what you did to me. I have hated you and your entire family with a force that gave me the will to live and return to finish what I started. I had one more incentive, however. That day I also learned that you were in possession of something precious."

He stretches a hand out and wraps it around Amira's neck, then he extends his other hand in my direction.

"The amulet."

I swallow thickly.

Cuervo, where are you? Hurry!

Orys can have the amulet. I don't want anything to do with it. All I want is for things to go back to the way they used to be.

Amira.

I put my hands up. "I'll give you the amulet, all right? Just don't hurt her."

377

He narrows his eyes.

"I don't have it with me, but we can go get it. We can . . ."

Behind me, I hear a familiar screech accompanied by the flap of wings. Through the open doors at my back, Cuervo swoops in. He circles once over my head, then lands on my shoulder, one talon digging deep into my flesh.

I wince, and as I look at him sideways, I see The Eldrystone clenched in his other talon.

He tosses it up, and I catch it. My fingers close around the gem while the chain hangs loose. It vibrates, making my hand tingle, warming my chest, and taking me back to the day I saved my father, the day Mother died.

The Eldrystone's power courses through my body once more, awakened by my fear.

It seems to take Orys a moment to realize what has happened, but when he does, he tightens his grip around Amira's neck and renews his threat.

"Hand it over, or I'll break her neck like a twig." Gray eyes glare at me from his ruined face.

The sounds of clashing swords ring throughout, but still no one comes to our aid. My heart hammers as I take a step forward. Cuervo croaks in disapproval, jumps off my shoulder, and flies directly at the sorcerer.

Orys twirls his hand and releases a blast of energy.

"No!" I cry out.

Cuervo dives to one side, swoops down, then goes back up. The magic shoots wildly and strikes the ceiling. Fragments break off and rain down.

Fiercely and with his talons outstretched, Cuervo goes for Orys's face. One of them hits true and carves a long gash along the sorcerer's already hideous face. He lets go of my sister to cover the wound, while Cuervo flaps his wings and flies out of reach.

"Leave, Cuervo," I shout. "It's an order."

He croaks in displeasure, a sound I know well. He obeys nonetheless and exits through one of the balconies. I'm relieved to see that my friend is unharmed. I didn't think I'd be putting him in danger once more. I will never do that again. Yet, I'm grateful for his help, grateful for the amulet held tightly in my grip, and for the confidence surging inside me.

Orys lets out a feral growl and grabs my sister again, smearing blood on her neck.

"Unhand her," I say, "you filthy hijo de puta." I'm not afraid anymore. I don't understand how, but I know I will make him regret what he's done.

"You will pay for your insolence." Orys's hand starts glowing around Amira's neck.

Even in her unconscious state, she lets out a whimper.

My free hand goes up, palm towards Orys.

"No," I say simply. Certainty and power surge through me, suffusing every single corner of my body.

My word is law.

Orys's arm freezes, his espiritu sputtering, then flickering out like a candle.

He shakes his head, confused. "You are a half-blood. Unworthy."

"And you're a murderer. You killed my mother. You destroyed

379

our peace, my father's spirit. You will *not* harm my sister and our legacy."

I advance a single deliberate step, my eyes locked on to his. "You will die. Today."

The words carry a weight that seems to saturate the air, heavy with my deadly intent. With a swift, almost casual motion, I flick my hand downward, and Orys crashes to his knees, and the dreadful sound of bones cracking fills my ears.

My sister crumples next to him, free of his magical hold.

Orys struggles to his knees, making a strangled sound as if he's choking on his own incredulity. His eyes bulge as he stares at The Eldrystone in my hand, his greed to possess it palpable. Desperately, he weaves his hands in a spell that doesn't come.

"This is for my sister," I say, jerking my hand to the left.

His right arm snaps, and he cries out in pain.

"This is for my father." I bend my hand right this time.

His left arm cracks and bends at an odd angle. He nearly falls on his face but manages to stay up. Through his pain-twisted face, his hatred still pushes through. I feel it like the slash of a dagger over my skin, stinging and true.

"And this is for my mother." My hand makes a cutting motion, like my rapier slicing the air.

A wound opens across Orys's neck and blood spills like water from a fountain, soaking his clothes and staining the marble floor crimson. He falls limp to the side, eyes open, wound agape and seeping. I stare numbly as the crimson puddle grows bigger and bigger. It reflects the light from the lonely chandelier left above.

I'm dimly aware that all the sounds around me have died out.

As my vision slowly expands to encompass more than just that ever-expanding puddle, I notice movement at the fringes of the ballroom.

In a daze, I lift my gaze. Hooded figures stand in a circle all around me. Right in front of me, a tall and commanding veilfallen, whom I immediately recognize, takes a deliberate step forward. He's twenty yards away, but I feel his presence like a change in pressure all around me: River.

Don Justo lies at his feet—dead? Or unconscious? I have no idea.

My sister stirs. She blinks her eyes open. It takes her a moment to focus, but when she does, Amira weakly kicks back, pushing away from Orys's discarded husk of a body. He is now pale, his pink-stained teeth showing through his disfigured, half-open mouth.

"W-what . . . what . . .?" Amira stutters, unable to finish her question.

Does she remember what happened in the last three weeks? Does she know that Father is dead?

"Amira," I say.

She looks up, and at first, I'm afraid she doesn't recognize me, but then she glances around the room, takes in the horrible tableau, and asks, "Val, what happened here?"

She's barely finished uttering this question when her body goes stiff, then slides backward at a prodigious speed, pulled by some invisible force. Before I can even think of what to do, she's in the grip of a veilfallen's magic, the same female who confronted Orys just moments ago.

Despite being smashed against the floor and her obvious injuries, the female's espiritu remains undaunted as she propels my sister upward and sends her soaring toward the towering fifty-foot ceiling.

Amira's legs kick, and she cries out for help.

Renewed rage takes hold of me. I grip The Eldrystone tighter. "Let her down, or I'll kill every single one of you."

River's voice rumbles in that calm way he has of speaking. "Try anything and the queen falls to her death."

"She won't," I assure him, a wicked, lopsided grin stretching my mouth. The amulet's power still *zings* through my veins. I can do anything I want.

"Don't let that feeling deceive you," River says. "It can be a treacherous thing."

The surety in his tone gives me pause. How does he know what I'm feeling?

"Are you willing to take that risk with your sister's life?" he asks.

I glance up at Amira, who is nothing more than a floating small doll with a terrified visage.

I don't have to listen to him. All I need to do is bring her down, and then I can take care of all these intruders. They will pay for daring to invade my home.

Bring her down, I think to the amulet.

Nothing happens. Amira remains pressed to the ceiling, helpless and afraid.

I try again and again with the same result.

My gaze falls on Orys. It was so easy to undo him, but this . . . this is different.

"Give me the amulet, and I will let her go," River says, and I hear a hint of amusement in his voice, as if he knows I've just failed.

He takes a step closer, hand outstretched. "I'll make it easy for you. Toss it."

"No."

"Then she will die." He points a careless finger upward.

"If she dies, we all die," I hiss through clenched teeth.

"I'm not afraid of death, little princess. Do as you will."

Little princess.

Little princess.

Little princess.

There's a tremor in my chest. Something in his voice has released a terrible foreboding feeling inside me, a feeling I choose to ignore.

"If you want it, come and take it." I hold my hand up, though I don't release my tight grip on the amulet.

Little princess.

Little princess.

Little princess.

He comes closer, but not close enough. His eyes are still obscured by the heavy hood.

"You must really want it," I taunt, resisting the urge to break him like I did Orys.

If I do, his lackey will drop Amira. I'm sure of it. What I'm not sure about is if the amulet would break her fall when I call on it. I can't risk her life. I need certainty.

River takes a few more steps and stops a short distance from me. I can finally see his eyes. The first thing that I notice is the scar etching its way across the left side of his face. It emerges from beneath the cowl, slashing a jagged path over his dark brow and tanned eyelid, before vanishing once more beneath the concealing fabric.

The scar is distracting enough. It makes me wonder where it starts and where it ends. It makes me wonder how he got it. Was it a sword? A dagger? Animal claws? I have to tear my mind away from all those questions to really pay attention to those black eyes.

It gets harder to breathe. My stomach clenches, and bile rises to my throat, burning like hot coals.

Little princess.

Little princess.

Little princess.

"Take off your cowl." I hate the way my voice trembles, the way my knees threaten to shatter and leave me wasted on the floor, another broken thing part of the destruction.

"As you wish, little princess." In one swift motion, he grabs the top of the hood and yanks it off his head.

The sight of him is like a physical blow, a fist to my gut, a hammer blow to my chest. My heart cracks with the impact. I nearly bend over, and it takes all my strength to remain upright.

It's Bastien.

Bastien with a scar running from his hairline to the middle of his cheek.

Bastien with lustrous onyx hair, as shiny as Cuervo's.

Bastien with pointed ears.

Bastien, a fae.

39

VALERIA

"We will lift them from the depths of their ignorance."

Habid Elharar – Moro Scholar – 120 BV

My vision blurs. A painful knot forms in my throat, and I can't swallow it down.

River is Bastien.

Bastien is River.

"Now," he says, his voice a couple of octaves lower than the one I'm used to, "give me the amulet." He puts his large hand out. The same hand that caressed me, the same hand that touched my most intimate places and made me quiver.

"H-how could you?" I whisper, the question barely audible even to myself.

"You know well what you hold in your hand, princess. You've done everything in your power to keep it to yourself. I've done all in my power to retrieve it."

"It was all a lie."

"You are extremely naïve for someone who grew up . . . *here*."

He makes a dismissive gesture toward the broken pieces of Nido all around us.

His words shatter my heart a little more, spider web cracks spreading and wrapping around the aching muscle.

None of it was real. All along he was after The Eldrystone, lying in wait until this moment.

Danger lurks. Ready yourself. He only said that because he was planning this.

"You're vile," I say. "Worse than Orys."

There's a slight tightening around his eyes, but it doesn't last. He blows air through his nose in fake amusement to deliver a bad joke. "I suggest you compare notes with your sister before you decide who is worse."

"I hate you."

He's unflinching, his mouth thin as a shard of glass. His hard expression tells me these words mean nothing to him.

"You could have made all of this much easier on yourself, if you had not decided to keep the amulet to yourself. It does not belong to you, princess."

"It does." My words slice the air with the conviction of an expertly wielded rapier. "My mother gave it to me."

"It was not hers in the first place. But I have no time for this. Enough! Give me the amulet now or watch your sister die."

I glance up. Amira isn't struggling anymore. She's limp, probably unconscious from shock. Gods know I cannot let her die, but I can't allow the veilfallen to gain the power that The Eldrystone would give them. This male is heartless. He would destroy us all. The veilfallen despise Castella. They blame humans for their exile. I cannot allow this sort of power to fall into his hands.

"*Tch, tch, tch.*" I shake my head. "I'm afraid I can't let you have it."

Loyal as always, Cuervo did not leave and find safety. Instead, he responds to my call by swooping back into the ballroom like a flying arrow. We've played tossing games many times, the two of us, and when I lob the amulet up in the air, my timing is perfect.

River's dark eyes follow the jewel's upward trajectory. He lurches forward, hand outstretched, ready to catch it.

Cuervo beats his wings, dives down, and snatches the amulet as if it were prey. With The Eldrystone grasped securely in his talon, he darts away and flies through the doors at the top of the stairs. Volleys of magic and arrows chase after him, barely missing him, but he makes it out, taking the object of Bastien's—no, River's—real lust with him.

"You bitch," the female who holds my sister with her magic cries out. "She dies." Pulling her hand back, she cuts off the magic's flow.

My sister plummets.

Without thinking, I run and position myself right under her. As she rushes in my direction, I know there's no saving her. But it doesn't matter—not when I'll go with her, and River will never have The Eldrystone.

At least the Plumanegra sisters' deaths will mean that much.

"Stop her fall." River's command is unequivocal. "Stop her!" he repeats when the female ignores his order.

Too late, she lifts a hand and releases a burst of magic.

It's not enough.

Amira crashes on top of me, and the world goes dark.

40

RIVER

*"Loreleia and Simón made my already miserable life unbearable.
I harbored thoughts of repaying the favor, but with their absence,
perhaps their children can bear the weight of retribution."*

Rífior – Veilfallen Leader – 21 AV

Valeria sleeps, strapped to the cot in the corner. Calierin's magic didn't slow Amira's descent in time to avoid a collision. Despite the clash, the young queen seemed fine when we pulled her off her sister. Valeria, on the other hand, suffered a broken collarbone, and perhaps a concussion. Calierin mended the broken bone, and I've been watching Valeria closely, ever since we left Nido.

Nothing can happen to her.

Not until she tells me where that damn bird took The Eldrystone.

I searched her bedchamber before making our escape, but Cuervo was nowhere to be seen. That creature has been nothing but trouble since the beginning. I should have snapped his neck when I had the chance.

We left Queen Amira in the rubble. I'm sure her people came to help her and will set her right. She never was of any importance to me. Calierin and the others are angry because I didn't let them kill her. In their minds, that was our goal for invading Nido, but I deceived them, and now they're demanding an explanation. I still don't know what to tell them. How to keep the amulet's nature a secret from them after what they witnessed, after they supported me in Nido, despite the way I changed our plans.

The last thing I need is more people vying to possess The Eldrystone.

At least Orys Kelakian is gone. He was always a blight on my kind. I know enough about him to be glad he is no more. Over two decades ago, he left Tirnanog to escape punishment for his crimes. When he unexpectedly attacked Nido the very day I installed myself as a guard, I thought he only wanted revenge, but when I realized he was also after The Eldrystone, things grew more complicated.

As best as I could, considering how busy I was with Valeria, I tried to keep an eye out for him. I imagined he was puppeteering Amira from afar or within, but it didn't occur to me that he was posing as her closest adviser. I didn't know Orys had that level of power. It is uncommon for anyone to pose as another person for an extended period of time, and he did it for hours on end during our journey to Alsur, so I discounted him.

He was skilled and powerful. I have to give him that. But of course, no one is a match for The Eldrystone.

Simón Plumanegra's death was unexpected. I had hoped to be the one to bring about his demise, but that satisfaction was denied to me. Nevertheless, Orys's intervention provided me with valuable insights into who possessed the amulet. He had come to confront Valeria because she was the one who thwarted his initial assault, the very person who disfigured him and the reason he was incapacitated for over a decade. There was only one way an eight-year-old child could have accomplished such a feat: she had worn The Eldrystone on the fateful day that Loreleia Elhice died.

It only took one overheard conversation between Amira Plumanegra and Emerito Velez to confirm my suspicions and discover that the new queen was also after the amulet. Without fail, the greed for power infects all of those who learn about Niamhara's conduit. It is a curse for which the goddess made no considerations, a curse that has dealt me the cruelest of misfortunes.

After that, my focus belonged solely to Valeria. I searched her possessions before Amira was able to do so and determined Valeria was keeping the amulet well hidden. At that moment, it seemed to me that she was fully aware of what she had in her possession. Then I discovered evidence to the contrary.

It was then that my fortitude failed me. From the instant I laid eyes on her, something that had stayed dormant awakened in me. Her zest for life captivated me, made me remember my younger self when fate hadn't yet dealt its merciless blow. The spark in her dark eyes, the tilt of her smile, the curve of her hips—all merged to create a seductive charm that eroded my determination day by day.

While Valeria obstinately kept the amulet hidden, I believed that earning her trust would be a more effective strategy, yet it proved to be a mistake. I hated the lies I told her, even as I convinced myself they were necessary. And in the end, getting closer to her tested my mettle and revealed my weakness.

She made me want to forget, made me feel as if her embrace was the heaven I've always needed. Yet, it was but a fleeting moment of madness, and any uncertainty about surrendering myself vanished when I saw The Eldrystone in her grasp and the glint of its power in her eyes.

Valeria stirs now. Her head moves from side to side on the pillow, and she makes whimpering sounds as if lost in a frightful nightmare.

I stare at my hands as I sit on a low stool, elbows propped on knees. There's a bucket with cool water next to the cot. I could wet a rag and press it to her forehead, but I dare not touch her.

Her lids flutter open. I watch quietly as her eyes rove drunkenly over the damp walls, the flickering torchlight, and at last, my face.

There is such sadness in her expression that I must fight the urge to get up and leave, just so I don't have to witness what I have done.

"Amira?" she says in a raspy voice.

"She will be fine. We left her in Nido. You are now my prisoner."

She turns her eyes away from me, closes them, swallows thickly.

"I will never give you The Eldrystone," she says, and even though she's staring at the wall and her voice is broken, I feel her conviction in the depths of my bones.

"We will see about that," I say.

"I would rather die than let you have it."

"Death is swift and merciful compared to all the possible ways this could go for you."

Now, her eyes meet mine again. "It will be my pleasure to suffer in order to deny you what you want."

"Feeling jilted?" I mock, trying to appeal to her womanly pride.

"You bet I am," she responds, surprising me. "I trusted you, *Bastien*."

I hate that name on her lips.

Tears fall and slide down her smooth cheeks. "I had feelings for you."

I stand up abruptly, knocking the stool down. This admission . . . Where is her pride? How can she admit her weakness? This is not the Valeria I know.

"You broke my heart," she goes on, each of her words embedding themselves like hooks into my being.

"I don't give a shit about The Eldrystone," she spits. "I would have given it to you . . . had you asked, *Bastien*. But you, River of the veilfallen, you will never have it. Never."

I throw my head back and laugh. "You almost had me convinced, but you're like everybody else. Power corrupts the weak, and you've had a taste. Now, you will do everything in your power to wield it again. But you should dispel that notion, little princess. Because here, without the amulet, you are nothing, and you will forever be nothing unless you give me what is mine."

"Forever may be a long time for you, fae, but I'm only human and fragile. I assure you, I will break, and it won't be in the way you are hoping. I'll take the secret of The Eldrystone's location to the grave. I'll let Niamhara's conduit be lost for all eternity, the same way you are." Her voice devolves into a whisper as her eyes drift closed and the sleep of the unwell sweeps her away.

Lost for all eternity, the same way you are.

Her words leave a lingering echo in the dimly lit cavern.

Angry, I run a closed fist over my mouth, wishing to erase so many of the things I said.

How does she know my deepest fear? I need The Eldrystone. Ever since her mother, Loraleia Elhice, took the amulet from me, I *have* been lost.

I don't care what it takes, however. I don't care if I have to break her down and rebuild her a thousand times, Princess Valeria Plumanegra will not deny me what is mine.

CONTINUE VALERIA AND
RIVER'S STORY IN . . .

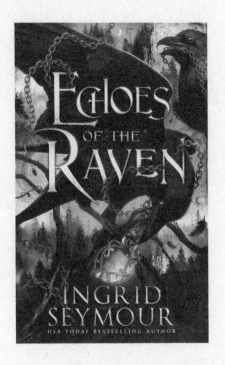

COMING SOON

HEADLINE
ETERNAL

HE NEEDS MY HELP,
BUT HE'LL BE MY DOWNFALL.

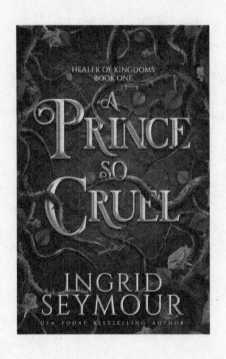

OUT NOW

THE PRINCE WOULD CHOOSE
TO SAVE HIS REALM.
BUT THE BEAST WOULD FOLLOW
HIS HEART . . . TO ME.

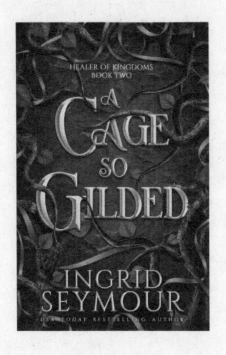

OUT NOW

HEADLINE
ETERNAL

THE FINAL BATTLE LOOMS,
AND OUR LOVE HANGS IN THE BALANCE.

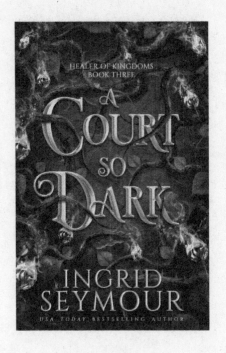

OUT NOW